SILENT CIRCUIT

MYSTERIOUS FIELDS
BOOK TWO

CELIA LAKE

Cover design by Augusta Scarlett.

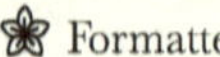 Formatted with Vellum

THE MYSTERIOUS FIELDS TRILOGY

Need a reminder of what happened in *Enchanted Net*, book 1 of the Mysterious Fields trilogy? You can find it on my website at https://celialake.com/en-summary or at the end of this book. (Look for "Enchanted Net Summary" after the Author's Note if the link doesn't work on your reader.)

These three books follow Thessaly Lytton-Powell and Vitus Deschamps through their lives in 1889 and into 1890. I promise there's a happily-ever-after in book 3 (*Elemental Truth*), but more events are unfolding before they can get there.

I

JULY 20TH, 1889 AT ARUNDEL

Thessaly didn't know what to do with herself. Everything felt off, as if there were some tremor of the magic or the land - or both. She had slept abominably for at least three reasons. First, it was a strange bed. Second, she'd not dared bring her sleep talisman with her. And third, last night's supper had been a duel she'd lost over and over again.

Worst of all, she understood some of why she felt horrible, but not all of it. That alone made doing anything useful about the horrid bits difficult. Beyond her, and Thessaly did not like to admit things were beyond her. The good part was that she was only staying one more night. Then she could go back to her own room and at least have a little space to figure out something different and hopefully a tad better.

Entirely better was, of course, impossible. This had been supposed to be a small family gathering with her fiancé's family. Thessaly was in formal mourning for her much loved aunt, who'd been killed a month ago. Instead, last night's supper had involved the immediate family, as she'd expected. The Dowager Lady Chrodechildis, Childeric's grandmother, had reigned from one end of the table, and his father Lord Clovis from the other. But instead of a small group - just Lady Maylis and Sigbert, Childeric's brother - there had been half a dozen other guests.

Thessaly had been marooned between people she didn't know, who'd kept a close eye on her and talked over her. Much of the conversation had been in a mix of English and French, scattered with references to people and events she couldn't follow, not without context. Possibly context and a good list. She knew - no matter how her brain had felt like cotton wool a lot of the last month - that she wasn't stupid at all. Supper had made her feel irredeemably so.

Worse, every time she glanced up, she found either Childeric or Lady Maylis watching her. The rub of it was that there was gossip. Thessaly knew there was gossip, and yet she didn't know the details. One of Mama's friends had spotted her talking to Vitus - quietly, well out of the way, but in public and entirely properly. But it was the sort of thing that gossips loved. Vitus Deschamps might be a young man on the cusp of a career as a gifted talisman maker, but gossip didn't care about that.

First, Thessaly was betrothed, and Vitus was nothing like her fiancé. Childeric Fortier - as with all the Fortiers - was one of the leading families of Albion, the magical community of Britain. Several dozen young women would gladly have thrown themselves at his feet given the opportunity. In due course, he'd inherit the land magic from his father. He'd be responsible not just for the estate she currently was standing on, but the land magic of the whole of western Sussex.

Vitus was of a respectable family, but decidedly of the

professional class. His family was the sort that got invited into someone's home for a bounded amount of work. And perhaps, if that someone were feeling generous, he would receive an invitation to one or two gatherings to thank the client families and professionals the landed families relied upon. That sort of event made a show of the hosting family's largesse and prosperity, before the little people were sent away.

Of course, like the Great Families did, there were marriage agreements. The Fortiers preferred she come to the marriage bed a virgin, but she was not expected to be eternally chaste within the marriage. It was common among women - and men - of their class to have an agreement spell out what was permitted. She was explicitly - anchored in blood and oath - permitted to take a lover. There were conditions, of course. The agreements obliged her to ensure any child she bore was Childeric's. And naturally, she could not cause gossip by her actions. Which came right back to the essential problem.

She was sure - Vitus had confirmed, in fact - that Childeric had a lover of his own, and Thessaly was fine with that. She wondered about the other woman, of course. It was natural to be curious. But if it kept Childeric sweeter, Thessaly got the benefit of that. Theirs was a marriage about politics and family alliances and what their magical lines might do if mingled. It was not for love, and no one expected them to adore each other. They were expected to support the family interests, be duly attentive in public, and avoid scandal.

Second, Thessaly was in mourning. Enough time had passed that it was permitted - even by the stricter standards - for her to return to work on her apprenticeship. But she was supposed to go there, go home, and avoid any other public social event or other interest. Only Vitus had worried about her. Vitus had wanted to see her, and she'd walked with him to Trellech's cemetery. Where they'd been spotted by one of the worst gossips in the city.

At least Thessaly had been fairly sure that Mistress Pembroke hadn't seen what had happened a few moments before she spotted them. Vitus had been very careful about Thessaly's commitments. He had sense, after all. It was one thing she liked so much about him. Monday last, as they'd talked, first he'd delicately said that he'd like to kiss her. And she'd wanted that. Oh, she'd absolutely wanted it. When she'd said she did, the kiss had been everything kissing Childeric wasn't. The kiss had been kind; it had been curious; it had been about figuring out how they were together, what they might create. That kiss hadn't been a battle for control or for space or for anything.

At any rate, it was excellent Mistress Pembroke had not seen the moment itself. Only, of course, she'd seen them together, sitting close on a bench, and she'd been all over questions. And now Thessaly knew - she'd known last night - that gossip had spread. Mama might not actually have heard - being in mourning for her own sister, and thus receiving only a few callers. Father wouldn't dignify gossip with a response unless it seemed likely to disarrange things.

For good or ill, it would take a lot more than gossip to undo Thessaly's marriage agreements with Childeric. That was part of what had her up so early this morning. The gathering had gone late last night, from a supper that started after nine through games of cards that lasted well past one in the morning. Thessaly had retreated to the guest room, set apart from Childeric and Sigbert's rooms, and had gone to bed uncomfortable in every dimension. She'd woken not long after six, with sunlight coming in the window at an angle and landing right on the pillows of the bed she was in. Half an hour later, she'd given up on burying her face in her pillow, got up, and put on a walking dress.

Now it was still before eight, and she'd made it down one of the long paths away from Arundel, or at least from the manor house. Thessaly knew she was still on the estate. She could feel the warding around her, but not in an area she'd been to on previous visits. She had wanted to be away from people. Now she followed a line of fencing down, away from the rising slopes to the north. Down near the south west corner, there was a building, what looked like some sort of outbuilding. Not a tithe barn, it was the wrong shape, but maybe intended for storing ploughs or harvest equipment.

But the roof was burned through, charred around the edges of a hole that spread across at least a quarter of the length of the building. She was about to go closer when she heard a voice behind her. "Thessaly?"

She turned, startled. She had heard no one nearby. Then she saw Childeric's brother, coming with great long strides. He looked a bit out of breath. "Good morning, Sigbert." Thessaly nodded. "I thought a walk might do me good."

"A walk is a fine thing, but not just round here. We had a lightning strike a few weeks ago, we're not sure the roof's stable. And if you were all the way out here, no one could hear you call for help. Here, let me walk with you, back toward the house. We can go through the orchard." Sigbert offered his arm, angled almost as if he wanted to contain her somehow. "You haven't been out on the estate much, have you, further than the gardens and the salle?"

"No." Mostly, she'd been here for formal events, or the sort of thing where her frock couldn't stand up to the kind of energetic walk she'd otherwise prefer. She didn't have it in her to argue, and the building did look more than a bit unsteady. Or perhaps that was Thessaly herself. The lack of sleep wasn't helping anything. "The orchard sounds lovely."

They walked back up the slight rise in the ground, then turned toward the east, walking along a path between fields. "How much of the land near you is planted?" The fields were pleasant, but they weren't even growing hay. Clover, but that was what a field might grow if no one did much with it.

"Thinking about the good of the land already?" Sigbert said it lightly, but it made Thessaly shiver. She thought she hid it well enough. Sigbert was enough younger - four years younger than Childeric and nearly three years younger than Thessaly - that she might manage it. At least he went on without apparently noticing anything. "Sheep, though they rotate through the pastures. The primary fields are beyond the manor wards. Too many people coming and going. It drives Grand-mère up a tree, her and Father. They're the ones who are attuned, of course, though Childeric will start taking some of that on soon... sooner than later."

That was interesting information, and it made her wonder if one of the two of them had sent Sigbert off after her. "I'm glad you found me then. I'd likely have kept wandering out. How do I know where the bounds are?"

"Oh, we can give you a map, so you know where you won't find yourself in trouble. We can do that when we get back for breakfast. We have time, too. I don't mean to pen you inside. Childeric will be asleep for ages." His voice shifted. "And Maman. You know she's heard a few things this week. People seem to delight in bringing her that sort of gossip. Do you want to tell me what actually happened? I can see if I can get a word in your favour?"

It was an exceedingly odd conversation to be having

with Sigbert. In the usual scheme of things, it would ideally be with one of the women in the family. But Bradamante Nevill, Sigbert and Childeric's aunt, had been absent last night. She was in France with her family, apparently for the Paris Exposition, an unexpected trip for the summer. Though Bradamante's eldest daughter, Rosine, had moved there with her husband, they did something in perfume materials. And Laudine, Sigbert's aunt by marriage to his uncle - well, they'd been absent last night too. Dagobert Fortier had been poorly since right around the time Aunt Metaia had been killed, with no explanation. The two of them and their son were at their estate in Essex and hadn't been seen even at family events.

Well. Most family events. Thessaly had had the most curious and puzzling conversation with Laudine a fortnight ago. She couldn't stop thinking of the day Childeric had announced he was going to challenge for the Council seat left vacant by Aunt Metaia's murder. Thessaly still did not know what she felt about it, other than it was many things layered on top of each other and pressed into confusion, like fossils.

Honestly, the Fortiers as a family were horrendous at explanations. Sigbert was at least offering some source of information, as Laudine had. She did not know if she could trust what either of them said, but she also could not continue thrashing around in the fog and dark.

Now, she let out a breath, because she had to say something, or she'd look distrustful. Or untrustworthy. Both. "You know Vitus Deschamps." His family were a client family of the Fortiers. His father handled business matters for several of the associated families and allies. "We've been talking a little about the challenges of illusion work and stones. And, of course, he knows a lot more about stones. He was kind enough to check with me on Tuesday, and to escort me when I wanted a little fresh air before going home. It's - Mama's still beside herself, with grief, and there's nothing I can do."

"Oh." Sigbert let out a breath of his own. "You did nothing untoward? Just talked?"

This was where she had to make a split second decision. "Nothing outside my agreements. Of course I wouldn't." The kiss wasn't. But also, if anyone had seen the kiss, the gossip would be entirely different. "And Vitus has been very careful. He's said outright that he doesn't want to cause any difficulty. People get the oddest ideas in their heads." Then she made one more split second decision. "And he's been kind, and it's a time I could use a bit of kindness. I feel all odds and ends and entirely too emotional.".

"Well, I suppose that's understandable. And it's commendable you loved your aunt, of course." That came out of Sigbert's mouth a little awkwardly, the words he was supposed to say in this exchange, and yet somehow not quite right. "Look, I'll see what I can do. Just, you should know Childeric's in a mood about it."

Childeric was often in a mood about something. This just gave him a plausible cause. Thessaly nodded. "I appreciate whatever you can do. And of course, I'll do my best to avoid anything that might even look wrong." At least until the wedding.

2

JULY 20TH, AFTERNOON

Childeric was - at least outwardly - amiable at luncheon. He suggested they go riding, that Sigbert had mentioned she was interested in learning more about the estate. And Thessaly had, in fact, brought a riding habit. She rarely rode to hounds, but she'd guested with the magical hunt in Northumbria more than a handful of times.

An hour after luncheon, she had introduced herself to a placid bay, and one of the grooms had helped her mount. Linden was an older mare, retired from more active hunting, but she had not yet shown any bad habits. Thessaly took a moment to sort herself out. An unfamiliar saddle always took a little adjustment. She was competent as a rider. Thessaly did not permit herself incompetence in front of other people, even Childeric and Sigbert. Perhaps especially Childeric, now she'd had the thought, and that was uncomfortable.

Thessaly had seen Sigbert on his liver chestnut gelding before, a leggy hunter who knew his work. Childeric's black stallion, on the other hand, was being a tad difficult.

He was showy, rather deliberately. Now, he was dancing from one foot to the other, as Childeric checked on the state of the path he wanted to take. Without saying much to Thessaly, he set off, picking up a canter almost as soon as they were clear of the stable yard.

He was well ahead before Thessaly and Sigbert got into motion, and Thessaly saw no particular reason to rush. Besides, it was a pleasant day, and it felt unduly good to be out and doing something a little different. Aunt Metaia, of all people, had understood that, the need to listen to her body and what made it more comfortable, especially in the midst of tension or politics. Not that tension and politics were actually possible to separate, in Thessaly's understanding.

Childeric went well ahead of them, down one long line of fences. He and the stallion took a fence at the far end, did a loop, and came back, taking the fence on the way back in stride. Another twenty strides brought man and stallion up to meet them, and Childeric nodded, as if pleased with it. "Pardon, Boaz needs a good run before he'll settle down."

Thessaly tilted her head. "Boaz?" It wasn't a name that she'd expected at all. "What does the name mean, please? And you looked splendid. He covers ground well, doesn't he?" She had absolutely no problem praising the horse, who despite his nerves seemed to be a fine example of horseflesh.

"Oh, the man who bred him said it means strength or speed." Childeric patted his mount on the withers, agreeably, and he seemed happier than he had at luncheon. "Now, I thought we'd do a fair loop of the estate, a good hour and a half. Sigbert, you had to be back earlier. Do you mind cutting back from the lower fields?"

"Not at all, brother." Sigbert inclined his head at Thessaly. "Are you settling in?"

Thessaly made all the proper agreeable comments, and Childeric wheeled Boaz around and took off again, though this time at a more sedate walk. They got through a couple of gates, then Childeric said, "Feeling up for a bit more, Thess? We can get a nice canter down the road, take a few fences." It was a statement rather than a question, but Thessaly had a better feel for Linden now, and she nodded. Besides, if she felt the fence was a bad idea, she could always pull up and find the long way round.

That, thankfully, turned out not to be necessary. Linden kept up well enough, both in the canter and taking a fence or two, as they went through field after field. From the road they circled back, following the line of the river up a riding path past a mill. "Mind if I stop and check on that repair quickly, Childeric?" Sigbert asked it easily, but Childeric grunted. Sigbert added, almost hastily, to Thessaly. "Don't dismount. I'll just be a moment. You know how tenants are, yes?"

Thessaly didn't, not like they did, but a mill was an important thing in the estate, she knew that much. She wasn't sure what this one did - was it for grain, or for something else? She didn't see anyone coming and going, or anything that looked like it might be storage. Just a stone and brick and wood building, and the large wheel sticking out over the river, spinning slowly.

Thessaly offered into the silence. "Thank you for showing me more of the estate. I want to understand, better. And it's beautiful, so much of it."

Childeric grunted again, then he added, though as if it took a bit of effort, "It suited the afternoon."

Once they got to a dip in the land with the manor

rising up in silhouette north of them, Sigbert touched his hat. "I need to get back. See you at supper, Thessaly."

She nodded, and Childeric did the same, sharply. As soon as Sigbert was well away, Childeric nudged his stallion into a trot. It was the least comfortable gait sidesaddle, even on a mare with a comfortable trot, and Thessaly did her best not to bounce around. Another field, and then Childeric pulled up to a stop, Boaz taking a step or two backwards, as if Childeric had overdone the signals.

Thessaly glanced around, not seeing anything in particular of interest here. They were outside the wards of the demesne estate proper, though still on lands held directly by the Fortiers. Tenant farmers, she thought, with the farmhouse a little further south. She could feel the difference, though, being outside the warding. Besides, Sigbert had brought her a copy of a map of the estate, and she more or less knew where they were. They'd cut directly west from the river. "Something..." She was about to say a bit more, but the expression on Childeric's face made her stop.

"Thessaly." His voice was rough, a burr in it, even on the few sounds of her name. "You forget yourself."

She froze, and her own mare took an uneasy step. Thessaly made herself breathe. It wouldn't help to have Linden upset. Or for Thessaly herself to faint.

"Childeric?" She tried to make it an uncertain question.

"You know there's gossip." She opened her mouth to say something, then closed it. And besides, Childeric kept talking, giving her no chance to catch up. "And you know you are not behaving as you ought. You are to be my wife, you are becoming a Fortier. You will behave like one, always, in public and in private. If I have to say any of this again, you will regret it."

Thessaly bit her lip. She wanted to say so much, but here and now, she knew she couldn't. Even if she could get the words out, and she wasn't at all sure about that.

Childeric went on, wheeling his horse around to face her. "Let me make this absolutely clear. I cannot stop you from continuing your apprenticeship. It is - alas - part of the formal agreements. I can, however, make you regret any indiscretions. We are bound, and I will make certain you bring no shame on the family, or on me." He then shrugged once. "Or, I suppose, on yourself." It was obvious, painfully obvious, that he didn't care a thing about what she thought or felt.

Thessaly swallowed. "I— I did nothing wrong."

If they'd been standing, she was suddenly sure he'd have struck her. Not on the face, probably, not somewhere it would show. But on her arm, to leave a bruise on her ribs, something that would remind her for days of how she'd been foolish and misjudged him. She could see the twitch in his shoulder even before Boaz danced a step or two in place, shifting and snorting.

"I never ever want to walk into Bourne's again and hear how you have been seen with another man. Oh, in a chaperoned setting, a shop or some such, I suppose. We'll have to find you a suitable duenna if anyone does ever want to consult with you. Though, until I can trust you'll behave, perhaps it would be best if you didn't take any commissions outside the family." Another twitch of his shoulder. "Or I suppose the Powells or Lyttons, if you do as you're told."

Thessaly winced, and worse, she let it show. Every part of her was losing this duel. She'd mocked - even if only inside her head - his magical duelling skills. This was where all the skill was, spotting the things she wanted to protect and slicing them away.

"And mmm, I should be entirely clear, shouldn't I?" Now he was leaning forward a little in his saddle, as eager and bloodthirsty as some predator on the hunt. "It won't just be you who suffers. Deschamps is in such a delicate position. So many things can go wrong with someone establishing themselves. It wouldn't even take much to destroy his reputation. No respectable woman would want a talisman from him, and no man whose reputation mattered to him. It would be so easy to put around the word that he created something that did more than he'd told, that let him take advantage. I'm certain I can come up with something that would destroy him."

"No." It came out of her in a rush of breath. "Please. None of it's his fault." She had more sense, even in the pounding of her heart, to not promise whatever Childeric wanted. He'd twist that and use it against her, over and over again. "I understand. Of course I'll ask you if I'm not sure. I won't see Vitus in private, just the two of us. And perhaps a duenna would be a help in time. You could be more sure." She didn't much like the idea, but living under constant supervision in public was likely better than living under constant suspicion in private. She wondered, all of a sudden, if Childeric would demand her oath on it, bind her by magic, or whether that would conflict with the oaths on the marriage agreements.

"See that you do." The words were clipped now. "You are to be my wife. A Council wife, in due course. Lady, when it comes time for that." Other men might have added a comment about how they hoped their fathers would be a long time before dying, and Childeric did not. "I will tolerate no scandal." He went silent, a stony silence that boded nothing good. Thessaly thought he might be done with the lecture, then he said, "He hasn't sullied you?"

Her breath caught. No, he hadn't. Vitus had done nothing other than kiss her, and that wasn't what Childeric meant. They both knew it. She cleared her throat, the line from one of the ancient Arthurian tales popping into her head. "No man has been between my legs, Childeric." It was a tremendous risk - that was Iseult, speaking of Tristan in disguise, long after Tristan had become her lover. On the other hand, Childeric was not exactly a student of either literature or legend. Not those legends, anyway.

Childeric nodded once sharply. "See to it there is no doubt. We have family magics to tend on the wedding night." Then he turned, picking up a trot again and leaving Thessaly to follow uncomfortably behind him.

They came up the low rise of the hill, back into the wards, before he spoke again, slowing to a walk until she came up beside him. "You asked, before, why I didn't tell you about my uncle. This is why. I can't trust you in a simple social situation, the rules laid out. I know you know them. How could I possibly trust you with anything more complex?"

She wanted to shout, complain, argue, somehow. But it wouldn't do any good, and it would almost certainly make things worse. After a moment - giving it due consideration, maybe he'd read it like that - she nodded. "I understand, Childeric."

"Good. Don't make me speak of this again." Then he took off at a canter, and he kept up that pace until they were back at the stable yard. He dismounted, leaving her in the hands of the grooms, striding back to the house without looking back at her.

Four days ago, Vitus had walked away from her, not looking back. He'd done it to keep her safe, he'd done it to take care of her. This was completely different. This was Childeric deciding she wasn't any sort of danger, that she wasn't worth bothering with. She wasn't even worth listening to.

And she was going to have to marry him. Unless there was some way of breaking the agreements that she could do, she was bound already by oaths and law. Aunt Metaia had offered her help, and Aunt Metaia wasn't here anymore. Thessaly was on her own.

Thessaly took a deep breath, waiting for Childeric to disappear inside the manor, before she made her own way back and up to her rooms. Changing out of her riding habit could be stretched out to take a while, at least. That was time when she only had to pretend to the maid that all was well and as it should be.

3

JULY 23RD IN TRELLECH

Vitus was trying not to take his current mood out on anyone else. Not on himself, not on Mama and Papa at home, and definitely not on Niobe. His apprentice mistress had been nothing but generous with him, and none of his mood was her fault. Vitus had done something foolish and whatever he was feeling now, he'd earned that feeling.

Not that it helped anything, of course. That was why he was up here in Niobe's storeroom, warded a dozen ways, going through an inventory of the gemstones for her. It was a tedious task, even though everything was labelled and they had a well-tested method for checking stones in and out that involved a triple check every time a stone was taken downstairs to show a client.

Vitus was trying to help himself settle. He'd arranged things on the table in the storeroom, and now he was checking the box of imperial topaz. The stone was known for brightening, easing a foul mood or muting irritation. Usually, he loved the play of the light through the stones, whether they were more golden or tending to the red-orange. These stones had all come from the best of the current mines in Brazil. Niobe had gone to some lengths to get them, as they were excellent for solar talismans. Those were always popular, people always wanted to shine and excel, after all. There was a steady market in it.

He was working one stone at a time, taking each box out of the drawer that held them. Then he checked the label against the inventory, confirming that the stone matched, then updating the inventory. Part of it was also taking a moment or two just to hold each stone. He could argue that it was to let him get a sense of each individual piece and what it might be best used for. But honestly, right now, it was to get him out of the tangles of despair.

It was a sign of Niobe's trust that she let him do this on his own. He'd gathered from conversations with other talisman makers that wasn't usual. But Niobe had her own customs. He'd learned that long since. Vitus had been working for perhaps an hour this session. He'd lost track of time, he often did, but he was almost done with the topazes. Once he put the drawer back in its cabinet and locked it, that would be a good time for a break.

Just as he pulled out the last stone, he heard the chime that indicated Niobe would like him to come downstairs. It was the pattern of taps that made it clear he should be timely, but that it wasn't an emergency. A customer, perhaps, that would make sense. On the other hand, she knew what he was working on. And that it would take him a minute or two to finish up properly with what he was doing and lock up.

Vitus did his best to be prompt. He finished the last topaz, slid the drawer into the empty space in the cabinet, and closed, locked, and warded the storage room behind him. Finally he washed his hands, glancing in the water closet mirror to tidy up. A bit of his hair was refusing to lie flat. He added a charm, straightened his tie, and then he made his way down the stairs. As he got to the bottom, he heard, "Office, Vitus."

The office had two people in it, as he'd expected, but he hadn't guessed who. Niobe had settled behind the desk, and the guest chair had the head of the Council seated in it. Council Head Rowan was dressed in muted blue, with black trim, what might be taken as a nod at mourning or not. She was a good generation older than Niobe was, and she looked not only proper but deliberately in control, from her hat and hair to her clothes. Vitus waited for a suitable moment and made a small bow. "Council Head, good afternoon. Niobe, what may I help with?"

"Your conversation, please. Pull out the other chair, would you?" Niobe was watching him, closely. "Hereswith asked if she might have a word or two with you. Both professional and personal."

Vitus couldn't make sense of Niobe's tone now. Usually, he did just fine with that. She'd been good about explaining when he started. She could have a dry wit, and it had taken him a bit to learn when she was teasing and when she wasn't. In private, it was never a problem; he asked, and she explained. Now he was nervous until he saw her tiny nod as he sat down. Whatever Council Head Rowan wanted to ask, Niobe knew what it was, at least in outline, and approved.

"If I can be of help with something, please ask." Vitus tucked his feet under his chair, feeling like he was taking up the wrong amount of space somehow.

"The professional, first." Council Head Rowan spoke clearly and unexpectedly gently. "I understand you have a commission from Theo Carrington." She lifted a finger. "I learned that from him, though Niobe confirmed it."

"Yes'm. We've discussed his priorities. I am meeting him on Thursday to choose a stone. Is there a problem?" Vitus kept his voice as even as he could, but he wasn't sure it was working. The commission could make or break his reputation, and the chance at it in the first place mattered a lot.

"I am asking Niobe to create some of the temporary talismans we use as part of the Challenge. They help manage some of the coordination on the night. However, there can be unexpected effects if those are created at the same time or in the same location as a talisman carried by a challenger. Not always, but we do like to be cautious. There are plenty of other risks in a challenge. I find it best to reduce the ones we can."

"Oh. Absolutely." Vitus swallowed, glancing at Niobe, who gave him an encouraging nod. "I am planning to move into my own working space. I should be settled there by the beginning of August. I'll need three weeks or so to do the talisman work, and a bit more to mount it properly and do the final enchantments. But I can certainly wait to begin any of the active work on it until I move, and my chosen date for the enchantment work is the beginning of September."

"That would do nicely as I understand it. Niobe?" Vitus realised that Council Head Rowan was using the informal name and a tone to go with it.

"I can also wait to begin until Vitus is settled in his own space. Though, Vitus, I would appreciate some of your time helping with the preparation. You have a deft touch with it, and it would save me quite a few hours."

"Of course, Magistra." Vitus used her formal title now, to make it clear he gave her that sort of deference. Though in Niobe's case, it wasn't just that he respected her as his apprentice mistress, but she'd gone well out of her way to help him. Several times over. "And I'd love to learn a little more about what's involved in the process, whatever you can share."

"You do always want to learn everything." Niobe said it fondly. "There, that's tidy. I'll expect to have them to you by the end of August, Hereswith, and I'll let you know if there's any delay or change to that."

"Grand. And you're always reliable on that count. I'm glad you've not taken on any direct commissions yourself."

"Ah, well, the Fortiers won't come to me. They certainly wouldn't come to Vitus. I gather they're talking to Antonius Whitesnake, which is certainly a choice." Niobe did not, as a rule, comment on their fellow talisman makers to customers, though she certainly had plenty of opinions about them. Vitus frowned, before catching himself and smoothing out his expression. Whitesnake did competent enough work. But he took on commissions Niobe wouldn't touch. Certainly, he cared more for the status of who was hiring him than what they did with the work.

Though at least in this case, they all knew what it would be used for. The kind of talisman someone brought into something like a Council Challenge would be of use elsewhere, but not in many other places. Vitus did not know what happened in a Challenge, but people went in prepared for fighting, for ancient magic, for all the things that could go wrong with both. Most of them came out in one piece, the vast majority of them, but not everyone did. Sometimes there were injuries. More rarely, there were deaths, though there hadn't been one since well before Vitus had left school. Arabella Connington's challenge in 1878, and he thought there hadn't been one before that for a while. It made him think of something, and he cleared his throat inquiringly.

"Yes, Master Deschamps?" Council Head Rowan nodded at him, giving him the courtesy title he had not yet entirely earned.

"I was wondering about the preparations in case something goes badly. An injury, or—" He let his voice trail off.

"If you had time, we could use another talisman to stabilise after injury. Either of you, I'll let you decide who. Standard rates for that, of course." It would be a nice bit of work, those were time-consuming to make, and therefore costly. But they could be done with a good garnet, so the materials costs were reasonable. She went on, leaning back and watching Vitus directly now. "We have a Healer on site, of course. But the challengers can come out in any order and spacing. Sometimes there is a great deal going on all at once that needs tending. More than a few of our number have training in emergency healing, of course. It is relevant often enough."

Vitus nodded. "I appreciate that, Council Head." Then he remembered there had been something else. "You had two things you wished to discuss with me, please?"

It made her snort, some amusement that he didn't try to make sense of. He knew he wouldn't understand why. "The personal, yes." Her voice turned warmer, but a cautious sort of warmth. Vitus had seen her in public, at the Council rites. He'd heard her speak more than a few times in other settings, but now she was turning all that focused power on him. Not harshly, not in any way that seemed a threat. And Niobe was sitting there, comfortably, not moving, her hands folded in her lap. "Have you heard anything from Thessaly Lytton-Powell recently? The past five days?"

He had. The question was what he said now, because it had been telling and also confusing. Vitus took a breath. "May I ask why you ask?"

"You know there's gossip." Vitus nodded, since he did. The parts he'd heard were overblown and vague. In most cases, it would have drifted away when people picked up some other topic. Only she'd sent that letter. Council Head Rowan went on, her voice now far more gentle. "Her aunt was one of my dear friends, and I am worried about Thessaly. I cannot call on her, not at the moment, without making a very large fuss of it, the kind of fuss that would not be much of a help. I am asking if you know anything more, so I can decide how much to worry."

Oh. That put a different picture on it. If she was saying so, Vitus began to think he should be even more worried than he already had been. He considered and then decided that perhaps honesty might serve. He couldn't have said why he chose it, except that a conversation with his brother flashed into his head. What seemed like years ago, Lucas had asked him about Thessaly, and when Vitus had answered him, Lucas had said Vitus was going to get his heart broken. He'd handed Thessaly his heart - or at least enough of it - ten days ago. And now he was worried about her. Whether or not she ever talked to him again, he'd be worried.

"She sent me a note on Monday, two days ago. It was posted from Trellech, the box in Portal Square." Which was about as anonymous as could be managed, without going to a lot of trouble. "It was very brief, just that the Fortiers had spoken to her about the gossip. She could not communicate with me. Not now or for the foreseeable future."

"They have decided ideas about how one should behave." Council Head Rowan sounded displeased. "And have you written back or seen her?"

"She said I shouldn't write back. That if she could contact me again, she would, but - she didn't sound hopeful about that. She didn't say so, of course, but I could tell." He let out a breath. "I'm worried about her too, but I can't do anything. And you can't do anything, you said."

"Not at the moment. It is possible matters will shift again." Then he felt Council Head Rowan's full attention on him. "What do you want for her?"

"Her happiness. Her wellbeing. Her to choose what she wants, who to talk to. I— I don't like that she can't do that. I mean, I'd like to talk to her again. She's clever, very clever, and she's skilled. We were working on a project, and besides, I think she needs a friend." It came out in a rush, and he looked down, flushing.

Whatever else was true, those things were also true. Vitus wanted to offer her a great deal more, and the kiss they'd shared had made him want more with her too, the way she'd trusted him. Most of all, though, he wanted her well and happy.

He looked up again, warily, to find Council Head Rowan nodding once. "It may be a few more weeks, but I hope she may have a little more, mmm, flexibility in due course." Then she considered. "I might get her a note."

Vitus shook his head. "She asked not. I trust she had a reason for that. If she'd meant not by the usual methods, she'd have said so." Thessaly hadn't even hinted that he might leave one near the orchard gate, where she'd let him in to talk twice. She must have good reason. "And I won't put her at risk by trying."

"So you don't care for Childeric Fortier either, then." Council Head Rowan nodded. "Good to know. I won't tell anyone." Then she stood. "A pleasure, Niobe. Let me know when you've the talismans for me, or if you need me to choose a stone. I'll have my man of business bring the deposit by— tomorrow or Friday?"

"Friday, by preference. Any time during the day should

be fine then. I've a piece I need to do some work on tomorrow." As the Council Head stood, Vitus stood as well, and then he moved to get the door. Council Head Rowan nodded once at each of them, sailing through, and Vitus ducked ahead and past her to get the front door.

4

A MINUTE LATER.

As Vitus closed the door, he heard Niobe call out, "Lock up, please, and come upstairs. I'll put the kettle on in the kitchen."

Vitus was rarely invited up to Niobe's flat, which had half the space of the first floor and all the second. He never went further than the secure storage room without a direct invitation. He hadn't, he realised, been up there since before he left on his Grand Tour, and he wondered whether anything had changed. Now, he locked up, bringing up the warding carefully to prevent anyone from coming in, and turning the sign to "Closed."

By the time he'd dimmed the lights and gone upstairs, he could hear Niobe moving around in the kitchen. She'd left the door to the private rooms open, and he paused in the doorway. "May I?"

"Sitting room, please. Just a minute." He heard a bit more - cups and a plate or something of the kind - as he went and found a chair. There were five, though he did not know who she entertained up here, with a low table between them and side tables as well. The room had not, in fact, changed much since he'd last seen it. All he could see was that the door to her private study had a new hanging on it. The new one was a piece of tapestry work depicting mountains and a sunset, done in what looked like silk thread.

He claimed one chair, tucking his feet under him again, and then feeling awkward. Vitus wasn't sure what to do with his hands, and that was a metaphor made flesh for the rest of him. He did not know what to do with the conversation he'd just had, or what Niobe wanted to talk to him about now. All he could do was wait until Niobe told him. She would, or at least enough of it, he knew that. She wouldn't have called him up here to let him squirm and guess.

Fortunately, the tea didn't take too terribly long. She brought the tray out, setting it on the central table. Then she poured him a cup, and one for herself, as well as handing him a small plate with three biscuits. He blinked down at it. "Three?"

"You might need some cushioning," Niobe said, agreeably. "Besides, I want an excuse to go by the bakery again. They have a new set of flavours this week." She favoured a bakery two blocks away who did a series of rotating biscuits based on the season, the current events, and the baker's whim.

Vitus studied his biscuits, in the absence of any further direction on the matter at hand. One had a blackberry jam in it. One appeared to be a vanilla shortbread dipped in chocolate. The last one - well, he'd figure that one out when he tried it. It was uninformatively lightly browned around the edges and beige. He took a breath, tried a bite of the shortbread - excellent as always - then set the rest of it down. "Cushioning?"

Niobe nodded. "First, do you have questions about the

conversation just now? And second, you know I generally leave your personal life to you, and you leave mine to me. But we have reached a point where we really ought to talk about a thing or two."

Someone else might have bristled at it, but Vitus just couldn't. For one thing, he was entirely at sea with what he felt and what that meant about what he should do about anything other than actually making talismans. Making them, he was fine at. Finding people to buy them, that was an entirely different and complicated problem. And he may well just have undermined all his chances for that. "Yes'm."

"First, do you have questions?" Niobe guided him back to that point relentlessly.

He did. Ones he could ask, even. "May I ask how long you've known the Council Head? And, erm. I've never heard you talk as openly about other talisman makers. To me, yes, but not to clients."

"Ah, those are good questions. Have another bite of biscuit while I figure out where to start with that." She considered. "I did some talisman work for Oscar Willett - second most senior to her on the Council, these days - back when I was just done with my apprenticeship. She trusts his judgement. And it was a delicate piece. He's a specialist in Flora, it was stabilising the conditions in one of his greenhouses. I've done a number more for him since." Her chin came up. "Though the downside of getting good longevity out of a piece is that he's stopped building greenhouses and doesn't need more. Not of those."

Vitus chuckled a little. "Problem of the profession, yes." A well-made talisman could last for years, decades, depending on how much it was used and how much the user's own vitality could feed it. Some designs had to be fed deliberately, some restored themselves by being around ambient magic - a thoughtfully warded home, for example. And some just kept going, long beyond all reason, if everything came together right in the making.

"As to talking about other makers, you've never seen me do it. But you're near enough done with apprenticing. We're just waiting for you to demonstrate your skills with the current pieces. And it's certainly nothing I haven't said to you." Niobe shrugged. "Some clients get more honesty than others. I wouldn't say that to just anyone on the Council, but I would to Hereswith. Oscar. Arabella Connington. People I've done work for."

"Not Metaia Powell?" Vitus couldn't help asking. It came out before he could reconsider it. But also, if they were being honest, he'd ask that question.

"I never did a piece for her. I'd want to do that to get a feel for someone, their magic. And there are people whose commissions I might not take. Hesperidon Warren, for one, not that he'd ask me. He'll only go to someone he respects, and women are not in that category as a rule. He, I am sure, is just waiting for Hereswith to retire or die. Hopefully the first, she's earned a bit of quiet ten times over."

"And Antonius Whitesnake?" Vitus took a sharp breath in, then let it out. "And the Fortiers?"

"You've seen enough of Whitesnake, you tell me. And then, yes, that would be the other thing we need to talk about." Niobe leaned back, cupping her hand around the mug of her tea. Vitus tried to gather his thoughts.

"Whitesnake has a reputation. No one's ever successfully caught him in making a nasty one, but he's one of the people who'll help you get one. If you wanted." Vitus did not have that need. If he were going to use a nasty talisman, one that snared the mind or harmed by its presence, he'd have the commitment to his goals to do it himself. Not that he actually would, but it was the principle of the thing, to do it with his own work if he did it at all. "And he's got an apprentice right now."

"A year in. Have you met him? Daniel Rollings. I don't think they were at the last guild discussion." The guild of talisman makers, such as it was, was more a loose affiliation. All of them - even Niobe - kept their secrets and their techniques close. But there was a benefit both in setting the base prices for certain kinds of standard work, and in having a sense of what others might take on that you didn't do yourself. A well-placed referral could benefit everyone: client, referrer, and the one who did the work.

Niobe shrugged and went on. "The Fortiers like Whitesnake because he won't give up their secrets. He doesn't complain about the oaths they make him take. I'm fairly sure he owes them a complicated favour or two, and not the sort that get him invited to the posh parties, like your family. Though of course, for the more honourable sort of work, they favour Ambrose Gallagher, as you know."

Vitus froze for a second, then he said carefully, "Not me at the moment. Or at least I wouldn't dare turn up."

"That is a sensible thing for you to realise." Niobe let out a breath, slowly. "What actually happened? Or what will you tell me, anyway?"

"You hadn't asked." Vitus looked up. "And I don't— I don't want to hurt her. Even accidentally."

His mentor considered. "All right. If I summarise it as you wore your heart on your sleeve - I can still see the outline, though I think you're hiding it with most people - and she did not slap you in the face, am I right?"

"And then someone came who knew her, who - I don't think she saw anything directly, just that we were talking, more privately. That's bad enough. More than enough.

She didn't say directly, but I think she fears the Fortiers. Or at least Childeric."

"Well, she has seemed - from what you've said and what I know - to be a sensible young woman. She should be scared." Niobe blew out a breath, the wisps of hair that had come out of where her hair was pulled back moving. "The Fortiers are determined sorts, and they don't care much who gets hurt between them and their goal. I don't think they'd bother to ruin you unless you press the issue, but they certainly won't care if they cause you trouble. And Childeric, more so." She considered. "There's some gossip about him, but the most I know directly is that he does not have a sense of proportionate response, shall we say."

Vitus considered this. Then a question popped into his head that he couldn't dislodge. "Do you know what Council Head Rowan thinks about Childeric challenging?"

"It's not the most promising field. We talked about that a little before I called you down. Childeric Fortier. Theo Carrington, obviously, who has yet to prove himself. Like Fortier, honestly, though he's more honest about cutting a swath through willing women. Cyrus Smythe-Clive, who's very much the black horse, no one's seen much of him since the death of his wife. He's still finishing his apprenticeship, I think, but almost done. And Heliotrope Masterson, though from what Hereswith said, no one thinks terribly well of her chances. Hereswith thought they might get one or two more. Some people take a while to commit to it."

Vitus nodded. "And none of those appealed much to her? Not that anyone understands how the process works, even the people who go through it."

"No one talks about it much at all, even the people who try and fail. I mean, I assume there's an oath, or something as good as one." Niobe shrugged. "So. What are you going to do? About the Fortiers, and about Mistress Lytton-Powell."

"Thessaly." It came out of him automatically. He sighed, and then he flushed. "Sorry."

"Be careful. That's all I ask. And that expression on your face, that's not careful. Not anywhere anyone else can see. Your family, I suppose."

"I just— she needs a friend. I want to help. And I know I can't now. I was foolish, and I fouled things up, and now she's on her own dealing with - whatever. And missing her aunt terribly, I know that."

"She is a Lytton and a Powell. They can take care of themselves." Niobe said it a touch dryly. Then she tilted her head. "Usually. I won't deny the woman could use more friends than she seems to have." Then she brushed her hands together, abruptly changing the subject. "I want you to put together a list of the gemstones you'd like. Same arrangement as the other stones we've decided on. You pay me back at cost, and if I have a need for them, you give them back. We renegotiate at a year, for whatever you haven't needed, and I let you go in with me on any further buying trips."

"It's too generous." Vitus sat bolt upright. This was at least a distraction from all things Thessaly. "It's not part of our agreement."

"Our agreement was for your apprenticeship. This is about after your apprenticeship." Her mouth turned up and then she was laughing. "Oh, Vitus, I would never let you go off and scrabble on your own. It reflects badly on me. You'll need to justify what you want, and some stones are too dear for you. No one will pay you enough to cover them yet. But you know that. Choose from the rest."

"If you insist." He'd been assuming he'd have to boot-strap everything, make enough of the simpler talismans from common rocks to build up stock. "I suppose I'd best go round to the flat and look one more time. The warding specialist is coming tomorrow afternoon. If I'm to have gemstones as well..."

"That would be why I told you today. Off with you, and come finish the inventory in the morning. We'll talk about your lists when Hereswith's man of business has been and gone Friday. He always turns up between ten and eleven. And you'll have an idea by then about Carrington's stone, as well."

"Yes'm." He glanced down at the biscuits. He'd eaten the jam one almost without noticing. He took a few bites to finish the beige one, which turned out to be vanilla seasoned with spices, more cardamom and nutmeg than anything else. Then he bobbed his head. "Thank you for the tea and the biscuits and the common sense. Tomorrow?"

"Tomorrow. Off with you." She waved a hand at him, clearly planning to linger a bit over her own tea. Vitus nodded one more time and then took himself off across town to the new flat. On the way, he glimpsed what he was sure was Thessaly, but well across the street. He couldn't even risk the ordinary polite gestures of acknowledgement, tipping his hat or nodding.

5

JULY 27TH IN NORTHUMBRIA

Thessaly sat uncomfortably on the chair she'd been assigned. Father had gestured at it, a raised eyebrow and one slight nod. Mama was posed on the end of the sofa, veil pulled back from her face, looking like a statue.

It had been a terribly uncomfortable week. As soon as she'd come back from Arundel, she had been kept on a tight schedule. It had often involved Father escorting her to her apprentice work or Mistress North walking her back to the portal afterwards. Or sometimes Mistress North had deputised one or another of the staff or her relatives to do it. Thessaly had been given no chances to even consider a conversation with Vitus, and she hadn't dared risk a note by the orchard. Even if she'd been able to get out there without someone wondering where she was. She'd just managed the one she'd dropped in the mail box at Portal Square when Father had been drawn away by a conversation for a few minutes.

She had admitted at least temporary defeat and had spent her evenings teaching Hermia to play increasingly complex variations on card games. It was a useful skill among the women of the Great Families, when they were banished to a drawing room after supper. That was the time when the men smoked and drank and talked about whatever men talked about at such times. The trick was in being able to match the skill of the other players. Or, specifically, to lose gracefully by the right amount to flatter or win by the smallest margin, so it felt like a fair game.

Thessaly vastly preferred an honest match, but if that wasn't on offer, she'd build the skills to manage what there was. Playing with Hermia was good practise, anyway, her sister had a good mind for cards. And when they'd played a game or three, Hermia could usually talk her into doing some illusion work, a chance to practise doing them on the fly. They'd deal out a few Tarot cards and Thessaly would make a story out of them, most commonly.

Now, however, Hermia was firmly upstairs. It was Mama and Father and Cousin Owain, and two of Father's brothers, and one of their wives. Just Aunt Amia. That meant Aunt Lysanne was ill, pretending to be ill, or had been told to stay home. Knowing which one of those was true would help Thessaly with how this conversation went.

She could do the maths, though. Mama and Cousin Owain, compared to Father, Uncle William, and Uncle Edgar, and Aunt Amia. Four to two, with Thessaly firmly in the middle, were uneven odds. Especially since Mama was really not in her best form at the moment and hadn't been since Aunt Metaia's death. And Thessaly didn't blame her. Mama and Father had been arguing - Thessaly had heard a little through closed doors. When they weren't arguing, they were ignoring each other, or emotionlessly tending to what needed doing.

More than that, though, Mama looked quite a bit at a loss. Thessaly had been thinking, on and off, how much Aunt Metaia had mediated some of the familial interactions. Not directly, very often, but her presence had counterweighted things. She had argued the harder points, the ones Father didn't want to concede, and it had let Mama focus on others. Now, all of it fell to Mama, and Mama was not sufficient to the challenge. Thessaly wasn't either, or at least her current position wasn't. She could not blame Mama for having the same problem, and yet she desperately wished the situation were different.

Father coughed once, and the quiet conversation of Thessaly's uncles stopped. "Now, we have some choices to make as a family." Father glanced at her. "Thessaly, you are being permitted to join us, since your upcoming marriage is a key part of the consideration here, but you are not to speak unless given permission."

That was unfair, but not entirely unexpected. Father did not take well to people questioning anything. Especially when the questioning came from Thessaly. Hermia had a better knack for it, but she was younger and Father doted on her a hair more. Thessaly was supposed to be competent, and quiet, and not interfere.

"Now, with Metaia's death, as with all changes, the politics of the Great Families are shifting. When Sioned and I married, it was a decision of both our families, hoping to produce children with potent magic. A son would have been preferred, but daughters also have their uses."

If there had been a son, if Thessaly had been a boy, or if she'd had a brother, this particular line of the family would continue on. Thessaly was marrying out - marrying a Fortier, the Fortier Heir. There was no other option. Hermia might have someone marry in. It wasn't impossible. Father more or less had. That's why they were the Lytton-Powells and not the Lyttons. Though he'd insisted on the double surname, rather than becoming a Powell.

"Thessaly will marry Childeric Fortier next March, at the completion of her apprenticeship. This coming September, she will be there, waiting, as he emerges from a successful challenge. I gather from his family that there are plans to ensure Thessaly understands her obligations as a Council wife. I have told the Fortiers they have free rein in that regard. The Lyttons and the Powells are both ancient respected families, but the Fortiers have their own customs as well as the tending of the land magic. You will defer to their preferences in all things, Thessaly. Am I clear?"

Thessaly wanted to argue, but the thing about it was, he was right. She was committed to the marriage, unless something dramatically changed. Or she died, which would be a dramatic change, but not actually one she remotely wanted, so that was no use considering in any practical sense. Breaking the engagement would mark her as stained in some way, inexplicable. It would certainly preclude any other marriage of the sort that would help Mama and Father and Hermia - or their extended families. And it would leave Thessaly herself to the whims of fate.

And while illusion work was a specialty that could earn a respectable living, she had been focusing on learning all more decorative. She was familiar with the nuances suitable for a woman of means, not any of the forms that were a more reliable income. Or, for that matter, also not much at all about managing a business. She'd learned the rudiments of managing accounts, but it was assumed that her mother-in-law would teach her what was needed for the estates in due course. The Fortier estates, in specific, but until the betrothal, there had been a placeholder there, the mother-in-law she acquired by marriage, whoever she married.

Now she just nodded once. "You are clear, Father." He wasn't asking for her to formally agree to it or make oath.

Thessaly certainly wasn't going to suggest that. She had more than enough oaths binding her as it was. She wouldn't add more willingly.

Cousin Owain cleared his throat. "Certainly, it is proper Thessaly be here. Some of this concerns her." It made Thessaly pleased to hear it, but Father immediately glared at Cousin Owain. Father said nothing, but Thessaly could read it clearly. Cousin Owain had never married, certainly had no children to guide. He might be on the Council, he might be Mama's cousin and Thessaly's, but he was here somewhat on sufferance when it came to family decisions, apparently.

Father immediately launched into his particular goal. "Which brings us to other considerations. Metaia was— my dear— not nearly as devoted to influencing matters for the good of the family as she might have been." That 'my dear', directed at Mama, sounded anything but. Cousin Owain shifted slightly in his chair. "Which raises several questions."

"Pardon, before you go on..." That was Aunt Amia. "May I ask if there is any further information about her death? It seems to me that might be relevant in the next steps."

Father looked stone-faced, not saying anything. Cousin Owain cleared his throat. "If I might? Hereswith has been getting regular reports and making sure I was available to hear or read them. There are ongoing concerns that it was related to Metaia's Council work."

"Go on, then." Father waved a hand at Cousin Owain, and moved to sit on the sofa, on the other end from Mama, who barely looked at him.

"All Council Members have a general remit, the good of the land magic and tending to the agreements with the Fatae. But we also have our own personal interests and concerns. We do not think this was any matter related to the general work of the Council, but something personal to Metaia herself. She had mentioned to Hereswith that she was investigating something, that she had more information she'd discuss after the rush and the obligations of the Solstice. But she— we— never got the chance."

"She didn't mention anything about the topic, nothing at all?" Uncle Edgar leaned forward.

"Hereswith knew her well - they were close friends, as well as colleagues, had been since early in Metaia's time on the Council. Closer than Hereswith and I are, the sort of closeness that meant they had tea together, regularly, were in and out of each other's homes without a formal invitation. Hereswith knew she was working on something, quite long hours, the few weeks previously, but not what."

"And that's when she changed her will." Uncle William coughed. "Any idea about that?"

Father actually flinched. Thessaly wouldn't have seen it, except she was looking right at him. "The timing is worrisome. We have taken steps to have the will fully proved in court. They expect to do so in mid-August. Apparently, there have been some bottlenecks with the scheduling, a courtroom needing renovation and key personnel not available."

Cousin Owain got an odd look on his face at that, but he didn't say anything. After a moment, Father went on. "Now, the goal is, of course, to preserve the family lines, to increase our influence. And given our situation, that means beginning to consider marriage agreements for Hermia. Possibly also apprenticeship, but she has not shown a strong talent in any direction thus far."

Thessaly bit her tongue to avoid commenting that it wasn't as if Hermia's current education encouraged that. Nor unless her magical talents were enhanced by painting porcelain or light and refreshing music. Fortunately, before Thessaly did herself some damage, Uncle William said, "How about having her come and try her hand at several things on our side? See if she shows any knack worth developing. She's of an age now. Perhaps the Powells might also come up with a few options. Sioned? Owain?"

Owain glanced at Mama, and then nodded. "I'll ask around. A couple this summer. A week each, that sort of thing?" It was late July already, so there was only August and a little of September. "And perhaps an aim of more next summer?"

There was a little chatter about that, and the end goal of finding somewhere between three and six options, reasonably balanced between the families. Thessaly let them go on about who might be willing, listening attentively to what the suggestions were so she could tell Hermia. She was fairly sure Father and Mama wouldn't think to.

Unfortunately, it didn't give her much warning when Aunt Amia said, "And Thessaly's ensuring there won't be more gossip, I'm sure."

This time, it was Thessaly who flinched. "No, Aunt Amia. Father's been very clear. And so has Childeric. Of course, I won't do anything that might cause more difficulty."

Father immediately added, "She spent last Friday to Sunday at Arundel. Of course she can't socialise in public yet, but we thought that would give them a chance to make sure of the expectations."

"Yes, Father." Thessaly swallowed hard, tasting something foul in her mouth for a second. "Lady Maylis was very thorough, explaining some of their customs. And I went out riding with Childeric and Sigbert." She wouldn't

- couldn't - talk about that conversation. "Just on the estate, of course."

"Well, now, they've got a fair amount of estate to ride on." Uncle Edgar sounded more cheerful. "I wonder if we might ride with their hunt sometime this autumn, William, Harold. I gather they've a splendid kennel master right now." That at least devolved into conversation about country sports, and Thessaly could listen with one ear again.

In due course, Thessaly was dismissed - and so was Mama, who retired to her room. Father clearly intended to keep chatting with his family. Cousin Owain paused as he was gathering up his hat and stick in the foyer. "Walk me out as far as the gate, Thessaly, would you? We've barely spoken."

Thessaly bobbed her head. "Of course."

Once they were a good way down the path, Cousin Owain turned to look at her. "I know your aunt didn't care much for your marriage arrangement. Can you hold on a little longer, and we can see if there might be some adjustments to expectations? Nothing I can share right now. Please don't ask."

Thessaly blinked at him. There was something earnest there. "If you say so, Cousin." She then let out a breath. "Perhaps if you have a little time next week or the one after, you might come for tea, and talk about something, work through some skills with me? I get my regular illusion work in, but nothing else right now, and I feel, I don't know, sluggish."

"Some of that's understandable, my dear. Grief is hard on a body, and hard on our magic. I know that whatever else you're feeling, you miss Metaia as much as I do and as much as your mother does. As you should. But yes, I can bring some of my sort of exercises with me. Let me go home and consult my diary, and I'll make arrangements. Or you might reasonably come to us, if you'd like to be out of the house. There, will that give you a little something to look forward to?"

Thessaly nodded. "It will, thank you." It was a change from the monotony of the days. And also a relief from the tension-filled visits to Arundel that were to be part of her life until that was where she lived. "Here, let me get the gate." She went to open it. Cousin Owain tipped his hat, and she waited until he was walking down toward the portal before she latched the gate and turned back to find Hermia.

6

JULY 27TH IN TRELLECH

Vitus had completely lost track of time. He'd come into Trellech early Saturday morning. He'd spent the day alternating between getting the flat set up the way he wanted and staring at the design for Carrington's talisman. Now he was up to the point of creating a larger-than-life diagram of the chosen stone. The next step was to determine the layout of the inscriptions and consider how to align this diagram with the three-dimensional reality of a stone for the optimal effect.

He'd chosen the stone itself with Niobe yesterday. That was part of why he couldn't get the project out of his head. This stage was where the painstaking work came in. Talisman work was partly about gem cutting, partly about precision, and partly about understanding what a particular stone was suited for. Unfortunately, it also required a snap of ideas coming together, and that part had remained out of his grasp.

Vitus had time, still. He had all of August; he didn't need to do the final attunement for the stone until the beginning of September. On the other hand, the astrological timing for beginning the work favoured the beginning of the month, though such things were almost always a tradeoff. In the end, Vitus - after consulting with Niobe - had presented three choices. Carrington's response to them had been informative, as Vitus had hoped, as much as choosing a stone was itself.

The thing about talismans is that there was almost never one and only one road to a goal. For example, a piece Vitus was working on for his own use, for a growing and stable business. One could get to stability by volume of work, a steady, earthy determination. A talisman for that road might support stamina, putting in long hours to keep the doors open and the new items coming. Or one could build a business by making the right connections in the right moment and having the gift of the perfect thing to say on your tongue. That was a far more Mercurial sort of enchantment.

Others might favour the burst of luck and expansion that came with a talisman focused on Jupiter. Sometimes it was the sort of business that made a difference. Someone who sold perfumes or other sensual luxuries might do best with something honed by Venus, making a mirror of the divine beauty so many people aspired to touch.

Vitus was more or less set on something that leaned into thoughtful, clear-sighted understanding of how to help his clients with their chosen road, building relationships over time. That wasn't entirely Mercurial. He didn't want the thread of the trickster getting tangled in there. He didn't do well in that mode at all. Vitus wanted an underlying honesty, playing to his actual strengths, not talking up illusionary ones.

That just made him think of Thessaly, of course. He had been thinking of her, on and off, all week. Not so much when he was focusing on something else, in an actual conversation, thankfully. But any time like this, when he was alone, some passing consideration would draw his mind back to her, as promptly and unerringly as a compass pointing north.

She spent her time in illusions, but there was something fundamentally real about her. Some of that realness was how she was entangled in a situation that not only concerned Vitus but also apparently other people. Council Head Rowan had asked about it for a reason. But some of it was how she was. Grounded, like she was made to connect to the earth, in an essential way, not dance away into the air like a sylph out of Fatae tales.

That brought him back to considering the choices Carrington had made. Vitus had, in keeping with the different paths to a goal, presented four stones, wanting to see if Carrington had a powerful reaction to or against any of them. Of course, he'd suggested carbuncle, garnet in this case, which was a classic protection stone. Niobe had a fine almandine garnet of deep red in her stores, and Vitus had brought back a pyrope garnet in a vibrant red from Germany. The name echoed a glowing coal, a burning ember that could keep fires going.

The garnets were more about Mars and conquest and rising to the challenge. But the lore also spoke to eternal love and faithfulness in some uses. That would not play to Carrington's strengths. In fact, he'd laughed when Vitus had laid out the associations, and clapped Vitus - rather hard - on the shoulder. It wasn't the stone he'd chosen, but the conversation about it had opened up the rest of the discussion beautifully.

Vitus had next offered a delicate piece of peridot - not an optimal colour in most people's eyes. The olive green didn't flatter many. And that also had connections to chastity, when worn. But it needn't be worn anywhere visible or even often. That was the trick with a talisman for a particular goal, of course. One could wear it when needed, and remove it otherwise, so long as the magic was tended properly.

That was a Mercurial stone, the sort that would favour someone like Odysseus or even Orpheus out of legend, quick-tongued and clever. But it also had associations with and took charmwork well for healing, as well as being excellent for personal protection and the ability to communicate.

Then he'd laid out a golden and warm-glowing carnelian for courage. That one was more straightforward as stones went, in some forms, all Mars, but in perhaps a different beam of light from the carbuncle. Carnelian brought patience and calmed anger. Carrington didn't have a reputation for needing either. He might proposition any woman plausibly in his path, but there had been no hint of that kind of ferocity in the gossip. But it also brought courage and it could be engraved with a man with a sword in hand to keep one free from enchantments and vices.

Finally, Vitus also suggested coral - though that was rather more complex to work as a talisman - for protection from danger and the gift of wisdom. Vitus almost wished they'd had a suitable blue opal. That was good for wishing. But opal really needed a proper setting for the talisman work to anchor in. An opal couldn't be carved or shaped using most talismanic techniques without shattering the fire inside.

Carrington's hand had drifted over the options. He'd taken his time. Then he'd settled on the peridot. He was, it seemed, a man who wanted to be thought clever, quick-witted, and able to decide in the moment, even more than he wanted to win. That was an interesting thing to know about his client, and Vitus had filed it away, along with some ideas for future work if this went well.

The other part of the consultation had been getting the measure of the man's magic, running through a set of standard diagnostic charms that gave a sense. Between that and the fact they now had a working relationship, Vitus was now in an excellent position to contact Carrington about particular stones as they came in.

None of this was actually getting the design any further, but before Vitus could get his attention back, there was a knock on the door. It startled him - no one but the landlord and the neighbours knew he was even here yet. But it could, Vitus supposed, be someone looking for Philip, not knowing. He stood, going across the narrow hall to peer through the tiny hole in the door. He blinked when he realised who it was, his hand automatically going up to open the warding. "Lucas!"

His brother was laughing. Then he took a step into the hall, letting Vitus get the door and wards behind him. "Mama and Papa are going out. I still have the evening on leave, and you hadn't turned up. Mama gave me the address, of course. Perhaps we could find somewhere here in Trellech? You know I rarely get a chance. My treat." Lucas then gave him a broad hug, pounding Vitus firmly on the shoulder, all cheerful energy.

When his younger brother let him step back, Vitus snorted. "And you wanted to see the place. You could have asked."

"And you'd have said you weren't ready yet. I want to see where you're settling in. I don't care that you're not unpacked or whatever. Show me around, do? And I mean it about supper somewhere out. My club, your club, a pub, I don't really care."

Vitus gave in. He always did, because his brother was a

boundless source of energy, and honestly, he wanted to see what Lucas thought. "Consultation room and office, first, workroom, bedroom?" he suggested. "This, as you can see, is the hallway. I am open to ideas about artwork for the wall, something small but professionally engaging." The entryway was small, and perched at the top of the stairs from below. The hall ran back parallel to the stairs, toward the tiny kitchen and bathing room, with the door to the workroom nearest the entry. To the right was the bedroom, which had almost nothing in it, and across the hall diagonally to the left was the consultation room, which other people might use as a parlour or sitting room, or something of the kind.

"As you wish." Lucas tucked his hands behind him, following Vitus like an eager puppy, glancing around down the hallway, then coming into the consultation room. "Oh, the light! I see why you like it. That's lovely, plenty of good light, no shadows to cause you trouble. And it's a grand big room, isn't it? Was that his desk?"

The great wooden desk under the window had indeed been Philip's. "Magistra Landry offered to let me keep the furniture she didn't need - and some copies of books, reference books, that they already had." It had been an odd offer, when she'd made it three weeks ago. If Vitus took over the lease of her dead son's flat, she'd make it worth his while. He'd been nervous of it until he'd realised she was hoping for someone to spot something left behind, and be the sort to tell her rather than sweep it away. "The desk, some of the storage furniture in the workroom - he kept a lot of materia in there, there's a lovely cabinet. And the bedframe, though I got a new mattress brought in this week. Not that I'm sleeping here or expecting to, often."

"And that's where he died." Lucas considered. For someone actually in the Army, albeit in a cavalry unit that hadn't often seen direct service, he could be a tad odd about death.

Vitus coughed. "Magistra Landry was clear - and I do not know how she knows - that he died elsewhere. Found here. And yes, that's exactly the sort of thing I'm not going to poke at further. I know better. Anyway. It's too generous an offer to turn down, especially given the light. And the landlord's been reasonable to me, I think partly because he was terrified I'd back out of the arrangement and he'd have to deal with Magistra Landry again."

"Can't blame him. Even if he doesn't know all of her reputation. All right. Nice big desk, glowing light, plenty of bookshelves to start with. Do you want a sofa for the fireplace or a side chair or two?"

"Either? There's some space. And I'd like somewhere to read and take a break from my work. The table there, mostly for consulting work, but I might refinish it to something better suited to looking at stones. Or get a few suitable tablecloths. There's a woman who can do meals for me - we've planned for lunches, starting next week - and she'll also add what little laundry I have when she takes hers."

"There, all the proper comforts. And does she also do the cleaning?"

"Mmm." Vitus had been less sanguine about that one, because of the protections on the stones. "We're working that out. I've interviews with two people Mistress Burley - that's the woman next door - suggested. Not the workroom, and timed when I can be here and supervise."

"I'd say you're too cautious, but you have chapter and verse and citation about it, so I won't." Lucas grinned at Vitus's acknowledging snort. "I like the room much more than I expected. It's comfortable, isn't it? The proportions, the height, the placement of the fireplace. Large and structured enough for consultations, but not off-puttingly formal."

Vitus nodded. "Exactly. And that's the sort of setting I'd like to do my consultations in. Niobe's space is a little more cramped, the layout is different, and the office feels more formal. But of course, she has the living space above, too. Here, this way." Vitus gestured them down the hall, to the narrow kitchen and the bath. That had a functional but slightly narrow tub taking up half the room, a sink tucked into an alcove. "All the conveniences, but not much space. But again, if I'm not actually here day in and day out, not such a problem."

Lucas nodded. "The workroom?" He asked it hopefully, and Vitus snorted, going and pressing his palm on the warding panel, then murmuring the opening charm under his breath, tapping his fingers in a particular pattern as he pulled his hand away. It needed all three - or two more checks, if it wasn't Vitus himself. Niobe knew them. No one else did, or likely would. "And there's an alarm that will warn me - I've got something on my watch fob now - and the man who set it, if there's an attempt to break in." He opened the door.

The one flaw of this room, for his purposes, was that it had a window. However, it also had the cabinets Philip had used, and the entire set could be and were additionally warded. He'd set a desk under the window, along with additional warding. The shutters opened inwards for a further layer of protection, as well as charms to obscure what was going on inside from anyone outside. That was expected, if it were being used as a bedroom, it wouldn't attract much notice. The rest of that wall had the cutting equipment, the various wheels and tools needed for the actual work with the stone.

Lucas took a few steps in. "Space for more bookshelves.

And your storage. That looks sturdy. It's also functional for you?"

"It's always a little awkward to open multiple layers of warding, but that's part of the work. I'm still figuring out how to arrange things. I don't have nearly as much stock as Niobe, but I want to get used to where things are. I'll work it out."

Lucas took a step back, eyeing him. "And you like it here. You think you can do what you do here. Well."

"It's not about the location." Vitus swallowed. "No, it is. But I think I can do well here. I want to." He swallowed hard. There was a lump in his chest. "I liked Philip. I told you that. He deserved better, whatever happened. And I like to think he'd appreciate a crafter being here, a magical one. I like to think the flat wants someone like that. I don't know, it's making a talisman out of a flat, all the little details and alignments."

Lucas blinked, then his smile grew broader. "Oh, now, that makes sense. Why didn't you say that first off? And look, I might know some people who have furniture. One of my unit - also magical, he went to Dunwich, originally. His parents have a shop, furniture and things for the home, some art. Reasonable prices, I gather, and they'd like the challenge of finding things to suit."

"Glad to talk to them." Vitus let out a breath. His brother approving mattered. "You've an eye for colour. Come look again at the consulting room, and help me think through what I might look for."

"Something to suit your stones. But yes." Lucas patted him on the shoulder again. "Then we can go find somewhere nearby to eat. Let them get used to seeing your face around."

7

AUGUST 2ND AT ARUNDEL

Thessaly felt decidedly uncomfortable. The Lammas land rites were not exactly a social event, more an obligatory ritual, which is why Thessaly was there. She was marrying into the land magic; it was important she understand the rites. This time next year, she'd be a new bride, taking her place as the Heir's wife for the first time.

There were many first times coming her way, she knew that. It began with Childeric's challenge for the Council. She'd never attended a Challenge before. Then there would be her wedding, the entire day a flurry of firsts, ending with her first bedding and whatever specific rituals the Fortiers had around that. There'd be the first morning waking up married. After that, there'd be a string of smaller firsts, strung like pearls. The first letter or notecard or invitation written, the first supper party as a married woman, the first gala, those would all build, one on the other. Eventually a first child, and all the naming and rituals and other firsts that went with that. And of course, the first time she went through each of the land rites and the Council rites as one of the family. That would take the entire year.

This was not yet that, but she was expected to be here, whether or not she was in mourning. Father had come with her, at least, which gave her an excuse to hang back and be quiet. They had arrived that morning, and they would go home that evening, when the events of the day were over. The Fortiers had nodded and welcomed them, but none of them had lingered to talk. Instead, she and Father had been left to amuse themselves.

Of course, Lord Clovis and Lady Maylis were quite busy. There were rituals to prepare for, guests to welcome, and they - and Childeric and Sigbert - had been kept busy with all of that. Dowager Lady Chrodechildis had been enthroned on a wooden chair brought out to the field they were blessing for the purpose. She was holding court, with people circulating around her. Thessaly had made her proper curtsey and greeting, but then she'd stepped aside to let others, more favoured, have time.

Along with the chair, there was a large pavilion. It was big enough to hold twenty people comfortably, but the sides were drawn down, hiding whatever was inside. It was brilliantly purple, with accents in gold and black, again the Fortier colours.

What surprised Thessaly, however, was seeing Dagobert and Laudine Fortier. She hadn't seen Dagobert since the Council rites on the summer solstice, before everything went horribly wrong. Childeric had said his uncle had been seriously unwell, the sort of unwell where Childeric had implied the need for strong attendants.

Honestly, Dagobert looked like he'd been unwell, indeed, but in a way that had shrunk him. He was pale, even at this point in the summer, like he hadn't been outside at all, and he was leaning heavily on a cane. No one had offered him a chair, and that seemed unreasonable. His wife Laudine was standing next to him, ready to offer an arm. Garin, their son, was quietly at her other side.

Laudine had made an overture weeks ago, and Thessaly still did not know how to interpret it. She couldn't go over now, though. The rest of the family would absolutely notice. And while Dagobert and Laudine were here, they weren't exactly being included either. Even by the Dowager Lady Chrodechildis, Dagobert's mother. As Thessaly watched, Laudine bent down to whisper something to Garin, and Garin nodded solemnly. Then he made his way across to his grandmother, saying something to her.

Whatever was wrong within the family, Chrodechildis wasn't taking it out on a nine-year-old. She listened intently to Garin, then explained something, gesturing at the pavilion, then nodding at Thessaly and her father. Garin made a little bow and came over toward them, pausing a few feet away. "Pardon, Master Lytton-Powell, Mistress Thessaly? Maman wondered if you would like to know what is going to happen, and Grand-mère said I might explain."

Thessaly blinked, but then managed a little smile. "That's kind, for your mother to think of it, and for you to explain. Please, I'd like to understand more."

Garin stood up a little straighter, as if this were some missive from a king in some earlier legendary age, controlling himself rather than babbling away. "First, we make offerings to the land. Uncle Clovis and cousin Childeric will walk around the bounds of the field, that takes a bit." His nose wrinkled up. "It's a different field each year. This one is bigger than most."

Thessaly nodded, not commenting on his expression.

His parents, she was sure, would have called attention to it, or his aunt and uncle. The boy was nine; he was doing a good job explaining. Thessaly would not scold him for being nine. "And then? Oh, and do you know what the libations are?"

"We have wine to drink, of course, but there is beer for this." Garin lowered his voice. "I don't care for it, but everyone gets a sip, and it's very traditional."

Thessaly nodded again, solemnly. "And then?" She prompted Garin one more time.

"Then Uncle Clovis and Aunt Maylis and Childeric and Sigbert go into the pavilion. And Grand-mère. Last year, Father and Maman did as well, but not this year. There are beds in there, um. Portable beds?"

"Cots?" Thessaly suggested. Her father had stepped away, she noticed, speaking to a couple of others there. He obviously had his own agenda for the day, one he had absolutely not shared with Thessaly. She would have to be furious about that sometime later and safer. "Do you know why?"

"Oh, that's even more traditional. They sleep, and then the dreams are interpreted." Before he could explain more of that, there was a beating of a drum and some sort of horn blown, calling everyone to attention. Garin made a little bow and promptly headed straight back to his parents. The rituals unfolded more or less as Garin had said. There was the libation, there were Clovis and Childeric processing off around the field, more like taking an afternoon walk. People chatted quietly while they were gone, then there were cups of sharply bitter-smelling beer passed around, with calls for a good harvest, a libation for bounty, and so on.

By the time the senior Fortiers retreated to the pavilion, Thessaly was entirely ready for luncheon or at least a seat.

The guests were taken off to a flat area near the house, but some distance away from the dreaming, and fed.

Thessaly hadn't known what to expect here, but the luncheon gave her enough time to get a better sense of who was invited and who was not. It was not nearly as large a gathering as May had been. There were perhaps fifty people here, all close and established connections to the Fortiers.

Magistra Landry was nowhere in evidence, but of course she was still in deep mourning for Philip. Thessaly had seen her a few times, at a distance, on the estate, so she was here at least at times, and not in Trellech. But she had not seen or heard any of the Fortiers offering her any particular comfort. That might simply be that Magistra Landry's every move forbade thinking she might need anything from anyone else, but still. Philip had grown up here from the time he was twelve, surely the Fortiers felt some sorrow there themselves?

It was hard to tell about anyone's actual emotions right now. Everyone was on their best behaviour. But Thessaly had a sense that many of the people here were here because they had to be, because the alternatives were more terrifying. She didn't know what to do with that at all, what that meant about the hold the Fortiers had or might have, and what it implied for herself.

It took some time for this part of the rites. The plates had been cleared for maybe fifteen minutes before there was any movement near the pavilion. Certainly it was long enough for everyone to go through four or five sets of polite conversations in different combinations, never touching on anything risky.

Then there was a movement. One corner of the pavilion opened and tied to allow those within to emerge. Thessaly focused almost immediately on the way Childeric was moving. He was leaning in to talk to his father, something urgent and bringing him to strong emotion. She couldn't hear the words, of course, but she'd seen him like that when he'd threatened her.

Only he couldn't be threatening his father. That made no sense. For one thing, Lord Clovis had far more power in the world than Childeric did, though after Childeric's challenge, that balance would change quite a bit. But Lord Clovis didn't look like he was arguing back. Maybe a minute later, Lady Maylis emerged, rubbing her temple as if she had a nasty headache, the sort of lightning bolt of pain that happened sometimes. Sigbert came out a little after that, offering his grandmother his arm. She looked shaken, but Sigbert also looked pale under his tanned skin from a summer outside on horseback and foot.

The five of them talked, huddled together, for several minutes while the guests tried hard not to stare. Finally, Lord Clovis offered his wife his arm, and they made a small procession. Childeric jerked his chin and gestured for Thessaly to come join him, and she went over. She didn't dare hesitate. It would make things look worse. He immediately took her arm, murmuring. "Chin up, make a good show of looking like you know what you're doing."

Since no one other than Garin had actually explained anything to her, this was harder than it ought to be. But apparently what they did now was make a small procession around the immediate environs of the house. They circled clockwise, of course, sunwise from the front lawn and the dovecote through one set of gardens, and into the back and the kitchen garden.

That was where the bee swarm happened. Or had been happening. Thessaly was not an expert on bees, but she understood swarms to be both natural and not an instantaneous event. All at once, there was tumult and commotion, and people screaming shrilly as bees were found in unexpected places. The staff shepherded most of the guests out, but Childeric lingered to see to whatever needed doing, and Thessaly found herself by the garden fence, watching from a safer distance.

Sigbert had said something. Or at least that's what Thessaly thought, because Childeric was gesturing fiercely again, as if refusing to admit some truth. She'd seen him do that duelling, before, when he couldn't admit that someone had been better or just plain more correct than he was. When he came back to Thessaly, the only reason she couldn't hear him stomping twenty feet off was that he was wearing outdoor boots, designed for traction in soft ground, not noise on paved paths. There was just the low, vibrating thud.

"Is something the matter, Childeric?"

"No." He almost spit it out. Then he took a breath. "There are certain things that could be read as a bad omen. Of course it's not. Swarming bees are actually quite lucky, so long as we know where the swarm lands. Our beekeepers are tending to it."

She could see people in the proper gear, veils and covering jackets and gloves, with the little lamps that poured out soothing smoke. "Perhaps we should get out of their way? Where do we go next?"

Next was, unfortunately, also not a good omen. They arrived at the edge of the river, some lengthy walk later, to find that Garin had slipped down into a boggy bit. There was an ongoing debate about how best to get him out. He was about knee deep in muck, and there was nothing to hold on to. Thessaly cleared her throat, when it became clear that no one had an actual idea. "Please, could we fetch three or four good long sticks or posts? Six to eight feet. We want to overlay them enough to give him something to pull on, don't we?"

How she said it must have worked. The words themselves certainly weren't any great feat of rhetoric. But she had experience staying calm when some accident happened - it was common enough in duelling practice - and people did seem inclined to listen to her. It took a good fifteen minutes, but eventually they had some strong farmhands with sturdy bits of wood. That was enough they could brace them against each other and give Garin something solid to pull himself out of the boggy bank. One man caught him up, pulling hard, and the mud gave way with a sucking sound.

Thessaly didn't have time to say anything to him, not more than to see he'd lost at least one shoe in the process. But he was safe. The man was taking him firmly back to get cleaned up and checked over, and Childeric was pulling at her.

"We need to finish. Make the right show that everything's well." Thessaly didn't argue, just let him escort her.

It wasn't until they'd looped through the long drive that led to the manor up to the portal, then around the edge of the lawn on the far side, that Childeric spoke again. "We'll be wrapping up earlier than expected. Grand-mère has a horrible headache. Dreams, visions from dreams, they're a longstanding tradition, but these were—" He almost went on, then he cut himself off. "Do you have any tendency to premonitions?"

Thessaly certainly wasn't feeling particularly well herself, at this stage in the afternoon. Despite - or perhaps because of - the bright sunlight, she felt faded. Or maybe like a silhouette puppet, projected upon a wall. The land also felt odd, though she didn't really have words for it. A little hollow, a little as if the wood of a floor had begun to rot out and crumble. She swallowed, gathering her words into something more useful. "Not generally, no. Shall I tell you if I have particular dreams, anything that might be relevant?"

Childeric stopped walking then, as if he couldn't think and walk at the same time. Then he nodded. "Yes. Please do. I'd ask you to stay and keep the party going, but Maman made it clear we can't ask that of you. Not until equinox, when you're out of mourning."

At least Thessaly would have time to prepare herself for that. "I appreciate that. This has been a lot to take in, all the customs. Perhaps sometime, when there's less to do, we might talk through more of them, so I can make the right show of things?"

"Perhaps." Now Childeric started walking again, the single somewhat dismissive word the only thing he said until they were back among the other guests. He left her with her father, almost immediately going off to see to whatever other tasks demanded his attention. Or whichever was more interesting to him. Possibly both.

8

AUGUST 3RD AT THE COUNTRY ESTATE OF THE FOUR METALS

Saturday night found Vitus at the door to one of the workrooms at the country estate for the Four Metals. It was one benefit of the society, having plenty of space to spread out and experiment without people looking over one's shoulder. The estate had belonged to the society for a good two hundred years, with new outbuildings popping up like mushrooms here and there for different needs.

Tonight, they were in one that had once been a tithe barn, the floor now paved over with stone, and intended for use for larger or heavier sorts of rituals. Not the forge, of course, or the kiln. Those were elsewhere. They had their own particular requirements. There was a long table near the entrance for people to leave their bags and supplies. As Vitus set his bag and satchel of supplies down and came over, Merryn waved at him.

"There you are. Hope it wasn't a problem to get away on Saturday night?" Merryn Penforth was the person who'd put this together, and currently somewhat a senior among equals in the society.

"Not a problem at all, Merryn. Good evening. My fault

I didn't leave enough time for Portal Square. I hope I didn't keep you waiting." Vitus nodded politely. He knew three of the five people here well enough now, though to varying degrees, but he only knew the other two by sight and reputation.

"Not at all. We were just chatting about Lammas rites in the various places." Merryn's voice got cautious at the last.

"Nothing but what we did at home for me this year. Papa had an invitation to the Fortiers, but thought it better not." Vitus shrugged slightly. It wasn't as if people hadn't heard the gossip. And here, if he wasn't exactly among friends and allies in the ordinary sense, everyone had sworn to the wellbeing of the society and their fellows in it. Then he inclined his head. "Magistra Remmerton. Magister Hollington. And Daedalus, Amays, evening."

"Oh, first names, please." Thirza Remmerton waved a hand. "I'm glad to talk, and to see your work directly." The last time he'd seen her had been at the society's private memorial for Metaia Powell. Thirza had been the one within the Four Metals to first become aware something had happened with Metaia. From what little Vitus had heard later, they'd been supposed to meet up for the Midsummer Faire, and Thirza had become extremely worried when Metaia had not turned up as expected. Vitus knew even less of Philemon Hollington.

It was an interesting assembly, and that was part of why Vitus was here. Oh, he'd have come anyway, because Merryn had invited him particularly, and her last several invitations or suggestions of that sort had been working out well for Vitus. Merryn herself focused on stone carving for larger markers and warding, but she also did some enchanted devices, smaller ones like toys. Amayas had a knack for storage boxes and devices.

Daedalus loved devices of all kinds, great complex contraptions like his namesake in legend, and also tiny cunning ones. He knew Thirza did work with colours and pigments to support enchantments, and Philemon had an interest in the rituals that enlivened a magical piece.

Now Vitus spread his hands. "Merryn only teased me with what you had in mind, enough I could bring the right tools and materials. I'd love to hear more."

The plan, it turned out, was to do some exploratory work to figure out a better way - no, better ways, plural - to connect materials with the rituals they were part of. It explained why Merryn had invited Vitus. That was core to the work of a talisman maker, but of course, they wouldn't be working with gem quality stones, but in other materials.

Vitus leaned back on his back foot, considering. "What's the goal here?"

"Well, for one thing, you've seen some of the research about electricity. You've been at a few of the lectures, you've said." Daedalus had too. Of course, it was right and properly aligned with some of his interests. "I was thinking about some of what was at the one two weeks ago, about making circuits. How with electricity you can encourage or impede the flow in different ways, for various effects. Greater storage ability, or moving it over longer distances."

It made Vitus blink. That was the sort of very large, very complicated, and decidedly dangerous idea that changed the world. Of course, people had been considering various things with electricity and magic for years, but this was more ambitious in several directions.

Now, he considered the people there. "You're thinking of using stones of some kind to anchor it. Stones and metal, I assume." None of them specialised in it, but anyone in the Four Metals had some basic skills to work wire or cold hammer copper. And it'd be copper they wanted for this, almost certainly.

"Thirza for pigments to anchor what we're doing, enchant it, frame it in a particular mode." Daedalus said. "And Philemon, for a ritual format for it, something to give it boundaries, magically. You because it's an application of a talisman."

"And because even with the little Merryn told me, I thought we'd want amber," Vitus said, amused.

"Electron." Thirza's voice was quiet, but everyone else gave her space for it. "That's what the Greeks called amber originally. Usefully conductive of vitality, whatever other properties it has."

"More to the point," Vitus said. "It's not the cheapest of stones to get in quantity, but there's plenty that's no use for jewellery or talisman work, and that should do for this. I brought a fair bit, though I'm assuming we'll split expenses in some sensible way?" Merryn had implied that. And all the other five were well-established in their fields, less concerned about the costs of something like this.

Thirza chuckled. "Since Merryn invited you, we've coordinated funds from the society, within reason. Unless the price of amber's gone up substantially since I noticed, we should be able to cover the expenses comfortably. And we realise this is something else on top of you establishing yourself and your other work."

That was true. On the other hand, if they could figure out how to make this work, Vitus could think of a dozen applications for talismans. And especially those used in a stable setting, like a home or business. He'd share them with Niobe, of course. That was the decent thing to do, when they could be shared. But it would give him potentially a significant edge over other talisman makers. "I appreciate that. And the fact you're including me, of course."

It made Merryn grin at him. "All right. Perhaps we begin by talking through the overall idea, figuring out who has ideas for what. Bring your notes, bring your amber, Vitus, if you would. I've a cloth we can use to lay everything out."

Vitus nodded at her. The next three hours were taken up with all six of them tossing ideas back and forth. They started with pieces of amber on the cloth, to mark locations and patterns, talking about how to chain the pieces together in sequence. They got little experimentation done - they'd need wire, drills for the amber, and proper structure for the ritual. But they did get as far as specific ideas to research and try.

Better than that, it felt fair. Vitus had started a little uncertain about chiming in, but all the other five specifically encouraged him, asking particular questions. Where group projects had always been tricky at school - Vitus was often the one left with the tedious grunt work because he'd get it done - this wasn't like that. Each of them cheerfully sorted out what they'd work on before their next meeting. They also established the best contact points.

It was at that point Philemon blinked. "Wait, I know that address. Wasn't that Philip Fortier's place? Same building?"

Vitus rubbed his face with his hand. "Same flat." He turned his hands over. "Magistra Landry asked if I'd take the lease over. I'd done a consult with him a few weeks - well, before. I'd been hoping to get to know him better. And she didn't want to deal with the landlord, and the landlord didn't want to have to find someone new. She was polite but terrifying when she asked. Emphasis on the terrifying you wouldn't want to say no to."

"Were you at the funeral?" Philemon considered Vitus as if seeing him in a new light.

"I was. Why?" Vitus could think of several possible answers to that question.

"Just there's a lot of unanswered questions about his death. I gather the Penelopes couldn't find evidence. The Guard's still investigating, but they don't have much hope of it. My cousin's a new Captain. Of course, she couldn't say much, but no magical traces. And aside from an odd burn, nothing quite like they've seen before, there wasn't a mark on him." Philemon added, "You're a brave man."

Vitus considered. "I think it'd take even more bravery to say no to his mother about it. And the flat's gorgeous. Not big, but the light is fantastic, both my consulting room and the workroom. That's hard to come by, or anything in that location. People tend to stay put."

"The funeral, I heard they didn't explain anything. Just the ritual." Philemon considered. "I don't suppose you know more about it?"

"Thessaly..." He cleared his throat. "Thessaly Lytton-Powell, erm, before the gossip, she wondered if it was a sort of ritual duel. And I asked Magistra Landry about it, and she said to tell Thessaly she was on the right track. I don't know if that helps you any."

Philemon got a predictable look in his eye. Vitus knew perfectly well that meant the other man was going to be up all night looking at reference material. He added, a little hurriedly, "I don't think Magistra Landry would talk about it more than that. And Alexander's out of the country for a good while. A year, at least, from what I picked up."

"Huh. Odd, he still went. You'd think his mother would want him home." Philemon shrugged and turned away, packing up his last things. It took Vitus a little while longer, and he looked up to find Merryn and Thirza were the only still left.

"Glad I asked you along, then?" Merryn was a little teasing.

Vitus nodded. "Very. I'm looking forward to next time. It's an interesting puzzle. And promising, if we can make it work." He nodded once at Thirza. "You aren't regretting adding me?" He felt he could risk teasing just slightly.

Thirza shook her head. "No. I was inclined to, mind you. Metaia liked her first impression of you." She stretched, sobering for a moment. "You weren't in school with Smythe-Clive, were you? Cyrus?"

"Thessaly was, I'm sure you know that. We just overlapped by a year, different houses. My younger brother did some things in duelling club with him, but Smythe-Clive was competent, not best in the year or anything."

Thirza nodded. "There's gossip about him. Burning the candle at every possible end, as far as anyone could tell. And I— it was Metaia's seat, and she'd not want anyone destroying themselves in pursuit of it. I just wondered if you knew anyone who might talk sense into him."

"If his sister can't and hasn't, I don't know who can. Lucas knew her a bit better. They were the same year, though she was Fox House, and Lucas is Boar." Vitus spread his hands. "I'm doing some work for Theo Carrington, so even if I thought he might listen to me, I'd be the wrong person. Conflict of interest."

Thirza tilted her head. "Huh. I won't ask what. That's prying. I'll be curious to hear the results. Will you be there?"

Sometimes, those assisting with pieces got an invitation, but Vitus certainly wasn't making assumptions. Carrington had suggested that if the talisman work went well, he might see his way to it. On the one hand, he didn't want to deal with the Fortiers. On the other hand, it was a chance to build connections. And on the third hand, Niobe was doing some work for the Council side, and that gave both of them a reason to be in attendance. "Probably. It depends if Carrington likes how the commission came out before he can truly test it."

"Well, I hope that goes well, then. I might be lending a hand with some of the behind-the-scenes coordination. Friend of the Council, all that." Thirza waved the idea along before turning and gathering up her bag. "Anyway, I ought to get off home. Have a good night."

She turned and walked out, leaving Merryn and Vitus alone. Merryn shrugged and Vitus helped her put the few bits of furniture back in order, before they went off to the portal, all with little further conversation. He got the sense Merryn was chewing on something important too.

9

AUGUST 4TH IN SOUTHERN WALES

"Here, through here." Thessaly looked around curiously. She'd never actually been to Cousin Owain's home, he'd never offered before. Of course, the Powell family events, if they were at one of the family homes, tended to be at the main estate. This house wasn't any part of their direct line.

Thessaly counted through it in her head. Cousin Owain was her second cousin once removed, Mama and Aunt Metaia's second cousin. They both descended from Thessaly's great-great-grandparents. Like Aunt Metaia, he hadn't married, but he lived with one of his aunts and his sister in a large house, one of the family properties.

Enfys, his sister, was married, but her husband mostly spent his time travelling for business, some sort of import and export work, and their children were still in the nursery. The three sets of adults each had their own spaces. Thessaly had expected she might see Cousin Tegwen and Cousin Enfys, but she wasn't expecting anyone else.

She'd always called him cousin, as a title, because that was a good way to be proper, without it taking a minute to say any ordinary sentence. If he'd been closer in, she might have called him Uncle, but Mama had frowned when someone had suggested that. And even at five or so, Thessaly had known never to do that again. So Cousin Owain it was.

He had invited Thessaly out for a quiet tea conversation, and some discussion of ritual theory. Thessaly had expected Mama to object and tell her she needed to stay home. Instead, Mama had suggested she go, so long as she was back before Father came home in the evening. That implied many underlying currents, only some of which Thessaly could even glimpse.

Thessaly hadn't been able to decide if Mama was encouraging her to spend more time with the Powell side of the family. Or, conversely, if Mama were simply wanting to get one up on Father right now, by encouraging something Father would dislike. It was a secret sort of game play, because if Father actually knew, he'd be upset, and there would be more arguments. Either way, Thessaly desperately wanted time out of the house that wasn't at Magistra Aldine's or Arundel, and she had leapt on the chance to say yes.

Cousin Owain had met her at the portal, inside the stone walls of the estate, but tucked away in a corner near the road. Not that there was much traffic on that road, they were not as remote as Bryn Glas was, up near Snowdonia. But there were few people to bother them, apparently. The Powells, as an extended clan, owned properties all over Wales by now, and a few in England as well. They were brought into the family one way or another, and then kept up for the family. It wasn't at all like the land magics, except for the family estate on the north coast, west of Bangor. Only it was. It was a network of land, and now she was going to have to think about that more when she got a chance.

Now, though, she was being shown through the entry hall, down a passage, and then out into an open courtyard. It had far more people in it than she'd expected, seated at chairs, small tables holding glasses of lemonade or tea, and small pastries and cakes. She counted five heads besides her cousin.

"Pardon, Thessaly, but we wanted a word, and this was the most effective way to manage it. And, we hope, not one that will cause you trouble at home." That was Cousin Tegwen, Owain's aunt, who'd been a tremendous beauty in her youth. She'd been in Fox House, and she'd honed her beauty so that people forgot she also had brains and strategy. She'd been married, but her husband had died young, and she had not remarried despite a number of offers. "Come sit, please, dear."

It wasn't as if Thessaly was going to flee through the house, out across the fields. She was not dressed for running, for one thing, and for another it would serve no purpose. There was a chair waiting for her. "Cousin Tegwen. Cousin Enfys." Then she took a breath. "And Cousin Alwyn, Cousin Siorus."

All of them were older than she was, by a good bit, a generation or more. Cousin Tegwen, of course, was two generations older, and so was Siorus. But none of the elders of the family were here, and that puzzled her. They all nodded, waited for her to be presented with a lemonade and plate of her own, and then the staff withdrew.

Cousin Owain coughed. "I did not bring you here under false pretences. I would indeed like to work through a few things with you - the workroom is right there, convenient. Alwyn and Enfys thought they'd join us, if you'd be willing."

Thessaly had been about to take a sip of her lemonade, but she set it down, then nodded. "Of course." Both of them might have some useful ideas. Alwyn did some quite systemic work with incantation magics, and Enfys had a knack for colour design, though her magical work mostly involved embroidery. Then she deliberately picked up the glass and sipped, hoping someone would say something else.

Tegwen picked up the thread, thankfully. "Owain told us about the discussion with your family, your father's family." She took a breath. "I was struck that it must have put you in a rather difficult position. We are also concerned about the wellbeing of the family, but I wish to be clear that this also includes you. And to be entirely honest, we are curious about what information you yourself have, and what you are willing to share with us. While understanding that you are caught between at least three points, and that is no steady ground to fight from."

The duelling reference made Thessaly relax, suddenly. Well, the reference and the fact that they at least wanted to hear what she had to say, in some form. She turned to Cousin Owain. "First, may I ask what you told Mama? And who else you intend to talk to about what I say?" She then added, a bit daringly, to Tegwen, "At least six points, though it depends on some definitional clarification." Her family and especially Hermia, the Lyttons, the Powells, the Fortiers, Vitus, and Thessaly herself. Not that she really got to count herself, exactly. She was at the centre, not one of the points.

He chuckled. "I suggested that we might get more information from you by asking you, but perhaps not when your father's side was looming. And she agreed. But it is up to you what you say. We will not press."

Thessaly considered that, because it was both soothing and confusing. "Why not?"

Tegwen spread her hand out. "Your mother is an exceedingly clever and socially deft woman, Thessaly. Metaia was magically much more sure of herself, of the two, but your mother has the ability to make plans decades in the making. Your marriage is one of them. An alignment with the Fortiers - or a small number of other landed families, none of whom turned out to have sons the right age who weren't already promised elsewhere - is the sort of thing that takes that kind of time."

"And then children." Thessaly kept her voice as neutral as she could, but then realised that was itself a problem. "It isn't that I object. I understand the obligations. And the agreements." She was expected to do her utmost - spelled out in an embarrassingly frank addendum - to bear two children, optimally at least one son, unless three separate Healers unbeholden to the family agreed it was too great a risk or impossible. That would mean a fair bit of somewhat invasive inquiries, as well as dealing with Childeric's expectations about how the whole thing should go.

Two months ago she'd been reasonably sanguine about it, but so much had changed since then. She hadn't expected she'd be passionately in love with him, but she'd expected they'd work together for their shared goals, cordially and companionably. Now, she was fairly sure about at least some of Childeric's goals, but the rest of it was far more worrying.

"Your father's family does have many thoughts about breeding magic for children. And your own magic is quite deft." Cousin Owain made it clear with his tone that was an actual compliment, not just politeness. "As I said when we arranged this, you have things you can teach me. And while I can see Metaia's hand in a lot of your work, you have your own approaches. You just need time to develop and hone them."

It was perhaps the nicest thing anyone had said about her magic in ages. She could see the gaps herself. It was a skill she'd learned in her duelling training. Thessaly had been faster to learn there, in some ways, or more flexible in the learning. Her illusion work had suffered from being in contrast to some things she'd had to do at Schola. She'd had to relearn a number of assumptions about magic and perception, then build her skills in making a convincing illusion. She considered her options, like a duel, and then she said, her voice as clear as she could make it. "Mama and Father have been arguing a great deal. They haven't told me, even Mama. But Mama said I should come today, just be back before Father is."

It made Enfys snort. "Well. I suppose that says a lot. Owain said that your parents were putting pressure on you to make things easy with the Fortiers." She glanced at her brother. "We've heard the gossip, of course. But may I ask, how much of it was true?"

Being asked outright was not how anyone else had done anything. Thessaly let out a breath. "I enjoy Vitus's company and conversation. We'd been working on some illusions properly giving the depth of lapis lazuli. I had other ideas. We have done nothing outside my betrothal agreements - or wedding. We talked, most of all." She took an instant to close her eyes and try to feel what path to take here. "I have had no one to talk to. About the pressures. The Fortiers."

Out of the side of her eye, she caught Cousin Owain go still, the sort of stillness she knew how to read. He had information, nothing he could or would share, she was sure of that. He didn't speak. Instead Tegwen nodded. "The Fortiers are dangerous to cross. You know that. You've heard some of the stories. I could lay out a dozen others, just in my adult life. They are known to be ruthless in pursuit of their goals, in business and in magic. You know enough about the troubles the Harrises have had the past few years?" Thessaly nodded once. That had been a chain of catastrophes. "At least two-thirds of those can be laid at the Fortiers' feet. Nothing that's gone against the law, but a few things that came close. And the Harrises provoked some of it. There were multiple insults from their side."

Thessaly would have to dig into the news about that rather more. She was sure Childeric wouldn't talk about it, and asking him was itself an invitation to a duel she could not afford to have. And there were a few other stories like that. She might be able to arrange time in the library in a month or two more.

Cousin Tegwen went on. "Your mother aimed you for them, and some of your betrothal is that you are, in fact, a catch by any standard in Albion anyone might want to name. Some of it is chance. Who else might be considered, around your age or a bit younger? And some of it is that, well. There has been some gossip, very quiet, about the strength of Childeric's magic."

Thessaly considered that, and the realisation she'd had when he'd been so angry. "I don't know, honestly. He won't duel me anymore, he hasn't for a couple of years. I thought that it was that I was better than he was, which I am. A problem of ego, not magic."

Siorus snorted. "Well, certainly also ego. Not a man who likes losing." Mostly he'd been sitting, listening attentively, making an occasional note or two, but not so much that it was anything like the complete conversation.

Cousin Enfys added, "There's some talk about how it's not just Childeric. That several around your year aren't showing skills or magic to the degree anyone expected. I have theories, and nothing has disproven them yet. That's part of why your father was considering various marriage proposals for you. You visibly are in good health, your magic is demonstrably strong, and you come from a good family."

Thessaly considered that, but she didn't have an answer for any of it. Whatever other offers might have been made, she was promised to Childeric. And whatever her magic was or wasn't, well. She hadn't heard details from others and she wasn't likely to. Not until she was married and a mother and tied into the networks of matrons plotting for their own offspring. That was, at best, near enough two years off.

"Nothing of that sort is a problem with you, to be clear? It occurs to me no one might have asked." Cousin Owain leaned forward. "Metaia would have noticed, I expect, if there were any concern, but she might have kept it to herself."

That made Thessaly feel more fond again, and also miss Aunt Metaia profoundly. But she shook her head. "Nothing's changed for me. Oh, I'm sometimes fatigued after the social events at Arundel, but nothing out of proportion, I believe. There's a great deal going on. I cannot draw on the land magic like Childeric and his family. And it's all new, on top of that. New things do take more out of one."

That got a chuckle of agreement from the others at the table. Then Owain sobered. "In terms of specific events, you should know this. If Childeric fails in the challenge, I have a plan to let you get away on your own until he's settled down. It is the sort of matter where I felt better putting some options in place, even before speaking with you. Hereswith was glad to agree, there's no bother there."

This was a suspicious amount of behind the scenes

plotting on Thessaly's behalf. None of which could be entirely explained by kinship, by friendship with Aunt Metaia, or by Thessaly herself. On the other hand, whatever Cousin Owain and whoever else were up to, she liked the sound of it more than being left on her own with upset members of the Fortier family. "Thank you." That was honest enough. "I don't know a lot else, honestly. Except that - you heard that Dagobert Fortier had been quite ill?"

"Not seen in public since solstice." Siorus nodded. "Long enough it's been causing some comment. Normally he and Laudine would have been at half a dozen parties, very much on display."

"He was at the rites at Arundel for Lammas." Thessaly took a moment to consider what to say. "He was using a cane. He didn't look at all well. Very pale, like he'd barely been outside, and Laudine didn't leave him." It wasn't the done thing to talk about the land rites, the sort of thing that was rude but not against any oaths she'd made. On the other hand, this part was relevant. "Part of their rites involve dreaming, a vision, or at least making the space for one. Normally Dagobert and Laudine would take part in that. This year they didn't. Garin told me that much."

That got a range of expressions from everyone in the courtyard. "Not what I expected. How did the family treat them?" Sirous was leaning forward now, his pen scratching at the paper with some reminder.

It was a far more troublesome question to answer. "They were included in the places where it would be obvious? But there was distance, and if it was visible to me, surely other people. Father noticed it, but of course he didn't discuss it with me. Dowager Lady Chrodechildis was definitely aligned with Lord Clovis, though. But the rites were - several things went wrong. No bad catastrophe, just off."

"That would be enough to unsettle anyone, I suppose." Cousin Owain nodded. "That's a bit more than we had. And we intend to use it to keep our own family interests in mind. That includes you, to be entirely clear." His mouth twitched. "I am fairly sure Metaia will haunt me if not, but we'd do it anyway. Powells take care of their own. It's just that sometimes we disagree extensively about what that actually means in practice."

That might well explain a lot of the trouble with Mama right now, beyond her actual reasonable grief. It made Thessaly wonder about Aunt Metaia, the ways she'd done her best to take care of Thessaly, until she couldn't. There was no help for that now.

Cousin Owain stood. "I did promise to get you back in good time, and Aunt Tegwen has places to be for tea. I am hoping in due time we might have more to offer you in the way of meaningful support. But until that's the case, I can at least offer some pleasant magical theory and experimentation. The ritual room's this way, unless you wish to wash up first."

Thessaly shook her head. "I'd love the chance, thank you." She inclined her head to the others, as Alwyn and Enfys stood to come join them. "Cousin Tegwen, Cousin Siorus, thank you for your time." They nodded back and were obviously going to pick up some further conversation. Cousin Owain showed her to the well-appointed and comfortably used workroom, and she let herself fall into the much more pleasant complexities of crafting a compelling illusion.

IO

AUGUST 9TH IN LONDON

"I am pleased to meet you, Master Deschamps." The man behind the counter came out, offering his hand first to Niobe and then to Vitus himself. They had come to London to make the rounds of her usual suppliers, both of stones and of the other materia necessary for their work. The shop itself was tucked among non-magical shops in Hatton Garden, the entire area was a nest of gem cutters and jewellers. "Charles Wentworth." He was older, perhaps in his early sixties, with silver-white hair and a neatly trimmed beard. Nothing so long it might catch in any of the cutting tools or foul them.

"Magister Wentworth." Vitus shook his hand, making a slight bow as well. Niobe hadn't had to warn him. She'd talked about the Wentworths, but this was the first time she'd brought Vitus along for the visit. The Wentworths, as a clan, had little patience for amateur fumbling. They sold to a chosen set of clients, magical and otherwise. They also had an eye for what stones might become fashionable in the next year or three that was likely enough a smidge of precognition.

"And a pleasure, Niobe, as always. I gather Mister Deschamps is up to snuff, then?" Magister Wentworth went to the front door, flipping the sign in the window and pulling the blind down behind it. Light still came in from windows above the door, but of course, this shop was not for showing off the gems to outsiders. "I have the list of what you were interested in. Some rough cut, some uncut, as you requested. Here, come have a seat."

Magister Wentworth led the way to a table, bringing up a charmlight above. "It's too grey outside to rely on the natural light, but of course, I'm glad to hold things briefly for the next bright day." Beyond the table, in the middle of the back of the shop, there was a massive vault door, the sort that had both mechanical and magical locks. Of course they'd need both here, as opposed to Niobe's protective warding. Now, Magister Wentworth opened the great vault door, propping it open with a massive ironwork piece. "Do sit here, M Deschamps. I'd like your comments."

More like he wanted to examine Vitus, but that was what Vitus had expected. And if he wasn't prepared for this, it was his own fault. "I've been following the news about the Burma ruby mines with some interest, but I've not had much chance to see specimens yet. Niobe mentioned you had connections there?" The Burmese mines had only opened properly for trade just two years ago, after the British Empire had expanded and taken over the Mogok region. Though, of course, they'd been mined for decades, so Europeans had some idea of the range and value of the mines.

"Those, yes, and some royal sapphires from the same region. And I have a few emeralds of interest, and then a number of other stones. Do you have a need for an aquamarine?" Wentworth asked Niobe the last, and she just smiled an enigmatic smile. Part of why Vitus was here - besides the introduction itself - was for a masterclass in the bargaining involved.

Vitus's role was to be interested and curious - no hardship there - while not actually expressing any desire for any particular stone. He did have a way to signal Niobe if he saw something of particular interest. But of course these stones were well out of his budget, even with how generous she'd been getting him set up. Or, well, depending on the prices, he might venture one notable ruby or emerald or sapphire. Perhaps especially if there was one that might be flexible for a range of needs. Likely only the one. And better if it were uncut, that would mean more risk for Vitus, but a better price by far.

Wentworth snorted, amused, and then went into the vault, bringing out a tray of stones. "We shall begin with the rubies, then. Some cut, some uncut." He set the tray down, then removed the cover, setting it well to one side. The small stones in the centre were displayed on pristine white velvet, letting the red of the stone glow through.

"The colour is startling, isn't it?" That was the thing about the Burmese stones. They were known for the depth and vitality of colour. The stones in Thessaly's engagement ring, those weren't Burmese. He was glad of that now, because they'd have looked even more like blood.

"Pigeon's blood, as they call it." Wentworth considered. "Take a look, tell me which you think are the highest quality."

It was fundamentally an unfair question, and they both knew it. This wasn't comparing apples and oranges. It was more like comparing different kinds of apples, for different purposes, cider against eating, early against late. Vitus forced himself not to rush. There was the evaluation of the stone itself, as a gem, what might turn up in any necklace of the wealthy and well-decorated. But then there was the question of the stone as a talisman or an anchor for enchantments, and sometimes that required entirely distinct qualities. An inclusion could make a gemstone unique, but it could also shatter a stone on cutting. At the same time, those exact inclusions could allow for unparalleled options for magical work.

He heard Wentworth and Niobe start chatting, while he looked at each stone, then handled them lightly and precisely, before finally pulling out his loupe and examining them. Five minutes later, maybe ten, they had a pause in the conversation, and Vitus cleared his throat. "Those two are the higher quality gemstone. It's a question of cut preference. I would love to see this with a rose cut. I think you'd lose less of the depth of colour. And this, as a mixed cut. But for a talisman, I'd favour this. The inclusions would align it against the base, for an outward reaching enchantment, naturally. Some protective charm, the sort that has thorns to ensnare and entangle. The three here, they'd do either way, but they're not top quality."

Magister Wentworth listened intently. "And the last one?"

"The last one is a spinel. As I'm sure you knew. It is entirely possible to catch me out, but that one? No." Vitus looked up. "Besides, there's no pleochroism." That had to do with the direction of the light. Rubies radiated it in multiple directions, spinel did not.

"As I expected." Wentworth nodded at Niobe, who looked amused. She wasn't surprised, of course, it was one of the first things she'd drilled him on. It helped train the eye.

"Niobe, if you'd like a look? And of course if you'd like to consider any of them for purchase. Perhaps the emeralds, next? I have a couple from the Egyptian mines." They had become somewhat less rare with the opening of the mines in Columbia. "The current prices are about what they've been the last few years, no tremendous changes."

Niobe accepted the tray of rubies and Wentworth went back into the vault, bringing out a tray of emeralds. These were, in fact, all properly emerald. He did the identification charm under his breath to make sure. An essential property of emerald, as one of his books had put it. No one had fully identified why there was a distinction. Or for that matter, between emerald and aquamarine and other beryls. But the charms could tell even when the eye wasn't as sure about nuances like depth of colour.

These were a joy to touch, and Vitus wanted to linger over them. He kept coming back to one, the way it felt in his hand. Soothing, nourishing, something deeply restorative. He wasn't likely to get asked to make a ring for anyone holding the land magic, not anytime soon. But it would be superb for that. Niobe had finished her own review, and now she was watching him. "That one in particular?"

Vitus glanced around, and Wentworth was at the end of the room, making tea. They'd be doing this in stages. The eye and the mind became fatigued too quickly otherwise. He shrugged one shoulder. "It would need the perfect client, and I can't expect that." He wanted to see what Thessaly would do with it, actually, though it was a stone sometimes used for truth enchantments rather than illusion.

Wentworth came back - the kettle was coming to a boil. "You've a good eye." This time it wasn't a test. "We'll come back to considering them." He took the trays away, setting them back in the proper places in the vault. Then the kettle sang, and it was another minute or three before he brought the tray with the pot and cups over. "You were in

Germany, weren't you? They've interesting lore about the stones."

Vitus felt himself blushing. "You have heard the gossip, sir." He took a breath. "If Childeric Fortier gave Thessaly Lytton-Powell an emerald ring, it would not turn brown and prove her unfaithful. She has done nothing against her oaths and agreements. She is a woman of her word." Saying that, though, made him want to see the stone on her hand, and he couldn't. He absolutely couldn't.

Wentworth nodded. He didn't press, other than offering Niobe a cup, then Vitus. They continued talking, quietly, for another few minutes, until Vitus had drunk half his tea and listened. Niobe asked, once they'd come to the end of the gossip, "Have you been seeing odd orders for things? I was trying to lay hands on some decent tourmaline, but there wasn't much to be had."

"No. We're near enough out. The only pieces left have inclusions. And I had someone round asking for large quartz crystals, and for copper ore. Not wire or fittings, of course, we don't deal in those, anyway." He seemed baffled, but also as if this were outside their usual sphere.

Vitus frowned, trying to track down some memory. Then he remembered one lecture he'd been to, that series they'd been running. "Wasn't there something recently, a paper, the last month or two, about the electrical properties of crystals and stones? Perhaps someone's doing testing? In quantity." His voice trailed off. "Piezoelectricity? I was talking to some people about that recently. Though we were working with amber at the time, so the electrical spark, instead, in practical work. And we weren't using anything gem quality, so a bit different when it came to vitality."

"Huh." Wentworth considered Vitus. "Not just content

to be a talisman maker, then? The gems aren't enough for you?"

That was politely said, and without obvious heat, but it was just as obviously a challenge. "The opposite, sir." Vitus straightened his shoulders. "I'd like to extend the art. I'm seeking understanding of why certain enchantments work best not just with certain kinds of stones, but certain cuts or varieties, or whatever other combination work best. Niobe has trained me well to trust the feel of the stone and the intuition about it, but the more that intuition is informed, surely, the better the piece."

Niobe looked triumphant, and Magister Wentworth raised an eyebrow, then lowered it. "I believe I would like to toast to what you come up with in the future. You are welcome to call on your own accord, by appointment. Once you are established, properly, I am glad to discuss favourable terms, such as Niobe enjoys. An early look at likely stones, and reasonable payment timelines once you've funds on record with - which bank do you use?"

"The Scali." His accounts there were rather barren, but vouching for his business practices was part of their service, once there was something to vouch for.

They finished their tea and then began working through the other stones. The process now was more conversational, certainly more relaxed, and Vitus moved round to sit next to Niobe so they could talk back and forth. She selected two dazzling sapphires, an aquamarine of the purest shade Vitus had seen, several diamonds, and a glowing piece of jadeite. Wentworth brought out a tray of cut and polished opals, just so they could both admire them. Though opals were delicate enough that most talisman makers avoided them unless they were mounted in a larger piece, they still deserved to be appreciated.

Finally, Niobe cleared her throat. "And that emerald

Vitus liked." Vitus knew better than to say anything. Wentworth brought it out, wrapping it all up securely, before Niobe tucked the box with the stones into the inside pocket of her skirts, sealing it up securely. They made their farewells, leaving the shop for other customers, and emerged out into the grey weather.

It wasn't until they were back at Niobe's shop, upstairs in the gem storage room, that Vitus felt he could ask. "The emerald?"

"This way, you know where it is. I don't expect I'll have a client for it in a rush. If I do, I'll use it. If I don't, well." Niobe shrugged. "We can discuss terms." She had all the stones out on the table, and she transferred that one into its proper storage box, then slipped it into the drawer of emeralds.

"She won't talk to me, of course she won't. Too much risk." Vitus said. "I can't— anything." His voice trailed off.

"That is now. Times change. Circumstances spin, like the wheel. I can sit here and quote platitudes at you for hours. I'll win. Go back to your own workroom and do what you need to do, and I'll sit here and be optimistic for you. On your behalf."

It was a cheerful, stubborn, unwinnable battle, and Vitus knew better than to try. He made a little bow and went out, setting the warding as he left so she wouldn't have to come downstairs.

II

AUGUST 10TH AT ARUNDEL

Thessaly found herself again in another unexpected gathering of people. She had been given a day's warning for this one. It involved an invitation to Arundel for tea with two women in order to discuss the expectations of a Council wife. Thessaly had put on the most stylishly made of her mourning dresses, and had her maid do her hair so it would lie smooth, flat, and elegant. And then she'd girded her patience, because the entire afternoon would be a duel, or at least close enough to need every strategy and skill she could muster.

Lady Maylis had at least let her know in advance. If it had been up to Childeric, Thessaly knew now there would have been no warning. But of course, Lady Maylis hadn't mentioned who else would be attending. That particular question occupied Thessaly for most of the early afternoon, trying to decide who they'd ask. She knew all the possibilities, after all.

The thing of it was, Thessaly knew enough of the work of the Council, more than most people. Aunt Metaia hadn't been inappropriate about it, sharing details that needed to be kept confidential. But Thessaly had a decent idea not only of the range of time and activity involved but also the more routine work and the seasonal aspects.

On the third hand, being the wife of a Council member - or she supposed a husband, though that had different social rules - differed from being on the Council itself. Thessaly was sure there was a whole layer of expectation in hosting and which events she should plan to attend. It was, in one respect, an excellent argument for an early pregnancy. Strategically, it would mean she could use the excuse of the risks of portal travel in pregnancy to keep out of the way until the gossips had some other target.

Not that it was actually an option until she was married, so she had six months of social events to plan for, at a bare minimum. That included the extremely visible ones at winter solstice. So, on the whole, best to go into this meeting willing to learn what she could, whether that was the intended lesson or not.

When she arrived at Arundel, a footman was waiting to escort her from the portal to the house. They went through the Great Hall and into the Great Chamber. She'd been here once or twice. It was the formal parlour for the Lady of Arundel, with a fireplace, a door to the gardens outside, a desk for dealing with correspondence. And right now, the chairs were occupied by three women. Lady Maylis, of course, but Thessaly immediately recognised Griselda Warren and Leda Grimly.

She'd considered Leda Grimly as a likely guest. The Grimlys were allies of the Fortiers, and they had the same sort of sharply applied magic that worried people about the Fortiers. Leda was in her early forties now. She and her husband, Fletcher, had two children. Thessaly had been in the same year at Schola as Ruan, but he'd been in Owl House like his mother. He'd been studious in class, like was expected of an Owl, but not a duellist. Selwyn had been a year ahead of Childeric, also in Fox, but he hadn't made much of a public reputation for himself since leaving school.

That was, now she thought about it, odd. Rather like Childeric, as well. Selwyn was married, a year ago, but his wife had been privately educated and Thessaly didn't know her well at all. The family went in for alchemy and ritual work, the combination of them. Casting her mind back, she thought that Council Member Grimly had been a protégé of the late Lord Vauquelin Fortier. Bearing that in mind would give her a better shape for what the afternoon held. Maybe. Hopefully.

The other woman was younger, in her early thirties. Griselda had married Hesperidon Warren six years ago, the year after he'd made his Council challenge. They had no children. Several times Griselda had disappeared from public events for a few months, in the way that women who were being cautious about the early stages of a coming child often did. Each time, she'd reappeared later without comment. Well, without Griselda or Hesperidon making any comment. Gossip certainly had comment to make, some kinder than others.

Thessaly was a bit more surprised to see her here. Aunt Metaia did - her mind caught - had not particularly cared for Hesperidon Warren. Thessaly thought, from a few scattered comments, that he disapproved of both what Council Head Rowan did and how she went about it. Griselda Warren herself was of a good family, but not a powerful one. They were known for steady magic, but not anything that might be described as passion or bravery. Such women were the pillars of Albion's elite, however, and gods forbid if anyone went against them.

Now Thessaly made a proper little bob of a curtsey,

aimed at Lady Maylis in her role of Lady of Arundel. "Lady Maylis, Mistress Grimly, Mistress Warren, a pleasure."

Lady Maylis gestured her toward a seat, to make the point of a triangle. The three women were arranged all in a row like the foundations of a pyramid, all focused on her. Thessaly did her best to ignore the discomfort of butterflies in her stomach while tea was poured for her. She declined a cake for the moment, because she was sure she couldn't eat it without it exploding down her frock.

They began by examining her, thoughtfully, but it was Leda Grimly who began the questions. "Now, of course, Maylis has given us a full detail of your background. Good marks at Schola, you are proceeding well in your apprenticeship, and there's no denying that skilled illusion work is a significant benefit to a hostess. Even if one hires out the work, you've a far better understanding of the quality. And you're pleasant enough to look at. That always helps as well."

Thessaly had, of course, been too young to pay much attention to two of their debuts. But while none of these three women had been the most beautiful of their respective years, they all knew how to use the looks and bodies they had as a tool and as a weapon. At the moment, they very much had the advantage there. All three were wearing brilliantly hued afternoon dresses, chosen for the vibrancy of summer. Griselda Warren's perhaps flattered her most, a teal that brought out her dark hair and green eyes. "Thank you, mistress." It was the safest thing to say.

"However, being a Council wife, that has higher expectations." Leda Grimly picked it up so promptly that Thessaly was sure they'd planned this out, rehearsed it. That made her wonder whether these two women were allies differently than their husbands or families might be. "We understand Childeric has made his expectations clear there."

"Yes'm." That particular honourific had all the hints of submissiveness needed for this moment, and Thessaly wouldn't turn down that tool in a time of need.

"All of Albion looks to the Council - and their spouses - as a model. We may or may not be the most beautiful or the most fashionable. But we are all in demand as hosts and hostesses, as guests, and as exemplars of what a woman of Albion might best be. Never go out in public without making sure your clothing is tended to, that there is no stray thread or sagging lock of hair. You will need a superb lady's maid. Whoever is seeing to you now is respectable for your current position, but you will need someone more polished before September." Leda Grimly pursed her lips. "Or perhaps more training for yours."

That was an argument Thessaly did not want to have with Mama. Having two lady's maids - of that sort of standard - in the same house would lead to difficulties in the servant's hall. They also didn't exactly have somewhere to put another lady's maid who would expect her own room and not to have to share the bathing room with the lower housemaids. Right now, Alma saw to her, and Alma was the senior of the housemaids. But she was fairly sure it wouldn't be kind to bring Alma here when she married, and maybe it would be better to hire someone new, with that in mind. "Perhaps, Lady Maylis, you'd be willing to advise, with an eye to a smooth fit with the household here in due course?"

Lady Maylis looked somewhat pleased at that. Thessaly couldn't quite tell whether it was the chance to have that much more control over Thessaly, the deference to the needs of the household, or something else. "I will give some thought to the best option, certainly." Now Lady

Maylis considered Thessaly. "I will say your manners are good, and your skill at conversation, so long as you don't let your own interests take over." She added to the other two guests, "Young women will press on about their current hobbies and trifles more than ideal, of course. We've all had to learn to hold our tongues."

"On that note," Griselda Warren said, coming in smoothly. "Speak far less than you think is reasonable. First, it prevents awkward moments. And second, you will hear quite a lot to your benefit, over time. Gossip, hints of some concern emerging, someone willing to extend themselves to flatter you, who gives something away your husband can turn to advantage." That last was more overt than Thessaly had expected, but Lady Maylis smiled at it.

Leda Grimly nodded. "If you must have your interests - and you will need things to fill your time - we recommend some sort of craft that is portable. Embroidery is traditional, but it needn't be the most common forms of handwork, so long as it is elegant and can be picked up and put down at need. Nothing that needs a tapestry stand, unless you prefer that for a quiet afternoon or evening at home. Keeping up on the papers and the news, of course. That goes without saying. But it is best if you also make time to read the currently popular books so you can find the proper opinion to express. The same with exhibits at the museum or evenings at the opera."

It was an extremely analytical way of going at the world. That did not precisely surprise Thessaly, but she was not entirely sure why these women were being so open about expressing it. Some of it was obvious, certainly to any woman who had survived and even thrived in Fox House. "I'd welcome recommendations, of course. My apprenticeship is still keeping me busy. But I've made a habit of reading the current novels in favour and such - it's a help for illusion work, of course."

There were general sounds that seemed more like approval than disapproval. Then, carefully, Griselda Warren cleared her throat. "Perhaps we might have a moment, Maylis?"

Lady Maylis stood. "I'll just take a turn around the garden." This had blatantly been pre-arranged, everyone knew that, but everyone kept to the fiction that it was an impulse.

Once Lady Maylis had gone out into the garden and closed the door behind her, Griselda focused on Thessaly again. "There are things you will learn - that we do not know, either of us - about being married to the heir to the land magic. And in due course, a husband who is Lord of the land. But there are things we know about being married to a man who has proven his skill in the most arcane of ways that Lady Maylis does not."

That was as true a statement as could be made. Certainly Thessaly could not argue with it. She simply nodded, forming her face into its most attentive expression. Leda picked up, her voice smooth, even a touch too much so. "You are a duellist, we understand, of skill. Treat every conversation outside the Fortiers and their allies as a duel. Treat every conversation within that group as a place where you must always think of the outward form, what others will take from it. Never contradict Childeric, there is no longer anywhere private for you, bar perhaps your own rooms with all due protections up."

Griselda nodded. "Such spaces are a privilege and a treasure, and I encourage you to show Childeric and his family that you can be entrusted with them. Everywhere else, people will look for signs in everything you do. Which dressmaker you do business with, which jewels you wear for what event, certainly any sort of more visible enchantment like a talismanic piece. How you hold yourself, who you speak with, how long, all of those will be measured and weighed by hundreds of people. But within the Council, there are also circles of allies and those who do not agree. Your Aunt was on one side of those, and Owain as well. Childeric will be on another. You must demonstrate where your loyalties are until no one can question them. Until you shape yourself to them, waking and sleeping, no moment unguarded. Do you understand?"

Thessaly went entirely still. Then she nodded once. She knew, the way she knew which way was down, that these women lived like that. Aunt Metaia had not. She was fairly sure Cousin Owain did not, and now she desperately wanted to ask him about the politics. But a Fortier, someone with these women as allies, would have to.

"I understand. I appreciate your clarity. Might we perhaps talk through, erm, the expectations for the day of the challenge itself, so I can do everything properly?"

That was an easier conversation. It involved understanding each step, where she might show excitement or adoration or whatever other emotion seemed supportive and encouraging to Childeric. There were also places where she was not to draw any attention to herself. They were clear but brutal in their explanations, and in the details of how much time a position on the Council took. There would be late nights, schedules upset, a husband come home in a foul mood because his particular project had been thwarted or a plan disrupted.

Thessaly thought that perhaps that presumed a bit more of a work ethic or a passion for hard work than Childeric showed reliably. Perhaps that would change in his challenge or in the days after. It certainly wasn't anything she could ask about, exactly what their husbands had been like before. By the time Griselda went to let Lady Maylis know to come in, Thessaly's head was spinning and beginning to throb a little.

From there, the conversation was at least simpler. The three ran through the relevant gossip of a great swath of Albion's Great Families, focused on the Council connections. Much of it, Thessaly knew something about, but all three were deft and skilled at weighing different social connections. Listening to them talk was a master class in the art of social management. It was not a hobby Thessaly had particularly wanted to pick up. But learning from some of the best was never a waste of time, and gods knew she needed all the tricks she could pick up.

12

AUGUST 14TH IN TRELLECH

Vitus came into the library on Wednesday afternoon. It was the evening they were open late, to align with the fact that there was often some lecture or another. Today, perhaps because of the summer, it was near enough empty. There were a few librarians working at the main desk and one more in the first nook as Vitus came back.

He knew some of what he was looking for, and the rest was one of those things where he'd know when he found it. The research project with his fellows in the Four Metals had exchanged some notes in the past few days, with a growing sense of where to focus first. He wanted to pick up a few more books about electricity and circuits in particular. Some of the books he'd somehow inherited from Philip Landry had him rethinking a couple of the common approaches to household talismans. It wasn't the books themselves - Vitus had read most of them at one point - but the marginal notes Philip had left.

It was possible to know someone best, at least in some ways, by their library. That thought distracted him, what his library would say about him, while he made his way along to the back. As he went by a bay, he stopped for a moment on the far side. He hadn't been looking at who else was there, of course, between his own thoughts and his desire for politeness. Or to be left alone, that too.

But just for a moment, he'd thought that was Thessaly. Whoever it was had her back to him, a black dress with little decoration. A black veil trailed down her back to the waist, covering most of the colour of her hair. Then he took half a step back, near silently, just as she turned around.

Immediately, he ducked his chin. Thessaly had made it clear she couldn't be seen with him. He would keep walking, he had to keep walking. He'd lifted his foot, about to step away, to find some far recess of the library until she was done with what she needed. Then she glanced around and crooked one finger in his direction.

It was like it pulled him in, as tidy as a fish on a line. Of course he went, of course he wanted to know how she was. It had been a month since he'd dared to kiss her in the cemetery and since gossip had flared up. It was a hair less than that since she'd made it clear that she could not talk to him. Now he went and stood beside her, looking at the shelves, when he wanted to look at her. He was doing his utmost to keep up the pretence that he was here for the books. Books on, apparently, inheritances and contractual agreements. He'd have a hard time coming up with some suitable story about why that interested him.

"Is there anyone near?" Thessaly's voice was quiet, shaky despite the fact she said only a few words.

He shook his head. "There's a librarian down near the front, two bays from the entrance. I haven't seen anyone else."

Thessaly hesitated, then he felt a brush of magic, the sort of thing that had a radius. A duellist's trick, more than anything practical, it didn't work well in a space where there wasn't a fair bit of magic. But they were, in fact, in a magical library and knowledge was one of the many weapons a duellist might wield. Whatever she got from the charm, it seemed to satisfy her, because she turned toward him. "I only have a few minutes. Mistress North is meeting me at half-four."

Vitus automatically glanced at his pocket watch and then set the alarm to sound - quietly - at five minutes before that. It gave them maybe eight minutes at the outside. "Thirteen minutes. I've set an alarm." Then he let out a breath. "I'll go away if you'd rather. Whatever you need."

She shook her head, just once, then her hand was resting on his wrist. She'd taken her gloves off to handle the books. "Please. If you don't mind. If you'd rather go, though. Was it awful for you?"

"Gossip. It died down, mostly, though it's been awkward for Papa." Vitus looked up, finally meeting her eyes, and she looked sad. Haunted might be a better word, actually. There was a complicated depth there, the sort of secrets you didn't tell anyone. "You?"

"Childeric made it clear that he'd make things awful for you if I saw you again. If he had any hint of it. That's why I wrote. Why you couldn't. There's nothing safe enough. Every place I am, someone might tell him."

"Oh." Vitus could feel the thoughts rushing through his head. What it must be like for her to worry that anything, no matter how innocent, might put her at risk. "Did he threaten you?" That mattered more than the threats to Vitus.

She shrugged and didn't answer, and that was answer enough. Childeric had terrified her. Vitus was suddenly sure of that, even if she absolutely wouldn't admit it. And of course Vitus would not press. Certainly not when she was meeting someone in a bare few minutes. Whatever emotions she had, they weren't kind ones, and they would be difficult to tuck away in a moment.

After that silence had lingered, Vitus swallowed. "I am glad to see you. Even if it's just for an instant. Please, let me reassure you I won't write. I won't do anything you don't want. But if you, if things change, please, I so want to talk to you. Listen to you. Whatever you're wanting." More than talk, he wanted to touch her, even this light and hesitant touch of her fingers on his wrist. He would love to kiss her again. The memory had intruded in the most painful and pleasant way all month.

Thessaly nodded once, then she lowered her eyes. "I missed you. I missed knowing I might talk to you. That you'd listen. That there was something outside this net I've found myself in. No way out, certainly nothing I could plan on." She glanced back at the shelves.

"Not your usual subjects, these." Vitus said it as gently as he could. "Not a topic I know too much about either, beyond some of what Father's mentioned. Wills and such are not his line of work. He passes those off to colleagues."

"They're reading Aunt Metaia's will tomorrow, and no one would tell me what to expect. I mean, not the specifics. I understand that, but not why it's taken so long, or what the process is like." Thessaly glanced up at the shelves, as if she was overwhelmed with choices.

Vitus could at least make a little sense of it. "Are you going to the solicitor's office, or somewhere else?" He didn't know the details, but he knew enough of how this sort of thing went. He'd gone along with Papa to some, when there were business interests, and Father's usual assistant wasn't available.

"No, they're coming to the house." Thessaly looked

back at him, and then she dropped her hand. "A solicitor, someone from the courts. We expect Magistra Rowan and cousin Owain from the Council. Maybe other people. Father and Mama have been arguing for ages, right after Aunt Metaia was killed. Murdered." Then she swallowed. "Why does the location matter?"

"If they're doing it at your home, it probably means that all the details relate to your family. If it was, I don't know, half your family and half other people, I'd expect it to be somewhere else. Solicitor's chambers, the courts itself, the Council Keep, something like that. And if they're doing it at your house, that means there's no formal ritual needed, either." He remembered that part well enough. "Sometimes they have to make someone swear under the truth oaths or make an oath on their magic that has specific requirements."

"Oh." Thessaly sounded even more confused now. "Is there a book? Do you know a book that might explain? That I could read tonight?"

Vitus managed a little smile. "A librarian would be better, but let's see what I can spot. May I change places with you?" She nodded and stepped into the corner, then pressed between him and the table to take the spot where he'd been standing. He could feel her skirts press against his legs, how close she got to him, the way her magic brushed his. Then he began scanning the shelves, looking for something that would be a reasonable overview.

"Are you doing all right? Your work? Beyond the gossip, I mean." Thessaly's voice was tentative now, but with a note of something interested there. He glanced to his right, and she was leaning forward a little, as if she wanted to hear what he had to say.

"Well enough. So much has happened." He considered what they'd last talked about. "I'd told you Henut Landry asked if I'd take over Philip's lease. I'm properly moved in there now. The light is gorgeous, and the workroom is set up well now. I still spend a fair bit of time at Niobe's, but it's good to have my own space. Council Head Rowan asked us to work on some talismans for the Council's use for the challenge. I'm helping with that." He kept scanning the shelves.

"And the piece for Theo Carrington? I'm not asking details, of course." Thessaly took a half step closer to him, so she could look at the shelves as well.

"In progress, and I'm quite happy with it so far. When this is all over, if we can talk, I'd be glad to talk about it more with you." Vitus let his fingers trace along the shelves, then pulled out a moderately slim volume. "Here, this is from someone who worked in the inheritance courts for decades. It's partly about the process in general, and partly about some of the more notable cases he worked on and could talk about. That might make more engaging reading than dry law."

"Thank you." Thessaly's hand was resting on his arm now, and she leaned in, enough he could feel the warmth of her breath on his cheek. "Anything else? Just. I like you talking. Sharing."

"Sharing." He echoed the word. "Whatever we can, yes?" He caught her nod out of the corner of his eye. "Niobe's been very generous in helping me get set up. Both stones and contacts, far more than I'd expected."

Thessaly inhaled, the sort of sound that had complexity behind it. Then, very softly, she whispered, "If the Fortiers ask you for a talisman, turn them down. Please. It'd likely be a trap."

"As you wish. I'll find some suitable excuse, that's easy enough. If it comes up." Vitus didn't know what made her say that, but he would trust her analysis of the terrain. And besides, it was certainly more likely than that they wanted to do him a favour. "I wasn't intending to be terribly noticeable to them anytime soon. I've been making contacts of my own, too."

"Good. I enjoy thinking of you being out there, doing good things, being free to choose them." Unlike her, and she didn't have to spell that part out. "The sleep talisman. It's been helping. I don't know what I'll do when - when I marry."

"Perhaps by then we can come up with something less obvious or visible. Or enchant some other piece for you. I'll start thinking about it, all right?" It was a weak and faint promise. He could already think of a dozen challenges. A piece under her pillow or her bed could be found by a maid. A piece of jewellery might be spotted by any of the ordinary charms to notice new enchantments. But he could think through that, given time and a number of conversations with Niobe. Perhaps layering the magic on a piece might work, with the obvious layer being for attractiveness or charm or whatever other visible need would pass without question.

Before he could say anything else, the charm on his pocket watch chimed. "Five minutes. You ought to go check this out. This one too, it's more of a history. I'd read the overview first, and the history as you have time."

"Thank you." Thessaly covered both his hands with hers as he handed her the books, leaning in as if she wished for a kiss, and they didn't dare. "When we can. If we can. You meant what you said?" It was as if there were some circuit, yearning to connect and be made whole, and it was blocked.

"I promise." Vitus swallowed hard as she dropped his hands and stepped back, going the other way around the table and chairs. This time, she was the one walking away.

She didn't look back, she didn't dare, just took steady steps up toward the front and the librarians waiting to check the books out.

Vitus set the timer on his watch for ten minutes, pulling out a chair and staring at a book he pulled at random from the shelves. When the second chime went off, he put it on the cart waiting for books to be shelved, and went off in search of the section he'd wanted originally. Oddly, a number of books in that section seemed to be checked out, as if someone had recently borrowed a good fifth of them. More than one someone, probably.

13

AUGUST 15TH IN NORTHUMBRIA

Thessaly had, of course, left her apprenticeship early today, to be home at three in the afternoon in good time for the reading of Aunt Metaia's will. The front parlour was a tad crowded. Naturally, the immediate family was there, Thessaly and Hermia, their parents, and Cousin Owain as well. But there was Mistress Collins, from Aunt Metaia's household, over in the corner. And there were five others who hadn't been entirely explained. Council Head Hereswith Rowan had folded herself into a chair. Then there was a solicitor, Master Phipps, and an unnamed assistant. Magistra Clement and her assistant, a Master Morgan, were both from the Courts. Master Phipps and Magistra Clement were both well established, maybe in their fifties. Master Morgan looked like he was in his early thirties, tidy and precise but quiet.

The whole thing had begun with a series of formal oaths - that was part of what the people from the Courts handled. They'd made an explanation that it had taken some time to get to this point. Apparently, various parties - multiple, unnamed - had questioned the legality of the will, and it had taken some time to prove it fully and undeniably. It made Thessaly wonder why they weren't doing this in the Courts proper. The book Vitus had found for her had been very helpful in a lot of ways, but it didn't explain how decisions like that happened. Obviously - Thessaly was of Fox House, after all - there was a political aspect to it, or trading of advantages or something of the kind. But she didn't have nearly enough information about any of it.

The first part of the will reading had been fairly straightforward. They'd been the smaller bequests. Aunt Metaia had left money - a substantial sum, actually, two years of wages - to each of the house staff. She'd named an additional substantially larger sum for Mistress Collins. There were bequests to a number of different individuals, some with an accompanying note. One was to Magistra Hereswith, one to Thirza Remmerton, a dozen others to people Thessaly knew Aunt Metaia had been close to. There were donations, and Mama and Father's reactions made it clear they were also substantial ones - to several charitable causes. Aunt Metaia had favoured the central library roof, the Schola library collection, and a few others.

Then Master Phipps cleared his throat. "Now it comes to the family bequests. We come to a somewhat unusual situation. Mistress Collins, you may return to your home, and one of our staff will be round to convey the bequests to the other staff later today, around five, if convenient. As we discussed, the will hopes the staff will stay on with the new owner of the property, but of course, you are all free to make other decisions."

Master Phipps went on. "Council Head Rowan was one of the witnesses of the will, and is familiar with the contents already. She has requested to stay in stewardship of a particular aspect. A trifle unusual, but permitted in this case, and we have the judicial orders to confirm it."

Both Father and Mama looked odd. It took Thessaly a moment to realise that they were furious, actually. She'd never seen that before. They were the sort of family whose disapproval was sharp words and ignoring the other person, or framing everything to jab in the point. This burning anger, she didn't know what to do with. It was both of them, at each other, and at someone else. Maybe at someone else, Thessaly didn't know how to read it. Instead, she reached for Hermia's hand and squeezed it.

Master Phipps waited for Mistress Collins to make her way out, and then went on, as if he were entirely ignoring the emotions swirling around. "The remainder of the bequests are for family." He listed out a substantial one for Cousin Owain, along with a letter, then a larger one to Mama. And then one, the same size, to Hermia. Thessaly could feel herself frowning, unsure what to make of the fact she'd been skipped over. The amount for Hermia would pay for an apprenticeship and set her up well with a dowry if she wanted to marry someone who expected one. It was the sort of money that would fund Vitus's business for a good year or three, even working with more expensive stones.

Finally, she felt a shift in the room's magic, something that had to be one of the people from the Courts. Master Morgan, she thought, the way he was focusing. Master Phipps confirmed it a moment later. "I am sure all of you, except perhaps Miss Hermia, are deft enough to feel it. Master Lamont Morgan has called the truth enchantments on me, to confirm that I speak the truth, as established in the will and subsequent decisions by the Courts." There were various small nods around the room.

Master Phipps went on. "The remainder of the estate, including the home Bryn Glas, the surrounding estate, all buildings, properties, chattels, goods, materia, books, clothing, the contents of all vaults and accounts, along with any other item previously owned by Metaia Powell, portable or imobile, is granted exclusively to Thessaly Lytton-Powell, for her chosen use. It may not be granted in marriage or otherwise dispersed. The Powell family retains the right to confirm a successor to the property. A trustee appointed by the Courts must approve all sales over the amount of a month's wages for her staff. Transfers from Mistress Lytton-Powell's vault or accounts over the same amount must be independently verified by the trustee and, if deemed appropriate, the Courts under oath, to ensure no coercion. A trustee will remain in place until one of three things happens. Those are that Mistress Lytton-Powell entirely fulfils her marriage agreements, becomes a widow, or makes petition for independent status in all terms as a parthenos who will not marry." He inclined his head. "Understanding, of course, Mistress Lytton-Powell, that your marriage agreements were known to your aunt and taken into consideration."

Thessaly had that number for sales in her head, and that number would buy a particularly ornate frock, give or take. Master Phipps continued while her head was swimming. And she didn't fully understand that next clause. She was sure she didn't, but didn't that mean that the Fortiers couldn't compel her to turn over the accounts either, not just the property?

"The trustee will also provide guidance should Mistress Lytton-Powell desire independent evaluation of financial choices, besides those of her family and her family by marriage. Mistress Lytton-Powell, as you bank with the Scali as a family, they have offered one of the senior men of the family as a trustee. They would be glad to meet with you early next week for a discussion about who might suit your needs best. The Courts have approved all four of the current senior generation in principle already. If you prefer someone else, we will explain the process for approval. It cannot be a family member by blood or marriage or any person who benefitted or might benefit from Metaia Powell's estate or from yours. We advise you to make your own will promptly."

This was a space where Thessaly was supposed to nod, so she did. The world felt vast now, and also complicated. What had Aunt Metaia known? When had she put this in? Had this been the change she'd made three weeks before her death? Thessaly did not know where to begin thinking about it. This was nothing like any duel she'd been in.

"I must also make clear - and again, I am speaking under the truth enchantments." Master Phipps was speaking to Mama and Father now. "That any attempt to interfere in the proper transition of the property, whether through direct action, undue influence and pressure, alchemical means, or any other method, will be seen and dealt with promptly and directly by the Courts. The common penalty is the binding of magic and restriction to a limited estate."

Thessaly flinched. She wasn't at all sure she wanted to be here, under the same roof, and all at once she actually had somewhere else she could be. That was another thought she didn't know how to handle at all. Mama's spine, from the side, looked like sharpened iron, and Father was clenching one hand and his jaw, but not saying anything.

"In addition to the physical property, the remainder of the estate includes funds on account with the Scali, and a full accounting of those will be provided at your meeting next week, Mistress Lytton-Powell." Master Phipps made a slight bow to her. "In short, however, you are a wealthy heiress, with more resources at your direct disposal than about half the landed families and significantly fewer expenses than most of them. I am sure you must have questions. Are there any you wish to ask with everyone here? Council Head Rowan and Council Member Powell have some thoughts about options for the immediate future."

Thessaly swallowed hard. She had hundreds of questions, all chasing around her head. What came out, finally, was about where this came from. "I had not realised Aunt Metaia was so wealthy." She glanced at her parents. "I'm not sure any of us did? May I ask, pardon, where the money came from?"

It was Cousin Owain who spoke up, though Thessaly saw Magistra Hereswith lean forward for an instant before he did. "Your aunt had the same inheritance from your grandparents that your mother did. However, she built up her resources with a combination of highly skilled consulting - both at the customary fees the Council pays, and for others. She made a series of deft investments, multiplying her funds over and over again. Metaia had a knack for spotting which materia would be in high demand, a year or so in advance, and the contacts for arranging for suitable imports. You will find her private accounts interesting reading, I expect. You have some of the same eye for it."

Thessaly nodded, managing a weaker, "Thank you, cousin." Then she thought of another thing. "I thought the house, the estate, went back to the family, always."

This time, Cousin Owain looked almost amused. "Oh, that we had a long argument about, over ten years ago, the senior members of the family. The agreement was that she might bequeath it to the person of her choosing, so long as it remains in the family. And so long as the grove is properly tended. You have the option to pass it to a child of your body or blood, but not to a husband. And when it comes to the grove, we are certain you are capable of what is needed. I or Hereswith or someone else from the Council will show you what is involved."

"On that larger count," Hereswith Rowan cleared her throat. "One of your first obligations is to reset the wards. That will take most of a day. I have arranged for your aunt's warding specialist to come out tomorrow, unless you would prefer to make a change. He advises, and I concur, that you limit access to the property and estate for at least six months. The usual recommendation is that the established staff may come and go as they have, all others you would need to greet and admit each time they arrived. He will explain that, the options and variations tomorrow. It allows the wards time to fully settle. And..." The Council Head lowered her voice, "Given the circumstances of Metaia's death, that precaution is advised for your well-being. A year and a day would be better. That is standard advice in unsettled circumstances."

That brought things home properly. Though at the moment, the idea of a house where only a handful of people could enter seemed compellingly glorious. There would be problems with it, she was sure, but an entire house where she could decide what to do, could be on her own, not guarding herself anywhere.

Thessaly nodded. "The warding, tomorrow, please. I want to make sure the house is safe, and so are the staff. And obviously, I'll need to speak to them." She felt faint with the number of things she suddenly needed to do. "I need to write to Mistress North, I need to..."

Cousin Owain cleared his throat. "I thought perhaps you might wish to pack a case for the night, and stay with me for the evening. A chance for the rest of the family to assess the situation. And then tomorrow, we could go on to Bryn Glas, and a maid here could pack up your things."

Thessaly looked to her parents, wanting them to say something about having her stay, but then she saw their faces, the way they were fixed on some plot or goal that had nothing to do with Thessaly, not really. She could not sleep here tonight, whatever was mended or talked about in the coming days. "Thank you, cousin. I think that might be the best for everyone. Hermia, you'll be all right?"

Hermia nodded and then leaned over to whisper. "I can go stay with a friend if I have to. I can come visit?"

Thessaly got her arm around her sister, murmuring back. "Of course. When I get things sorted." The only fear she had about Hermia was what she might let slip to Father. Or Mother. The world shifted in her head, as she thought it, as if Mama was a dress set aside that no longer fit. She would have to sort through that later. Then she looked up at the various officials. "Is there anything else that is necessary here today?"

Magistra Clement, the woman from the Courts, shook her head. "We have witnessed that you have heard the key points. We would be glad to discuss the details, the implications, and the various decisions the Courts made in this case at your convenience. And it would be fine if that were a week or a month in the future. We do understand your situation has changed rapidly in ways you did not expect in any way."

That last phrase made Mother speak. "You truly had no idea, Thessaly?" There was such an odd note in her voice, something ancient, hollow, and broken.

"I knew Aunt Metaia was comfortably settled. I knew she loved me being there, that I adored Bryn Glas as much as she did. But she said nothing about this to me. Not before, not when she made changes." That brought her attention back to Magistra Clement. "Is there a history of that? What changes she made?"

Magistra Clement nodded. "There is, though those files do not leave our archives. And Council Head Rowan was witness to all of Metaia's wills once she joined the Council. She can speak to the changes as well, if she wishes." Magistra Hereswith just nodded once, as if she'd expected that to be said and had already agreed to it.

"In that case, if you don't mind, I'd like to pack a trunk. I'll be as brief as I can." It would be better, on the whole, to bring anything she valued with her. She did not trust Mother not to do something with anything she left and claim it had been accidentally lost.

"Of course." Magistra Clement considered. "Would you object if I came with you, to make sure everything goes smoothly. I can therefore provide a witness to what you take now, in case anyone wishes to question it?"

That would solve that problem. "No, of course not. We all know that your oaths and commitments make you excellent witnesses." And she was a woman. "Let me summon Alma, my maid, and it won't take long."

In the end, it didn't, less than half an hour. Thessaly was tidy. And she had been keeping lists in her head for years of what pieces of jewellery were hers in her own right and what were family pieces that had come down through Mother or Father. Magistra Clement stayed out of the way, just observing as Thessaly and Alma packed up her personal items. A change of clothing for the day and her nightgown and toiletries went into a case for the night. She added a notebook, her writing case, her seal and sealing wax, though maybe she'd need a new seal made.

Most of her wardrobe for the autumn and winter was still being made at the dressmaker's as soon as she was no longer wearing mourning. That included the dress in progress for Childeric's Challenge. The other mourning gowns went into the trunk, though. She tucked in a couple of her favourite shawls as well. The clothing here wasn't what she needed to have with her, whatever came next.

She packed her own small collection of books in the trunk, putting the library copies in at the top. She only had a few of her own books on the shelves here. Most of her illusion books were at Mistress North's, and many of her beloved copies of children's stories had been Hermia's for years now. There was an old and much loved doll, Anna, of course, Aunt Metaia's garnet pendant, which she slipped around her neck. She could use the protection, absolutely, as well as the comfort of the gift. Finally, she rummaged under the pillow, bringing out the jasper talisman and tucking it into the pocket under her skirts. Now Thessaly looked around the room one more time, and she knew she'd never sleep here again, with the sort of certainty that meant something she didn't yet understand.

"May I have just a moment, while Alma gets a footman to bring the trunk down? I'll leave the trunk open. You can confirm I didn't take anything."

"You are not the one we've concerns about, Mistress." Magistra Clement's smile was warm for just a moment. "Of course." She withdrew to the hallway, while Alma went back down to get someone to bring the trunk down. With the charms on it, it wouldn't be heavy, but it was large and awkward to carry. Thessaly closed the door, then made one final circuit of the room, the way she'd pace out a new duelling salle, feeling it in her bones and her blood. She took one last look out the window, toward the orchard. Three last breaths.

Then she turned and opened the door, nearly surprising the now four people waiting outside. "I'm ready. Thank you, James and Peter." She went down first, then

Magistra Clement. In the foyer, she kissed each of her parents on the cheek, once each. Then she hugged Hermia tight. Finally, Cousin Owain offered her his arm and escorted her out, Magistra Hereswith just behind them, and the trunk behind that.

It wasn't until they went through to Cousin Owain's home - the trunk had gone ahead to Bryn Glas, with Magistra Hereswith and the solicitors - that Thessaly let out a breath. "Who contested the will, please?" Her voice didn't quite shake as she said it, but if she'd said more words, it would have.

"Both your parents, and backed by the Fortiers, though of course they are a secondary party in this case."

She was going to have to think about that. A great deal. That both her parents had wanted to contest it, that the Fortiers had. Childeric was likely going to be furious that she had resources, she had anything that he couldn't control. He was going to explode when he realised he couldn't enter the estate. She didn't want him to. She certainly didn't trust him to. "What do I do tonight? I have some letters I should write, Mistress North." The Fortiers, in some form, somehow. She didn't even know the proper form for that, how you explained that in polite words.

"We have a room set up for you. One of the maids can draw a bath. You may eat in your room or with us, whichever you prefer. Write your letters. The maid will bring them to the portal when you're ready. In the morning, we'll have a good breakfast. It will be a long day."

Thessaly nodded. "I am, I am exhausted, I think." Here, now, she felt she could admit it.

Cousin Owain patted her arm. "Anyone would be. Let's get you somewhere comfortable for the moment." He hesitated, then added. "I'm glad you came. I didn't like to think of what the evening would be like for you, otherwise."

Thessaly held still for a moment, then she shook her head. "Me either. Thank you for giving me a choice."

She had choices now. Thessaly did not know what to do with them, but she had them. Many of them, all swirling around, entire lists of things she needed to do. Then she realised one thing. She could write to Vitus. She would.

14

AUGUST 18TH IN TRELLECH

Vitus did not know what to expect. Friday morning, at Niobe's, there had been a letter for him. It had come in the first post, and it was sealed with a blank bit of grey wax and three charms, no sign of who sent it. He'd been planning to see Niobe that afternoon, but she had sent a messenger to tell him to come round in the morning, in case it was urgent.

Once he was staring at it, though, he did not know what to do. The envelope itself gave no clues, just his name and Niobe's address on the front in perfect block handwriting. Out of caution, he asked Niobe to open it carefully, and the charms had resisted her. The wax and the paper had parted easily for Vitus, though, as simply as turning a page of a book.

The letter inside had been entirely confusing. This was in Thessaly's hand, or at least it looked like the other notes she'd sent him. Though, as her handwriting had been trained to look much like every other young woman of good breeding, it wasn't anything to rely on. The note was on thick ivory paper with a black border. There, in carefully precise lines, it asked him to come from a portal not in his usual orbit, to a portal address he'd never seen before. Not that he knew all of them, of course, but he knew the common ranges. And it asked him to come at around three on the Sunday.

If he wasn't able, there was a place to send a message. That made no sense to him, either. That went through the Scali bank, addressed to a particular number. The Scali wouldn't give up their secrets, it was an explicit part of their services. No need to reply if he could come. He was expected.

Vitus had stared at it for a good five minutes. Niobe hadn't pressed him about it, though she was obviously curious, barely restraining herself. Finally, he pushed it across the counter to her. "Thoughts?"

Niobe frowned at it, her finger hovering above the paper where the address was. "I'm fairly sure that's northern Wales, but I don't know where. I've only been to a couple of the public portals up there." She looked up, meeting his eyes. "Are you going to go?"

"Yes?" Then Vitus swallowed. "Yes. I think it might be Thessaly, but there's nothing certain there. I'll tell someone where I'm going."

Niobe raised an eyebrow. "Besides me, I hope? I can alert someone if you don't turn up, but I'm no good at charging into dangerous situations."

"If it's actually dangerous, I don't know if anyone would be any help. My brother, too. He's got leave for the half day on Sunday, he's coming for the afternoon. Cavalry man, he's had training in some of this. And duelling."

"Fair enough. You tell him I'll be here in the afternoon

if he needs more help, all right? I don't have plans I can't change."

Vitus had blinked, stammered about her having more care with him than he knew what to do with. She'd patted his hand and sent him off to go look at agates for which ones he might want to bring over with him. He'd spent the Saturday and Sunday morning in his own new flat, continuing to work on standard sorts of pieces, mostly to keep himself from fretting into shards of anxiety.

He'd followed the instructions, of course. Multiple portal trips were harder to track, and especially if you went through a couple of busy ones, like Trellech or London. And, of course, with multiple trips, some to remote spots, it was harder to miss someone who was following you. He knew the theory of it.

He'd taken the portal from Trellech's Portal Square to the one in Brighton - he'd been there on holiday a few years ago. From there he went to London, Southwark, then to near Lake Windermere. For good measure, he'd walked from one portal to another to add another break in the chain. It also gave him a breather to get his wits back. That many portal journeys in close succession made him dizzy. Finally, he set the location for the address he'd been given.

That last hop brought him out into a lush green patch of ground, with a ruined stone tower rising just to the left of him. For a moment, there was no one visible at all, and Vitus wondered if he'd somehow set the portal wrong. There were trees to the south, blocking most of the view of what lay beyond. To the west, the ground rose sharply upward, the lower part of a mountain, maybe. He'd looked up the portal address, of course, and while he hadn't been able to get the precise address, it seemed likely to be somewhere around Snowdonia.

He was left on his own for maybe three minutes. Not quite long enough that he turned around and went away, but certainly long enough he was thinking about it. Then there was a movement, from some fence or gate beyond a hedge, before a figure appeared, behind the fence. He braced himself, but it didn't approach, instead calling out. "Vitus? When is the last time we talked?"

That was Thessaly's voice. "May I come closer?" It was the only reasonable reply. He could understand why she was being cautious.

"Please. Just don't touch the fence." Vitus walked forward toward that voice. As he got closer, he could see a gate in the hedge, a narrow one, just big enough for a small cart for deliveries. On the other side stood Thessaly and an older woman. Thessaly was in mourning dress, but it was a black tea gown, something of the kind, rather than something more fitted.

Once he was standing three feet away, Vitus could see her face more clearly. "We talked in the library, on Wednesday. I chose a couple of books for you." He glanced at the other woman, who looked pleasantly impassive.

Thessaly nodded at her once, and she took several steps back as Thessaly reached to do something to the gate. It wasn't just opening it physically; it was also magical. Vitus couldn't make sense of the enchantments, but he could feel they were there. "If you'd take my hand before you cross the boundary?" Her hands were ungloved, and she held out her right hand as she stood where the gate was ajar.

Of course he'd take her hand when she offered. He drew off his own gloves and put his hand in hers. She felt solid and real, even if none of this made sense at all. Then she was stepping back, like the movements of a dance no one had taught him, bringing him inside the fence. Inside the wards, he was sure of that. Once they were through, Thessaly dropped his hand and nodded at the other woman. "Tea on the terrace, please. As we discussed."

The older woman bobbed slightly, acknowledgement and agreement, but not a curtsey, and disappeared off toward the house, covering the ground in efficient steps that didn't look hurried. Vitus looked after her, then back at Thessaly. "Are you all right? I don't understand, erm, any of this? But I hoped it was you, the note. I thought it must be."

Thessaly swallowed, and he saw all at once that she seemed to be on the edge of tears. He held up his hands. "Please. I shouldn't press. You take whatever time you need."

She closed her eyes for a long moment, the sort of trusting gesture that hit Vitus hard. When she opened them again, they were glistening, but she was more resolved. "We, there's a lot to talk about. Will you come and have tea?" She motioned toward the terrace. "The terrace. We're still working on the wards for the house and the other buildings."

"Of course." Vitus felt those sentences also raised several questions, but now they were walking slowly through the field, and he could get a sense of what those buildings were. They skirted a grove of trees. Then he could see a tidy house, bigger than his own home, but not by much. Another broad building, probably a barn, stood beside it, two storeys tall and just as long. There were other stone buildings beyond that, and the entire front of the barn and house were covered with flowers and ivy. Roses, among them, but a whole swath of other colours, some blooming, others not.

To this side of the house, he could see a terrace, a small

space with a table and garden benches. Thessaly led the way there. Once they were seated, she finally spoke again. She'd taken the bench facing him, a table between them, arranging her skirts automatically and evenly before she looked up. Vitus didn't ask anything, he just waited. Something in the moment felt magical in complex ways, like asking would break the enchantment and shatter it.

In the end, she looked off across the meadow they'd just crossed, back to that ruined tower and the trees. "This is mine now. The house, the estate. Aunt Metaia left it to me." It sounded hesitant, all the way through, as if saying it made it real for her in a way she hadn't quite managed yet.

What did one say to that? The etiquette books, anything Mama had taught him, none of that had an answer for this situation. Vitus took a deep breath. "How do you feel about that?"

Her expression changed, multiple times, and then Thessaly had her hands over her mouth, the sort of uneven breaths that might be sobs or laughter or both. She hunched a little, before finally it settled out to a little chuckle, and she lowered her hands. "Very complicated. But Aunt Metaia wanted me to have it. Wanted to ensure no one could take it from me. People have tried, already. Mother and Father, in the courts. With the Fortiers' support. They never told me what they were doing, none of it."

There were whole layers there that Vitus felt entirely incompetent to untangle. He was not made for that sort of family internal feuding, if that was what it was. "But it's yours? That's what happened on Thursday?"

Thessaly nodded again, then settled her hands on the table between them. "The books, the ones you suggested, were very helpful. And Cousin Owain was too, that night.

He had me come stay. I didn't want to be home with my parents." There was a slight movement by the door, and Vitus saw her startle, then nod. The woman from before came out with a tray with a teapot, two glasses of lemonade, and multiple cakes, arranged on a pleasantly informal pottery plate. It was nothing like the fancy porcelain he'd have expected.

"Vitus, this is Mistress Collins. The housekeeper here."

Mistress Collins nodded once. "Sir." Then she added, as if she were sure Thessaly had not yet mentioned it. "It is not possible to enter the property beyond the field with the portal, without Mistress Thessaly's permission." She caught herself. "Mistress Lytton-Powell's."

Thessaly's mouth twisted a little. "We are still getting used to the new way of things. Thank you, Collins. And yes, I will do my best to eat. These look lovely." There was something definitely affectionate there, a little relaxed. The housekeeper turned to go, and once she'd closed the door behind her, Thessaly said, softly. "She's known me since I was tiny. I'm glad she's staying, all the staff are. It makes things easier. Also harder and better, all at once."

"You have a lot of history here." Vitus considered it. "And you're going to make more. Are we up by Snowdonia, then?"

She nodded, gesturing up toward the mountain. "Eryri, properly, but yes. You probably know more about the geology than I do, though I've climbed it some."

"The geology. The Belin, those under the mountain." That was one of the agreements with the Fatae, made at the time of the Pact. He knew that, though he'd never had anything to do with the agreements that meant mines weren't interfered with if they'd been managed properly.

"I'll learn." There was a fierce commitment there, suddenly, and Vitus suddenly did not want to be between her and her goal. Not unless he was actively helping and she knew it.

Now he took a sip of the lemonade, set it down, and asked, "What do you want me to know? I am glad to come, very glad you wrote. But I don't understand."

15

THAT AFTERNOON AT BRYN GLAS

Thessaly hadn't known why she needed to talk to Vitus. Or, rather, she knew some of it, and it wasn't anything she could put into words. But she had a place where she could, and that had been one of the few things holding her together the last three days. Now, she took a breath, drawing on all the tools she'd learned in duelling. She'd already broken down once. More wouldn't help anything.

"You're not trying to get anything from me. You're not making me into something you want. Besides, you do that with stones, with magic. You're not doing that with me. Do you understand what I'm trying to say?" She looked down for an instant, then back up into his eyes. "You're one of the few people I know who hasn't. I mean, Cousin Owain and Magistra Hereswith have been very helpful, but I'm sure they've also got reasons that aren't about me. Not really."

"She was worried about you earlier. Magistra Rowan, I mean." Vitus was polite, of course, and formal. "A week after, erm." He then sucked in a breath, and what came out next was a huge rush. "I didn't mean to make things so difficult for you. I didn't want you hurt. And then you wrote and said I shouldn't write, you would if you could. And now you have, but I don't know what you mean by it."

Thessaly was reaching for his hand before he ran out of words. Then the table was entirely too annoying. "Would you, could you come round here? This side?" It might be easier without the space between them. Or at least different. "You walked away, when that was what would keep me safe. And you're here now. That's, that's a lot more than most people have done. You listen to me."

"Why shouldn't I? You have words, you say them, surely you know how you're using them, what you want to say." There was utter bafflement in Vitus's voice now, but he stood, coming around to join her on the other half of the bench. Their legs weren't quite touching, but almost. She could feel the brush of his magic. "It's all right here?"

That, at least, she had some straightforward answers for. "The staff is sworn not to talk about anything of mine outside the household. Magistra Hereswith was very thorough. Wards, limits on who can come through the portal, the oaths, all sorts of things. And I told Collins the truth about the gossip when I sorted out inviting you."

Thessaly watched Vitus suddenly have a whole new set of questions. His eyes went wide. He might not have been born to her sort of family, but he certainly knew enough about how some of it worked. "She's afraid for you. Magistra Rowan." Then he straightened up. "Let me, may I confirm a few things, then ask you more questions?"

Thessaly nodded once. "Whatever order would help you. I'm still so tangled up, I don't know where to start. Talking it out, honestly, would be a help."

"Right." Vitus looked down, as if that made it easier for him to think. First, cautiously, he offered his hand, and she immediately slipped hers into his. It felt better, immediately, as if he had made himself into some talisman that was steadiness and calm and comfort, all at once. "How is your family taking it?"

Thessaly let out a breath. "Badly. Very badly. First, Aunt Metaia had a lot more money than any of us realised, even Mother. Magistra Hereswith knew. Cousin Owain, too. I've got meetings with the Scali on Monday, but it's all set up so I can't grant it in marriage or have it taken from me. Children of my own, yes. Husband, no. My sister's got a good dowry. I don't need to provide for her. And I don't understand all the nuances, but I understand Aunt Metaia was trying to keep me safe. And it's a lot of money, the kind people get very energetic about. The solicitor said more than about half the landed families, on my own. Just one estate, whatever repairs it needs. And not supporting dozens of nieces or nephews or cousins."

"Why is your family upset, then? All your family?" Vitus squeezed her hand gently. "They knew, before Thursday?"

"They knew. Not the details, the amounts, but that I was the primary heir." Cousin Owain hadn't talked a lot about the details, but he'd been clear about that much. "Mother and Father and the Fortiers. They're all furious. Childeric has tried to force the portal twice. His parents have sent two letters. I'm waiting until I can talk to the Scali. Mother and Father have written, um, six letters in total, one from both of them. Hermia's gone to stay with a friend, thankfully."

"Your sister." Vitus paused, as if he was thinking through things. "That must be terrifying. Even with the warding." Thessaly felt herself shiver, and then Vitus was dropping her hand, slipping an arm around her shoulders, immediately and instinctively. Then he froze, and asked, "Do you mind?"

"I like it. I like how I feel with you. Not as lost, not so much flailing." Thessaly let out a slow breath, trying to get her heart to stop racing again. "So Magistra Hereswith was worried, you were saying."

"She came to talk to Niobe about some things relating to the challenges. And she'd heard the gossip, and I'm still sorry about that."

Thessaly turned her chin, nudging him with it. "You asked if you could. I said I wanted you to. It's not your fault. If it's a fault, it's both of us, together." Then she sucked in a breath. "I don't want to think of it as a fault." Then she realised there was an entire set of things she hadn't told Vitus, and they mattered. "There's something you need to know, though. Why I told you to be so careful coming. Not just the gossip. You need, if you decide you don't want the risk, you walk away, promise me that?"

Vitus frowned. "Not without hearing it."

Well. That meant forging onward. Thessaly tried to get her thoughts tidy. "Childeric was furious about the gossip. About any idea that you'd been close, he threatened you if you— again. I should have told you in the note, but of course it would be revealing, if anyone saw it, and you know how some people are." The words came bubbling out of her.

Vitus went still, for long enough that Thessaly was worried, even though she was looking at him, watching for any tiny reaction. "Thessaly. Are you— are you scared of him?"

Put like that, bluntly, she had to nod. She could only nod. There was something in her throat that felt impossible to speak around. Then she managed. "Yes. I wasn't, before. Cautious. Aunt Metaia had been worried about him. She'd talked about it the day she— the day someone killed her. It's why the warding, I mean, there are other reasons for it."

"And you're sure of the warding." Vitus shifted, this time squeezing her shoulder again, first cautiously, then more steadily when she leaned into him again.

"Very sure. You can come through the portal. I named you specifically. I can. The household can come and go, but there are oaths on what they say outside the house. But anyone coming past the fence, I need to bring them in right now. For a good while, I expect."

"And you're staying here, then? For however long?" Vitus's voice cracked. "Until you marry?"

"Probably." Now Thessaly's voice got tiny again. "There isn't a way out of the marriage agreements, not just because I want to."

Vitus hesitated, then he cleared his throat. "I'm prying, but why?"

"I said you could ask things. Haven't taken it back, have I?" It came out of Thessaly's mouth sharper than she meant, and she immediately murmured, "Sorry. None of this is your fault, remember? I agreed to the terms. I thought I was doing what my family needed, what would keep them steady. What would give my sister more options and more freedom? Only now..."

"Only now your family is being awful, your sister has some options, and you're like a fox in a trap. You could pull away, but what cost?"

Thessaly winced at the image, but it was true. "If Childeric goes against it. But even what he's threatened so far, that wouldn't. And things are more delicate, before we're actually wed."

"And your apprentice mistress, she's..." Vitus seemed to struggle for words now. "Niobe keeps surprising me with the ways she shows me care. I didn't expect that. We've always got on well, but this is, she's helping me set up properly. Introductions, supplies, all sorts of things. And yours isn't like that."

Thessaly shook her head. "We do all right. I've learned a lot? But she wishes I wouldn't get distracted by other things going on, and she knows I'm never going to be focused just on illusion work. And she took me on as favour to Father's side of the family. She won't get in the way, but she won't help. She's quietly annoyed at the moment that I have things I need to do on Monday and maybe Tuesday. Mistress North is a good teacher, but we are not close, and I don't think we can be." She paused, turning that over and over in her head now she was thinking about it properly. "My parents chose her. I suppose that says enough, doesn't it?"

Vitus winced, visibly. "I'm sorry that you haven't had that either." He sounded sincerely sorry, too, like it was something she should have expected to have. Then he changed the subject, as if that would ease something. "The Scali, you said. Why them?" Vitus shifted a little to lean back against the bench, and Thessaly moved with him. She liked very much how it felt to have her head on his shoulder.

"Aunt Metaia insisted on a trustee. That's until I've fulfilled my marriage agreements, become a widow, or gone through the process of declaring myself a parthenos. That means legal standing as a spinster, independent of anyone else's financial obligations. And if I do that, there'd be all sorts of pressure on me, so I won't, not anytime soon."

"A lot of people - not just the Fortiers - would find you a very excellent catch." Vitus cleared his throat. "I don't know how to think about that much money, actually. It seems utterly unreal."

That just made Thessaly start giggling, and it took her a good while to stop. Vitus patted her on the back once or twice, which didn't help. Finally, she got a proper breath again. "I don't know how to think about it at all, either. I mean, I suppose there's philanthropy in my future, but I know enough to know that's complicated too. So I get to pick one of the senior Scali family as a trustee. They approve everything over a certain sum. Which eases things for me. And I can send letters through them - if you'd written back, they'd have sent along the letter promptly. And that's probably how we ought to write. If I write to you, it'll go to them, then get dropped in the post. They won't look at it."

"Especially not if you seal it like you did. No, that's fine." Vitus swallowed. "I don't want the Fortiers angry with me. But it sounds like, from what you've said, that I can write you through the Scali, and come here when we've arranged it. Taking some precautions so no one realises where I'm going. If I do that, it should be private."

Thessaly nodded, and now she was watching him again.

"And you'd like it if I did." His voice had gone soft, but not tentative. Hopeful. Maybe that was her hearing what she wanted to hear, but she thought not.

Again, she nodded. "Very much. I can't— it's not fair if I beg, is it? But I feel better with you. Safe, no masks, nothing I have to hide. You listen, you're not out to get anything from me, or make me be someone else. And I, I think I really need that right now. Even if that's not really fair to you."

Vitus considered for a moment, then reached across both their bodies with his free hand, taking hers in his fingers. "I have the chance to hear you say things like that. I suspect, in due course, you'll have some interesting talisman commissions of your own, as you settle in here. And I would like to be your friend. When things are a little less overwhelming, I'd love to get back to talking magical theory with you, about the lapis lazuli and whatever else we become curious about, together."

"Curious together. I like that very much." Thessaly looked down at their hands. "I can't, um, it's easier to manage Childeric if I do nothing I'd have a hard time answering questions about. I can manage seeing you, but anything else, I ..."

"Certainly not right now." She hadn't expected Vitus to be willing for that, to understand that, but his voice was solid now. "If, in the future, circumstances change, we can talk about it then. I would enjoy other things with you, I'm sure. But I also enjoy talking, and knowing you're enjoying it. I know what I'm choosing."

Thessaly looked at him for a long time. She could hear her heart thumping, over and over again. Then she just managed a smile. "If you need a change, promise me you'll talk to me? Not just assume what you should do."

"Promise." Then Vitus let out a long breath. "So. Would you show me a little about the garden? Tell me about that ruined tower, perhaps?" Those were questions that were bittersweet, of course, because it was Aunt Metaia who'd told her all the stories. But they were also safer, and it would let them walk the bounds of the meadow, hand in hand, just enjoying the moment. She would keep any moments like that she could, as long as she could.

16

AUGUST 18TH AT VITUS'S HOME

Vitus came home a bit warily. It was still fairly early, half five, but he wasn't sure when his parents were due back. They'd gone out for tea, they expected to be home for supper with Lucas. But that left a fairly broad window, between now and half seven, when they might turn up. And how he wanted to be with them, at least right now, was different than with Lucas.

As soon as he got into the front entry, however, Lucas was leaping out of the chair, hugging him and patting his shoulder. "Mama and Papa said to expect them around half six. Your room? The garden? Where would you prefer to talk?" Then Lucas took a step back, hands grasping Vitus's shoulders, and peering at him. "Good grief, what else has happened? She didn't break your heart, did she?"

No, she hadn't, but that didn't actually help anything. Vitus let out a slow breath. "Somewhere private, please. My room. Your room. The far end of the garden, I don't care which."

"Mine, then, my warding is better. And I think I've still got some brandy." Lucas kept a bottle for the rare nights he spent at home and wanted a nightcap. Lucas took a step back, then nudged Vitus with two fingers along his shoulder. "Do you want to change?"

"Yeah." Vitus mostly felt tired. Putting on a smoking jacket and relaxing a little wouldn't hurt, and Mama and Papa wouldn't mind. It was just family tonight, as it usually was on Sundays. He went upstairs before Lucas had to nudge him again, hearing his brother go along the hall and into his own room. Five minutes later, he'd changed, washed his face and hands in cool water, and looked in the mirror. Hopefully, he'd improve a bit more before his parents got home.

Then he went along to Lucas's room. The door was ajar, and Lucas was already perched on his bed, leaving the chair for Vitus. There were two glasses poured, not a lot of alcohol, but enough for a little buffering and restoration. "Was it Thessaly?" His brother was leaning forward, looking insistent.

"It was. Though it's also complicated." Vitus sat first. One thing at a time, he was fairly sure he wasn't up for multiple things at once right now. That conversation had been confusing, even the parts about it that had been good, that had absolutely felt good. Thessaly trusting him, when she obviously needed people she did trust in her life right now. The way she'd felt leaning against him, how she'd relaxed into that, how they'd had long enough and privacy enough that she could. But tangled up with that were all the implications of what she'd told him, of her family, of the Fortiers, and everything else that went along with it.

"What's complicated about it, then?" Lucas had slippers on. Now he toed them off and pulled his feet up on the bed. "Did she hurt you? I'd have to go have a talk with her if she did."

It made Vitus smile. "Not like you mean. And besides,

you couldn't get to her if you wanted. That's part of the complicated." He contemplated his glass for a moment, took a swallow, and set it down. "She inherited from her aunt. A great deal of money, the estate - that's up in Wales, near Snowdonia. And she's sure her parents are furious and so are the Fortiers."

"That makes no sense." Lucas grimaced. "What sort of money and land are we talking about? Enough they'd hurt her to get at it?"

"That won't work. I am Papa's son, just like you are. I thought of that. Her aunt hedged it round, really carefully, and she told me the outline of that. One of the senior Scali men as a trustee, she has a meeting with them tomorrow. She can't grant any part of the estate in marriage. It is explicitly exempted from her marriage agreements, all that sort of language. She can pass down the money to her children, and possibly the estate, if they meet the Powell line's requirements for tending it. There's a grove or something - I don't know if it's related to the Belin or to some other Fatae, but it's supposed to be tended. I didn't pry about that."

"Not our sort of thing, no." Lucas grunted. "Is she safe right now?"

"You can only get through that portal - it's a private one - if she's permitted it. The staff there, they had all been with her aunt for years. Her. Me. I don't think that many other people? And no one but the staff and Thessaly can actually get into the warded space, the fenced in area and the house and buildings."

"Huh." Lucas considered, fiddling with the cufflinks he was wearing. "She is a duellist, but that implies she's thinking several steps out. Or someone is? Does she have anyone else she's talking to?"

"Her cousin, Owain Powell, also on the Council. She

didn't share details - why would she, necessarily? But Council Head Rowan also had a hand in it, I'm sure. She was one of the witnesses to the will."

"I'm stuck on why her parents are furious. It doesn't make much sense?" Lucas frowned. "And, well, people react all the time from emotion, but this doesn't seem like that, not exactly. You'd think they'd be pleased she'd become a heiress."

Vitus grunted. "That doesn't make any sense to me, either." He shook his head. "Except, of course, that they want her to not have any choices other than Childeric Fortier for some reason." Vitus did not like that thought at all, though of course he was terribly biassed about some of it, and couldn't avoid being.

"And the money?" Lucas turned his palm up. "A lot, then. Enough to change all the calculations?"

"From what she said, middle of the landed estates, which is a lot of money indeed, and not a lot to maintain." He considered what he knew about the Fortiers. "Arundel's well off, but they've got multiple estates that need upkeep, not just a house and whatever buildings close in. They've got tenants to manage. Client families who might reasonably demand aid in various ways, some of which are most easily solved with money and loans."

"They've been spending, too. Not just Childeric and the wedding plans and all that, though I'm sure that's cost a fair penny." Lucas tapped his finger. "I heard something in the Den this afternoon, I was catching up with someone there. Lots of orders going through the portal for them, all wrapped up tight. Not just recent, but there'd been another on Thursday, maybe Wednesday, with some odd shapes and instructions. You know how people notice odd shapes."

"And odd instructions." Vitus echoed it. "Nothing more about it? Anyone you could ask?"

Lucas considered. "Maybe. I'll drop a note, see if we can get a drink next time I can get away. No promises, and it might be a bit." Now he leaned forward, elbows on his knees. "You're still pretty taken with her, aren't you? Even after the gossip and not seeing her, and all."

"I ran into her in the library on Wednesday. The will reading was Thursday. She was trying to find books to explain what no one was telling her. And..." Vitus swallowed, looking away for a moment, off to the dresser in the corner. "She trusts me. She feels comfortable with me. And that's not so true anywhere else right now. Think about what it means that she's walled everyone else out, because she's not sure what they'll do."

"Seems to me her aunt gave her an edged gift. Not a kind one." Lucas kept turning it over, the way Vitus would turn a stone over and over, finding the shape to cut it to and what sort of talisman to make.

"A necessary one. Her aunt was worried about Childeric. About him becoming hurtful, method unspecified. Now she has a way out. She has a place he and his family can't touch, not without bringing down all sorts of trouble on their heads." Vitus shook his head. "He's going to hate that. He already hates that." Then he hesitated, before going on, because he knew how Lucas would feel about the next part. "She also told me he'd threatened me."

"Wait, what? That's the sort of thing you start with, you. Some of us might want to do something about that." Lucas had bolted upright at that, taking a step closer, as if he wanted to let out all that energy now.

Vitus touched his hand. "Not a physical threat. At least not unless I provoked it. The gossip got him badly, even though Thessaly's made it clear it's nothing against her agreements. She's scared of him. I encouraged her to talk to the Scali at least for right now, about someone who could accompany her in public. You know the sort of thing, a chaperone ready to duel."

Lucas snorted and took a step backwards, sitting down on the edge of the bed again. "I might know a couple of people. Can you get a note to her? Privately, I mean?"

"Mmhmm. Via the Scali, one of their many services when you have that much money on account with them. Whenever I like, they'll make sure it goes through and can get picked up. The private bank portal, too, those are harder to mess with." Vitus looked up again. "You might know someone?"

"Not well, but it's not as if the women of Boar House can go into the Army, now, is it? And there's some call for that sort of work. Not that it'd help with her actual marriage." Lucas's voice got suddenly careful and gentle. "When she marries him, she'll have to be alone with him. On their estates, at least sometimes. That will not sit well with you."

"Wrong verb tense. It doesn't now. Not because..." Vitus stood, suddenly, a rush of movement like something thrown into the air, tumbling against the sunlight, to go stand at the window. "She said she trusts me because she doesn't have to wear a mask with me, she doesn't have to hide, she doesn't have to protect herself. I can't give Thessaly that by wanting to control her. She's a duellist, she knows how to judge risk. Better than I do, almost certainly. She absolutely has more information to work with." He turned back. "Maybe Childeric will settle down. Maybe the Challenge will give him something else to focus on. I don't know."

"And their wedding's still, what, seven months from

now? A lot could happen in seven months." Lucas offered it carefully. "Maybe they come to some better agreement. He gets less grasping. I don't know." Then he let out a sigh. "Still going to worry about you. And her, now. That's annoying."

Vitus had to smile a little at that. "She's not some princess in distress in a story. The stories are far too simple. More than that, just rescuing her wouldn't help, even if she wanted it. And she doesn't, quite, because it doesn't solve the problems. Even if she feels safer where she is now, it doesn't solve her coming marriage, what it means." He then shivered. "I don't like the thought of her alone with Childeric, no. Especially not knowing her aunt was worried. But why aren't other people concerned? What sort of lever do the Fortiers have on the Lytton-Powells, or, I don't know, some faction of them?"

"Those are excellent questions. Also not ones I have an idea how to answer. Do you think Niobe might have any ideas? She knows a lot of people."

"But she's a generation younger, and most of that tier don't come to her for talismans. I can ask, though. She's heard enough about it already. She won't give me a hard time." Vitus made a mental note to think about it. "I offered to do some talisman work for Thessaly, as she thinks about what she wants in the house."

"Did you see anything about the house? What's it like?" Lucas considered. "If she's got it well warded, I suppose she knows what she's about there."

"Not inside. The wards were still settling. The terrace, the garden. I met the housekeeper, who'd obviously been told a little about me. What, I don't know, but it was the sort of look you get from someone who's evaluating you for truth, you know? The way Mama sometimes does."

Just then, they both heard the chime from downstairs

that meant people had come home. "Speaking of." Lucas stood up. "Let me think about it a bit and lay out a few practical steps when you walk me down to the portal. And I'll be in touch with some names for you to pass on."

"Grand. I can leave a note with the Scali to give to her on my way in tomorrow, let her know there will be more coming." Vitus stood as well. "It helps to talk it out, thank you."

"You're still going to get your heart broken. Just, I can't even be upset with her for doing that. She's not trying to hurt you. She's in an awful place, not much help for it. And you're a decent person who cares about her."

"Loves her, wants what is best for her." Vitus had to say it, saying it ached but also helped, in some odd way. "Got to keep going, anyway." Then he took a couple of steps around the bed, to the door, opening and waiting for his brother in the hall before they went down together.

17

AUGUST 20TH AT THE SCALI BANK

Thessaly was waiting for her mother. She had spent almost all of Monday in this very room, one of the small meeting rooms the Scali kept for meetings with their clients who need privacy and security. Yesterday had filled her head with dozens of things she needed to consider and decide upon, ideally promptly. She'd talked to all four of the senior men of the family. After lunch - and being able to see him interact with his wife - she'd settled on Amadeo Scali, the oldest of the four brothers, as her trustee.

The Scali men - and several of their wives and two daughters - had spent all day with her. They'd begun by checking what she understood of what she'd inherited. Then they'd talked through each aspect, the financial and legal implications. They'd given her advice, but they had not forced her hand. Most importantly, they'd agreed that she needed some sort of ongoing personal security and had offered someone temporarily. Miranda Foresby was a former Guardswoman, still active and now in her fifties, and she was waiting by the door.

Second, and just as importantly, they were arranging for a solicitor up to the demands of dealing with Thessaly's many and varied legal needs. Or rather, the Scali would present a choice of options for interviews later in the week. She needed a will, and promptly, but not before she understood what she was leaving. And, in a couple of cases, until she'd been able to confirm some restrictions with the courts.

But one item on that list, an essential and pressing one, was a conversation with her mother. Thessaly refused to go to Northumbria for it. She knew, with the sort of lurking fear that she felt when she thought about being alone with Childeric, that if she went there, she'd have a hard time leaving. Something in her would break or change or be destroyed, she didn't know which. She didn't want to know. Nor was she going to risk it until she was in a more secure position herself.

Now, it was just waiting to see if Mother would appear on time, or keep her daughter waiting. Which meant Thessaly was sitting here, on one side of a table, with her notebook and file copies handy. Fortunately, precisely at ten, just as the clock in the room chimed, there was a knock on the door. "Mistress Sioned Lytton-Powell is here." Miranda waited for Thessaly's nod, then opened the door, holding it. Mother stood there, her veil over her face, in the most severe of her black gowns.

Thessaly nodded once at Miranda, who went out, closing the door behind her, and gestured at the seat across from her. There were, of course, protections on this room, both those that could be triggered and those that were more subtle. Thessaly had a button, beneath her side of the desk, that would alert Miranda, bring her back through the door, with others behind her. But there were also charms on the room against certain kinds of magic, and layers of intention magic against threats seen and unseen. The Scali were exceedingly thorough.

"Do have a seat." Thessaly kept her voice even and steady, refusing to think about how well Mother could read her. "We need to talk."

"We could have done this at home." Her mother sat, however, with the rustle of silk and slight crackle of crepe.

"No, Mother, we couldn't." Thessaly was fascinated - horrified and delighted, both - to see her mother flinch at being called 'mother'. "We are, however, quite private here, unless I indicate I need assistance."

Her mother took a breath, let it out. "If you insist."

"We are both daughters of Fox House, Mother. You know what that means, or you ought." Thessaly folded her hands in her lap. No sense in giving away anything with a gesture that could be avoided. "I have many questions. The answers will determine a number of my choices."

"I suppose you do." Her mother adjusted the chair slightly. "Begin, then." Her voice was crisp and clipped, and Thessaly refused to think about how much she wanted something warmer. Something like before.

"I want to know not only why you contested the will, but why you didn't tell me anything about it. Did you know I was the primary heir?" Thessaly kept her voice as even as she could.

Mother did not look terribly surprised, but it was the most logical question. "It is a matter of family politics. Not personal ones."

"I am an adult, under all of Albion's laws. I am engaged to be married. I am nearly done with my apprenticeship." Thessaly laid it out beat by beat. "And it is also my family. Why didn't you want me to inherit?"

Her mother looked away, over Thessaly's shoulder, not meeting her eyes. "All marriages are a balancing act, a series of judgements, about preserving the family you have made together. You do not - yet - know that in truth. Metaia did not. Metaia refused to."

"If it is a balancing act, you are sending me unarmed, my vitality and magic drained, to a duel I cannot do my part in." Thessaly chose the metaphor, fully knowing it would annoy Mother. Again, she got a brief twitch in response. "The Fortiers do not tell me anything. Childeric does not tell me anything. You do not tell me anything, either you or Father. What am I supposed to do? Meekly do as I am bid, be a broodmare for the Fortiers, all my own magic and skills set aside but that?" Thessaly saw the answer long before her mother said anything, the way Mother collapsed inward. "Did you and Aunt Metaia argue about it, then?"

Mother stood abruptly, going to face the fireplace, still far enough away from Thessaly that she had no physical worry, but Thessaly shifted her chair slightly so she could move if needed. When she spoke, it was to the stonework, not to Thessaly. "Metaia understood we needed you to marry well. For money, but also for leverage. The Lyttons wanted it, the Powells wanted it. You were the culmination of decades of planning. And the Fortiers agreed, which is at least half luck, that you had little other competition among women of your age. Childeric liked you well enough to say yes, and everything you were bred and raised to be suited the family as a whole."

It made Thessaly feel entirely like some horse, or pig, or sheep bred only for bloodlines. Perhaps a hunting hound, that had some use in more than one way. The worst of it was, she'd known that was how it was. She'd agreed to the marriage knowing that it wasn't about love or even companionship. It was about duty and power and anchoring the family's place in the world. For an instant, she closed her eyes. Then she opened them again, because no matter how she felt, she needed all the information she could grasp. "Aunt Metaia didn't argue to start, did she? But later, she did."

"After the marriage agreements, after the betrothal. I don't know what set her off. She didn't tell me. But in, what was it, I don't know, at the end of April, she came to me again. Asking if you had said anything about Childeric, how things were going with the rest of the Fortiers." Mother turned back, part way. "I told her you were going along as expected. You were a good daughter. You understood how things were done. Metaia was never competent at that part. She always went at the world with a twist."

"Foxes are traditionally tricksters too, as much as Seal," Thessaly pointed out. "And then?"

"And then she came back. It must have been the week before she changed her will. She was worried about something, but she wouldn't say what. Do you know? Will you tell me?" Mother turned fully, coming over to take her chair again. She waited, the sort of expectant waiting that was hard to ignore. The thing about Mother is that she knew exactly what Thessaly would react to. It gave her an entirely unfair advantage.

Thessaly considered. "Aunt Metaia was concerned that Childeric would abuse me. She talked to me about it carefully, delicately, when I was dressing with her. Solstice afternoon. Before..." Thessaly couldn't help letting that show, and swallowed hard. "Before."

"And since?" Mother rested her right hand, the fingers, on the edge of the desk.

This was a particular choice in this duel, and Thessaly was clear it was a duel. She was holding her own, but that wasn't the same as winning. It certainly wasn't the same as getting to her actual goal, which was information and a way forward. "I have been thinking she was right to worry."

"Oh?" Mother leaned forward a little now.

"Well, for one thing, Childeric stopped bothering being charming - or even polite - as soon as the betrothal was final. Nearly before, in fact. Even at our betrothal, he went off to gamble with his friends for some of it. He has not given me the most basic information so that I could give a show of support. I had no idea that he was announcing he was challenging for the Council seat before he did, none."

She was about to go on, but Mother held up a hand there. "Clovis and Maylis thought he had told you. Or they would have made sure to do so themselves. They agree it was no suitable thing to surprise you with."

"He also did not tell me - until well after it was relevant - to be cautious about what I said to Laudine Fortier. Or about what the expectations were for the Lammas rites, and someone could certainly have done that for him. As it was, Garin explained. I think we can agree that when a nine-year-old is the one who notices the gap in information, there is something quite wrong."

Her mother winced again, but nodded. "Your father told me about that. Is there anything else?"

"Threats. About the gossip, in ways that made me fearful. And then, multiple letters over the past few days, several attempts to get through the portal. It's barred to all but the household and a few necessary people. None of the family, none of the Fortiers, certainly. Some of that is the wards settling, but some of it..." Thessaly's chin came up. "You understand I do not feel safe anywhere right now, except there."

"Safety is a luxury we rarely get." Her mother's voice came out low and sharp, and that put a whole different angle on the problem.

"Has Father threatened you?" Mother did not answer for a long moment, but Thessaly could read enough of it. "Not physically, then, but other ways?" That got a small nod. "So Aunt Metaia gave us all as much freedom as she could."

Mother's mouth twitched, and then she looked away. Thessaly knew she had made her point. She wished she could ask how much Aunt Metaia had supported her sister, all the ways that were now visible since her death. But Mother wouldn't answer that. Instead, her mother's chin came up. "Money isn't power. You know that. Daughter of Fox House. My daughter." Then she added, carefully, "It may give your sister more freedom. We will see."

"I want that. I want all the things for her I couldn't have." Thessaly let out a long, slow breath. "I had the Scali look at the marriage agreements, but I need to hear it from you. There are very few things that could break them now, correct?"

"Correct." Her mother opened her mouth, about to go on, then stopped. "Your father wanted to contest the will for control, and because he knew you having independent property would upset the Fortiers. I wished– my sister, my own sister, gave you more choices than she gave me. And I hated that."

"And Father has threatened you in some way that matters." Thessaly would name it that far, no matter what else.

"Yes." Then Mother cleared her throat. "To break the marriage agreements, you would need the sort of accusation that held up in the courts, the kind of thing that has lasting serious consequences. Or the sort of harm to you that could not be hidden by magic, beyond what the truth telling magics could bring to light. I do not want the second for you."

Thessaly didn't much either. She knew enough stories of just how bad that could be. Just like she knew enough stories of how men - and a few women, but mostly men - controlled their partners. She hadn't been able to get Lady Teague out of her head since Aunt Metaia had mentioned it. There were a thousand ways to cage someone, trap them in a net of their own complicity, because the costs of breaking free were too high. "And if I broke the agreements, I'd be ostracised by Albion's society."

"Just so. No one would duel you, no one would invite you to any gathering, no one would employ you. And you might not need to work, now, but—" Her mother spread both hands now. "You want to find a place that suits you. Idleness at home, even so lovely a home as Bryn Glas, is not that. You could go to America, to somewhere in the Commonwealth, but I do not think that would suit you either."

It wouldn't. Not now she somehow, miraculously, had Bryn Glas. Certainly not without giving up on the obligations to the staff and the land and the grove of trees she'd taken on. And she knew that even if she went, Vitus couldn't consider following. He loved his family too much and all his professional connections were here. Their lives relied on the network of vouches and referrals and agreements made over generations and years. Finally Thessaly nodded. "If it comes to that, something that might break the agreements, may I call upon you as a witness? The proper sort, with a solicitor and the truth enchantments."

Mother nodded. "And—" Now she hesitated. "Perhaps we might arrange for tea in a private tearoom next week. Myself and you and your sister?"

"Let me see how things go along. But yes." Then Thessaly hesitated. She hadn't been sure she would share this. "Hermia can come through the portal if she needs to, but I would need to let her into the estate. Not you, not Father. But if she needs somewhere to be."

"Thank you." That, now, had all the warmth and relief in it that Thessaly had wanted to hear on her own behalf, and hadn't heard. But she would claim it for Hermia, who was far more blameless in this. "I'll go now. I'm sure you have plenty to do. And I do not want to be away from home long. Your father..."

Father was keeping track, obviously. "Of course. And you can write, care of the Scali, they're forwarding letters twice a day."

Mother stood, not attempting to come closer for any sort of physical touch or affection. She just nodded once more and went out, opening the door and going through. Thessaly leaned back, not closing her eyes until Miranda was back in the room. "Tea, then?"

"Please. And if you'd let Amadeo know that I'd like to talk to him this afternoon, when convenient to him? I want to go through some accounts first, again, and make as much sense on my own as I can."

18

AUGUST 22ND IN THE TRELLECH LIBRARY

Thursday afternoon, Vitus was back in the library. He had no expectations of seeing Thessaly here, of course. He'd sent along the note with a few names Lucas suggested on Monday. Yesterday morning, he'd got back a note via the Scali, thanking him and letting him know the names had been useful. It was unsigned, of course. It had asked when he might be free to call again, but that she had obligations both Saturday and Sunday.

He'd written back immediately. Now, he wasn't exactly at loose ends - he had plenty of work to be doing. But Vitus had needed a break between a long afternoon working on the details of Carrington's commission and an evening working on smaller pieces to ready them for potential sale. The library was, he hoped, a productive pause, in the main. He'd get some books, he'd pick up some supper on the way back to the flat. Then he'd work until he was just able to get himself home, and he'd do it all again tomorrow.

As it was, he was contemplating last night's lecture. It had been another on electricity, this time about the development of high voltage direct current systems in Italy. The discussion afterward had got into larger systems, chaining devices together to serve different purposes. Vitus wasn't entirely interested in electricity itself here. Rather, he was taken by the idea of pieces of the system enhancing or stabilising the flow. That was right in line with what the Four Metals group was working on. In particular, he was wondering if there was a better, more efficient way to line them up. Ideally, one that would let them get the effects supporting each other rather than draining potency.

He was working his way through the books on the shelves, looking for anything interesting, when one of the younger librarians came by with a cart. "Oh, let me get out of your way for a moment. Plenty of other books. I can come back."

"If it's not a problem." Her eyes flicked to his collar and hands. "Master. You've been in here quite a lot?"

"Vitus Deschamps. I'm a talisman maker by profession." He managed, at the last moment, not to add the 'apprentice' in there. He was, for all intents and purposes, done. Niobe had told him to stop disclaiming so actively in social contexts, though he still had to stand up before their guild and do the last presentation of his pieces. That would be late September or early October, after the Challenge. "So, plenty of other things of interest."

"It'll just be a minute, if it's not a bother." When Vitus stepped away, she immediately went back to shelving books, making tidy little spaces. She must have twenty or so to shelve on her little wooden cart. Vitus drifted two bays down, toward some works on geology. If he went to the proper collection on gemstones and mineralogy, he'd be there for hours, and they'd have to pry him out when they closed. He selected a book or two about Eryri, since he'd like to brush up more on the geology of that great mountain.

The librarian was efficient. Three or four minutes later, the cart went past where Vitus was standing, and there was a quiet chipper voice. "All set, Master Deschamps. Please let me know if you're looking for anything and can't find it."

"Mostly browsing, thank you, but I'll let you know." Vitus finished up scanning the shelf he'd been looking at, and then went back to the electricity. This was a more precise process, so many of the books didn't deal with anything that was immediately useful. He had got the impression - nothing had changed his mind - that electricity was currently like one of the new magical techniques.

Everyone had an idea how it worked, only some of them would play out. He could be a bit of a snob there, talismanic stones were one of the older forms of magic. But he knew that some of the sympathetic magic techniques, earlier in the century, had seen the same ebb and flow. Now, it had mostly settled down. Electricity would do the same. Mesmerism more or less had. Sometimes.

That one, he held a grudge about, because well-meaning women kept suggesting to Mama that it would solve all her problems. She had, in fact, tried it, one seaside holiday. It had done no great harm, but it certainly hadn't solved a lasting cough or weakness. With some determination, he refused to get distracted by that frustration, and turned back to the books, considering the ones that had just been returned. He hadn't noticed titles, but he had an eye trained to notice shades of colour. It made pulling the re-shelved books out easier. They didn't match his mental image of the shelf as it had been.

This one, bound in a bright green, that hadn't been

there. He'd have noticed it. Or this one with the blue. He pulled the first out of the shelf, flipping through it. It was, as expected, about electricity. But it was leaning into experiments that had something to do with fields of energy or magnetism, as much as the direct passage of electricity from one point to another. He flipped to the back cover when his eyes caught the name on the checkout card tucked into the neat pocket. He pulled it up with his thumb, then considered it.

Dagobert Fortier. The way Dagobert wrote his initial D was unusual. Vitus had noted it before, with one of those loops that was second nature to the writer and chaos for anyone else. Vitus set it aside and then looked at the blue book he'd noticed. That had the same thing. Now, of course, he was fascinated. Setting his bag down, he pulled out a notebook and pencil.

Beginning at the head of the section, he took out each book. If one of the Fortiers had checked it out, their name on the card, he wrote down the title and the dates. It seemed rather like sneaking around, and perhaps it was, but the card was there in the back of the book, for anyone to read. When he was done, he had a list of fifteen titles, all focused on electricity and specifically on the creation of fields or spaces defined by it. Or at least Vitus thought that was it, piecing together what he'd learned in various lectures.

He picked out three of the books, plus two others that were closer to his original goal. Then he stopped in the fiction section for something pleasant to read, choosing from one of the newer titles. He'd read a review, saying *Three Men in a Boat (To Say Nothing of the Dog)* was quite funny, and others saying that it catered to the lower classes. It was, as the title suggested, three men and a dog boating on the Thames. Non-magical, of course, but that seemed like an interesting change from the rest of his reading at the moment. Certainly, a pleasant break from everything he was thinking about. Three men, a dog, and a boat were not worried about the intricate demands of the Great Families. Or probably even much about whatever Vitus's situation with Thessaly was. That was, admittedly, because his situation was definitely tending to the unique.

That done, Vitus brought the selection up to the desk, waiting for the librarian - the same one who had been shelving - to check the books out. She smiled up at him, and it suddenly struck him that if he hadn't been thinking about Thessaly, he'd have considered striking up a different sort of conversation. Perhaps seeing if she'd like a walk. But things were as they were, and he wouldn't do that. It seemed unfair in several directions, or rather unfairness added to what was already in his life. He did smile back, though, the sort of neutral professional smile. "It's grand you re-shelved when you did. Several of them look interesting to me."

She drew the cards out, pushing them over for him to write his name. Vitus did so, then presented his library card, the little cardstock square that - with an added charm - confirmed he'd been loaned the books. She matched it to a card in the drawers to her right, and each of the cards from the book lit up obligingly green. "I'm glad you found plenty to read. Oh, and you're in luck with this." She tapped the slim green volume. "You're the first to read it. We just put *Three Men and a Boat* out this afternoon. While you've been here, I think."

"Ah, now, that's a treat, to be the first with a book. I'll treat it gently, then. Not that I don't ordinarily. Book rests and book snakes and all that, when I'm studying, too." Vitus gestured slightly at the other books.

"You said you were a talisman maker. I suppose that

would mean having books open while you're considering some diagram or something of the kind." She considered. "I'm Elsie Norris. Would you perhaps be interested in talking with our senior librarian at some point? I know she was considering additions to our collections on talismans and on stones, but of course we know books, not every specialty they're about. She would welcome some ideas of what titles would be most useful."

That, now, was an interesting question, and one Vitus had opinions about. "Of course. My card, if she'd like to write and arrange a time? Late morning or late afternoon, a little before closing, both tend to be better for me, but it varies. I'd be glad to ask Magistra Hall, too, my apprentice mistress. She has far more opinions than I do, I'm sure. And there have been titles where I wanted to check something, not the whole work, and had to borrow a copy from some private collection."

"Well, then." Mistress Norris looked pleased. "Magistra Holland will be in touch, I'm sure. She was just saying this morning how it was hard to tell which books had new information, which are just duplicating a shared source, all that."

Vitus nodded at that. "Well, best be off. Reading to do, obviously." He carefully loaded the small stack of books into his satchel, touched his hat, and went off with a final "Good evening."

Once he got back to the flat, he put on the kettle for tea, and then settled on the sofa to consider the books. Thumbing through the first one, nothing leapt out. The second one, he started reading after a decorative illustration that caught his eye. Ten minutes later, he was at his desk; the book propped open, as he tried inscribing a particular pattern onto a river rock. He'd need quartz or amber to test it properly, but he needed to translate it into three dimensions again. Or rather back into three, because the thing about electricity was that it started that way.

Vitus did not make it home that night, glad he'd decided on a bed in the small bedroom next to his consulting room. His feet nearly brushed the wall on the far end - the room was quite narrow - but it was comfortable enough, at least for a night.

19

AUGUST 22ND IN SOUTHERN WALES

Thursday afternoon, Thessaly had come straight from her apprenticeship to Cousin Owain's home, accompanied by Miranda. Monday, she would interview candidates for the long-term position. At least there was a list in progress for that. The Scali had continued to be superbly helpful. Miranda was excellent, finding a mix between her duties and being too stiff and distant. But she did not want to live in Wales, even with generous time off and easy access to a portal, so that wouldn't do long-term.

Collins was already setting up a pleasant room in what had been the coach house, with more than sufficient privacy and space. And Thessaly had made it clear that she would stay within the wards when she was, in fact, home. Which she expected to be most of the time for the next few months. On the other hand, she was apparently obliged to be out at Arundel on Friday and Saturday evening, and the days, too. Miranda was competent enough to serve as lady's maid, at least. A woman of many skills.

Now Miranda was looking around cautiously. "You know where you're going, Mistress?"

"Just there." Thessaly nodded at the door to the house. "See, there's Cousin Owain, coming out. And he's a Council Member. He has his own protections well up to snuff." She could feel them, she was certain Miranda could.

Miranda snorted. "He does. I'd like to talk to whoever does his warding. Interesting texture to it." That was an unusual term to pick for it. People more often said flavour or perhaps shape. That would be a topic for some other time, perhaps later this evening.

Cousin Owain met them part way. "Grand to see you, Thessaly. We're up in my sitting room, more private, though Enfys and Tegwen might join us later." He nodded politely. "Mistress."

"Miranda Foresby, my current guardian," Thessaly said. "Miranda, Owain Powell, my cousin."

"Mistress Foresby, you're welcome to check the warding, but I'd like to ask you to wait outside for a little. Delicate topics, even though you come highly recommended." Cousin Owain said it smoothly, with no stall, which was interesting. But it also made clear that this was far more than a casual social visit or even checking in on the current state of Thessaly's well-being. "We've a comfortable chair. I'd be glad to offer a book or whatever refreshment suits while you're working."

Miranda tilted her head, deferring to Thessaly. Thessaly snorted, a bit bemused. "Do check the warding thoroughly. I know you want to. But I trust Cousin Owain and Magistra Hereswith." She then added, teasing her cousin a little, "If they wanted to be difficult, they'd have done it a good while ago, or it would be so subtle you being in the room wouldn't help."

That made Cousin Owain chuckle. "Just so. We mean you well, we're glad to make that more clear." He led the way into the house. Miranda did take a couple of minutes to look at the room and the warding. Then she declared herself satisfied and installed herself in the chair by the window at the end of the hall. A minute or two later, there was a knock on the sitting room, and Cousin Owain opened it.

Thessaly stood, only to be waved back into her seat. Hereswith Rowan came in, wearing a simple tea dress - quite informal for an afternoon. It made it clear she was not out in public. Cousin Owain gestured her into a chair, and then set about putting out tea and small plates of biscuits where they could all reach. Thessaly looked on, curious.

"We don't mean to be entirely opaque, Thessaly." Magistra Hereswith settled in a chair she clearly knew well, spreading her skirts. "But we wanted privacy for this, for reasons I think will be obvious. You are both a clever and observant woman, thank the gods."

That was a tidy little compliment, tidy enough that it made Thessaly cautious.

Cousin Owain began somewhere simpler, though. "First, we'd like to know how things are going, settling in. And if there's anything further, at all, where we might be a help. Recommendations for professional attention, all that."

That made Thessaly consider him. "With a purpose, cousin, yes?"

He spread his hands. "With a purpose, yes, we are getting to that. But the question is honest. How are things?"

"The warding is settling - thank you again, Magistra, for getting the specialist out so quickly. I am obliged to be at Arundel on Friday and Saturday night, but he is coming round Monday afternoon to check on everything. Miranda - you saw her outside - feels it's quite secure, but of course still adapting to the changes."

"Excellent. Magister Fulton is quite my preference for anything remotely delicate. He has a deft touch with it. And with wards related to intention, in particular, which seems potentially relevant here."

"Quite. And he had a colleague in the Portal Keepers, who has set it so only a limited number of people can come through the portal in the first place." Thessaly considered her options. "We might come back to that?"

"Of course. And the household? You had a good sense of it, and of course you've been raised to expect to manage your own in due course." Magistra Hereswith leaned back. None of this was a surprise to her, so Thessaly wondered what made her relax. Perhaps that Thessaly was being reasonably forthcoming.

"Mistress Collins has everything exceptionally well in hand. She's arranging quarters for whoever takes on the long-term position of guardian and visible companion. The rest of the staff are relieved, and they're all quite willing to stay, even with the additional protections and the limitations involved."

"I'm glad to hear that," said Magistra Hereswith. "If it would be any help, when you have a little time, I'd be glad to loan Bess to have a look and see if there's anything that needs attention. I know your Mistress Collins is incredibly efficient, and she's made it clear she intends to give you the same loyalty she gave Metaia. But sometimes a fresh set of eyes is a help, especially since you will have different needs."

"You are being very generous, Magistra." Thessaly inclined her head. "I would be glad to accept. But, now, may I ask why you are being so attentive? This goes beyond care for Aunt Metaia or the house. At least on your part." It would be interesting to have Magistra Hereswith's companion's commentary, though, and while Bess would take some of it back home, certainly, Thessaly thought it wouldn't be anything Magistra Hereswith didn't already largely know.

Magistra Hereswith flicked her fingers. "As I said, you are an intelligent and observant woman. Owain, would you?"

Cousin Owain stood, going first to the door and then to the two windows, tapping in a particular pattern. Thessaly felt something like the weight of a cloak descend, flexible but undeniably present. Magistra Hereswith went on, her voice the sort of even that meant she was suppressing a great deal. "Metaia was murdered. The Guard does not have much in the way of a meaningful lead, certainly not regarding motive."

That implied something about the method, or perhaps the murderer, and Thessaly opened her mouth to ask. Cousin Owain said, quietly, "In a moment." Thessaly closed her mouth again, folding her hands so she wouldn't fidget.

"As you know, in broad strokes, all the Council have our own projects. Not just whatever consulting we might do, or our personal interests, but in our remit as members of the Council. We know Metaia was concerned about something, but we have not found any direct references, and she did not share any details with us. It was at a delicate stage, the kind of thing where a breath in the wrong place might bring everything crashing down." Magistra Hereswith looked deeply sorry for a moment. "And likely did. But we do not know which breath, where."

Thessaly inhaled herself, thinking about the breath.

"You want to know what that was. If I've seen any sign of what it might be, or if she said anything that in hindsight makes a horrible amount of sense."

"Exactly." Magistra Hereswith leaned back, and Thessaly felt the full weight of her consideration. "Will you?"

"I am, as you say, trained in a number of things. One of them is not to make agreements too quickly, if it can be avoided." Thessaly ticked off on her fingers. "You can't compel me, or it would be a matter for the Guard. You wouldn't be asking like this. You must certainly have arranged for a look in the weeks of the investigation before the will was read. And I know Aunt Metaia trusted you both, but if she didn't tell you, she had reason. I don't know what that reason was, so I don't know if it still stands."

Magistra Hereswith blinked, and then she chuckled. "Ah, you delight. Not so many will stand up to me anymore. I am glad you are one of them. I am not asking for a promise here and now. Just laying out what we are thinking about. If you come across something that is relevant that you are willing to share, I hope you will consider it in whatever circumstances you feel comfortable doing. And explicitly, under whatever protections you feel are needed. If the truth enchantments would ease things, with a set list of questions, we can do that. If a room like this would be better, we will gladly arrange that. And so on."

Thessaly inclined her head, considering her options. The thing of it was, these were two of the most powerful people in the country. They could no more break her marriage agreements than she could, but telling them might open a doorway or a lever or some small thing Thessaly could use. "I have worried about the last conversation I had with her in private, the afternoon of the rites."

Both of them leaned forward, just slightly. They

weren't trying to hide their reactions, and they certainly both could. Thessaly would be staring at the ceiling thinking about that tonight, and on other nights to come, she was sure of that. "Whatever you can share."

"She gave me the garnet, the pendant she'd worn for her Challenge." Thessaly reached to touch it. She'd been wearing it every day since she'd fled her childhood home. They must surely have some idea of what it did. "And then she told me she was worried about how Childeric was treating me. It's— it's worse since then. She gave me as much freedom as she could, but it's been made clear that nothing he's done would break our marriage agreements."

"Ah." Magistra Hereswith leaned back, tapping her fingers. "That was the Scali advice, and your solicitor?"

"Yes'm." The honorific came out automatically, and Thessaly looked down and away. "And Mother's advice, as well. Though under the circumstances, confirming it with more neutral parties is obviously sensible."

Cousin Owain said, gently, "You've spoken with her, then?"

"Tuesday, the Scali were kind enough to facilitate. And Miranda loomed properly." She nodded toward the hallway. Then she raised her chin. "I agreed to the marriage terms because I thought Childeric would do his part. It is clear I was wrong about a number of aspects, but having money of my own that he can't touch is a help. Currently infuriating him, and I expect that to continue. It will not be a pleasant visit."

"No." Magistra Hereswith's voice had a weight to it. "And Miranda or someone of her calibre will be with you throughout?"

"Oh, yes. Childeric has not seen fit to prevail on me physically beyond the usual sort of kiss. And I am still in mourning for Aunt Metaia, even if he and his family find it increasingly inconvenient." Thessaly contemplated, then added, "To give you an idea, he did not tell me he was intending to Challenge, before they made the announcement. The Fortiers made arrangements for me to observe from the gallery above their Great Hall. That gives a sense of it, I'm sure."

"It does, rather." It was easy to forget, sometimes, in all she'd done since, that Magistra Hereswith had had a career of some note as a competent diplomat, before her own Council Challenge. "Thank you for sharing that. I do not have advice for you, not right now, but if I learn anything that might be a help, I will tell you what I can. But I am not and have never been an intimate of the Fortiers or any of their allies."

That was frankly more than Thessaly had expected. "I will see whether I come across anything - notes, or whatever. But you know what Aunt Metaia's library and rooms were like, papers everywhere. I do plan to go through things piece by piece." She considered. "Many of her books are relevant to me. But perhaps I might make a list of the ones I do not wish to keep. And you might suggest if there are people or community spaces where they would be welcomed and enjoyed?"

"Certainly." Magistra Hereswith nodded. "That's another project to talk to Bess about when you're ready. I'll let her know you might be in touch about either at some point. It is not an offer with any sort of time limit."

Cousin Owain nodded, then cleared his throat. "Perhaps we might have a brief walk in the garden, and then tea properly with Enfys and Tegwen? They will be glad to see you, Hereswith. Tegwen has a new puzzle for you."

"I can't leave without hearing that, certainly, no." She

stood, waiting for Cousin Owain to open the warding, then the door. Thessaly did the same. She had certainly run out of things she felt competent to say this afternoon about anything complex. And perhaps tea and conversation with people who were not named Fortier would be restorative before Friday's challenges.

20

AUGUST 23RD IN TRELLECH

Vitus had not originally planned on attending the lecture on Friday night. He often didn't. They tended to be more full of people who were making a night out of it, and less about serious discussion. But it was going to the lecture or going home to worry about Thessaly. The lecture seemed the better option. In the end, he was glad he went, though most of it wasn't terribly relevant to his interests.

One presenter was a Healer, talking about how most of the devices designed to apply electrical current for health reasons did little good. Vitus knew Mama wasn't considering any of that, though she might well have been a target for that kind of quackery if they'd been living among the non-magical.

The other presenter, however, had spent about half her time talking about the different and competing sorts of electricity, and what that might mean for magical applications. It wasn't anything terribly new to Vitus at this point, but the way she explained the advantages and disadvantages of both direct and alternating current was more evocative than others he'd heard. She'd tied it into some of the classic magical theory.

Her approaches to the topic were all things anyone who'd made it through Schola likely knew, and a fair number of others with any exposure to sympathetic or ritual magic. But she'd also put it well, a summary that made it possible to follow the rest of her discussion more readily. It gave him something to think about, in how to talk about it, anyway.

On the other hand, leaving the lecture was rather more interesting, if also complex. Vitus had a word with a few people sitting near him, but he'd declined their offer to go on to a party somewhere off in Yorkshire. Instead, he waited for the crowd to filter out. Vitus wasn't in a rush. While he was waiting halfway up the aisle, he realised Dagobert Fortier was in attendance.

The man really did not look well. Vitus hadn't seen him in ages. Thinking back, not since solstice night. He hadn't been at Philip Landry's funeral, and he hadn't been at Metaia Powell's funeral, either. But then there were those books, checked out in his name. That implied he'd at least been at the library a fortnight ago. At any rate, he looked faded and exhausted, and as if he'd lost enough weight that his tailor couldn't keep up with the adjustments. But he also had the sort of stubborn look Mama got when the body wasn't obliging but the mind refused to give up. Now he was moving slowly down between the seats, one hand on the back of the row nearer the stage, the other on a cane, navigating cautiously.

Vitus stepped back to give him a little room. "Master Fortier."

The comment apparently made him stop, as if he couldn't both speak and move. Then he nodded back. "Master Deschamps." He was silent as he got to the end of the row, then out into the aisle. Fortier made his way slowly up the aisle, into the foyer, pausing out of the way. "My wife is meeting me. I suspect her own evening ran a little long."

It wasn't as if Vitus could offer to lend a hand, it would mean acknowledging the visible weakness. That wasn't the done thing, and especially not with a Fortier. Vitus considered what he could say that was both truthful and different. "Have you much interest in electricity, then? I've been at a number of lectures, but usually the Wednesday set. I've found they're a bit more focused, greater in depth."

Fortier shifted his free hand back and forth. "Some. I find the topic interesting, though I do wish people would settle to some sort of tested conclusions about it. Right now it's all at the invention stage, trying things out and not understanding why some of them work and some of them fail." He considered for a moment longer, then added, "Or what the risks are. I am an alchemist. I think about the risks more than some, I suppose."

Vitus inclined his head. "That's a perspective we don't seem to hear often enough, no. I'm principally interested in some of the discussions about sequences and systems. I'm doing some work with a few other people to apply those techniques to talismanic use or stonework. All very experimental still, and we are taking it slowly."

Vitus was no Fox to read this sort of thing clearly, but he thought the other man flinched at the mention of sequences. "Ah. Some people I know were trying something along related lines. It hasn't gone well." That last sentence had an echo with it. "Perhaps a different direction will do better." Whatever that was, whoever that was, Fortier didn't sound very optimistic about it.

"Hence the lecture?" Vitus offered, carefully.

"Perhaps. You said the Wednesday ones are better? I

might try that next week. Or perhaps the week after." He shifted, a little unevenly, then he focused on someone coming in the door. His wife, Laudine, was dressed for a night out, at some restaurant or gathering, in an elegantly designed dress of deep green that flattered her dark auburn hair. Vitus made a slight bow toward her as she approached. "Mistress Fortier."

She inclined her head, immediately focusing on her husband after that, one hand reaching for his. It was an affectionate gesture, one Vitus hadn't noticed them make before, not merely one expected by etiquette. "Master Deschamps. Dagobert, was it a pleasant lecture?"

"It gave me some things to consider. I am glad I came." They exchanged a look, the sort of thing Vitus's Mama and Papa did, though he couldn't guess at what this one meant. Then Dagobert cleared his throat, addressing Vitus directly. "Perhaps you might join us for a drink. Would we be keeping you from something? There's a restaurant along toward Portal Square, and I'd rather wait for the evening traffic to die down."

His wife didn't argue - she made no comment and certainly gave Vitus no hint. He considered his options, but he was very curious if Dagobert might say more about the electricity. "I'd be pleased to join you. And no, I had no plans other than going home. No one's expecting me at any particular hour. I often go out for a bite or a drink after one of these."

"Excellent." There was then a slow and somewhat unsteady procession out of the lecture hall, down the steps, and across two and a half blocks. They wove through the shops and restaurants, until Laudine Fortier paused by a smaller place, wood-panelled and lit with golden light. She was clearly known there. One of the staff in a smart uniform opened the door for her. "We will have a table in a moment, Mistress. For three?"

"For three." Laudine spoke evenly, her voice clear. A minute or two later, they were settled into a corner where it was quieter, and where Dagobert could lean his cane out of the way. They made pleasant but unmemorable conversation until their drinks arrived, mostly asking about Vitus's parents. Then Laudine tilted her head. "Any objection to a little more privacy?"

The trick of it was, when someone asked like that, they usually had a reason. And yet, asking about that reason was impossible. It wasn't likely they'd explain, not least because of whatever reasons they wanted the privacy for first. That went triple, at least, when talking to two of Fox House. Whatever Dagobert's current health concerns, it hadn't seemed to affect his mind much, though Vitus did not exactly have an extensive experience to match it to. Vitus straightened a little, shaking his head. "No, of course not, if you'd prefer."

Her fingers flicked, calling up a privacy charm twined to the table. Vitus could feel it, how it extended a little. That explained at least one reason for liking the place. Now, she cleared her throat again. "You have an interest in electricity, then, Master Deschamps?"

Vitus nodded. "I mentioned to Master Fortier that I'm doing some experiments - with due care, of course - related to systems and circuits connecting. Some of the electrical experimentation leads one to think in certain similar directions, about the flow of current, about those things that enhance or inhibit it." He very much had the sense that Laudine, in specific, was measuring what he said to the finest detail. "We're working with a variety of materials, including talisman quality stones."

"Oh, indeed?" She led him through a good five

minutes on the various properties of stones. Despite some of his caution, he found himself relaxing into it, replying to her easily about those parts that were more general and wouldn't give specifics away. Once they'd been talking for a bit, she asked, "May I ask your professional opinion on the quality of the tourmaline from Cornwall as compared to, say, Sussex?"

"Sussex is better for pyrite. Not much tourmaline, if you want a wider range, definitely Cornwall. Though some of the south Wales mines aren't bad for a range, either. For jewellery, for a talismanic piece? Pardon, I'm prying. Professional interest makes me pay attention."

She inclined her head. "I think at this stage of professional interest, I might reasonably ask you to call me Laudine." She said it like it was a simple sentence, but of course it wasn't. It had dozens of implications.

When Vitus didn't answer for a moment, her husband cleared his throat. "Likewise." He was following her lead, rather visibly, at least from Vitus's proximity, and that was also making him wonder about a great many things.

He had choices here; he knew that, but if he backed off now, they'd likely never offer this sort of opportunity again. And, to be honest, he was curious about the range of her - Laudine's - knowledge, and also about why they'd asked him for a drink. He nodded himself. "Please, call me Vitus."

"There, that's entirely civilised. You have questions, of course. You didn't expect this depth from me?" Laudine asked it, almost teasing.

"It was not what I expected from the evening, no." Vitus considered. "You have far more depth of knowledge than I'd expect from someone not in the field. Most people don't bother with the properties of the stones the same way."

"Ah." Laudine flicked one finger. "My father is a talisman maker, of course, though he's never made it his only business. And my sister married Helios Osbourne, six years ago now. Relatively early in your apprenticeship, if I have the dates right?" She said it lightly enough, but that was more than sufficient information to make Vitus realise the implications.

Helios Osbourne and his wife had left Albion rather abruptly, because of a family scandal. Not Helios. The aftermath had been fairly clear about that, and not his wife. His father, Vitus thought, not that he was going to stumble and ask. He could consult the papers next time he was in the library. That was recent enough the archives were readily accessible still.

"And you have some interest yourself, beyond the familial?" There was a brief flicker there as he said the last word, but then Laudine was all pleasant expression and agreeable comment.

"Yes, my own training was in sympathetic magic. I still get a fair bit of use from it, and I'm thinking of some projects of my own. I wasn't so much thinking a talismanic stone, though that is worth considering, but a focal stone."

"In that case, it would depend on how you wanted to balance the local aspect, the piezoelectric factors, and the appearance." Vitus considered it. "I don't normally work pyrite. It doesn't take as well to inscription, but there are some beautiful marcasite pieces. That's a misnomer, of course. Actual marcasite reacts more easily, and no one needs sulphuric acid on their fingers or person. Pyrite is notably safer."

"No, indeed." Laudine made the words low and somehow echoing some mystery. "Perhaps you might consult privately, at some point?" There was another one of those quick glances at her husband. "I understand entirely that you do not wish to draw attention from the rest of the Fortiers."

Vitus froze, feeling suddenly trapped. "Madam?" It came out not quite as a squeak. He took a breath, then did his best to answer. "I am always glad to discuss a professional consultation and see if we can come to some suitable agreement. I had not wanted to presume at the moment, of course, though I am grateful for the family's support in the past."

Laudine's mouth curled into a slight smile for just an instant. "We entirely understand that you might not want certain attention focused on you at the moment. Neither do we. Dagobert and I have our own resources and interests, of course, distinct from Clovis and Maylis and their children. We are staying at the Essex House at the moment, and expect to be for some time. Rather more privacy."

Vitus managed a nod, but he didn't know what to say to that. He was intrigued, certainly, but there were a dozen implications there about the balance of power and influence and danger.

Laudine considered for a moment before going on, not waiting for him to say anything. "I will be seeing Thessaly tomorrow. We're invited out to Arundel. Last I saw her, at Lammas, she looked well, though we got little chance to speak." When Vitus said nothing further, Laudine shrugged. "I can't promise to get a message to her tomorrow, not private, but it's not impossible in the future."

Vitus swallowed. "I appreciate the offer, Laudine, Dagobert. But I couldn't put you in a difficult situation. And—" He hesitated, because he didn't want to give anything away. "She made it clear an attempt to contact her would not be welcomed by others. I would hate to put her to any kind of discomfort. I want only the best for her."

"Mmm." It was on the surface a non-committal noise.

After a moment, Dagobert picked up a little cautiously. "You've been attending some of the lectures on electricity for a while. May I ask where your own reading has taken you?" That was a far easier line of conversation, at least at the moment. It gave Vitus a chance to work the conversation around to a few of the titles he knew Dagobert had been reading, without revealing his knowledge outright. When that conversation wound down, perhaps twenty minutes later, Vitus murmured, "I should perhaps let you get back home. I hope Garin is well?"

"Very kind of you to ask, and to think of him. He is—it has been a more difficult summer than we would like, but I have been enjoying being able to spend a bit more time with him. We've been teaching him a bit about alchemy and some of the materia work related to it, the things a child can learn easily enough." Dagobert said that part warmly, enough that Vitus was sure of the genuine fondness there.

"He has always struck me as both clever and attentive. I hope that goes well." Vitus waited for them to stand. Dagobert tended to the bill, waving off any offer from Vitus. As Vitus waited for them to go through the door, he caught one last odd gesture, private communication. Then they all went the last half block to Portal Square, and on their separate ways.

21

AUGUST 24TH AT ARUNDEL

"Thessaly." Childeric's voice immediately made Thessaly brace herself. "Walk with me, would you?"

It wasn't remotely a request. The family were out in the gardens, and Miranda had been lurking properly about ten feet away. Thessaly had made appropriate conversation with Lady Chrodechildis about the history of the gardens. Then she'd talked with Lady Maylis about her dress for the Challenge, and with Sigbert about a bit of history of the estate.

Twice, a conversation had gone in an odd direction. There would be a reference to a concern about the harvest, and Lord Clovis or Lady Maylis would immediately change the subject. Certainly, while the grounds looked well-tended, there were signs that not all was right. Some leaves were browned along the edges, like they'd been singed by drought. It was particularly obvious in contrast to Bryn Glas, which was abounding with green health. Thessaly felt odd being here, as if these were things she were seeing that none of the family acknowledged. It made her wonder if the problem were her, somehow, except that when she was at Bryn Glas or in Trellech, she did not feel the same way.

Childeric had been absent until five minutes ago, though neither of his parents had commented on it. Now he was waiting, his arm out at a slight angle, making it visible what she should do. Thessaly stood, slipping her arm through his, and he set off. For once, not at his usual pace that overmatched her shoes. "Must you continue wearing mourning? It is only the family here."

"Yes, Childeric." She bit off a comment about how that was especially true since she'd inherited from Aunt Metaia. Wearing black a little longer seemed relevant. The black itself felt insignificant, some of the time, or too restrictive at others. But on the whole, it felt right, like there was a necessary boundary marker in her life that deserved her respect. It was like the walls of the duelling salle that way, or the boundary of the Pact and the Silence.

He walked her in silence to the end of the formal garden, through the break in the hedge to the French garden. When Miranda followed behind them, he turned. "You're not needed."

Miranda said, her voice clear, "The terms of my employment - as determined by Mistress Lytton-Powell's trustee - state that she is to remain in line of sight at all times when away from home."

Childeric grunted unpleasantly. "Wait there, then. We will not leave this garden." The garden, mind, was a good fifty feet on a side. Thessaly knew perfectly well that there were many things he could do that she would regret before Miranda could cross the distance. Childeric tugged her on until they were two-thirds of the way down the side. "It won't save you on our marriage night. Or as many other nights as it takes to get you with child."

There was utter ugliness there, a brutal nastiness that he wasn't remotely bothering to hide. Thessaly twitched, and he moved his hand, suddenly twisting his to pinch the skin between her thumb and forefinger, just where it hurt most. Thessaly nearly yelped, but it wouldn't do any good, and she didn't want to give him the satisfaction.

"I want to be very clear. There will be no nonsense with a bodyguard when you live here. You might hold Bryn Glas in your own name, but you won't be visiting there. There will be no place you are permitted that I can't go. You will bar no door to me, no portal. Tell me you understand."

Thessaly swallowed hard, against all the desire to fight that was welling up in her. She bit her lip, holding her silence.

His fingers dug in again, harder this time, enough to force her to take a breath at the pain. "Tell me." She looked at his fingers, and she could see a flash of turquoise on his ring, her mind fastening onto it rather than the pain she felt.

"I understand, Childeric." She didn't think it would hold. Thessaly was going into this marriage with more armour, more weapons, than she'd expected to have. She had months to lay out plans. There was time to work out with Amadeo Scali how best to handle restrictions, how to set up checks against Childeric's grasping jealousy. "But surely there will be some nights you are not at home, when you are off with your mistress."

He dropped her hand, taking a step back, about to slap her. She was sure of it. His hand went down and then out, his shoulder moved to put his weight into it. Then Childeric must have remembered Miranda was watching. "Don't you ever say such things. Not to me, not to anyone." He was furious now, his nose flaring with it, his face increasingly red. He took another step back, and Thessaly braced herself, a proper duelling stance with both her hands free, and sensible shoes on beneath her skirts. "You forget yourself. And you forget what I could do to your pathetic follower. Surely, he only cares about your money. It's the only reason anyone would."

That was bad logic. Vitus had been interested in her conversation - and perhaps other things, but indisputably also her mind and her knowledge - from the first.

"Have you seen him since I forbade it?" Now Childeric's voice was a growl, and Thessaly also felt weak. It was an out of proportion reaction to the pinch, but she could feel her knees wobble.

"We were both in the Trellech library at the same time last week." That was true, honest, and also public. "Of course I made it clear of the risks of writing, or of being seen near me again."

"That is some small thing. You are not entirely foolish, then. It would be a bother to ruin him, but I will, if you give me any provocation. As I will destroy whatever else you hold dear if you don't keep your place. Your sister, for example, she's still so young, and gossip can be so cruel."

Thessaly inhaled sharply. A week ago, she'd have said her parents could keep Hermia safe, she'd have told them this threat. Father would have been annoyed, Mother would have taken steps, but Hermia would have been safe. Now she knew there was no such certainty. "You've made your point, Childeric. Surely you've other enjoyments than threatening me?"

He grunted at that, though there was something almost amused now. "Oh, but what if it turns out that I find threatening you a most intriguing pastime? I will make you bend, I will have you begging me. I will find out how to bring you in line." Now he reached to touch her, but this was a single finger tracing along her jawline. "We have so very much to look forward to, together."

At that, he wheeled on his heel, and strode off, taking long steps. Thessaly stared after him, unable for a moment to do anything other than see everything she loved shattered. Bryn Glas as a ruin, every bit of her work ground to dust, anything she showed any sign of caring about. It didn't matter that it wasn't reality - Bryn Glas would go back to the Powells before it could be ruined. She'd have nightmares about it, she was sure.

At the far end of the garden, Childeric brushed rudely past Miranda in the hedge archway. Miranda only stepped aside at the last moment. Thessaly looked off after him, then found herself rubbing her hand where he'd pinched. Miranda stayed near the hedge, watching where he'd gone, presumably, as Thessaly eventually made her way closer.

"Are you injured, please?" Miranda's voice was strained. "You ordered me not to interfere, but that..."

Thessaly sucked in a breath, letting it out, then held out her hands. "He pinched me there. Where it won't show. I don't suppose you know a charm?" Then, before she could lose her courage, there was the thought that had occurred to her just now as Childeric stormed off. "Could I get him to hurt me enough to break the agreements, but not injure me permanently, do you think?"

Miranda had cupped Thessaly's hand in both of hers, but then she froze. "I would not advise it, mistress. As a professional, it is a tricky thing to pull off, especially in the spaces that he might permit as the duelling ground."

"Well, I don't know that I can advise being married to him, either. There is a certain appeal in risking everything once, and getting the aftermath over with." It was an entirely fatalistic approach. "That is not yours to decide on. Could I do it, if I had to?"

There was a long moment when Miranda busied herself with a charm that brought a rush of slight warmth to Thessaly's hand, then relief from the ache. Softly, the older woman said, "You have more skills than others I know who have tried. Three were successful. But I know two who did, with similar ability. One lived the rest of her life as an invalid, an injury to her neck. The other died, a few days later, at her husband's hand. I cannot, as I said, recommend it."

"Oh." Thessaly let out a breath slowly. "I'm sorry for their losses, and for bringing up a painful memory."

"You are right to ask, to consider all your options. But I would seek many others before trying that. And of course, I'm glad to witness to the Scali what I saw. I know that whoever replaces me will, too, and perhaps you might arrange a charm piece that would let her listen as a regular part of her uniform."

"Ah." That was an interesting sort of puzzle, and that would help, yes. "Thank you. For now, well, guard my door in case he rattles it in the night, please."

Miranda harrumphed. "I'm fairly sure he tried last night, actually. I'll move the cot in front of it tonight." Then her chin came up. "Mistress Fortier, good afternoon." She dropped Thessaly's hand. "Mistress Lytton-Powell thought something might have stung her."

It was a passable excuse. Laudine Fortier inclined her head. She was less fussily dressed today than her sister-in-law or her mother-in-law, a simple afternoon gown of deep blue. "I'm glad that Thessaly has someone to check on these things for her. Might I have a word in private, Thessaly? Perhaps down at the end of the garden, where Mistress Foresby can keep an eye out for anyone who might disturb us?" She made the suggestion almost conspiratorial.

"As you wish, yes." Thessaly nodded to Miranda, and then walked with Laudine to the far corner, further than she'd made it with Childeric. "Your husband looked a little more recovered, earlier. I hope that's the case?" Dagobert had found a seat, talking mostly to his brother, though the conversation had seemed a tad uncomfortable.

"Improved, yes. Thank you for asking. A slow recovery." She did not explain - no one had explained - exactly what had happened to him. And of course, Thessaly wasn't going to ask. She'd told Miranda to keep her ears open when she was in the staff areas of the manor while they were here, in case there was any gossip. But she suspected there wouldn't be. The Arundel staff were too loyal or too cowed to talk about such things with strangers around.

What Laudine said next shocked her, though. The older woman leaned in a little, cast a charm - something that insured privacy, Thessaly was fairly sure. "There. Quite private. Though she doesn't enchant the gardens this far out, that's why Childeric brought you here for whatever he had to say to you. I cannot offer much help there at the moment."

"I would not expect it." Thessaly had intended to stop there, but then she considered and went on with a particular move in this ongoing duel that might open up a new line of interaction. "I have gathered you have your own challenges and priorities right now."

Laudine honestly smiled a hair at that. "I look forward to not being entirely alone with the, what do I call it, the intensities of the family. With someone else who sees them clearly enough. Though Dagobert has come round to my way of thinking on several points recently." She then went on, smoothly. "Dagobert was at the lecture in Trellech last night, on electricity, and we had a pleasant drink afterwards with Vitus Deschamps. He is well, and also clear that he does not want to put you at further risk. The young man made a good impression on me. I look forward to talking a bit more about a possible commission with him." Her eyebrow arched up. "Not one I'd mention to the Fortiers, of course."

There was no 'of course' about any of that, but Thessaly followed the line of thought. "Childeric has made it very clear what he thinks of my talking to Vitus. I regret that, I had been very much enjoying our professional conversation, the mix of illusion and mineralogy, for example. I wish you well with whatever project there is."

Laudine nodded. "Perhaps in a week or two, you might come for tea, if you wished? When we could have a more, mmm, private and lasting conversation. Of course, you must be quite busy right now, taking on an estate to manage. And no matter how competent the staff is, there are things that only the owner can decide. Perhaps we might talk through a little of that about the Essex House, if it would be a help to you. It's a more modest size, both in the buildings and the surrounding lands, than Arundel. And not in my mother-in-law's grip, despite her preferences."

That last part, now Thessaly couldn't hide a smile. "I'm sure. I would be glad to learn whatever you're willing to share, then, if it's convenient for you to have me to tea. And, of course, I expect the third week of September to be busy with all the preparations."

"Ah, yes. They do expand to fill up whatever time one might have. I'm sure you'll see your way through all of it. Shall we walk back? Do tell me a little about your dress for it. Maylis mentioned something but didn't bother to go into details with me." They made their way around the other two sides of the square, Miranda falling into place behind them. Returning to the rest of the group before anyone wondered too much about what they were talking about was a good strategy. Thessaly was fairly sure Laudine was using all her skills at that for her own reasons. The support she was offering to Thessaly, such as it was, was entirely tied into whatever those reasons were.

22

AUGUST 26TH AT BRYN GLAS

Vitus was not at all sure what to expect. He'd received the note first thing that morning, confirming that this afternoon would be a good time for another visit to Bryn Glas. He had turned up at half-five, as requested, to find the meadow around the portal clear. Thessaly was waiting by the fence, as she had last time, with her companion over her shoulder.

"Vitus." She opened the gate, then offered her hand, guiding him through. "I can invite you inside today. Magister Fulton was quite pleased with how the wards are settling. The library?"

Vitus ducked his chin. "Wherever you would prefer, of course. Though I am curious about libraries in general and this one in specific."

That made her smile, an honest and glowing one, which made him even more certain it was the right thing to say. Then Vitus got another look at her. "A difficult day?"

"Today was long, but much easier than Friday, Saturday, and Sunday. That's a topic for, well. Sitting down, at the very least." Thessaly sounded tired, as well as looking it. She was wearing a tea gown again, this one black and sleeveless over a deep charcoal grey underdress with sleeves that draped and billowed around the cuffs at her wrists. Somehow, the effect was even more of mourning than unrelieved formality was. Without saying much more, they made a little procession to the door. She did something to the warding, a shimmer of magic, and brought him inside and to the right, into a strikingly beautiful room.

He thought, at first, of a tumult of polished and cut stones, the way gems and crystals reflected light and colour in their myriad ways. This was not exactly the same. There were decorative patterns here, but the vibrancy and vitality of the room took his breath away. There was a sofa facing a tiled fireplace, each of the tiles picking out some story or sequence he couldn't place immediately. Stained glass in the transom over the door and over the bay windows added glowing light. And of course there were the books. This was no library of immaculately matched sets, barely opened. The volumes were all shapes and sizes and bindings, many of them visibly well-worn.

Mistress Collins appeared almost immediately behind them. Thessaly smiled. "Tea, please, and then if you'd let us be unless I ring?" The housekeeper nodded, disappearing for just a minute before she wheeled in a tea cart loaded with both tea and cakes.

"They are trying to tempt my appetite," Thessaly said. "It's almost working. Though I ate little while I was gone, and food is ..." Her voice trailed off. "I need to ask, before we go on, are you sure you're willing to take the risk of being here?"

Vitus was about to sit - she'd taken one end of the sofa, and he had thought he'd take the other. Space between them, and Miranda had disappeared entirely as well. Now he paused, hands behind his back. "Did he threaten you again?"

Thessaly said nothing, but she didn't need to. She might be a daughter of Fox House, raised to hide her emotions, but he could read the flash of her eyes well enough. Or something in her expression, anyway. Vitus squared his shoulders. "You trust the privacy here?" She nodded. "Then I will stay. I trust your evaluation of the risk."

Something in that shook her. He could see that. But she said nothing about it. Instead she looked away, toward the shelves behind his shoulder. Vitus gave her a moment and then turned his attention to pouring the tea. He was certainly competent to do that, and he assumed that whatever had been served was to her taste. She turned back, taking the cup and saucer from him, holding it delicately. "Will you tell me about what you're currently working on? Nothing private, of course, whatever you'd like to discuss."

It was not why he'd come here, not exactly. But he understood she couldn't bring herself to any more complex discussion just yet. Instead, he settled into some of the work he was doing to prepare a set of commonly requested stones. His plan was to bring them all to a point where the particulars could be added. There were stones for healing, for sleep, of course. The ordinary sorts of household needs were a steady enough sale. There were near infinite variations. "One trick of the business is to fulfil the current need in a way that will bring someone back to you in due course for the next. A talisman to aid teething in a baby, followed by something to protect a wandering toddler from bumps and bruises or worse, in the nursery."

Thessaly nodded along with that. "And then something

to, I don't know, encourage learning and study in the nursery classroom, then something for memory as they go toward tutoring school and the exams."

"Exactly. And along with that, a stone for one complaint won't ease others. May I ask how your talisman for sleep is doing?"

"Oh, that's been quite useful. Again, not so much the past few days, but I slept very well when I returned last night." Thessaly inhaled. "I was invited out to Arundel, Friday to Sunday. Not the sort of thing I could decline."

Vitus nodded, lowering his gaze to his cup. "I ended up having a drink after one of the lectures in Trellech with Dagobert and Laudine Fortier. They mentioned they expected to see you."

"And she told me you'd impressed her. She was considering a commission." Thessaly leaned back. "That's interesting. She's obviously trying to make a bridge, trying to go in a different direction than the rest of the family. I have absolutely no idea if I can trust any of it." She let out an aggrieved breath. "This is not a duel in the salle. I cannot manage this. I really can't."

Vitus took another sip from his own cup, then leaned forward to set it down on the cart. "Will you tell me a little more about what happened? I am certainly no Fox. You have experience and training I do not - at many things, not just duelling. But I often find talking out a problem is helpful."

"Do you, then, with someone?" That had distracted her from her other emotions, apparently.

"Oh, yes." Vitus had to smile at it. "My brother, Lucas, for one. Though we have to cram it all into his visits home for Sunday supper."

"You said he's a cavalry officer. Posted somewhere he

can get back, then?" That was also apparently diverting as a concept. "Weekly, or near enough?"

"Just so. His unit hasn't been abroad for some years. Training and such, and training up mounts that then go on elsewhere, a fair bit of the time. He's hoping to end up in that line of things. It suits him very well. Lucas was in Boar House at Schola, a specialist in the martial magics. But mostly, he just really likes a horse. Or most horses. Possibly all of them he's ever met. I haven't actually asked."

"But you also haven't heard him dislike one. I suspect that's telling, yes." Thessaly nodded again. "Who else?"

"Niobe. I still see her two or three days a week. Technically, I'm still her apprentice through the end of September or early October, when I'll be presented to our Guild."

Thessaly opened her mouth, then snorted. "When there's the evidence of the Challenge to work with. I'll spare you dancing around how to say that."

"Exactly. It doesn't entirely matter if Carrington is successful or not, just whether the talisman does what it's designed for. Though obviously, there are benefits if he's successful, on my end. I'm expecting it to be ready for him so he's got a full fortnight to attune to it properly." Vitus looked up, suddenly feeling more uncertain. "I'm nervous about it."

Most people, he thought, would have soothed him, would have said that it would be fine. Even Niobe had settled on reassurance that he knew his work, but of course she hadn't seen the finished piece. Thessaly tilted her head. "Why are you nervous?"

"I've done nothing quite like this before. All the separate pieces of it, yes. I've done pieces with this kind of nuance of design, or the precision of the inscription, or needing to choose exactly the right stone. But I've never put them all together in one piece. Certainly I've done nothing with this kind of visibility."

"See, this is where duelling would help you. Every duel is new and different, even if you've done it before." Thessaly leaned back against the arm of the chair. "What does your brother say about training a new horse who will need to go into battle at some point? Each is new, each is their own self, each can mean life or death, for the horse and the rider and maybe the people around."

Vitus opened his mouth, then closed it. "I'll talk to him about it." It was, in fact, an excellent idea, and he was sure Lucas would have some ideas. Just talking it out, with that framing, would help a great deal. He could feel it. "Thank you." Vitus shifted slightly closer to her on the sofa before he realised he had.

She smiled at him, and he would do a great deal for more of those smiles, especially if he helped them happen. She should have far more reason to smile in her life than she did. Thessaly set her own cup down, looking at the fireplace for a good twenty seconds, then she looked back. "Childeric threatened on Saturday. Me. You. My sister, Hermia."

"What did he threaten you with?" Vitus leaned forward a little more. "Will you tell me? Tell someone?"

That brought a sharp inhale out of her, like he'd hit a mark she'd not protected well enough. He reached out his hand, cautiously, the sort of move that was all offer and no demand. A moment later, he felt her fingers around his, then they tightened. She wasn't looking at him now, as if that would make it impossible to speak, just at a spot on the rug. "He was crude." Her voice was quiet. "That he'd be in my bed, as many nights as it took to get me with child, that's what he said. That I would not be permitted to come here. Certainly, I could never close any door to him. He hurt me - nothing that would show. He almost struck me, but he thought better of it at the last minute. Or at least the fact Miranda was watching."

"And in six months or so, he will have every right to demand you open to him." Vitus left the innuendo there, to cover both door and bed. He wanted to apologise for the awfulness and sheer nastiness, but apologising wouldn't do any good. Vitus wanted to offer his help, but unspecific offers weren't actually easy to tend to. He took a breath, then said, carefully. "I am here. I am glad to talk whenever you wish. I would be delighted to lend my skills to a talismanic piece, if you think of anything of use. Or a connection to others, for enchantments. Niobe has a broad network of people."

Thessaly squeezed his hand harder. "You don't - you don't find it distasteful? He ..." There was another sound, nearer a sob, and Vitus didn't dare look up. He knew it would shake her away from any further words. "He said you only wanted my money. And I know that's wrong, only it got stuck in my head like a thorn."

"Childeric is apparently just as incompetent with a calendar as he is in the duelling salle." Vitus tried to put a bit of amusement into that, though yes, he was concerned about what Childeric had said. Now he ventured a look up, to find her expression was startled. "I was interested in you - in whatever manner you would permit - from the first night we met. You are creative and talented. You had done more with your illusion work than almost anyone in that ballroom. You knew what suited you in mood and style, and you did something different - but just as well suited - for your aunt. And then, you were kind to me, and interested in me, when you needn't have bothered. That was long before any of this." He gestured at the room with his chin.

Vitus added, after a moment, "Also, not that it's relevant, but I paid attention when you told me about the terms of your inheritance. I know full well there's no shaking that. What is here is yours. If Childeric is so, so..." He ran out of words. "Well. He is misguided and ignorant about this, as with many other things."

Thessaly was blushing when he looked back. "Oh." She half-closed her eyes. "All I could hear in my head that night, yesterday, was how no one would want me. Even if I did break the agreements, it would be all awfulness. A different awfulness than marrying him, and I'm fairly sure a better one. But still awful."

There was nothing Vitus could say to that, because she was likely right. Certainly, she had more information to work with than he did, and more experience than he did about dealing with these kinds of complex negotiations. "All I can do is hope that some alternative, some good alternative, presents itself."

Thessaly nodded. There was another squeeze of his hand. "You aren't scared? Of what he might do?"

"I am. I just refuse to let him decide what I feel or think. You have a say in that. I choose to give you one." Even if it was not really a choice at this point. "He does not. Not that I won't take precautions. I don't want to bring you more risk. But here I am, and I am glad to return when you ask, while we can."

Thessaly inhaled again. "And if I asked you to kiss me again? Here? Would you?"

When Vitus looked up, her eyes were visibly damp, glistening with it. It was certainly a moment where action would speak far louder than words. "I would be delighted. May I?"

It only took one nod. Then he was sliding across the silk of the sofa, to sit next to her. He considered their positions, venturing to rest one hand along the back of the sofa, then cupping her cheek with the hand that had been holding hers. As he leaned in to kiss her, she inhaled, just once, then she was flinging herself into it, soaking up every bit she could. He let his hand move to her shoulder. Nothing more intimate. He wasn't sure either of them could stand that right now. Most of all, he let her guide the intensity of the kiss. It built and built, each of them breaking away for just long enough to breathe, all eagerness and mutual delight.

When Thessaly finally pulled back, she was breathless. Her hand had moved to his knee, and her eyes were half-closed again. Vitus let out a sigh, both eased and aroused by it. Not that he'd so much as mention the latter to her. "I will most certainly be glad to do that again, as often as you permit. I desire so many different kinds of pleasures with you. Kisses, talking, illusions, books, whatever it is. Do I need to convince you further?"

That brought her eyes back to meet his. "I might need a little more persuasion. Confirmation."

It made him chuckle, and he shifted to kiss her again. He took it slower this time, his focus on getting her to relax a little. He wanted her to trust that this one pleasure was not only for this moment, that they might find such chances again in the future. That she had something to look forward to that was kind and mutual and enchanting.

When she finally pulled away from that, minutes later, she leaned into the corner of the sofa. "I, I am overwhelmed. You are persuasive, though."

"Then I will be glad to let you rest. Perhaps, when you are a little recovered, you might tell me more about the library?"

It seemed the proper change in mood. After a little more restorative tea, Thessaly didn't move away from touching him, but she shifted to talking about the books. Mostly she talked about the various kinds of materials, and how she'd just begun going through them properly. Vitus could listen to her talk for hours, and did. It was near eight when he finally left. Thessaly - and Miranda - escorted him back to the portal, through the wards, and she promised she'd let him know when he could visit again.

23

AUGUST 31ST AT ARUNDEL

Thessaly was trying to stay out of the way, to avoid trouble. It was only nominally working. She had been invited to Arundel again, with Lady Maylis making it clear in the invitation that only dire and contagious health issues were cause for refusal. Even if Thessaly had dared to try, she was sure Lady Maylis would have inquired about the attending Healer and then subjected whoever Thessaly named to an interrogation.

It had, in short, been easier to agree. She had arrived after her apprenticeship on Friday evening and been given time to change before a substantial gathering. It was technically family, in keeping with Thessaly still being in mourning, but only by the barest technicality in a few cases. Laudine and Dagobert had not been there, but Bradamante, Lord Clovis's and Dagobert's sister, between them in age, had been. So had her husband, two of their three children, and their husbands. But whoever had made up the invitation list - Thessaly wasn't sure if that was the Dowager Lady Chrodechildis, Lady Maylis, or both - had included several more distant cousins.

It was meant, she thought, to be a model of how younger married couples behaved. Childeric was certainly taking no lesson from it. He'd given her the barest cordiality in company, spending his time talking with the other younger men. It involved something about gambling, a bit of horse racing, she thought. Or at least, the names being tossed about seemed more likely to be horses than, say, obscure strategies for card playing. Admittedly, as a duellist, she could not throw stones about odd names for techniques.

The women had not so much included her as talked at her, as if she had been dropped into a tennis match in progress. Statements were balls flying past her at speed, ready to bruise if she moved wrong. Some of it was about the current fashions, some of it was about the latest gossip. None of that was about Thessaly, at least. It had been long enough that her scandal, such as gossip made it, had fallen away unless someone deliberately brought it up.

And part of the conversation was about Flora Mortimer's baby daughter, her second. Flora was Bradamante's second child herself. There had been plenty of none too subtle commentary about Flora having met and exceeded the marriage agreements. Though Flora made it clear they intended to keep trying for a son in due course. It was exactly what other women praised. Thessaly listened, murmuring her own compliments in the appropriate places, but wincing internally every time.

She had six months before she had to think about being in bed, with conception as a goal, with Childeric. Maybe something would change. Maybe he'd soften. Perhaps he'd at least be persuaded by some of the comments Thessaly heard, about which approaches seemed most conducive to a quick pregnancy and a healthy babe. She could at least, when the time came closer, talk to these women about their advice for that. She wouldn't need to feign being a nervous bride.

The women's side of the gathering had broken up before the men were done, with various people dispersing to their bedrooms. Thessaly had been glad to retire, but it meant she had woken very early on the Saturday, long before the rest of the house was stirring. What she wanted was to be at Bryn Glas, looking at what needed tending for the autumn, in the gardens, in the house itself, in the property as a whole.

Instead, once Miranda was up and about, Thessaly went for a walk. She knew better than to go in the directions she'd been warned away from, the mill on the river, or the outbuildings. This time, instead, she went west, toward the family cemetery. It was tucked in a grove of trees anchored by yews.

She'd expected to be entirely on her own. It wasn't yet eight in the morning and the Fortiers as a whole took their time in rising. But as they approached, she could see a figure moving about in the most distant left corner of the space. It was a woman, also clad in black - Thessaly didn't think that was just the angle of the sun. That likely meant only one person on the estate.

"Miranda, give me a little space? I don't want to intrude too much." Thessaly glanced over her shoulder at Miranda, who looked bemused.

"I am supposed to protect you, and I can't do that from.... do you know who that is?"

"That is Magistra Henut Landry, and I don't think she currently has much interest in hurting me. Stay here, please." That done, Thessaly went forward, though she admitted, entirely inside her own head, that she was a little nervous.

She hadn't seen Henut since her son's funeral, and that

had been two months and more ago now. Thessaly hadn't been certain, but now she was fairly sure that was deliberate on the part of the Fortiers. They had not kept her from the estate, but they had not included her, not in any of the gatherings. She was, of course, in mourning for her son. And, though Thessaly was sure she had missed quite a lot, there had been very little gossip about the cause of Philip's death, in a way that made her curious now she thought about it.

Seventy days, she kept count of how many days it had been since Aunt Metaia's, like she kept track of which day of the week it was. Now, she kept her hands down, no sign of gestures that might be a charm, walking steadily toward the back corner of the cemetery. The front was reserved for the direct line of the family, of course, but it was an enormous space, and still had room for graves.

This one, though, was new, and not in the same style as the others. Most of the graves here had simple tombstones, with a name, dates, perhaps a phrase or carving of some particular symbol. The one Henut Landry was tending was newly turned earth, no grass growing at all, with a sandstone slab carved in what must be hieroglyphs. There were quite a lot of them, circling an oval that had Philip's name and dates, then another oval below, with what might be the same thing in Egyptian. Or at least, she assumed it must be Egyptian. That was the language that made sense.

Thessaly stopped about five feet away, clearing her throat. Magistra Landry ignored her, going about whatever tasks she felt needed to be done. They involved pouring of water from an earthenware pitcher, a smaller pitcher with some sort of oil in it, a series of prayers. It was all deliberate, all done the way the most potent rituals were, not for show or cosmetic benefit, but out of deep need.

It might be rude to stay, but Thessaly thought it was

also something that needed a witness. So she waited patiently enough. Besides, Childeric was not likely to come out here and be difficult. Understanding more of the family history in a broad sense was an admirable virtue for her right now.

Perhaps ten minutes later, Magistra Landry finished whatever it was she was doing, and turned to face Thessaly. She had kept her long silk veil down, but now she lifted it, folding it back with what looked like long practice made into skill. "Thessaly."

"Magistra Landry." Thessaly inclined her head. "I hope I have not intruded. It— I thought perhaps knowing someone else was here might be some slight comfort."

Magistra Landry had always been a touch uncanny, by Albion's standards. Not like the hedge witches of the rural countryside were, not at all, but neither was she like how the most polished and perfect scions of Albion's elite could be, in an entirely different form and wardrobe. There was nothing feigned about her, but there was also something undeniably not of Albion. She had made her life here for nearly two decades, Thessaly knew that, and yet it might have been only days or hours since her arrival from France. There was nothing particularly of the French about her, either, so she had clearly carried that timelessness with her for longer than she had known Albion.

Now, the older woman inclined her head, making no show of what she might feel. "You are deliberate. Did Vitus Deschamps pass on my message about your observation at the funeral?" The words were clipped, not her more usual fluency, as if she were translating out of some other language into English.

"He did. We were both curious." With anyone else, Thessaly would have made a protestation about not having talked to him recently. Here, now, she was fairly sure Henut

Landry knew, and second, that she did not care. Such things did not concern her, the foibles of others. Now, Thessaly nodded at the grave. "Was the stone just placed, may I ask?"

"Yesterday. He was buried first thing this morning, at dawn." The words were smooth, almost emotionless. "My family keeps the old traditions of mummification and that takes seventy days."

Thessaly inhaled. "I am sorry for his death, for your loss, and for Alexander's." It was the trite thing to say, and also it was true. "And it must be challenging to do that, knowing that people there have forgotten." She gestured back toward the house.

Magistra Landry tilted her head. And now Thessaly had the undeniable impression of a snake, considering whether to strike. Or perhaps what to strike. She wanted to stay still, not to draw more anger or venom. Then Magistra Landry's voice came more smoothly. "It must be more difficult for you. They do not ask me to dance attendance, ignoring my grief. They leave me alone. They do not give you that choice."

"No." Thessaly felt it was impossible to lie. Besides, it was obvious to anyone paying attention on this estate. "I am glad you have had that space. And that you..." She considered. "You chose to bury Philip here?"

"My husband had a distant connection to Vauquelin Fortier." She gestured at the most recent grave beside Philip's up in the section for the immediate family. It was still shining and largely unweathered. Thessaly knew it was only four years old. "We are family, here, or at least my sons are. I preferred him here. When I am gone, someone will tend his grave. And perhaps mine." Her chin came up. "Though I think perhaps not you."

It had all the weight and terror of an omen. Thessaly

knew better than to want anything like an omen. Omens ended badly. Now, she took a breath, trying to shove her sudden reasonable fear down. "Is there something I should know?"

Now, Magistra Landry smiled, a slow smile, just as worrying as the stillness. "You have nothing to worry about from me. I am glad to promise you that. You hold no blame for Philip's death. And besides, Alexander would miss you as a duelling partner when he returns to Albion. He might be a decent challenge for you then, don't you think?"

Thessaly could not, in fact, argue with that supposition. Alexander was still growing into his adult self, both in terms of his magic and in terms of his body. Whenever he returned, yes, he would be a more interesting challenge. She nodded, now. "I expect so, yes. He's a fast learner. It must be difficult to have him gone?"

Magistra Landry gave a slight shrug. "It is for the best. He understands, I understand. That is all that matters." Other people's understanding was apparently entirely irrelevant. Now she nodded one more time. "I have further prayers to tend to, but I am glad you were here when you were."

It was an absolute dismissal. Thessaly inclined her head, first to Magistra Landry, then to the grave. Then she took seven steps backward and turned onto the path up the centre of the cemetery to rejoin Miranda. It wasn't until they were well away, taking a large circle back, that Miranda cleared her throat. "There are rumours about her. And her family."

"I am sure there are." Then it occurred to Thessaly that Miranda must still have connections in the Guard. "No further news about the cause of his death, though?"

Miranda shook her head. "No. It was in the papers,

though rather buried, a back page. I suppose there's no harm in saying it. Quite a mystery, and unlikely to be solved. Those I knew still in the Guard are sure there was something done to cover up how he was killed, but they could not break through. And her family customs, they could not keep the body long in case of additional ideas, not without more compelling evidence."

"No. I suppose not." Some traditions didn't permit that, even the stasis magics were imperfect. They'd done an entire week on death rituals in her Ritual class at Schola one year. There were so many variations, but they came down to how to remember people and what aspects of body or heart or memory were treasured in which way. "Do you think we could do a full circuit, be gone until at least ten?"

"Oh, I'm fairly sure we can manage something. There are ducks or geese or something of the kind to watch, aren't there? They can absorb a lot of time with no need for an explanation." That said, Miranda gestured at the path that would give them a suitably long walk, and Thessaly turned to take it.

24

SEPTEMBER 1ST AT VITUS'S HOME

Vitus had been in the family library all afternoon. Theoretically he was working on some notes on the business accounts, so he could talk to Papa about them Monday morning before he went to Trellech and the flat. On a purely financial side, he wasn't entirely sure how to read it. Oh, he had enough to pay his expenses for a month or two. That would be even better when he turned over the piece for Carrington and got the last payment for it.

It was the longer term that was more uncertain. It wasn't even a bad sort of uncertain, just entirely nebulous. Vitus was a man who liked the solid and practical - that was talisman work. He was used to a certain amount of variation, of course. Which stone was most beautiful or most desired or most expensive was something that fluctuated with current fashion and that also depended on the individual preferences. But things there ran within ranges, like water in a river. Most of the time, the water stayed within the banks, granting a certain amount of predictability.

Now he ran his hands through his hair, and set to work on a fresh set of notes, the way Papa had taught him years ago. This one had the fixed information - his rent, for example, and the ordinary materials he went through. He had numbers for that, because he'd kept track of it for his work for Niobe. There were the various things for the stonecutting itself, wax to hold the stones in place while they were being worked on, all of that.

Next week, he had another meeting of the research group. They'd kept their word about funding the supplies, but he'd gone through two packs of notepaper already, and he'd need to pick up another. Also tracing paper, because the diagrams he was working on were easiest to manage that way, in layers. He made a note to stop by the stationer's tomorrow.

He was going through the papers for about the fifth time when he heard the rattle of the door. "Just a minute, Mama."

"Not Mama." That was Lucas's voice. "Aren't you glad to see me?"

Vitus pushed his chair back at an angle. "Always, don't be silly." He glanced at the clock over the fireplace. "You're early, though."

"Got off sooner than I expected." Lucas came over, pulling a chair over to the other side of the table. "What's all this?"

"Sorting out paperwork. Papa's got time to work through it with me tomorrow morning, first thing." Vitus shrugged. "I honestly don't know how to weight some of it. I'm too close to it. And I'm thinking about other things, too."

"You usually are." His brother considered. "Shall I get some tea in? Put some of that away, or at least fewer piles covering the table, if you don't want it embellished with a few drops of tea."

Vitus had to smile at that. Lucas was not the neatest of tea drinkers. He had a tendency to gesture with the hand holding the teacup at least once per conversation. He tucked everything away, his notes on top. When Lucas came back, a few minutes later, he'd changed into a more comfortable smoking jacket and looser trousers, and out of his uniform boots. "You're staying the night?"

Lucas nodded. "Most others are off. I didn't have stable duty tonight, and I put in extra time the last few weeks. And we're waiting for the new horses to come in, from the summer fairs." Getting them from one place to another was time-consuming, since they all had to go by train or foot, not by portal. "Not until the end of the week, and then, yes, I'll be busy. Like as not, won't be here next Sunday."

There was a knock at the door with the tea cart, and once they got things set up, Lucas snagged one of the fruit tarts. That was the glorious thing about summer, the berries in absolute abundance. Vitus had done his share of walking through the hedges, gathering up whatever had come ripe so Cook could make her rightfully famous jam.

Lucas took his own - two tarts and a sandwich to start. Vitus felt the cavalry was perhaps not feeding him enough. "How's the rest of it? Your commissions." His voice got more careful. "Mistress Lytton-Powell?"

"I saw her last Monday. But she thought maybe not this week. She's rather busy, and the Fortiers demanded she stay Friday to Sunday again. There are things she needs to do at Bryn Glas, and I don't know what else. She told me to thank you again for the recommendations. I gather she picked one of them."

Lucas grinned. "Emeline Harris, who could use the

work. She understands it might not last past the marriage, but it'd get her a good reference, at the least, and she's interested in the challenge. She was three years ahead of me, in Boar. Which means I can tell you that part of what your Mistress Lytton-Powell is busy with will be dress fittings. I was at the Boar's Head before this, catching the gossip." The Boar House club was good for that.

Lucas took a sip of his tea before continuing. "And then I went round to the Arthur for a drink and heard a bit more." It made sense that the officer's club on Club Row would be full of people talking up the coming Challenge. "There's quite a bit of betting on. I'm sorry to say Carrington's not the favourite. Of course, no one has an idea how to weight your talisman in the matter. He hasn't been too public about that."

"Is Fortier?" Vitus wasn't sure what he wanted there. He'd certainly heard nothing that made him think Childeric Fortier should be handed more power than he already had, and quite a bit to the contrary. Vitus certainly hoped Carrington came out of it well enough, but he didn't know much about what Carrington would be like on the Council. He thought seducing women wasn't a particularly relevant skill there, even if Carrington did generally seem to leave the women in question inclined toward him. That showed a certain amount of tact or diplomacy or decency, on aggregate.

"More or less." Lucas wobbled his hand back and forth. "The bets are running in Fortier's favour, then, curiously, Irene Hamilton." She'd been a late addition, one of two women. "Then Carrington, then Heliotrope Masterton. Cyrus Smythe-Clive is the dark horse, no one has any idea what to expect of him, he's barely been seen in public since his wife died."

"Well, to be fair to the man, he's got a baby at home,

he's still finishing his apprenticeship, and he's grieving. He might not be done up in full mourning gear like a widow would be, but it's clear he is in his heart." Vitus had seen him at a distance a few times, but always obviously concentrating ferociously on something, like he was cramming three days into every twenty-four hours. "He was the same year as Thessaly, actually. And the same house."

"That's an inside line on the betting. Not that she could. Obviously. I can't imagine anyone would take a bet of hers against Fortier." Lucas considered the gambling angle a little more. "What does she think of Fortier's chances, do you know?"

"Not something we talked about, honestly. Around the Challenge, yes. A little about the piece for Carrington. We got off on other topics. People trying different things. I didn't go into details about that project with the Four Metals, but she was interested in the idea of people experimenting." Vitus shrugged. "I am too. Obviously, I'm doing it. But the lecture last Wednesday got me thinking, too."

"Oh? Something new there?" Lucas snagged a scone, now taking a bite of it, then another, neatly enough.

"Something I've been noticing. Look, scientific advancement, magical advancement, is all well and good, right? Experimentation. If the Four Metals work comes off, we might do quite useful things. Maybe stabilise vitality for healing, for example, that would be a big help. Certainly something like maintaining warding more efficiently or some of the illusion charms that keep the non-magical out of where they oughtn't be."

"Just so," Lucas agreed. "I hear a 'but' there, though."

"But a lot of what people are talking about - usually not directly, admittedly. What comes up seems to be a grab for power, or people just haven't thought about what the practical applications are."

"By which I diagnose that what, a third of the people in these conversations are Fox House, that'd be the power grab. And a third are Owls, all interested purely in the theory." Lucas said.

"And the rest of us - and the other four schools - crammed into the last third, all a jumble." Vitus had to laugh at the image. He had the sudden idea of legs and arms sticking out of a great ball, like a tangled set of necklace chains or items from a kitchen drawer. All bright colours, of course, to go with the relevant heraldry of the house or school. "Like that, yes. And I do like the practical."

"That's why you were in Salmon. Being less prone to charging at your problems than I am." Lucas chuckled, then sobered. "I see what you mean, though. And it makes you wonder what people are up to that isn't so public."

"Exactly. I mean, I can tell you about the Four Metals. I trust you won't spread it around. And I suspect people might guess we're up to something. Being a reasonably secret society interested in the crafting of magic. But it's not as if we're publishing anything anytime soon. For one thing, we'd have to have something worth publishing."

"And it's early days there, you said. Testing, repeating it, refining it. And you said everyone was busy, so you can work on it, what, once a month?" Lucas asked.

"It gives us time for reading and new ideas between, but yes. And a lot of the experiments we want to take multiple people, we can't just push forward individually the same way." Vitus leaned back in his chair. "I guess that's my question. There must be groups of people doing things, but I don't have any idea who or what. I assume some of them are Great Families, but I don't know which ones, or how you'd tell."

"No hints at all? People who are showing up at all the

same lectures, anything like that?" One of Lucas's gifts, this was something Boar House had honed in him, was seeing straight to the point.

"I don't even know what to do with the information I have. Look, I told you about Dagobert Fortier and his wife last week. Earlier that week, I was at the library, and I noticed that he had checked out a number of books related to various electrical things. Circuits and such. But I only noticed because I was interested in the same titles, and was there when they were re-shelved. Otherwise, I'd never have looked at the loan cards. I didn't ask about it, of course, I know better."

"And you couldn't trust anything he told you, quite." Lucas agreed.

"Besides, Laudine was being very smooth about handling the conversation. She didn't let it wander." Lucas shrugged. "And he is an alchemist. He's got some ideas about healing potions and all that. It's obvious he's been ill. Perhaps he was exploring some of the electrical belts or healing baths or whatever. Though I can't say I'd much want to immerse myself in water with a current running through it, no matter how well tested."

"Some people have very odd ideas about improving their health. And no, I suppose if that's one of the options, asking about it is even more delicate." Lucas shook his head. "Look, has Mama had ideas about any of that, or Papa?"

"Not that I've heard, no. Are you worried she might?" Vitus worried about similar things, on his own, but if Lucas was also worried, that needed more attention.

"Just in a general way. Nebulous, the same way as all of this. I agree with you, it's not well tested. I might have a line on a Healer with some new ideas, though, I'll let you know."

Before Vitus could say anything else, they both heard the front door open, the sounds of Papa and Mama coming in. "In the library," Lucas called out. "And we have tea." That cut off the conversation tidily for the evening, though Mama was rather cheerfully full of the visits they'd made, and the pleasure of the autumn weather. They'd been out at one of the Deschamps cousins, and she was especially cheerful about having spent time with one of the toddlers, wandering about in the garden.

25

SEPTEMBER 4TH IN TRELLECH

"Do have some tea, Thessaly, dear." Odelia leaned forward. "We want to hear all about the dress fittings, and just all the everything!"

Thessaly felt trapped. She had far better things to be doing on a Wednesday afternoon. But she also knew how this dance went, or this duel, whichever word beginning with a D she wished to choose. Discourse, debate, and possibly also debacle applied. This invitation to tea was not one she'd been able to refuse, anyway.

Odile and Cosmerance had been her same year at Schola. They'd shared a dormitory for two years, and Fox House's shared spaces for three more. As well as classes, of course, though Odile had favoured Flora and Materia, and Cosi had gone in for Alchemy and Materia. Both Odile and Cosi had married well before Thessaly, neither had apprenticed. In fact Cosi was only just up and about again. She'd had a baby over the summer, her second.

Thessaly was fairly sure Mother had arranged this gathering, or possibly Lady Maylis. It wouldn't have taken much. A word in the right ear, woman of Fox House to woman of Fox House. And it certainly wouldn't have taken much persuasion. Both Odile and Cosi were well born, but not from the sort of families who naturally rose to the top of the social circles of the Great Families. Of course, they'd be delighted to borrow whatever snippets of reflected glory they might. It brought hopes of invitations to Arundel in the coming year or offered gossip to bring back to their actual friends.

She would resent it less if her week weren't filled with things like this. It had been the dressmaker yesterday for yet another fitting. Monday evening had been more pleasant, but that had been about Emeline getting settled at Bryn Glas and doing her own exceedingly thorough review of the warding and spaces. Master Fulton had come out, so that Emeline could be permitted to bring people into the warding, since that seemed a suitable and practical choice. They hadn't finished until well after nine that night, with just enough time for a quick meal and bed.

The rest of the week wasn't any better. Tomorrow she had tea with Mother and several aunts on Father's side, at one of the tea shops here in Trellech with private rooms. That would be a certain amount of rather sharper social duelling, likely littered with jabs at Thessaly's aspects that needed improvement. Thessaly could take that in the duelling salle, but doing it that way, over tea, with all the false niceness as a layer on top, did not appeal at all. The one bright side there was that Hermia was likely coming. Mother thought they might manage a few minutes alone.

And while she wasn't obliged to be at Arundel Friday through Sunday this week, she was expected out there all day Saturday. And from quite early until the end of the evening, for a gathering of the larger extended family. It gave her an excuse not to stay - several of the older generation would be - but it didn't give her time to work on matters at Bryn Glas, either.

Now Thessaly lifted her teacup, taking a sip to give herself a little breathing space. "Oh, we're not at any of the exciting parts yet, really. Later this month, of course. And then I'm finishing up my apprenticeship, and there's the wedding. Of course, most of that is being done by the Fortier traditions, as you'd expect." Which meant no one had consulted her about decisions, or likely would. She might get a choice of wedding dresses, that was on the calendar for October, so it would be completed in good time.

"Well, now, that's just part of why we wanted to have tea. We know, Thessaly, dear, that you've not much experience keeping a man's attention properly. Not one of the skills you practised assiduously at all hours." Odile smiled, but there were sharp edges to it. She had spent quite a lot of time making sure every hair was perfectly in place before she set foot outside their dorm, even at thirteen.

Thessaly dressed well. She knew how to manage her hair - and these days, how to make sure she didn't mess up what Collins had done for her. But she also believed in acting in the world, which meant touching things and walking about in places that might - horror of horror - have some dust. She enjoyed being outside when there was a breeze. All of that before getting to the duelling and the desire to move reasonably freely, at least given the weight of the skirts. She found the bustle wasn't the problem, but rather how tight the skirts were cut at the front and how much the whole thing weighed.

Now, she matched the smile, considering how to play that. "Ah, well. The marriage agreements were specifically detailed. I haven't done anything against them, and that means that no, I've not nearly the experience you both have, now, as married women."

The thing of it was, Thessaly didn't at all want to go to bed with Childeric. She'd been willing in March, she was decidedly less so now. She could, in fact, use advice on how to make it as tolerable as possible, beyond 'don't annoy him any time in the previous fortnight'. That, while likely sensible advice, neither dealt with the more intimate aspects, nor was it actually plausible.

It made Odile and Cosi titter, agreeably. "Well, we might just have to do a trip to one of the Paris modistes. Madam Cardolle's not magical, of course, but her sewing is delightful. Not the sort of thing dear Patros lets me splurge on, alas." Then Odile's eyes widened. "But that's not a worry for you now, is it? Oh, we could have such a delightful time."

Thessaly was not fooled by that wide-eyed, apparently innocent thought. Her wealth would indeed make any dressmaker, modiste, or lingerie maker quite willing to open their doors and tend to her every whim. That was true no matter how late at night she wanted their time or how quickly she demanded the items. That was not why Aunt Metaia had left her the money, for one thing. And for another, whatever else Aunt Metaia had instilled in her, it was a proper Welsh respect for hard work of all sorts. Aunt Metaia had never forgotten the work that went into the luxury, and Thessaly was determined to honour that memory in particular.

"It's awfully hard to get away, even for a day or two. Especially now, while I'm still in mourning. I've all sorts of people inquiring about gatherings, and of course the Fortiers have been inviting me to Arundel so often." She leaned on that phrase. As much as she hated the command performances and knew they'd just get more onerous, they were at least a shielding charm against a wide range of others.

A duellist used all her tools as needed, rather than turning up her nose at perfectly serviceable options.

"Oh, pah." Cosi batted her eyelashes, which did not have a particular effect on Thessaly. Cosi had spent most of their second year practising that, as well as the perfect arch of an eyebrow. Having seen the earlier attempts, the current ones - polished as they were - didn't land the same way. "Do think about it. And there's the Paris Exposition through October. That would be a lovely time for the city. You've been to Paris, yes?"

Thessaly had, but only twice for a day or so each time. "Briefly, but then, of course, it has such a lot of history. Did you talk to Jacinthe, by chance? Bradamante and Yves Nevill spent much of the summer there with their family, visiting their eldest. I heard a few stories, but it sounded like a splendid time. Outside the city, of course, the Percys are involved with perfumes, all the flowers of the countryside."

The new topic - the latest perfumes and scents - caused a quite respectable diversion from difficult topics for a good eight minutes. Not bad, by Thessaly's standards. But as with all such blessings, it ended. "Honestly, though, Thessaly, you really must give some thought to pleasing Childeric in the bedchamber. He's certain to have his own expectations. Beyond, well," Cosi inhaled. "Having an Heir in turn."

"I'm sure he does, but I wouldn't dream of inquiring in advance of what he wishes me to know. Or, I suppose, his mother or aunts." Thessaly offered that last out of instinct, and then saw Odile react a little oddly.

"Such a shame about Dagobert Fortier. People keep saying the oddest things. You know Patros knows Sigbert and all, they've a regular card game at Bourne's. Childeric doesn't join them often. But Sigbert mentioned, dear boy, that they'd really been quite worried. I can't imagine how Laudine shows her face."

"Not that she has much." Cosi picked that up. "She was supposed to be one of the chairs for the Albion Inheritance committee for the summer fete, and she just refused to attend entirely. Now, there's a way to make yourself enemies, Thessaly, dear. I know you know better than that."

Thessaly thought that the serious illness of one's husband might reasonably excuse someone from six or eight or ten deeply important planning meetings about what shade of beige the tablecloths should be this year. Or the slightly more interesting topic of whom to insult how, with which flower arrangement. That was the elevated mode. However, someone had to be on committees for decades before she was allowed anywhere near the flowers. She'd learned that from Mother long ago.

Mother, of course, was on precisely those committees. Thessaly wasn't a full member yet, only a junior one, but that was because she wasn't yet married. The invitation would come after the wedding, when she might reasonably have an inheritance to pass on for Albion, in the form of currently hypothetical Fortiers. Now she just nodded. "Mother's made it very clear what's expected there. But I must say, Dagobert Fortier really has been ill. He was at the Arundel Lammas, of course. And I know Laudine was quite worried about him, though I gather from the most recent conversation that he's been doing better. She's been very kind, of course, letting me know some of the family traditions."

"Well." Cosi sniffed again. "Though that reminds me. You know dear mama is on the committee for the Support of Indigent Daughters of Albion." Thessaly nodded her head once. "Well, they've had just such awful times with the home they use. Where the girls learn what's needed to go into service, of course, it's all about making sure they've a suitable employment for their station."

It was either going to be a request for money or to take on one of the girls. Neither of which Thessaly was going to do, though for very different reasons. Or, no, possibly both.

"Well, Mama was wondering when I mentioned I'd be seeing you, if you'd consider coming on a tour. Only, the roof really is a frightful problem, I gather. And then perhaps, if one of the girls caught your notice, you might..."

Thessaly blessed Aunt Metaia's foresight. And staffing. "Ah, I'm afraid it's no use asking me right now. There is a trust. I can't think of spending anything substantial - of course, there's reasonable allowance for clothes, especially this year - without my trustee. And that's Amadeo Scali, you know his reputation."

Odile wrinkled up her nose. "Do I ever. Patros was telling me he stopped, what, four different investments going forward, just last month, just by shaking his head. Really, you must deal with him?"

Thessaly had, in fact, discovered that Amadeo Scali was delightful. He treated her like an intelligent woman - as women of his family generally were, from what he'd said. She knew little about the kind of money she had now, but he'd been clear she could and would learn what she needed. He had a rather wicked sense of humour in the teaching, peppering in stories of people who had been unwise, without ever breaking actual confidences. Or giving enough information she could tie it to any particular person or business. She admired the deftness of how he did it, as well as the education.

And she'd enjoyed the conversations, not only with him but with whichever of the senior and expert members of the family he'd brought in to talk about their specialties. She'd been working with two of the Scali women to better understand her aunt's investments in imported materia. That was with an eye to making a few smaller attempts of her own in the coming months.

"Aunt Metaia's will was really rather specific." Thessaly managed without laughing. "As to the girl, I can ask Mother, but all of Bryn Glas's staff stayed on, and we've no room for anyone else. Besides, well, the security considerations. Adding someone new, unknown, even if they're vouched for, is rather a process right now."

She had not entirely expected that to divert them for the rest of tea. But apparently both of them had been reading rather Gothic novels of the dangers of large and unknown houses. Or, alternately, servants who had secrets beyond their presumed station, and who were up to dubious plots. Neither was remotely true, not at Bryn Glas, not at most places. But it was a far more pleasant line of conversation than anything previously, so Thessaly let them keep up with it until she had to take her leave.

26

SEPTEMBER 5TH AT THE CARRINGTON HOME

"Here we are, then. Thank you for being willing to meet me here, but I wanted to give it a proper test, and of course, that needs privacy. I suppose we could have leased one of the salles in Trellech, but why bother with that? Do you need anything before we get started? A spot of tea, something else to drink?" The offer to stay after was lingering in the air. Vitus knew how to spot that. Whether it happened would depend on what Theo Carrington thought of the talisman they were about to test.

For his part, Vitus was nervous. Confident, but also nervous, and that was an odd line to be walking. The talisman had come out just the way he'd hoped. When he'd actually done the inscription and enchantment work, it had been as smooth as writing with a finely tuned pen nib. The anchoring charms had taken perfectly, giving him the best ground to work on.

The peridot itself had come out splendidly. He had gone with an elegant form of Carrington's initials on the front, mounting it as a ring. The back, however, was inscribed as a dual talisman. One part, the enchantment scribed around the border of the stone, would mitigate magic sent at the wearer. It would ground it in a form that allowed it to pass along with far less harm. Possibly none, but of course Vitus would not claim that, untested. He suspected a truly lethal attack would fracture the stone, for one thing, and then whatever happened after that would end badly for the wearer.

The second enchantment, on the base, would grant clear speech and thought. As the stone of someone who would prefer to talk his way out of a situation, it should do very well. That was most of what the intricate web of lines and script on the back was for. It had come out looking handsome, too, the dark olive green an unusual shade, but one that went well with Carrington's suit.

Next, Vitus took in the space they were in. It was a large workroom; the sort used for more elaborate rituals or enchantments. The kind where there were either half a dozen people working together, or where the work required a great deal of space. He thought it was the latter, for the Carringtons, but he wasn't sure.

Carrington nodded at a man waiting inside. "Horace Fellingworth. My tutor, when I was younger, he's Father's assistant these days. He volunteered to help test the piece. Now, it's as we discussed?"

"It is." Vitus brought his satchel over to the table along one long wall that was waiting. "And as you asked, I brought the other piece I was working on, in case it suits." He brought out the ring box, opening it and presenting it with a slight bow.

Carrington took it out, looking at it closely, then he took a breath. Whatever else he was, with his flirtations and his affairs, he wasn't sloppy about his magic. He centred himself on his feet, he paused, and then he put the ring on, smoothly, but making it clear he was attentive to the nuances.

Another breath, and he held his hand out in front of him, then twisted it, palm down, palm up, to one side. Fellingworth, about ten feet away, cleared his throat. "Ten sentences on the topic of the autumn harvest."

Vitus wasn't listening to the words, not after the first few reiterating the subject of the declamation. He was listening to the rhythm of it, and feeling for the flow of the magic. The stone's effect was subtle, but Vitus could certainly tell it was working. Carrington looked like he knew it too. There was a slowly growing grin of delight on his face, not that it distracted him. When he came to the end, Fellingworth sent a charm his way, something meant to warp and discourage, and Carrington stepped tidily out of the way.

"Tell me you shan't." That apparently was a joke between them, because Carrington laughed first. Then he launched into another piece - not a set piece, this one, though perhaps one he'd rehearsed in his head. It was a delicate, funny, wickedly sharp takedown of his tutor's foibles, matched with gestures. There were glasses perched on the nose, the particular way some schoolmasters tapped something on their hand when they were running out of patience. And Carrington had the little lean forward, as if daring his charge to push just a little and find out the consequences.

Before Carrington could entirely finish, Fellingworth was laughing, his hands up in the universal signal of a duel won. "I yield, I yield. How does that feel, then?"

"Oh, I think that's your line, Deschamps?" Carrington turned back to him. "It feels splendid. Just what I wanted. No, more than I wanted, in the ways I did not - at the time - have assistance in articulating. Will you stay for supper?

I'm sure my parents would be interested in hearing more about the design and the work. Not your particular secrets, of course, but the overview."

Vitus made a little amused bow again. "Oh, it takes years to learn what secrets I have. Mostly it's a knack for matching stone and intention that I hope will make my name in due course. I am glad it suits, and I would be delighted to stay, I had no particular plans this evening."

Carrington snorted. "And no commissions beating down your door, either. We shall see about changing that one. Though I hope you'll continue to make space on your books for me if this does as well on the equinox as I think it will. And that you'll be there to join us"

Vitus let himself smile. "Of course, I'd love to know how it does in practice."

"Oh, please do plan on it. All the more reason to have you stay for supper, you can meet the rest of the family before the day. My sister will be along, too." He said the last one a little off-handedly. "The other work?"

This one was a handsome piece of carnelian. In the end Vitus had chosen a larger stone than he'd have picked for the Challenge itself, almost the size of his palm. On it, he'd carved, carefully as he could, the face of a lion, the lines of the mane following the curve of the stone, with the talismanic inscription on the flat bottom.

He drew out the box it was in, then the narrower box with the mirror plate in it. That would best reflect the light through and make the stone glow. He set it out, then stood back, letting Carrington have a closer look.

"I did not realise you were also an artist. You are right, then, that your work takes a long time to learn." Carrington sounded impressed, in truth.

"Oh, I have a fairly narrow range, all told. But making a stone look well, as well as holding the enchantments you wish, that's part of the art. You can see why I didn't want to promise it until I was sure the carving worked. And I'm more willing to risk carnelian than a gemstone proper."

"Hah. At the costs involved, I can see why." Carrington ran his fingers over the lines of the mane. "And what does this do?"

"It encourages a certain amount of social connection and bravery. Extending oneself just slightly will be rewarded, shall we say? Place it in a room where you wish to encourage conversation, especially more jovial, good-natured, shining a light. It might lend itself a bit to problem-solving."

Vitus had, in fact, made a similar piece, though not nearly so intricately carved, for his own use. He'd brought it to the research group meeting on Tuesday, and it had worked well there. Merryn had said, toward the end, that she felt like she had brought her best self. That was exactly what he'd hoped for. And such a thing might be of use to Carrington, whether he made it onto the Council or not.

"Might we employ it at supper and see what we think of it? Or would that drain the stone unduly?"

"No, that's quite a fair proposal." And besides, it was one he'd calculated, if he wanted the Carringtons and others in their circles to consider him as a talisman maker with some range.

They made some small talk then, for the hour between when Vitus had arrived and supper time. It was an informal meal, relatively speaking. Vitus was intrigued that they were a family who talked to each other in a way he suspected was less common in the Great Families.

However, he also had a certain sense of being eyed by Carrington's sister, Rhea. She was a few years younger - close to Thessaly's age, but he thought not the same year. Rhea had a fair bit of Carrington's own charm, though it was still muted by her age and the fact she visibly adored her older brother. Vitus was, of course, absolutely polite. This was just as necessary a skill in their line of work as any other of their skills.

After supper, when the women withdrew, Carrington's father had a matter to tend to. Carrington poured a drink for Vitus and then gestured with his chin toward the drawing room. "Please don't be bothered by Rhea. She's heard some of the gossip, from her school friends. She's curious about what might make someone forget themselves."

"That is a novel way of putting it." Vitus considered what else to say. "I'm afraid my affections are otherwise attached, entirely separate from the gossip." That was a true sentence, even if there was, of course, an intersection he wasn't talking about.

"I will pass that along and tell Rhea to mind herself next time we have you over. I do intend on a next time, I can think of all sorts of interesting pieces we might commission over time. Especially given some of your stories tonight. I hadn't known entirely what to expect of you as a guest, but you've a knack for making the tales interesting."

Vitus smiled at that. "I am glad the pieces please, and the stories. I've always thought the lore of the stones to be as glorious and many-faceted as the stones themselves, honestly. Some things the ancients thought are complete foolishness, others have seeds of genuine power and weight to them."

"Quite, quite. Oh, and on the business end, shall I call at the Scali tomorrow and make the transfer for the rest of the payment? I believe that's what you said you'd find easiest." Carrington was going to be a good client, indeed. Merryn had not been wrong about that. The transaction had been properly registered with the Scali, so the terms and deposit for materials were already on file.

"That would be superb, yes. And the lion, should you wish it..." He gave the sum. "A fair bit of that work is in the carving, of course. It does take time."

"And it has proven its worth. His worth, to put it properly. Of course, that's entirely fair. And I'll be glad to recommend you around to various others." Carrington took a sip from his own glass, not even questioning the sum. "How upset are the Fortiers with you, then?"

It was a sharp and incisive question, and Vitus only managed not to splutter because he was not currently drinking himself. "I have not pressed the issue, but I have had several conversations with Dagobert Fortier, since - well, since. And one with his wife. He's been at some of the same evening lectures I've been at." Vitus shrugged. He might as well be honest here. "To be fair, I didn't think the Fortiers would do more than facilitate a few connections themselves. They already have several talisman makers they prefer, and it's an individual sort of business."

"Ah, yes. I had a consultation with, who was it, Master Tambleton? I didn't care for him much at all. Older than we are, but somehow it felt like decades. Father thinks it's best to do a couple of initial interviews, and I can't say I disagree. It threw into rather sharp relief the difference in your approaches."

"It's been a pleasure to work with you. Your own background in incantation and enchantments made the process much smoother, figuring out what might suit. And you didn't go for the easy, obvious piece. I like that. Not that there's anything wrong with doing so, but the peridot was a more interesting puzzle to form the way I hoped." At that point Carrington's father came back in, and after a bit more conversation, Vitus took his leave.

That was a very promising evening. And at least he'd be at the Council Challenge. He'd have to check with Thessaly if she were all right with that, in the circumstances, but he rather felt like he wanted to be there. He had the nagging sense of needing to be a witness to something, as if the idea had been lurking in his mind for some time already.

27

SEPTEMBER 10TH IN TRELLECH

"I do wish Laudine had joined us." Lady Maylis had claimed the larger and more comfortable chair in the dressmaker's fitting room. It had apparently been a close call whether they came to the dress or the dress came to Arundel. In the end, though, they had come to Trellech. The dress was still in a somewhat delicate state. Some of the beading applied but not yet fully anchored with the charms that would be added at the last step. "But I am glad you could join us instead, Sioned."

Her mother made some comment Thessaly couldn't hear, but it must have been a query about where Laudine was. Emeline had accompanied Thessaly for the appointment, but she had been banished to the front room, facing the street. Otherwise, Thessaly could have asked later what had been said.

"Oh, she said she wasn't feeling very well. Honestly, she dotes far too much on Dagobert. She's far too worried over nothing, I'm sure. Or was it Garin this time? I honestly can't remember. There are so many other things that need tending. Even more without her help, of course."

Lady Maylis went on, the sort of complaint about being so terribly busy with everything needed that was two-thirds bragging about the reason for it. There was a complaint in there, though nominally couched as a concern, that of course they hadn't been able to ask Magistra Landry for her usual help with a number of things on the estate. Lady Maylis' tone didn't make it clear why, just that they were, in fact, obviously avoiding her, but with an edge of nastiness. That one couldn't expect Magistra Landry to behave the way a Fortier did.

When Thessaly thought about a time beyond the equinox, she found her mind sliding off of it. Obviously, there would be an October, and a November, and a December, proceeding on in incessant procession to the spring and a wedding date in May or June. They were still deciding on the optimal day, but the initial notes about that would have to go out soon.

Certainly, thinking about the actual wedding - or what came after it - was as challenging. The wedding was a blur in her mind. Except that she was sure she'd be wearing some ornate gown, with a train that needed other people to handle, the weight of it reminding her of her obligations and commitments. She expected there was no way to avoid rather intense embroidery as a demonstration of wealth. That took time to do, at least.

As for the wedding night, well, she'd had more than a couple of nightmares about it already, too strong for the talisman Vitus had given her to keep away entirely. She might ask, when she got a chance, for something specific to nightmares, but that would mean admitting to what they were. She liked Vitus far too much to put those particular images in his head as well. Bad enough they were in hers.

All of that meant she missed the next few exchanges while the dressmaker's assistant, a young Welsh woman named Myfanwy, with no surname given, was adjusting her underlying layers. Thessaly had been behind the curtain in the dressing room for a good five minutes already, standing patiently with her arms slightly outstretched. Myfanwy had been taking pains to make sure that the corset was adjusted perfectly. She'd also made certain that the folds of the chemise underneath and the cage of the bustle all hung as they ought. The dress in question was hung in three parts.

Objectively speaking, it was a lovely dress. The bulk of it was a green brocade, with a darker green creating a foliage pattern. It laced at the front over an underskirt of matching damask silk and a lace overskirt over that. Many of the details were exquisitely delicate, down to slits at the hem revealing the lace godets.

For someone else. Exquisitely delicate was certainly not her preferred mode. The one grace was that it was at least a dark colour other than the lace. Not the more proper lavender or purple for someone just out of mourning. She hadn't really expected that. In the Council Keep, that had other resonances, and ones she certainly wasn't about to claim. But she had hoped for a deep blue.

Green made sense, for the land magic connection - something none of the other candidates could claim. But the lace was going to catch on just about everything, whenever she moved. And it had short sleeves, so she'd be wearing full length gloves the entire time. The lace collar covered most of the exposed skin at the neck. But she'd not be able to wear Aunt Metaia's protective garnet with it. The dark red would clash horribly without something to make it look more intentional. She could wear it hidden between her breasts in the corset, though. That would do.

Now, the assistant was bringing down the underskirt, bustling it over Thessaly's head, then fastening it at the waist and smoothing it out. "Does your maid need a hand learning how to manage this, mistress?"

"Do speak up, please." That comment, no matter how mild, had caught Lady Maylis' attention. "And are you almost ready, dear?"

"Myfanwy was just asking if my maid would be familiar with how things go together, Lady Maylis. And just a moment longer, we want to make sure it's all sitting right. I'm sorry for taking so long."

Myfanwy ducked her chin and Thessaly mouthed, "Take as long as it needs". Then a little louder, she continued, "Yes, though perhaps she might visit and you can share any specific advice?" She'd be getting dressed at Arundel, not at Bryn Glas, that had already been made clear. But she'd asked to bring Collins with her, rather than have to burden the maids in the house who already had plenty to be doing.

Now came the overdress, and Thessaly could see the tiny beading glimmering. It was subtle, highlighting the foliage of the brocade, the lacing, the neckline, even where it was hidden by a fold of lace. When the piece was completed, they'd gleam like they were lit by candle light. Madame Foyet, the dressmaker, had demonstrated that when they'd done the initial planning. Thessaly's part was not to shine, it was to be a moon to Childeric's sun.

"I shall just see, oui?" That was Madam Foyet now, and she opened the curtain to peek in. "Move along, please, Myfanwy." That was pitched lower, and Thessaly suddenly wondered at the change in accent. Of course, a woman could be French, but have grown up in Albion, or have moved here as a young adult. Not that it mattered much. People should get to make their own futures. Thessaly believed that even more strongly now that she was getting driven into a very particular one.

"Pardon, mistress." Myfanwy busied herself with the lacings, tightening everything up, then reached to make sure the lace overskirt lay properly under the overdress. "There. Madam will need to see to the hem, and there's a little more to be done in the bodice, I think."

Thessaly nodded, waiting for the curtain to be held aside. The skirts were indeed long; they were dragging slightly on the floor. Thessaly made her way in proper small steps to the raised platform that would make adjusting the hem easier. At Lady Maylis's gesture, she spun slowly in place, slowly enough the fabric kept up with her.

It was a dress, in short, that was symbolic of everything the marriage would be. The gown was weighing her down; it was forcing her into a shape she would not choose on her own. It was lovely, and there were certainly fine and good things about it. But it would limit and restrict and make her seem different from what she wanted to be.

Lady Maylis considered, her head tilted slightly to one side, and then she burst into a flurry of rapid-fire French. Madam Foyet kept up with it, listening along, but it went too fast for Thessaly to catch all of it. Or rather, some of the language was technical, and not all of French dress-making carried over into the English terms for such things.

Once she'd made her point, Lady Maylis nodded once, and then switched back to English. "I don't know how much of that you followed, Thessaly?" It was more polite than asking her mother, certainly, and the one answer could be taken for both of them.

"About two-thirds. I should learn more of the specialist language, obviously," Thessaly said.

"Just so. We might think about a trip next summer to Paris. You would want it for that." Then Lady Maylis repeated the instructions in English, as Madam Foyet began working through the related tasks. Of course she hadn't given Thessaly any say in any of it.

Her mother, a little unexpectedly, spoke up. "That's not a colour you usually wear, Thessaly. It looks well on you, now I'm more used to it."

Lady Maylis tsked a little. "There are a number of traditions, of course, including those concerned with the land magic. I wouldn't expect you to know them, yet, nor Thessaly, but this is a start. Really, I still think it could have been a brighter green."

Thessaly managed, her voice rather smaller than she'd like, "I am glad we chose this. More suitable for the autumn than the brighter, perhaps? And the silk has a particular lustre."

"You know, I ought to ask Laudine if she'd lend - no." Maylis shook her head. "Not suitable, not yet. Laudine has a lovely parure of emeralds, a gift from her mother. But that's something for an established matron, known to have the best interests of the family in mind. Someone who has demonstrated it ceaselessly for years. Not for a maiden, not yet wed. Honestly, I'm glad Laudine doesn't wear them much. It suggests a seniority she does not have." And, per Lady Maylis, would not have at any point in the future, not if the title passed down through Childeric and Thessaly, and on from there.

Mother tilted her head at that, but said nothing directly. "Had you given thought to the wedding gown in more detail, yet, then?" That question was absolutely addressed to Lady Maylis, not at all to Thessaly.

"Oh, Madam Foyet and I have looked at some fabric and set some aside. We decided to wait, though, because there might be some aspect of the Challenge that should be highlighted." Thessaly, clearly, in this picture, remained a dim reflection of Childeric. At this rate, he'd be dressed in cloth of gold not seen for centuries, and she'd be wearing something that turned all the attention to him. "Purple, perhaps, something that suggests but does not tread on the Council purple. Childeric is consulting with his tailor at the beginning of October. Though it's possible we might go in quite a different direction."

Thessaly did not hate purple, certainly not on her. But she did, she found, resent the idea that she wasn't even getting that small a choice. Lady Maylis then glanced up, the sort of seemingly casual glance that was anything but. She added, her tone precise, "I know, Thessaly, that you have agreed to do as the family recommends in a number of matters."

She couldn't quite prevent a flinch, which brought with it the added sting of a pin in her thigh. That was going to hurt for a bit. She immediately murmured an apology to Madam Foyet, and Madam Foyet hummed a charm to staunch what bleeding there might be. Then Thessaly remembered she ought to say something. "You're quite right, Lady Maylis, of course. I look forward to what's chosen, of course."

From there, the conversation settled into more ordinary topics. There was a little gossip, a bit of Lady Maylis trying to get more out of Mother about the state of things with Father. Mother dodged that quite competently, of course. She must have expected it would happen. When the adjustments had been made and approved, Lady Maylis stood. "I have a little more shopping I ought to do before I return home. Thessaly, we expect you on Friday, of course."

"At five, naturally, Lady Maylis." There was another necessary obligatory Friday to Sunday there, another few days away from the sanctuary of Bryn Glas. Sunday was Thessaly's birthday, and she was certain none of the

Fortiers would notice. Certainly, there would be no congenial celebration with her parents, since congeniality was not on offer there. She'd have to see if Collins could arrange something quiet for Sunday evening.

Thessaly knew the entire matter of the schedule and the lack of consideration for any of her preferences was absolutely deliberate. Lady Maylis swept out after the proper farewells, and Thessaly was shooed back to the changing room. Once she was dressed again, Madam Foyet had disappeared and Myfanwy melted away, back to the front room.

"Is that the usual way things go?" Mother leaned in, adjusting a fold of the mourning dress Thessaly had put on again. "Ask Collins to have a look at this seam. I think that's not the only thread."

"If anything, milder." Thessaly took a deep breath.

"The demonstration of how things are is informative, dearest." Mother leaned forward, and now it was a whisper in her ear. "You handled it well, but nothing will please her but perfection."

Thessaly did not lose her temper in frustration, but it was a near thing. There were so many things she wanted to do, starting with asking if Mother hadn't thought she'd been imagining everything. "Of course, Lady Maylis thinks Childeric can do no wrong, and should have every good thing. I'm clear on what that means for me. You needn't scold." More to the point, Mother had given up every right to scold, by her own choices, and Thessaly's frustration did show through.

Mother stepped back, looking momentarily over-set, but then her expression shifted back to broad neutrality. "Didn't you say you had a little shopping to do? You'd best pick up your companion and see to it."

"Of course. It was good to see you, Mother." She

offered her mother a kiss on the cheek and then went off to the front room. Emeline immediately got the door, and Thessaly took off to the right for three blocks before remembering that what she really wanted was the stationery story in the opposite direction.

28

SEPTEMBER 18TH IN TRELLECH

Vitus had not expected to see Thessaly at this lecture. Oh, he'd certainly come to it because of her. But he'd thought that it would give them a comfortable topic to talk about when they could next speak in private. Something that wasn't the Council Challenge or Childeric Fortier, or his family.

He'd known, too, that wouldn't be this week. She'd sent a note, apologising, rather profusely, that she was obliged elsewhere from Friday afternoon through Sunday evening, and all the next week, through Sunday again. Perhaps the following week, she'd offered that cautiously.

Vitus had sent back a note that same day, through the Scali, that he would be delighted to come call when she was free. But also that he understood her time was not her own right now. He tried not to think about how much less her time would be hers in six months, whenever she was properly married. But at the same time, there was no sense in borrowing trouble.

Or at least, no need to go racing toward it faster than it was already approaching. If that was the right metaphor, which it probably wasn't. Thessaly might find it amusing, or it might inspire her to some better duelling metaphor. Vitus had taken two books on duelling out of the library last week, in fact. They were the sort that were a collection of increasingly unbelievable stories and situations, written to make the reader laugh and smile and be startled. It was right on the edge of sensationalist literature, but he was enjoying it.

Though it had made Mama regard him thoughtfully. He'd left it in the library, while he was seeing about more tea last night. It wasn't as if she'd snooped in his room. When he came back, she had picked it up, thumbing through it. Mama had asked just if it was a new hobby. Vitus had shaken his head, that he'd met someone who was a duellist, besides the fact that some duellists also bought talismans. It hadn't been convincing at all, and Mama certainly hadn't been fooled. She'd tutted amiably, and told him she'd love to hear about whoever it was when he had a bit of time.

Not this week for that, either. This week felt entirely too unsettled for Vitus, even if it wasn't a fragment of what Thessaly must be feeling.

He focused on not looking at her. That wouldn't do at all. She'd come in with several other women, Emeline trailing behind them and keeping an eye on the room. Thessaly was still wearing mourning dress, though this one had touches of a medium purple, as well as the black. The women with her - the glimpse Vitus had got - had been older, perhaps other former apprentices of her apprentice mistress, or colleagues of her aunt.

Either would make sense. This lecture was about applications of illusions in various settings, and specifically how they might be usefully anchored by materia or talismans. The latter made it a good choice for him, but he suspected he knew most of what would be said there. On the illusion side, the contrast was apparently more the thing for the two speakers, who intended to engage in a proper academic debate about the topic. It should at least be entertaining, especially if they were demonstrating any of the illusion work.

At any rate, he'd turned up early, but he was saved from the utter temptation of turning around to look at Thessaly by the arrival of several of the Four Metals folks, including Merryn. That meant he could let himself get caught up in the amiable chatter of the group, commenting here and there. And Thirza Remmerton, who of course had an interest in pigments used as materia. That meant that the opening of the lecture snuck up on him. Then there was a good hour and a half of listening, blinking at some of the example illusions. Everyone was leaning forward as the two speakers broke them down, piece by piece.

There was something about the layering techniques they were using. They were not dissimilar to the ideas Thessaly had been working on about how to make the illusion of lapis lazuli look real. It made Vitus want to dig into the theory a great deal more. And then, naturally, the applications. He was all about how to make that magic real, have an effect on the physical world.

Thirza was one of the last to stand, and she nudged him. "There?"

Vitus was shaken out of his thoughts, and he looked around. Not wildly, he was better trained than that. He followed where Thirza was looking. Thessaly was talking to one speaker, gesturing. The rest of the hall was emptying, people going along to get a drink or a late supper. Thirza said, her voice still quiet. "Maybe a word with Magister Oswald. If you want to find us, we'll be down at the Fourth and Seventh." That was a pub, often favoured by musicians, but the sister of one of the Four Metals folks owned it. She was glad enough to let them have the upstairs room if it wasn't already in use.

"I'll likely be along in a few." Vitus waited for Thirza to step out into the aisle. Then he did so himself, turning right to go down to the stage, instead of left like she did. There were a few other people waiting to talk, but fewer to Magister Oswald, who'd been the one on the materia side.

Thessaly's question, whatever it was, had drawn in several other people. Vitus's question had been about how the quality of the materia used affected the illusion, as well as how much was required. He'd got the sense from Magister Oswald, that small gem chips would do quite well, and could be of lower quality. If so, that was something he and Niobe both produced in some quantity. And more to the point it had little use other than going to the colourmen and their studios for pigments for ink or paints.

By the time he was done with that, the conversations next to him had ebbed and flowed. Vitus nodded politely in that direction, then caught Emeline signalling. Oh, the stair to the balcony. Everyone up there had gone. He gave one last nod and said farewell. Then he went to lurk in the stairs for a minute or ten. As long as it took for Thessaly to show up or for it to be clear he'd misunderstood.

He didn't have to wait long. Maybe four minutes later, there were feet coming up the stairs, and Emeline's "I'll just stay down here." Keeping an eye out, obviously. They wouldn't have more than a few minutes. The staff were cleaning up and would want to get home. But then Thessaly came up onto the landing between the floors and held out her hands to him. Gloved, she was in public. They both were, even if it was a sheltered public right now.

Vitus squeezed her hands back. "I didn't expect to see

you today. Are you all right, other than being kept far more busy than you want?"

The look on her face said it all. She went a little pale, looking away from him. "Dreading Sunday, really. There's not much to do about it, but brave face, walk forward." It had the ring of something she'd heard from people she trusted, and Vitus suspected it was her Aunt Metaia.

"You still don't mind if I'm there? It won't be distracting?" Vitus had been gnawing on that one. "I can put Carrington off."

"No, you should get to be there, you've earned it." Thessaly met his eyes again, then squeezed his hands back. "And I think I'd feel better if I knew you were there. Even if we can't talk, can't even look at each other. Besides, it'll annoy Childeric no end that you got an invitation he couldn't foil."

"I got the sense that the Carringtons don't care much for him. I've no idea why, and of course it's not the kind of thing they'd say. Not at this stage in our very nascent patronage relationship."

The way he put it made her giggle, then she clapped one of her hands over her mouth to muffle it. That made Vitus feel wonderful. Those moments of spontaneous happiness always did. They'd been few and far between for her, and with good reason, but that made them even more precious. If he were going to put it into poetry, he'd be talking about, oh, the finding of a sapphire in an alluvial deposit. Most wouldn't think it romantic or impassioned at all, but the way chance and ancient stones and the movement of the world came together in that image grabbed at him.

Also, apparently, at his tongue, because now Thessaly was looking at him, her head tilted. "You were thinking?"

"About poetry. And alluvial sapphires. I'll explain when

we get more time, shall I? I might even have a proof of concept to share." He would make a note of it as soon as he had both hands back, though he wasn't likely to forget the idea.

"I like the idea of having something to look forward to. Even if it's something most people would say sounded like nonsense." Thessaly reached to tap the tip of his nose lightly with one finger. "Not that I'm saying that. Just that other people might. I would like to hear the explanation when we can."

"Of course. As you wish." Now Vitus let out a breath. "Is there anything else I can do for you?"

"Come see me. When I get a moment to myself at home. Whenever that is." She leaned forward, now much more earnest.

"Always. You let me know when I can. Or for that matter, I could come see you first thing in the morning, if you don't mind losing sleep at that end of the day." He would, too, for all it would mean rising even earlier for him.

It made her tilt her head again, considering. "I'll think about it. And I don't mind getting up early with that waiting. Worse for you."

He shrugged. "I can go to bed earlier. No Fortiers demanding all my time. It might puzzle Mama, but that's manageable."

Before Thessaly could say more, they both heard Emeline from down at the foot of the stairs. "Oh, she was just looking for something on the stairs. Mistress Lytton-Powell, did you find that trinket yet, for your friend? The one you'd dropped?"

"Oh! Here it is, right in the corner." Thessaly rummaged in her reticule for something. She closed it, pulling out a small copper piece, the kind of thing people used for knitting or sewing markers, or something of the kind. "Coming, you're so kind." She didn't kiss him, there wasn't time for that. But she touched his hand once, then went down. He could hear her drawing whoever was there off to have another look at the hall where she'd been sitting, as if she'd lost something else. Vitus could hear her talking about a gap in her reticule. She'd gone upstairs just briefly to speak to someone, but now she didn't have the scissors she kept in there. Could he help her look?

It gave Vitus the chance to slip away, out the doors of the hall before any other staff spotted him. He was a block down the street, going toward the Fourth and Seventh, when he stopped to catch his breath. Then he squared his shoulders and decided to say as little as possible about where he'd been. They'd guess, or at least some of them would, but he could probably trust they wouldn't tease about it where others could hear.

In fact, in the way of their society, it had been long enough that there was an energetic debate going on, a four-sided one. No, five. Thirza raised an eyebrow at him when he came in, but she was arguing at some volume about the quality mattering. Vitus could fling himself into that with what Master Oswald had said. And he'd also come up with the beginnings of a proposal for actually testing it, if they could get the right people in place for it. That was, at least, a different sort of argument, with people tossing around ideas for proper variables, and it took them through the next two rounds of drinks.

29

SEPTEMBER 22ND AT THE COUNCIL KEEP

There was a protocol to their entrance. Of course there was. It went with everything else from the day so far.

Thessaly had been permitted to sleep at Bryn Glas both Friday and Saturday night, for a wonder. But she had been out at Arundel from nine in the morning past eleven on the Saturday. She'd been set to work helping with the arrangements for the grand celebration planned for Monday. Whatever happened tonight would be the family and whoever else they invited along, Monday would be everyone they could fit into the estate. More than for the betrothal, even. There were three separate tents set up on the lawn. And she'd been there from nine in the morning today, her only time without close observation while she was dressing in the afternoon. Or rather, being dressed.

Each of the tents had needed to have illusions set, and the Fortiers had decided that Thessaly, at least, could be of use with that. Within, of course, strictly defined guidelines. She was there to create what the Dowager Lady

Chrodechildis and Lady Maylis thought best, not to have any thoughts of her own. She'd tried to offer a comment, once, only to be told to keep quiet. What they'd decided would mean the illusions would fade more than they ought, without additional attention. Thessaly had resigned herself to giving each of them a little more magic on Monday morning and being exhausted because of it. If they failed, that would also be her fault.

Now, she was walking into the great hall at Dinas Emrys on Childeric's arm in a stately procession. He was at the head of it, of course, naturally, like there was no other place. She had her arm on his, her other hand managing her skirts, especially to keep them out from under his feet. Childeric wasn't having a care about that. He'd stepped on her hem twice, though thankfully nothing had torn.

He looked splendid. Where she was in dark green, he was in a vibrant purple that coordinated well with the green, flowing robes over duelling clothes, tall boots and breeches and a black shirt with billowing sleeves. The vest was cloth of gold, as was the decoration on the robes and shirt. There was a thread of green to match her dress, vines climbing up toward his head and an occasional leaf. And there was a ring on his finger, though he'd twisted it so only the gold band was showing.

They had gone into the portal first, and he kept walking as they came out, steadily on. Behind them, she could sense more than hear the others. Dagobert was escorting his mother. He'd had a word in her ear, Saturday, that Laudine was expecting, offering it as if Thessaly might find it indelicate. She'd assured him she was glad to know and wished them well.

It explained why Laudine had not been there Saturday morning, and then why she'd been set to even more tedious work than the illusions. And of course, why she wasn't here now, no portal trip for her. She'd come to Arundel the long way, by train and carriage. Portals were too many variables, Aunt Metaia had said, a few years ago, to judge sensibly.

And behind them, of course, were Childeric's parents, followed by Sigbert. It was an odd problem of precedence, and Thessaly tucked that away in case she needed something to think about while they were waiting. Now, she took in the hall, which was hung with purple banners, alternating the compass with the white rose, the two most dominant heraldic symbols of the Council. There were seating areas set up along the long sides of the hall, collections of sofas and padded chairs. Each had varying different flower arrangements that gave a nod to the challenger's Schola house and family heraldry.

Childeric's was up at the front. She could see the purple, gold, and black. Nothing else in the hall was quite that combination. As they reached the halfway point, Council Member Warren came forward, offering his hands to Childeric and barely acknowledging her other than a slight bow. "Master Fortier. We are ready for you at the front as soon as your family is settled. May I walk with you?"

Childeric almost dropped Thessaly's arm, but then he offered again and escorted her up to the front. He turned to bow his mother into her chair, and then his grandmother, before straightening up. Hesperidon Warren had waited by the entrance to the group of chairs. "One of the staff will be around with something to drink, Lady Fortier, Lady Chrodechildis. Please let them know if there is anything else you need."

"You are very kind, Council Member." Lady Maylis spoke fondly. "May I ask, is your delightful wife here?"

"Ah, no. I will pass on your greetings, of course." He bowed again, and Childeric turned to face his parents.

"Thessaly, I'm sure you will do as Maman indicates. Including making a proper show of it when I come out in triumph."

That rang oddly in Thessaly's ears. Maybe - probably - it was the hubris of the assumption, on the edge of something that ought to be treated as more sacred or holy or otherwise distinct from the ordinary. However, she knew her role, and she smiled. "Of course, Childeric." Then she glanced to the side, got the brief nod from Lady Maylis. "I have something for you. I know it's not a joust, not a duel, not like that. But I made you a favour, as the legends suggest." She brought it out from her reticule, unfolding a small length of embroidered silk, meant to be tucked into a belt, one part hanging free. It had the Fortier heraldry on it, of course, the two golden bees on purple above, the castle fortress in black on gold below.

"Ah." Childeric glanced at his mother, not at Thessaly.

"I suggested it, dearest. And Thessaly's embroidery is..." Thessaly was sure she'd been about to say 'adequate' or some other faint praise, before Lady Maylis remembered they were in public. "Charming."

"Of course I will wear it, then. You are kind to have thought of it." Childeric made the word 'kind' into something awful. She had not enjoyed embroidering it. She rarely favoured embroidery as a way to spend her time. If she were going to do intricate decorative work, she would choose illusions every day.

But she was playing her part as thoroughly as she could, and she wished anyone here could at least respect that. Possibly Dagobert did. She caught an odd expression on his face for just a moment before he shifted back into neutrality. Childeric tucked the silk into his belt, adjusting it so it hung just where it was visible under the line of his robe. "I shall go."

He turned, walking with an easy confidence, loose-limbed and even, going up to the front of the hall and bowing low. He took Council Head Hereswith's hand, kissing the air over it, then the other pleasantries. Council Head Hereswith looked a trifle occupied. Honestly, she must have a dozen things running through her head.

With Childeric, they had collected two of the five challengers. Heliotrope Masterson was there, talking to Council Member Palgrave, who was apparently sponsoring her. She was wearing something that looked rather unyielding, a small bustle and skirts, but Thessaly suspected there was some way to lift the fabric and allow easier movement. There, that was another topic she could amuse herself with while sitting quietly and waiting. What costume would she choose if she made a challenge? Or rather, what she'd choose if it wasn't duelling clothes.

The rest of the people waiting, that was a more interesting observation. There had been the polite nods of acknowledgement as the Fortiers had entered. But while there was a little conversation between people in the other small groups, no one approached the Fortiers. Thessaly had not been at larger social events since the summer solstice, but she suddenly wondered how the Fortiers had been treated there. There wasn't anyone she might reasonably ask, either. It would be too telling a question. Now, she could see - and feel - an essential and uncomfortable distance.

As Thessaly watched, Irene Hamilton approached, to be met by Fletcher Grimly. She'd seen his wife here, talking to the Hamiltons before Irene approached the front. Irene was wearing rather more practical clothing than Heliotrope. Not quite designed for duelling, but more ease of movement, and Thessaly was almost sure those were split skirts under a long overskirt.

Irene was a few years older than Childeric. She wasn't primarily a duellist, so Thessaly didn't know her terribly well. But she did a bit of duelling, the way certain people did to challenge themselves. Testing herself against the forms, rather than against an opponent, perhaps that was the right description. As Thessaly watched, she talked comfortably with the others - not Childeric, who was still pointedly focused on the senior members of the Council who were there.

It must take a lot of effort to make everything run smoothly. That was true even if - as Thessaly had been told by her aunt - the actual Challenge was entirely up to the magics of the keep. But there would be people here to welcome the challengers. There would be people upstairs, where the actual door to the Challenge was. And there must be quite a few besides the Keep's staff, making sure the food and drink and other needs were tended to. Thessaly hadn't had how to manage large social events drilled into her for nothing. There was a Healer who'd need space, cleansing charms that might be called on, many potential demands.

As Thessaly watched, the last two came up. They'd been positioned next to each other, and Theo Carrington had paused for a moment for Cyrus Smythe-Clive, who had been further down. Cyrus looked awful, in a way Thessaly could measure, because she'd seen him day in and day out for five years at Schola. There was some part of him, a large part, that wasn't here. It was somewhere remote. He'd stopped for a moment, to kiss his sister on the cheek and hug her once, then he'd turned. Theo had matched him in stride as they came up the central aisle together.

Of course, that gave Thessaly a glance at Vitus, too. He was right there in her line of sight. He had more sense than to acknowledge it, thankfully, then he turned his head and shoulders to watch Theo move. Theo was dressed sensibly, in comfortable duelling gear. In contrast, Cyrus had on a long, black, sleeveless ritual robe over a stark white shirt and black trousers.

There were deliberate choices in all the clothing on display, including the guests. But Thessaly thought Cyrus was the only one who had made it into a tool, deliberately. There was something timeless about him, a gravitas well beyond their age. Perhaps she'd have time to ask him about it at some point later. They'd never been close friends, but they'd been amiable acquaintances before. They might manage it again, if Childeric didn't become horribly jealous there as well.

Childeric probably would. Thessaly was learning to spot those better, though admittedly this took little skill. Was it someone Childeric felt might exceed him in any way at anything he cared about? If so, Thessaly should pretend that person did not exist. It was tricky, when that person was Thessaly herself, even before the other implications.

Now all five of the challengers were in place, there was the sound of a deep bell. The keep did not have a bell tower. It did not remotely matter. It tolled six times - the hour, then, not some other count. Council Head Hereswith opened with an elegant brief speech, welcoming the challengers and their families and friends. She laid out how the Challenge would go. They would draw lots for who entered in which order, proceed upstairs, and let matters take their course.

Everyone there knew how this would go, but it still had to be said. That was part of the point of a ritual, of a set of steps taken the same way every time. And the grounding of it, the habit of it, that was soothing. It was more so to the existing Council Members, especially. Thessaly could see the ones there settling a bit, the way their magic flowed differently. She did not, she realised, see Cousin Owain. He must be behind the scenes somewhere, and busy, or she was fairly sure he'd have at least come to greet her.

Perhaps, like Thessaly herself, being here - at the Challenge for Aunt Metaia's seat - ached in a way that didn't have any names. She had to be here, smiling and putting on the proper face for it. Cousin Owain did not, and she envied him that. And she was grateful that he could, at the same time. It helped, just a little, to know that both of them weren't miserable for the same reason and were on display.

Hesperidon Warren was bringing around the container with the lots— stones with numbers painted on them, drawn from within a small and decidedly opaque copper barrel. Each drew, and Council Head Hereswith announced them. "We shall have, in order, Heliotrope Masterson, then Cyrus Smythe-Clive. Third will be Irene Hamilton, then Theo Carrington, and fifth and last, Childeric Fortier."

There was a rumble from those watching. Lady Maylis leaned forward. "The order means nothing. Hesperidon told me that already. Often the last to go in comes out the first, and the numbers suggest most often triumphant."

That was an entire line of statistical analysis that must make some people thrilled, and that Thessaly had not bothered to check. There were far too many aspects to it, and she had not wanted to spend the necessary time keeping them straight in her head. Especially when it would have no benefit to her. Or rather, she might have fixated on it, and she did not need further incentives to insomnia.

With that announced, there was a beat of a drum, and the doors at the head of the Great Hall opened. Council Head Hereswith led the way, going through the doors and off to the left. Now there was waiting, for some unknown time, wishing and not wishing for a particular outcome.

30

THAT EVENING

Vitus felt entirely out of place. He still wasn't at all sure it was a good idea for him to be here. It probably wasn't. Simultaneously, it was an excellent idea for him to be here.

Lucas, bless him, had heard him out this afternoon. His brother had made a point of coming home first, rather than going into Trellech for a round of the clubs. They'd gone for a walk earlier that afternoon. Lucas had made friends with four different great draught horses on their day off, out in the fields. It might have had something to do with the dried apple pieces he eased out of his pockets, but it wasn't just that. His brother's honest love of a horse - and the adoration of every horse Vitus had ever seen him with - was an unabashedly good thing in the world.

Now Vitus tried to have that air here, that every person might be agreeable. And that if not, there were sturdy enough fences to keep it from being a fuss here and now. That was more or less what he'd talked about with his brother, how to be in this moment.

It was one time he missed having either duelling training or the sort of incantation training that had a performance aspect to it. He'd done a little of the latter at Schola, of course. It was part of the broader teaching of the field. But since he'd apprenticed, all of his focus had gone into the stones and the inscriptions, and how to do those enchantments.

Vitus knew he was dressed well. Mama had seen to that. She'd checked everything was perfect before she'd sent him off. Black suit, impeccably proper for the evening, over a vest with a print in darker golds and browns, a brighter golden ascot and pocket square. He'd arranged to meet the Carrington party there, but now that meant walking into the hall by himself. Fortunately, he spotted them halfway up the hall on the left. Theo was standing, talking with a number of gestures to his sister and parents. There were several others there as well, as Vitus had expected. An aunt, an uncle, Theo's apprentice master, the respectable and proud connections gathered together.

Theo caught sight of him, gestured more broadly, making it clear Vitus should join them and that he was welcome. As Vitus approached, he was full of introductions to the people who didn't yet - as Theo said - know Vitus and his skills. He was wearing the ring, of course, Vitus could tell before he saw the flash of the green. Theo had dressed to match it, rather than in the expected purple for Fox House. He wore a sleeveless ritual robe of the deep muted green. It flowed down from his shoulders over his own black suit, and his vest and ascot were patterned to match the stone. It made him look striking, especially with lighter hair and dancing pale eyes.

Vitus ventured, when there was a pause in the conversation. "The colour suits you. I thought, coming in, you were something out of a pastoral legend, the muted colour and the gold of your hair."

Theo laughed. "Most of that's Rhea's idea. She has an excellent eye for it. I was hoping for a brown suit, actually, but we couldn't get the proper fabric in enough time. Charm-woven woollen silk does not grow on trees, alas." That meant his suit had been made for the Challenge, all sorts of protective work woven and sewn in. Which explained why he'd been less concerned about a protective talisman, and more about one that would enhance his other skills. Vitus snorted and knew Theo would read it correctly.

They chatted for a bit, and then there was a pause, the room going quiet as the Fortiers made a procession in. Vitus near held his breath. He didn't dare move. Of course, he had to look. Childeric wanted to be looked at. Thessaly, beside him, was lovely in all the ways she was expected to be, but she was holding herself stiffly. It was, of course, the first time he'd seen her out of mourning since the solstice, and he wondered how she felt about that, that this was the first time other people were seeing her without any of the visible reminders.

And that gown, while beautiful, was a style he thought she hadn't chosen. It was demure, suggesting a pastoral innocence entirely at odds with Theo's choices, for all the same adjectives technically applied. Green, drawing on the land, flowing. Perhaps he'd have time to ask her what she'd rather have worn in the coming days. Once the Fortiers were settled, Vitus made himself turn back to the conversation, asking Theo's aunt and uncle about their particular interests. It was the sort of conversation anyone could do without concentrating, but he was interested in the answer.

Once that had gone on for a few more minutes, Theo glanced over to the left. "Ah, I see Cyrus going up. Wish me well!" There was an echo of good wishes, a mother's blessing, a father's pride, all in little phrases that obviously meant the world to Theo. He stepped into the central aisle, greeting Cyrus Smythe-Clive and walking side by side with him.

Vitus watched them, before realising someone was tapping him on the elbow. "Please, sit." Rhea gestured at a chair. "And someone will come round to ask if you want something to drink. We have wine, but if you'd like something else, I think it pleases them to be hospitable."

That was an interesting comment. Vitus smiled, settling down in a chair. Before he could say much more, there was a stirring up at the head of the hall, then Council Head Rowan called everyone to attention. Vitus half-closed his eyes, feeling the ritual and the anchoring of it roll over him, listening as they were greeted and named, then as the challengers drew lots.

It wasn't until the five challengers, their sponsors, and several others had disappeared that the conversation picked up again. The Carringtons were quieter than the Hamiltons next to them. Though the Smythe-Clives were quieter still. There were only three of them, Cyrus's parents and sister. Vitus knew Master Smythe-Clive via Papa. Papa wasn't their man of business, but he sometimes had dealt with particular contract agreements for them. Just the three, and that seemed very odd. Every other family here had at least half a dozen. And Cyrus had recently finished his apprenticeship, but his apprentice mistress wasn't here.

Not ten minutes after they'd gone upstairs, Heliotrope Masterson reappeared. She walked straight from the double doors at the head of the hall down the aisle. Her family stared after her, then stood, following her out, one of the Keep's staff trotting after them. Heliotrope's cheeks were red. Her gown was flaring out behind her, but she did not say a word to anyone, just kept walking at as fast a pace as she could.

The rest of the room fell quiet, confused. From the front of the room, there was a brief sound of a bell or a chime, something deeper. "Heliotrope Masterson has paid her respects and declined to enter the Challenge. We wish her well." Not, by that language, barred at the door. In his research, Vitus had learned it happened sometimes, though it hadn't previously in Hereswith Rowan's tenure as Head.

Slowly, the conversation began again, haltingly. Vitus wasn't sure what to say. Then he turned back to Rhea, to find she was watching him. "I beg pardon." Then he remembered what she'd said a few minutes ago. "You've been paying attention to the arrangements here, then?" It seemed relevant now.

Rhea beamed at him. "Few people notice what goes into a large event like this." She then tilted her head. "Well. Not as large in numbers as some, but with people touchy about their prerogatives." She nodded across toward the Fortiers, and Vitus carefully didn't look. He could guess well enough. As Rhea spoke, someone came around, checking to see if Vitus wanted anything. He said he was delighted with the wine, thank you, for the moment. A glass was pressed into his hand, and the conversation eased into something undemanding. It was the sound of people reassuring themselves that the rhythms of the world were as they ought to be, not tangled or fouled.

Whatever Theo had said to his sister about Vitus's attentions had worked. She was charming, interesting to talk to, but she did not press the issue at all. For his part, Vitus refused to look over toward where Thessaly was sitting. He couldn't permit it. Not looking might be noticed, but looking would be far worse, and likely more so for Thessaly.

Perhaps five minutes after that, Vitus was startled when he heard a voice over his shoulder. "May I join you?" Vitus looked up to see Council Member Owain Powell, Thessaly's cousin. Cousin at some distance, a different generation along with everything else, but she'd talked about him and his household fondly in a couple of their conversations. Vitus wasn't the one who could offer the invitation, but the Carringtons did immediately and gracefully.

As Owain Powell sat down, Vitus got a sense of something shifting. It took him a minute or two to realise what it was. One or more of the talismans he'd made with Niobe had been activated. That thread of magic that came from him was close enough and strong enough he could feel it. He could see, then, that there was a tense attention among the Council Members he could see. That wasn't all of them, of course.

Vitus glanced at Owain Powell, sitting next to him. The older man leaned over to whisper in his ear. "Best for you and I if we're somewhere public that can be sworn to if needed. Let's keep chatting, shall we?"

There was nothing sensible to be said to that. Vitus merely nodded, but now his mind was racing. Something had gone wrong, something that needed healing talismans. Or at least, where they thought they might be needed. It wasn't Theo, or surely Powell would have handled that differently. That he'd warned Vitus meant it might well be Childeric.

An injured Childeric seemed an even worse idea than an ordinary Childeric. He did not seem the sort to take injury well by anything Vitus had ever seen from him. He couldn't do anything about what had happened, though, other than agree that not being anywhere near it, being visibly seated right here, that was a sensible choice.

The chatting grew on and on. The Carringtons had noticed something odd— Rhea commented on it, briefly, but didn't linger. Instead, they were curious why Owain Powell was spending time with them. All three of them were charming, the same way Theo was. But there was a second question. Surely Council Member Powell had other things to do beyond spending so much time with them? Powell just stayed and stayed.

It was maybe half an hour before there was some signal from the front, and Powell excused himself. "Please, stay here. There may be some news shortly. A pleasure speaking with all of you." He made a slight bow to the ladies and withdrew. Great double doors opened briefly at the front of the hall. They were ajar just long enough for Powell to enter. Vitus could see for just an instant that he was talking to someone, suddenly gesturing energetically. The doors closed again, blocking any hint of what was happening. Except that those talismans were no longer engaged or active.

Ten minutes after that, Hereswith Rowan came out, accompanied by three staff members. They moved like duellists. That was the thing Vitus noticed first. She spoke quietly to the Fortier group, including Thessaly - this time Vitus could not help looking. Everyone was looking. And the Fortiers looked confused, most of all. They stood, and were escorted off to a door opening from the front corner of the hall, through the door. Thessaly brought up the end of the little procession, walking more slowly with Dagobert. The rest of the family had abandoned him for last.

When Vitus turned back to the Carringtons, they also looked entirely puzzled. "What do you think it means?"

Vitus cleared his throat. "I don't think anything good."

Then he pressed his lips together. "If— that's not how they announce the successful candidate. Niobe explained that. And none of the others have come back down."

"No." Theo's mother pursed her lips. "We will continue as we were, then, and I am sure there will be some additional information. At some point."

31

THAT EVENING

Thessaly wasn't certain what she was feeling. In part, that was because she was feeling a number of different things. Anxious was certainly in there, knowing that everyone in the room was aware of her and that many of them were watching how she reacted. Certainly, the people she was sitting with were marking every move she made.

They'd been arrayed in a curve of chairs. Thessaly's back was slightly toward the head of the room, while Lord Clovis and Lady Maylis had the seats of honour facing the front. Dagobert was next to Thessaly, then Sigbert, then the Dowager Lady Chrodechildis. She was reigning in state. She had a knack for making that visible as soon as she sat down.

Once the initial remarks had been made, certainly once the candidates had disappeared, conversation sprung up. Several of the Council came by to say good evening, the usual sort of pleasantries, but none of them lingered very long. Cousin Owain came by, and he made a point of speaking directly to Thessaly, and asking how she was. The others, she was just folded in with the Fortiers. She was, apparently, only of interest by connection, not identity.

It occurred to her after the third of them - Casper Roberts, who was also a duellist - that they might have thought they were being kind. Running through the conversations, that was more likely in two out of three cases. Not drawing attention to her, in ways the Fortiers might disapprove of. Council Member Roberts was in his mid-forties. If he were willing to give her a bout sometime, she suspected she'd learn a lot, but also have a good challenge. And of course, several of the Council Members who might have been more personal were busy with other things. She was sure Cousin Owain would have comments later about some of that.

Certainly, one thing Thessaly was feeling was boredom. Or a particular discomfort at waiting. She didn't entirely resent the waiting. It was a necessary part of the process. But this felt artificially awful, building tension that didn't need to be here. Or perhaps that was coming from inside her. The longer it had been, the more there was a pit inside her, something in her magic that was shouting in a way she couldn't quite hear or understand. It wasn't aimed at her; it wasn't engaging her duelling defences, but it made her shift uncertainly in her seat.

Before she could figure out whether to say anything, there was a commotion at the front. All of a sudden Heliotrope Masterton was walking furiously down the centre aisle. She disappeared out the far doors into the courtyard before her family could even stand, and they trailed out after her, followed by one or two of the Keep's staff.

Dagobert and Sigbert both picked that moment to

begin talking. Dagobert gestured at Sigbert, who settled into the obligatory wondering aloud what that was all about. Had she been denied entrance at all? Had she chosen to walk out? Obviously, no one was going to answer that question right in the moment, but Thessaly made a note to ask Cousin Owain later.

From there, Dagobert asked his mother about some minor thing on the estate, a detail no one was actually that interested in. Even Dowager Lady Chrodechildis. It did, however, keep the awkward silence from coming back.

While the others talked - Thessaly's opinion was absolutely not required on the topic of preferred rose bushes in the northwest garden - she noticed movement at the front of the room. It was subtle, but several of the Council excused themselves, not all at once. They each slipped through the doors, with no sign of what was going on. Cousin Owain had been talking to the Carringtons, where Vitus was, for some minutes, but even he excused himself, one of the last of the Council to disappear.

The odd feelings were more so now. Thessaly still couldn't label them. She wanted to be moving, to feel the ground under her and magic in her hands and her body, and she couldn't do that. She felt rather pinned in place, like a specimen of a butterfly. The lepidoptery pin was made of social expectations and sharpened by Dowager Lady Chrodechildis's glare.

Of course, they wouldn't alert anyone. Whatever had happened, it was for the Council to deal with. Possibly, that also included the Keep's staff. Most of them had also vanished, though a few were refilling drinks and bringing trays around.

Ten minutes after that, Council Head Rowan came out. She was flanked by three of the Keep's staff, and all three were duellists. They were all men, with strongly built shoulders. Thessaly noticed that immediately. And they moved in unison, used to matching each other without drawing attention to themselves. The Council Head came into the grouping of chairs. "Would you please all accompany me? We need to speak more privately."

There was no other comment, no sign - other than the formality and neutrality - of something wrong, but Thessaly knew there was. Childeric had been injured, perhaps, or something had gone wrong with the Challenge. She couldn't figure out what, though, and Council Head Rowan certainly was an expert in not revealing information she didn't want.

Slowly, the family rose. Thessaly fell in last in line, she knew her role here. Sigbert was escorting his grandmother, then Lord Clovis and Lady Maylis. A moment later, Dagobert offered her his free arm. She took it. Thessaly would not make a fuss. Not at him, and not at this moment. She knew better than that.

They were escorted in silence through a door at the right corner of the front of the room, a single door. It led into a hallway that Thessaly remembered. As they turned right, she glanced left to find Cousin Owain standing there. He nodded at her once, and followed them two doors down and into another room.

These were public rooms of the Keep, open to those not on the Council, but they weren't normally opened up during gatherings. She'd been in them a few times when she was with Aunt Metaia. The one they ended up in was called the Turquoise Room, for all the obvious reasons. The shade reminded Thessaly painfully of her aunt, though it was a bit more green than the bluer tint Aunt Metaia had most preferred. There were chairs, but no one sat, just standing there.

The room had double doors which opened onto

another room, but right now Thessaly couldn't remember which one. That kind of thought got stuck in the front of her mind, as if her mind wouldn't focus on the reason for the odd request.

The door from the hallway was closed. Two of the staff took places by the double doors that separated this room from the other, the third by the door to the hallway with Cousin Owain. Council Head Rowan waited until they were all in place and cleared her throat. "I am terribly sorry to be the one who must tell you this. Childeric Fortier died during the Challenge. It was quick, whatever happened. Healer Raddick examined him thoroughly, but there was nothing she could do."

There was utter silence for perhaps five seconds, and then Lady Maylis was absolutely wailing, keening. There were sounds from the others too, disbelief, hisses of whispers, but all Thessaly could hear was the pulse drumming in her ears. She was free. Somehow, miraculously, wondrously, she was free. She hadn't expected that at all, not remotely.

It would be wrong to say she hadn't wished Childeric dead a few times, but it hadn't had weight to it. Now, here she was, a solution to all the problems, out of the blue. Thessaly brought her hand to her mouth. She had to hide at least some of what she was feeling. They had loved their son, their grandson, their brother, and their nephew. At least, she assumed so. He had, perhaps, not been cruel to them, or not in the same ways.

"I must see him. You must be wrong, he must be, there must be..." Lady Maylis became increasingly shrill, her voice carrying over the others.

Council Head Rowan answered her, a much milder alto filling the room. "Are you certain? It is— there are marks on him."

"I will see him." Lady Maylis wheeled to the left to face Council Head Rowan, absolutely challenging her. "Where is he? Bring me to my son."

At a nod, the two Keep staff by the double doors opened them. On the other side of the doors, in the centre of the next room, there was a low bier set out. It rested on simple wooden containers, the same ones there had been for Aunt Metaia's funeral, but this time uncovered by linens. Childeric lay on top of it. His hands had been folded. Someone had closed his eyes, but Thessaly couldn't make any sense of his expression. Not from here. His robes did not show any sign of damage, but the favour she'd given him was gone, no longer tucked into his belt.

Lady Maylis rushed over, taking one of his hands, imploring him, begging, then begging magic itself, the sky, the land, whatever might have a single drop of willingness. Nothing changed except the sounds in the room. Lord Clovis came over, not quite touching her, his mother on the other side. Sigbert stepped forward, too, with his grandmother. It left Thessaly and Dagobert at Childeric's feet, though Thessaly took another step or two forward.

She'd thought his shirt closed, but it hadn't been buttoned, somehow. When Lady Maylis had grabbed his hand, something had moved. His shirt had fallen open. Thessaly could see two burned marks against his skin. They lay about where his necklace and watch might have been, and then delicate feathered red marks, the strike of lightning made flesh, running up his chest between the two.

Now Lady Maylis looked up and around. "Thessaly. Thessaly, you come right here. Love's kiss has tremendous powers. Here, you must."

Thessaly shivered, and no, she would not do any such thing. She felt a hand on her arm, one on her shoulder a moment later. The shoulder was Cousin Owain. He had come up behind her. The hand was Dagobert, and that felt oddly reassuring.

"Maylis." Dagobert's voice was shaky, but he was speaking. She could hear him speaking over the louder pounding in her ears. "Don't. We can all see there's no hope. Council Head, is there anything else you can tell us at this time?"

Lord Clovis growled, then waved a hand, a buffeting force of magic that caught Dagobert as a slap might have. It was a tremendous loss of control, especially in front of an audience, the sort of thing that could only be barely excused by the current tragedy. Dagobert staggered, catching himself on the cane, and Lord Clovis motioned at Thessaly. "Here, try."

It was not quite an order, and yet it utterly was. Thessaly shook her head. It was safe enough to let her actual fear show. It was a sensible choice in this duel she'd found herself in. "Please, no. It's such a shock, seeing him like that."

Cousin Owain's hand stayed on her shoulder. "We assure you, our Healer tried everything possible."

Council Head Rowan continued, picking up smoothly. "What we know is very little. He appeared on the landing outside the Challenge door. It did not open or close, as we would expect. He was soaking wet, then. We called the Healer, immediately, then brought him downstairs, in case any other charm or magic might help. It did not, so we brought him here, and laid him out, so we could tell you as soon as possible."

Lady Maylis turned, standing, launching herself at Thessaly. "You come here, girl, and you..."

Thessaly took a deep breath and did the only sensible

thing in this moment. She'd been holding all her own emotions at bay, and now she let them rush in like a deep tide, pulling her under. The last thing she felt was arms catching her as she gave herself over to the darkness and collapsed in a faint.

32

LATER THAT EVENING

Eventually, the conversation picked up again, though slowly. They were down to three families and associated friends. The Hamiltons, who were fairly numerous, the Smythe-Clives, who weren't, and the Carringtons and Vitus, who were in the middle.

He did his part, making sure the conversation didn't falter into complete awkwardness. Eventually, Theo's mother - who was increasingly visibly nervous - asked Vitus about his travels in Europe. He was sure no one really cared about the answers. But it gave them plenty to discuss with coming anywhere near complicated questions like 'why have the Fortiers not come back' and 'where is everyone else'?

There were one or two Council Members visible again, those more recently on the Council themselves. But they were just as distracted. The staff, too, seemed unsettled, glancing quickly at any noise. This was not how things normally went. And it certainly wasn't a quick resolution. Vitus thought that Council Head Rowan had escorted the Fortiers out before six-thirty, but time went on, past half seven. Not too long after that, Council Head Rowan came out, looking entirely sombre, flanked by half a dozen of the Council Members.

The gong rang, calling everyone to silence - not that people hadn't fallen silent already. She spoke, her voice enhanced by a charm to fill the room. "I am sorry to announce that Childeric Fortier died during his Challenge. His family has returned to Arundel, and there will be information provided about the funeral arrangements to everyone here who might wish to attend. Condolences may be sent there, of course, as well. Here and now, we recognise he died here, in the heart of the Council Keep, and we are sorry for that. To the best of our knowledge, the others are still proceeding as expected. Please continue as you were, but let the staff know if you have any needs." That was it, nothing about the manner of death or anything other than the barest circumstances that were already obvious.

And, Vitus realised, thinking back through it, she had said they were sorry, but the whole thing rather lacked any great sorrow at Childeric's death. On the one hand, that was somewhat to be expected. He was not one of their number. On the other hand, several of the Council had ties of various kinds to the Fortiers. Vitus looked up, considering who he'd seen and who he hadn't. Both Hesperidon Warren and Fletcher Grimly hadn't come out with Hereswith. Nor had Owain Powell.

Nor had Thessaly, who was not actually a member of the Fortier family. Nor would she be. Then it hit him. Childeric Fortier was dead. She couldn't marry him. He couldn't threaten or hurt her anymore. He brought his hand up to muffle what must be visible on his face, then excused himself to one of the water closets off the main hall. The staff directed him to the one near the entrance, of course, not anywhere he might overhear anything.

Once he was alone in the water closet - or as alone as he could be, he was sure there were ways to monitor here - he let the water run, then stared at the mirror. Thessaly wasn't engaged anymore. Vitus wanted to shout for joy about it; he wanted to dance. He wanted there to be fireworks and illusion charms and a parade. None of that was remotely appropriate. There were people who had loved Childeric, or at least that was the impression he had from how Thessaly had talked about the family.

He wondered, now, how Childeric had died. Deaths happened in Challenges, but this had seemed unusual, even by those standards. Certainly, the announcement had been proper, formal, but also stilted. And Hereswith Rowan had been a diplomat before she was on the Council. The form of it certainly wasn't accidental.

Vitus couldn't linger too long, but the pause, outside of anyone's obvious oversight, had been enough to get him back and focused. He couldn't do much about Thessaly right now. He had to assume someone was seeing to her. With a tiny bit of luck, not anyone named Fortier. He could, however, talk to her as soon as she liked and see how she was doing. In the meantime, he had to go back out and find out what had happened with Theo. With, he hoped, a vastly better outcome, and not just for the professional reasons. He was starting to quite like Theo and his family, and he'd like to build the business relationship and friendship more in due course.

By the time he'd emerged, there had been a change. Irene Hamilton had reappeared, looking rather unsettled, but entirely in one piece and not apparently damaged. As he sat down, murmuring a slight excuse, Rhea leaned over. "She just came out. Not successful, obviously, and there's a rather long ashy mark along her hip. You can't see it now. I don't think she had an easy time."

"Thank you." Vitus considered. "I suppose if it were a walk in the park, it wouldn't be called a Challenge, would it? She doesn't seem happy, though."

Rhea shook her head, and then picked up with a question about Vitus's visit to the mines in Germany, and about his visits throughout Italy. Maybe twenty minutes later - they were now at about eight - the double doors opened again. Theo walked down the central aisle, steadily, not looking like he'd had a difficult time physically. He made a slight bow as he turned into the chairs where his family were, embracing his mother, then shaking his father's hand, before Rhea launched herself into a hug. He patted her on the shoulder. "I'm entirely all right. Not successful, but I'm fine."

Once he took a step back, he added, focusing on Vitus. "They told me about Childeric when I came out. Nothing like that for me, but the talisman was quite useful, saved me from a nasty misstep. I owe you, Vitus, and I'll be glad to talk about additional work." Theo glanced back toward the doors, then up toward where the tower stairs must be. "And maybe, in due course, another try. Though perhaps not for a few years."

It was enigmatic, of course, but the Challenge was a ritual mystery. One couldn't expect either sense or details. Vitus offered his hand for a handshake. "I'm glad you came through well. Sit, please, can I get food or drink for you? The staff have been very attentive."

Theo nodded, mentioned a few things, and Vitus went off to find one of the staff and ask about them. He wanted to give Theo a few minutes with his family. If Theo was out, and Irene Hamilton, that meant Cyrus Smythe-Clive would possibly - probably, hopefully - be successful. But of course, there had also been instances where no one was successful. That hadn't happened for rather longer.

By the time he came back, food and some tea were in process, Theo waved him into a chair. "Mama asked, and I thought you'd be interested in the answer. She wondered if I had any idea while I was in there. And no, we were quite separate. I suppose it's possible that there might be a way to have us interact, but it wasn't like that at all. It was, hm. How do I put this? Designed for my mind, my way of being in the world. That's where the talisman came in so handy."

"I'd wondered when you'd made your original decisions. But as I said then, better to draw on your strengths, for one thing. And for another, I suppose it might be the sort of thing where the attitude you bring in with you is relevant." Vitus spoke carefully, especially at the end.

Theo nodded, looking pleased someone had said it, maybe. "Just so. And now I'm relieved, I've learned a bit more. We'll see about the future. Do we think Cyrus is likely to appear at any point soon? The waiting's hard."

It must be. Sitting around waiting seemed like a particular punishment. The people who made it this far tended to be more than a bit high-strung, rather like a racehorse. They wanted to be doing, or getting on with the next thing, not waiting for some unknown moment. Being patient, being visibly patient, was yet another strain at the end of a day filled with so much else.

That was the point at which food and tea appeared, and Theo dug in, rather obviously famished. Whatever else he'd done, he'd likely done a fair bit of magical work. Vitus knew enough about what that looked like in the aftermath. It was about another twenty minutes, then finally, the doors opened again.

Hereswith Rowan came out, with Cyrus Smythe-Clive

beside her. He looked startled, in a way Theo had not, in a way Irene had not. He wasn't just quiet. While she spoke, he was unusually still.

"I am pleased to announce that Cyrus Smythe-Clive will join us as the newest member of Albion's Council. We welcome him now, as we will continue to welcome him in the coming days. We thank Irene Hamilton and Theo Carrington for their willingness to Challenge. At such time there is another open seat, we would be glad to have you come to us again as a Challenger. Now, one moment of blessing, before I let you all go." At that point, she switched first into Latin, then into what Vitus was fairly sure was Old Welsh. He didn't speak the latter, not enough to do this on the fly, but he thought the basic shape of the blessing was the same. The words rolled out, and it was a bit like a blanket across the land, immediately nearby and further away.

When she finished, there were three echoing sounds from the bell, and then Cyrus was greeted by each of his new colleagues. They'd all lined up. Everyone else applauded, then waited for the greetings to be over. Finally, Council Head Rowan had one last word for him, then Cyrus was coming down the central aisle to greet his family.

His sister met him part way there, her skirt flaring behind her. She hadn't quite run, but it was a near thing. She flung her arms around him, hugging him tight, and Vitus looked away. It was a raw moment, an intimate one.

Then, and only then, did people start filing out. Theo shook his hand one more time. "We'll find a time for you to come round for supper. Not this week, maybe in a fortnight? Let me know if there are good days for you when you get a chance." Then they were off, and Vitus was left alone, letting the Challengers and their families go first. He could wait for the portal.

He did move down toward the end of the hall. That meant the staff could clean up, and the Council members could do whatever it was they did after this sort of thing. He was standing there, waiting for the last of the Hamiltons to gather up their cloaks and such, when he heard a cough by his shoulder. "Any message for Thessaly, when I get a chance?"

Vitus glanced over. "Council Member Powell." Thessaly's cousin smiled slightly, and now Vitus had to figure out what to say. "I wouldn't want to intrude, in a complicated time, but if she would like to speak to me, she knows how to reach me." He considered, then added, "I wish her the best, of course, in all ways, and especially in such a time."

That made the Council Member laugh. "Well said. Ah, there we go. I think everyone else who's leaving now is settled. Have a good night, Master Deschamps."

Vitus nodded, and he could tell a dismissal when he heard one. The last thing he saw of the Keep was a couple of people standing in the doorway, silhouetted against the light. He thought that was Owain Powell and Hereswith Rowan, but he couldn't be entirely sure.

33

THE NEXT MORNING

Thessaly woke up with a bit of a start, jolted to alertness by realising she was not in her own bed. Then it rushed in, everything that had happened last night, and she turned to bury her face in a pillow or blanket or something, before what she felt could show. She must be at Arundel, if she wasn't at home. That made a horrible and terrifying sort of sense.

There was a cough from what was now behind her back. "It's fine." Emeline's voice was dry. "You needn't pretend things you don't feel. How are you?"

"Where am I?" It seemed an entirely relevant question. That Emeline was here, however, was promising. That Emeline said she didn't need to pretend was more so. It was Emeline's job to be aware of the charms and enchantments on the room or in the room or on Thessaly herself. Thessaly pushed herself up on one elbow. She was wearing a long nightgown that wasn't hers, her hair was braided loosely. She felt as if she had slept for hours and hours, the sort of sleep that left you achy from not moving at all.

"Your cousin Owain Powell's home. I'm sorry, I don't know how to say the Welsh properly." Emeline flushed.

"There's something you don't know? I am actually shocked! Hen-aelwyd, it means 'old hearth'." Thessaly sat up properly. "Wait, how did I even get here? I remember..." That rushed back, how Lady Maylis had been, how it had been a deliberate decision to faint. It had been that or terror, honestly, and terror hadn't seemed like it would help anything. Well, terror or fury, and Thessaly was still reserving fury as a later option.

"I think that's where I should let the Council Member know that you're awake. It's about half-nine. You were asleep throughout the night, other than a bad dream or two. And I can sort a breakfast tray. Would you prefer tea and toast or something substantial?"

"Substantial, please." She'd barely eaten last night, and not that much at luncheon, either. Right now, she was absolutely famished.

"Just a few minutes. It's the same room you had before, I gather, if you need the bathing room or water closet." At that, Emeline disappeared. By the comment, that meant she was pleased with the warding, and Thessaly could be trusted to make use of either without risk. Thessaly did, in fact, do both.

Someone had thoughtfully left a dressing gown. Thessaly thought it was Aunt Tegwen's. It was the shades of purple she liked. She put it on, then used the water closet before washing her face and re-braiding her hair. The dress she'd been wearing the night before was hanging on a screen to the side of the room as she came back in. She had no desire to put it on before she had to.

Then she swore. She'd have to wear mourning dress again. For months. She'd have to pretend she was actually sorry that Childeric was dead, any time she showed her nose outside her own property. That was going to be miserable. It wasn't just the funeral, she could have managed the specific events that came with that. It would be everything else.

She'd settled on the bed, the blankets over her lap, by the time there was a knock on the door. "Come in?"

That revealed Cousin Owain, accompanied by a maid with a breakfast tray. The maid set the tray down, and then bobbed and disappeared back out the door. Cousin Owain nodded. "Do you need anything else for the moment? Or may we talk? How do you feel?" She nodded, and he closed the door. She felt the warding shift, but he waited until she'd had a few bites of food.

It was a somewhat complex question to answer, not least because it depended whether he was asking about her body or her heart. After a bit of restorative sausage, she had an answer. "Some aches, nothing significant. Confused, though of course I remember being told that Childeric was dead and that scene, up until I fainted. I would very much like information, please, cousin." Thessaly added the last, obligingly.

He waited until she'd had a few more bites of food, enough to take the immediate edge off her hunger. There were eggs, sausage, laverbread in little fried cakes, and hiding under the lid, scones. And tea. She had a whole small pot for herself. She poured and drank a little, then looked up. "Thank you. For - I didn't expect to find myself here."

"They wanted to take you to Arundel, and I was having none of that. I was sure you wouldn't want it, for one thing, and for another..." He winced, then pulled up a chair beside the bed. "You will go carefully now, please? I am glad to advise, if you wish, or Hereswith is as well. Others of your aunt's friends, if you like."

"You're not asking me if I'm grieving or sorry or I don't even know how to put it. I'm sure I'll hear the assumptions soon enough." Thessaly let out a breath. "What happened?"

"You are free, but not yet safe, there. That's a good way to put it. I know you're not grieving. Whatever you might have felt sorry about, I'm sure he crushed." Cousin Owain paused, lifting a finger while he thought. "We don't know, honestly. Not much more than you do, Hereswith told you most of it. They all entered. He was the last one in. Fifteen minutes later, at the most, his body was on the landing, soaked. You saw his chest?"

She nodded once.

"We saw that too. And we've no idea what it means. The others came out, then Cyrus." His expression shifted slightly. "You were the same year at school. I would very much, before next Wednesday when we meet, like to learn more about him, whatever you feel you can share. He was - honestly, the bets were about even between Childeric and Theo Carrington."

"Was Carrington all right?" That was a key question, because it might tell her something about Vitus.

"Quite well. I hope he makes a Challenge in the future, he had the right sort of attitude. And he was pleasant about the whole thing. Quite a few people aren't, which has always rather confused me. For all the mystery and awe of the thing, we are - if someone succeeds - colleagues and peers. You'd think rudeness wouldn't be the way to start that off, and whoever's challenging is certainly not in a suitable position for a duel for power." He cleared his throat. "I had a word with Vitus Deschamps. He wishes you the best in all ways, at such a time. He made it clear he did not wish to intrude, but that you know how to reach him if you'd like to speak to him. I assume you'll be sending around a note as soon as you know when your presence is commanded at Arundel?"

Thessaly grimaced. "Yes. I— that's rather a lot to think about. It's going to be awful. It already is awful, his family, it's going to continue being." She tilted her head, had a bite of sausage while she was thinking. "Was Lady Maylis as, as overwrought as I remember?"

"More so, probably. I think you missed about half of it. There was screeching. I feel sorry for her, it must be an awful experience. But that was an entirely proper and well-considered faint of yours. It gave us all the excuse we needed to see you tended to separately. I was able to get you back here, and then Emeline could be a help. She's quite a good choice. Keep her around, close at hand, for the foreseeable future."

"You think there's still risk." Thessaly half-closed her eyes. "It'll take me a bit to think through it. They don't have a hold on me anymore, and none of them will like that at all."

"More than that," Owain leaned forward, touching his fingertips, "People who are that badly hurt lash out. They might or might not actually mean to, but it hurts all the same." There was a note in his voice that made Thessaly look at him searchingly. He flicked one of his fingers. "All of us on the Council have had that kind of experience, I think. If not before we join, not terribly long after. That's part of why I'd like to know more about Cyrus in advance. I'd like to better understand where he is in that grief and change and how much he feels he's drowning in it."

Thessaly was suddenly certain that Cousin Owain had

lost someone he loved dearly, and she had absolutely no idea who. She'd not have heard about a romance at Schola or something of the kind when he was quite young, but she'd never heard a whisper. After a moment, she said, gently, "I am very sorry for your loss, whoever it was, cousin."

His mouth twitched. "That, you can say with honesty and care, and I thank you for it." He shrugged. "Not a tale for today, nor for a bit, I think. It has thorns." Then he resolutely turned the conversation back on course. "You'll have to figure out how to deal with your parents, too. I've had a note from both of them, separately. If you'd like to see them, we can arrange that here. If you wish to claim you are still overwrought, we can do that. What would you prefer?"

"I would like to go home. To Bryn Glas." Thessaly considered. "Once we've finished talking. And I suppose I need to see about a mourning dress, something for this. I do not expect to be going out much for the coming months, I think. I am not inclined to wear the visible signs of what I'm not actually feeling more than I have to." Thessaly coughed. "I may be an illusionist by training, but that is a bit much."

It made Owain chuckle, and that made her happy, because his expression when they'd touched on grief had been painful. "We can arrange some private gatherings here, with those who would understand. Or if you'd like some neutral space to speak with either of your parents. Hermia is a different matter. But I'd prefer you only spoke with your mother or father in a thoroughly warded room, like the downstairs parlour or the one we used last time."

"I appreciate that. I don't want to let either Mother or Father into the warding at Bryn Glas." She grimaced.

“They’re going to want me to get engaged again as soon as is proper.”

“They are.” Owain folded his hands again now. “I am glad to assist if I can, but there is, in fact, a limit to my power and influence. If you wanted to be sent on some Council task to some distant place, we could probably arrange that, but that only puts off the problem, not resolves it. Metaia gave you a great gift, but people will come sniffing around it, even if it is yours and only yours.” He hesitated. “I’m not asking about how you feel about Deschamps. That’s unfair, this morning.”

“We might talk about it later, though.” Thessaly offered it as a token of understanding. “Right now, I— how do I play things with the Fortiers?”‘

“Visible grief, all the markers of it. Use the veil to your advantage in company, and whatever illusions wouldn’t draw attention. Be scrupulous about your protections, including checking your food and drink. Do you have a good source for the protective lotions for bare skin, or charms for it? Hereswith has someone, I’m sure.”

“I’m sure Magistra Hereswith manages much of her own,” Thessaly pointed out. She was a specialist in Incantation, that was a help there. “I’ll think about what would work best. Especially if I’m expected to stay overnight again.”

“Not an easy road.” Owain glanced up. “I should let you eat, and if you wish to return home, we can lend you a wrapper for the purpose. It’s not as if anyone will see you going to or from the portal, this end or that, but trusted staff and family. Send a note when you know what the Fortiers are demanding of you, and I am glad to have a Healer confirm you should not strain yourself. You, of course, may define what strain includes.”

Thessaly nodded. “I appreciate that very much. Please,

if you don't mind, on the wrapper." She added after a moment, "And please thank Cook for me. I am not doing justice to her food." It made Cousin Owain smile again. He stood, bending to kiss Thessaly on the forehead.

"Let me go put things in motion. You should be able to go home in twenty minutes."

34

SEPTEMBER 27TH AT ARUNDEL

Childeric Fortier's funeral wasn't until the following Friday. Vitus wasn't at all sure why it had taken quite that long - three days would have been more usual. Besides everything else, it meant he hadn't been able to see Thessaly, or even exchange more than a note or two. She'd written on the Monday, saying she expected to be ordered to be at Arundel much of the week. She didn't know when she'd be home.

She had included a little more than that. That she was all right, but not at all looking forward to the necessary obligations. Thessaly had hinted things had gone rather badly during the announcement, but Vitus wasn't sure how to ask. Certainly he did not know how to do that in a note. None of his training in rhetoric or composition quite covered inquiring about the death of one's beloved's undesired fiancé under mysterious circumstances.

He had written back, of course. Vitus had reassured her he hoped she was doing well, at least, and offering some ideas for talismans that might be of help in due course. He'd finished with the simple desire to see her when it was possible, if she also wanted.

None of this made being at the funeral any easier. Both Mama and Papa were attending as well. Papa needed to. Vitus stuck close to them. Papa had been to a number of previous funerals in the family, and had shared the outline of their customs. And the Fortiers expected many people to attend. Including, it seemed, those like Vitus who might well not have been on the invitation list for any other event. There were hundreds here, at the least, many of them just as unsure what to do next.

The estate had been opened up, with footmen at the portal to direct those attending down the long line of trees, down the drive. Everyone had been assembled in a long row, lining both sides of the drive to the cemetery. Vitus wondered - he didn't know if he'd ever seen one - if there had once been a chapel in the manor house. Perhaps it had long since been turned into something else.

He could see that the main entrance was draped with lengths of flowing black silk, shadowing the doorway, but also making it stand starkly against the rest of the house. He thought he could just barely see a movement or two inside, from the great hall, but it was impossible to tell for sure. Vitus was standing there, his parents next to him, when he heard a voice on his other side. "Do you mind if I stand here?"

He blinked. It was Council Head Rowan, apparently by herself, not with any of the other Council Members or, for that matter, her husband. Vitus nodded. "Of course, Magistra. Please." Then he glanced around. "I noticed a number of the Council Members are here."

"Most of us. It seemed the thing." Her voice was quiet, and he suspected she might be employing a charm to keep it that way. "Were you wondering about the custom? Were you at Vauquelin's funeral, near five years ago?"

Vitus shook his head. "Mama and Papa came." He nodded to his left, where they were in equally quiet conversation with someone Papa knew well. "I did not, though. Now—" He hesitated. "I was there, of course, on Sunday. It seemed relevant."

Her mouth turned up just slightly. She was wearing black silk, not formal mourning on her own part, but the sort of dress one wore to a funeral when it wasn't a personal grief. "I paid my respects, in this case, inside. The coffin is laid out in the great hall. They've kept vigil the past days. Other than that, their custom is rather isolated. Each of the family eating in their own rooms, not speaking above a whisper when they need to say anything. The women of the house have been sewing the shroud, in various parts. That's also a common enough custom."

Vitus considered the particular horror that might be for Thessaly, isolated but where it would be quickly obvious if she didn't do her part in the sewing. He winced, once. "And the men? Is there a custom there?"

Again, Magistra Rowan's mouth shifted, just slightly. "Stoic silence and drinking, mostly. Or, here, it's a landed estate, walking the bounds. That is both tradition and gets one out of the house. I can understand why they might." Then she nodded. "Ah, there. It begins." She nodded towards the manor, where a hearse had drawn up, the black horses wearing great black feather plumes. They had pulled up far enough that those watching - at least at that end of the rows of people - could see the coffin carried out, feet first. Vitus could see Lord Clovis, Sigbert, and the other men of the family. He didn't know them all by sight.

Fortunately for him, Magistra Rowan did, and she shared the names. "That is Bradamante's husband, Yves

Nevill." She was the sister between Lord Clovis and Dagobert in age. "And all three of her sons-in-law. The Percys came from France. That might be the reason for the delay." Vitus nodded. Now she'd given him the certainty, Vitus could make out Hugo Percy, Lucas Mortimer, and Amalric Howard. Howard was the only one of the three he knew at all well. He'd been the year between Vitus and Childeric himself at Schola, and he was a gifted specialist in Incantation. They'd ended up with a number of the same lectures, especially Vitus's last year or two at school.

Behind them came Dagobert, leaning on a cane, with Lady Maylis on one side. Laudine was just behind, walking with the Dowager Lady Chrodechildis, and Thessaly behind them, all on her own, followed by Bradamante and her daughters. They slowly, painfully slowly, put the coffin into the hearse, sliding it into place, and then the carriage moved forward, leaving them as a procession. Now it was Lady Maylis and Lord Clovis directly behind the hearse, then Sigbert and his grandmother, then the others, the husbands escorting their wives. Thessaly was left awkwardly on her own, followed by Bradamante and Yves, then Dagobert and Laudine, and finally the rest of the family.

Thessaly was taking small steps, but of course she was veiled, and he couldn't tell much from her posture at this distance. At least he wasn't staring at her, rather at the whole procession, winding around the drive, down to the road that cut across. As the procession moved, he saw another figure, entirely in black, appear from the side of the house. That was, he was fairly sure, Henut Landry. She had a right, though she wasn't family, of course.

The hearse went by, from Vitus's right to his left. Slowly, the people on the far end of the row began falling into place, in pairs or small groups. Everyone was utterly silent. He could hear boots and shoes on the gravel of the drive.

It was his turn, or rather his and Magistra Rowan's - she hadn't moved, had sought no one else. After a moment's hesitation, he offered her his arm politely, and she took it. Mama and Papa joined them, and the procession inched forward. It was not a terribly long walk to the cemetery, where the hearse had been pulled up to one side of the entrance. People filled in the space all around the wrought iron fencing, to see what happened.

Just as painstakingly, the pallbearers brought the coffin out of the hearse, halfway down a row to an open grave. The dirt was mounded up to the side, waiting to be filled in again, and Vitus could suddenly smell the dampness of it. It had stormed here last night. There was still a hint of the rain on stone and a stronger scent of ozone. The six men processed, just as silently, to the grave, and the gravediggers lowered it in, using magic, naturally. The women had followed, standing in a line like statues, their faces all invisible behind their veils, though everyone could see Lady Maylis's shoulders were shaking.

He'd expected something like a procession past the grave, or perhaps some words spoken. Instead, two footmen came out, bearing a moderately sized axe, the other a large glass container of wine. The axe was presented formally, with a bow, to Lord Clovis. A moment later, Vitus could see the lid of the coffin brought up, again with magic, and then he was bending, lowering the axe into the grave. Next, he turned to his wife, and she shook her head, enough everyone could see. Lord Clovis then poured wine into the grave, or perhaps something in the coffin, handing the empty jar back to the footman.

Two others came forward then, each holding a basket, also black, with draping folds of black silk. Lord Clovis took something from it, brought whatever it was to his lips, and then tossed it lightly into the grave. Vitus blinked, glancing at Magistra Rowan, but she shook her head, obviously also visibly puzzled. The other family then came forward, one at a time, pausing and taking something from the basket, then doing the same.

Vitus couldn't stop watching Thessaly. She seemed entirely alone there. No one was paying her much heed. Not, really, that was very different from anything she'd described when Childeric was alive. Her parents and sister must be somewhere in the crowd, but he didn't see them, and he didn't think they'd be much support. Or at least not other than Hermia, who might be overwhelmed by all the complexity here.

Henut Landry was near the front of the ordinary mourners, she'd inserted herself tidily into the flow, but none of the Fortiers seemed to say anything to her, nor she to them. When she came to the head of the line, she held out her hand, palm up, to indicate she did not need whatever was in the basket. Stepping to the side of the grave, she nodded her head once, and tossed an item in. There was a brief hiss of a whisper, Lord Clovis twisting his head toward Sigbert, both of them watching Magistra Landry intently now. As the next man came up behind her, she moved to one side, making her way like a stately black ship out of legend to the far end of the cemetery. No one stopped her, at least. Likely, everyone had enough sense not to try.

Then, it became clear that everyone in attendance was expected to follow the custom. Step forward, take whatever it was from the basket, make whatever final blessing or comment they wished to make, and toss it lightly into the grave. Then each moved to the side and to the next path between the graves, back out to the drive, until all the other people had done the same.

When it came time for Vitus's turn, he finally got a look at what the objects were. They were tiny bees, made of copper. He rolled the one he'd taken through his fingers, judging it to have been made by a mould, and quickly. He could feel the edges hadn't been tumbled or smoothed in some other way. That was another reason for the delay, then, if they didn't keep such things on hand.

When Vitus bent over the grave, Childeric's body was covered, fully shrouded, which was a blessing. More of one for Thessaly, though presumably they hadn't covered his head, at least, until just before the funeral. Vitus noticed, too, a few gleams of gold and silver inside the coffin. Those must have been the bees from the family. He tossed his in lightly, then stepped away. He was guided through the cemetery to the other side, where there was a line.

Now, he had to make the entirely proper condolences. He managed them in French, after hearing a few people before him do the same. It felt less personal to him, and it meant he kept to the proper formal words, with no chance of misspeaking. He worked his way down, until he reached Thessaly, just before Childeric's cousins and their husbands. Of course, he didn't speak anything other than the most proper words in English, "My best wishes in this difficult time."

Of course he couldn't actually see her expression, and she didn't offer a hand— she hadn't been, he'd noticed that. But she did nod slightly as he moved down to the others. Once he was through the line, the guests were directed to rows of tables, chairs, and simple foods. That was a more common custom, given the need to wait. No one talked much, though Vitus could hear a few people wonder more about the circumstances.

It would obviously be rude to depart before everyone had paid their respects. Vitus found a chair at a table well out of the way and left his parents to the quiet conversations they wanted to have. He could see Cyrus Smythe-Clive with his sister, at another of the more remote tables. She had her hand on his forearm, whispering, and he looked more shaken than Vitus would have expected.

Vitus set himself to the moderately interesting mental problem of how he would design such bee tokens, perhaps with an additional layer of magical benefit, taken as an entire group. It would keep him from doing anything foolish, like talking to Thessaly.

35

LATER THAT MORNING

The last three days had, frankly, been rather like hell. The Fortiers had made it clear her presence was nigh essential. Essential, in this case, turned out to mean hours alone in the guest room she'd been assigned, including all her meals. Emeline had been largely exiled to the servants' hall, except for bringing Thessaly's meals and helping with her bath each day. As well as being present when Thessaly was sitting vigil downstairs. That had not permitted any conversation, however.

The whole of it was awful. The vigil was worst, being with Childeric's body in the Great Hall for four hours at a time, each of them taking it in turn. She wasn't able to move, barely to breathe, in case someone else in the family came by. She did her best to focus her eyes on the floor, well below the coffin and bier, and to repeat duelling figures in her head. When that failed her, she counted up by prime numbers, then down by a Fibonacci sequence.

At least now he was dead, he didn't leave her spent from the sheer strain of having to manage his moods, his threats, and his presence. She had not slept well, the last few nights, but the nightmares had gone, and so had that unending sense of fundamental exhaustion that had been here on her previous visits. The land felt odd, what little she could sense of it, but not hollow and drained. The leaves were still browning around the edges, but she supposed a few days - in September, no less - was not a time for quick changes in the foliage.

When she was not in the Great Hall, she could not lose herself in reading. No, she had yards of sewing to do. She had been given a long length of shroud to hem and seam, and she knew each stitch had to be perfect. The tiny, matched, even stitches processed down yards of fabric, making perfect French seams. It was not as if Childeric would be bothered by an uncovered seam against his skin, but Lady Chrodechildis certainly would be.

She'd hoped when she finished what they'd given her, that would be the end of it, but no, there were other things to sew. Hems, just as neat, for silk to be hung by the doors, for additional covers for the household's mirrors. No one had told her why or much of anything at all. That was at least consistent of them. But she suspected moths or something of the kind had got to some of the covers used for the late Lord Vauquelin.

When she was not sewing, she lay in bed, mostly staring at the ceiling. She had not dared to bring the stone talisman with her, and her sleep was full of uneven dreams. The one joy of the whole thing was waking and knowing that whatever this was, it was temporary. She was doing the correct thing, because it was a kindness and it would keep her safer in the long term. And the Fortiers missed Childeric, even if Thessaly did not.

There were deep undercurrents. She did not understand any of them, and of course no Fortier was explaining anything. Even Laudine, though Laudine had not really had any chance. Whoever had made up the schedule of vigils had made sure that they never succeeded each other. Thessaly came after Sigbert and before Dagobert, in some arcane pattern. And Dagobert had not spoken to her at all, beyond a silent nod.

Thessaly could retreat after the funeral, and hole up in a house that was hers, and figure out what came next. She could read something she enjoyed, she could invite those she trusted to come and talk. She could do many things not permitted to a woman mourning her fiancé.

Some of what she considered when she couldn't sleep was exactly how long to visibly mourn for. There was, so far as she knew, no fixed period for this. She'd have to consult the current etiquette guides and someone else experienced, preferably not Mother. It depended on what was decorous, how much she wanted to indicate she loved him, and all that. She would like not to demarcate anything of the kind, but that was a very poor choice. She refused to limit her future options that way.

When the day of the funeral came, breakfast was a bare minimum of toast and tea and a little broth. Thessaly eyed it warily, fairly certain it implied that a little further fainting was required in the day and they were glad to help it along. Fortunately, Emeline promptly produced a couple of hard-boiled eggs, some cheese, and an apple from pockets under her skirt, and Thessaly near inhaled them.

By the time one of the Fortier maids appeared to see if they needed anything, Thessaly was fully dressed. Emeline was finishing sewing the veil into place in Thessaly's braided and coiled hair. That ensured it would not come loose in a gust of wind. The bonnet went on over it. Still in silence, Thessaly was escorted downstairs, nodding briefly to the other women waiting. She certainly did not know what to say. Oh, she'd managed the proper condolences when she had seen Lady Maylis and Lord Clovis, and then to the others, but that had been brief and expected words. She'd been afraid Lady Maylis would turn up in her room at some hour in the early morning, wanting to cry on her shoulder, and at least that hadn't happened.

Now, she waited her turn, awkwardly and uncertainly. The others all knew how this went. It was their family custom, and all of them had been familiar with Lord Vauquelin's funeral five years ago. Thessaly followed their lead, through the procession, into the cemetery, into being told to take a small silver bee and toss it into the grave. She'd stood in line, through hundreds upon hundreds of people.

Most of it seemed to go as the Fortiers had expected, except for the matter of Magistra Landry. Where everyone else - including the Fortiers - had taken a bee from the baskets, Magistra Landry had brought her own. And hers had been undeniably gold, impossible to mistake, given how close Thessaly had been expected to be to the grave itself. She had not, however, heard whatever it was Lord Clovis said to Sigbert, she had been too occupied - along with Laudine - making certain Lady Maylis did not collapse in a faint.

Finally, she'd been released to go sit quietly at the head table. Emeline brought her food, but eating under the veil was tricky. Very few people approached her. Vitus wouldn't, of course, or at least she hoped he had more sense. The brief word in line had been more than she'd expected. Garin had not been made to stand through the whole procession, but she had seen him brought out by his tutor. He'd had time to pay his respects when most people had done so, then been taken inside again.

She was sitting, looking off toward a bit of far-distant green, when there was a cough. She looked up to see Cyrus

Smythe-Clive standing, his hands folded. "Pardon, I did not mean to disturb you."

He was wearing full mourning, unlike many of the men who were wearing some amount of black or a black armband, but not a fully black suit and accoutrements. "Cyrus." Thessaly made the comment as gentle as she could. "You're not interrupting at all."

"I wanted to offer you my condolences directly." He glanced down, then unexpectedly met her gaze. "I am sure you must miss him tremendously, and I know how awkward people have been with me. If you ever wish to talk to someone who understands more of that. Who is, well, young enough?"

Thessaly blinked several times, feeling like every direction had a snare. Cyrus was not, on the whole, prone to social games for power or entrapment. He never had been, and she didn't think that had changed. He was certainly competent, socially, if not always entirely in the same league as some of the Great Families who had honed the skills from birth. Now she took a breath. "You are very kind to think of me, Cyrus. I appreciate that no end." Then she saw her way through it. "It is a different situation than you and Tanith."

Cyrus glanced down at his hands, and she suddenly realised she hadn't seen him in anything except black and white since Tanith's death. She hadn't seen him often, mind, and it was a little more of a trick to tell with men's clothes. Men weren't expected to make it visible for years, not like women who were widowed. "Oh. I beg your pardon, then."

He sounded - and looked - suddenly hurt. Thessaly reached out to touch his hand, glove to skin. "Please. I appreciate you thought to talk to me. And perhaps we might speak more, at some point. I'm sorry people have left you, made you feel alone, about Tanith."

Thessaly had been one of them, though to be fair, she'd had a number of obligations in the time since Tanith's death. Even beyond her own flailing at what to say at such gaping grief. "May I ask how Gemma is doing?" She blessed the newspaper pieces for reminding her of his daughter's name. She'd otherwise have been worried she'd flubbed it. "Oh, and my congratulations, as well. I'm sure there are good reasons you prevailed. I know you well enough to know you want to do the thing right."

He flushed again, but the question about his daughter held him. "She is a delight. Just beginning to figure out walking, holding onto hands. Nanny suspects she'll manage it on the early side, given how she's going at it now. Very stubborn."

"She gets that from both of you." Tanith had been two years behind them, also in Fox House. There were a couple of deeply ridiculous tales from her year, the sort of necessary and fearsome grudges that only Fox House could manage. Cyrus didn't tend that direction, but once he'd made a decision, he was hard to shake from it. Which might well be why he'd succeeded in his Challenge. "I'm glad she's doing well. I'm glad you are too."

Cyrus looked up at her again, and this time, there was a little of the expression she remembered from their time at school. "Better than I was, thank you." He then touched his hat. "I shouldn't take up more of your time. Perhaps when you are up for accepting an invitation, let me know? Andie and I would be glad to have you for tea and you could meet Gemma."

Thessaly nodded. "I'm glad she's keeping an eye on you." Andie, his sister, had been doing that since the Challenge, she was sure. "And I would be delighted to meet

Gemma if we can arrange something in due course." She then saw Lady Maylis watching her. "Thank you, again. I should check with the family, I think."

"Of course." Cyrus excused himself, gracefully enough. Thessaly was considering how to throw herself into the fray again when she saw Sigbert approaching.

"Maman was concerned that he was being difficult. I hope not?" Sigbert did not look terribly well. Unrelieved black did not suit him, for one thing. "How awkward of him to talk to you. Do I need to have a word with someone?"

"Oh, no. Please don't. We were the same year at Schola together, and both in Fox, of course." She was fairly sure everyone had actually forgotten that. "He offered quite proper condolences. And it is not as if others were waiting to speak to me."

"Mmm." Sigbert offered his arm. "Maman would like a word. She hopes you might stay another night, now the formalities are over."

"Oh." Thessaly swallowed. "I— I am sure it would be a comfort to her, but it's been so difficult being here. I see him everywhere, here, everything he touched."

"I suppose that must be a challenge. Let us see if we can persuade Maman to let you go, then." Sigbert was, it seemed, positioning himself as a defender. It was far too little too late, for one thing— not that he'd have gone against his older brother. But she also wasn't at all sure about what it implied. Now, he escorted her over to Lady Maylis and Lord Clovis without further comment.

36

SEPTEMBER 28TH AT BRYN GLAS

Vitus was not at all sure what to expect. Thessaly's note had been waiting for him when he got back from the funeral, and he did not know how she'd managed that. He hadn't tried to talk to her, of course, not with every single Fortier - and a few who no longer had that surname - watching closely. Watching her, particularly closely, he'd thought, though she also hadn't been exactly included.

Now, it was eleven on the Saturday. He had stopped in Trellech for a few things. His bag held a handful of books, some cheerful flowers, and a couple of stones to see if any of them suited her desires for another talisman. He'd tucked everything but the flowers in his satchel. Then he'd hopped around the country by portal, including up to Edinburgh, before coming back to Bryn Glas. He was right on time, and he came around from the portal to find Thessaly standing at the gate, just on the other side, with Emeline behind her.

Before he could say anything, Thessaly opened the gate, and then she was running at him. He had just enough time to see she wasn't wearing anything remotely black. There were folds of glorious peacock teal, the flash of a well-cut labradorite, over a glowing daffodil yellow undergown. The two did not particularly suit her complexion, and it did not matter at all.

Besides, by that point, she was right there, hesitating suddenly, before he opened his arms and Thessaly flung herself into them. He hadn't touched her like this at all, not with all her energy and solid desire behind it. Also, he realised suddenly, absolutely no corset or bustle. She buried her face against his shoulder and Vitus just did his best to be steady. Finally, she pulled back to look at him. "Sorry."

"Don't be sorry." He did not know how to put the next part, that she could, that she was free to, that she chose to. That got him far enough. "I'm honoured that you're choosing to share your freedom with me."

It made her snort, the sort of sound that was half a laugh and half more complicated. "You don't think it's an insult?" She pulled back enough to take his hand - hers were ungloved, as well as the colours.

"I think you are at home, and you have earned every bit of your choice here, ten times over." Vitus let her tug him along back to the gate, and then through it. "The very opposite of mourning. You are the bright noon sun, and make me think of amber and topaz, labradorite and aquamarine." Then he considered. "Also alexandrite. It changes colour under different light."

That made her laugh and squeeze her hand. Once she'd closed the gate, she nodded at Emeline. "I don't plan to go out today. I'll let you know if I need anything." Emeline nodded and disappeared, walking swiftly back across the grass toward the back of the house. "Will you come in? I don't know where to start, not at all."

"Of course." Vitus lifted the flowers. "These are for

you, if there's a vase handy? I thought you might like something cheerful, not lilies and such."

Thessaly turned to him, beaming. "They will go well in the library. Or upstairs." Then she considered. "Perhaps you might come upstairs?" Now she was shy again. "There's a sitting room, there. I'm still getting used to thinking of it as mine."

"You haven't had terribly long to make it yours, have you? I gathered you'd been out at Arundel all week, as well as everything else." Thessaly made a sour face, nodding. "I would like, very much, to see your sitting room. Also to sit in it."

Without saying much more, she led him by the hand, back to the door, then up the stairs. They went down a narrow hall, into a space that took up the entire side of the house. Half was a sitting room, the other - he could see right into it - was her bedroom. Vitus shivered, squeezing her hand again. "Are you sure?"

"That I would much rather have you up here than..." Thessaly tilted her head to the side. "Than anyone else. Not just Childeric. That's a low bar, indeed." She tugged him along to the sitting room. "There's a vase, there, there's a bathing room through there." She pointed through the bedroom. "On the left. It's a ridiculous size."

Vitus took his instructions, leaving his satchel as Thessaly moved around the room, adjusting something or other. The sitting room was all bright colours, the same as what he'd seen previously downstairs, all vibrant. In the bedroom, the bedding on the bed was a bit darker. But the walls had an Arts and Crafts design in leaves of dark green on a blue ground, with red and golden berries to accent.

The bathroom was absolutely Metaia's choice of colours. There was much more of the teal and blue and gold here, like he'd stepped into some underwater kingdom. He filled the vase, feeling entirely underdressed for the occasion. Then he brought it back out, adding the flowers and spacing them a little before setting it back where the vase had been. That had pride of place on a side table Thessaly could see from anywhere in the room.

She had claimed the sofa, or rather half of it, her skirts tucked in on one side. Just to be sure, he nodded. "May I join you?"

"I was— would you?" Thessaly looked up. "I'm feeling terribly forward."

Vitus had to swallow a sound he shouldn't make, near enough a moan. He knew enough to be sure they had to talk first, to make sure she wasn't just flinging herself at someone very unlike Childeric. Mind, Vitus was rather proud of being so, especially right now. He sat, then turned a little toward her. "I like the idea of finding out what you think is forward. But we should talk a little first. I also don't want to hurt you."

"Or be hurt yourself?" She asked it before he could really think it, though that was true.

Vitus nodded once. Thessaly reached up to touch his cheek experimentally, then let her hand drop. That meant he could take it easily in his, the sort of touch he felt more manageable if he also had to produce words. "Let's see. How have you been? What should I know about everything since Sunday? Or before that." Though really, it was the challenge and after that probably mattered here. "And there's been some gossip. You might want to know about it. What you do about it, I wouldn't dream of telling you."

"I'm not planning on being visible much. Not for a while." Thessaly ran her thumb against his finger. "Going out in public, in black again, pretending that I'm grieving?

That's an insult to people who actually are. Cyrus, for example."

"I saw he was speaking to you. Was that a problem?" Vitus wasn't sure how to ask about this at all. He'd felt envious that someone could. And also baffled that Cyrus had dared.

"We've never been close, exactly? His family wasn't where mine were aiming me, you know? Well-bred, but not Great Families, no one notable for a few generations. But we were in the same year and the same house, and he's always been pleasant. Not anyone I worried about." Thessaly looked up. "Is it bad that it's him, and not Theo Carrington?"

Vitus shook his head. "Theo seemed very philosophical about it? I'm going out there for supper in the next week or two, to discuss more commissions. He was very pleased with how his went, he's recommending me to some others, as well. No problem there. And he doesn't begrudge Cyrus, either."

"Oh. Good. I'm glad." Thessaly hesitated, then she shifted, leaning a little on Vitus's shoulder. He moved his hand, making a bit more room for her, but not more than that. Not yet. Not until they figured out what they were doing.

"From what I heard - some of it from Council Head Rowan - the Fortier customs are rather gruelling. Are you all right? Did you get anything like enough sleep or food, or whatever?"

"Not much sleep, but I'm back here now. Last night was better. And having the talisman, I didn't dare take it with me." Thessaly tilted her head. She hesitated, then she said, "No nightmares. And honestly, while it was awful, I feel less exhausted and drained by the whole thing than I expected. A more, what's the word, understandable awful?

It had reasons I could point to. You don't mind me leaning?"

"I like it very much." Vitus couldn't and wouldn't lie to her. "And it seems to me you've not been comforted the last days. Were they awful to you?"

Thessaly grimaced, blowing out a puff of air. "Demanding, more like. From when they told us, I hadn't really even understood it, I think? And Lady Maylis was flinging herself at me, wanting me to kiss him, to make him live. It doesn't work like that. And he certainly wasn't some prince in a fairy tale."

"No." Vitus hesitated. "What do you know about what happened? All I know is that he died. That's all they told us. And gossip's been held very close."

"Cousin Owain didn't tell me anything much. Though I also didn't ask. After Lady Maylis was, well, like that, I fainted. Fairly deliberately, but it seemed like the only sensible way out of the situation. He insisted on bringing me back to his home. Aunt Tegwen and Cousin Enfys were there, and they sent someone for Emeline, and of course he knew the wards were safe. I'm very grateful. I have to think if there's something I can do to help them sometime." She shrugged. "I did see him. I don't know if you want to know."

Vitus considered. Talking about Childeric was certainly not his preferred topic, but on the other hand, it might matter. And he had a desire to know. "Would you? I promise not to tell anyone else." More hesitantly, he added, "And maybe it might be good to share it? Not be alone with it?"

Thessaly nodded. "He was - " She swallowed. "They hadn't done much, not really. Not all tended to. And it wasn't like Aunt Metaia; exactly. His shirt was partway open. Most of him looked ordinary, but there were lines running up his chest, like feathers. A bit like lightning."

"Oh." Vitus swallowed hard against a lump and the taste of something foul. "There's a name for that. I can find an image and bring you a copy, sometime. It's called a Lichtenberg figure or mark. It happens when someone's been struck by lightning."

"Lightning?" Thessaly blinked. "But he was inside, surely…" Then she stopped, her free hand coming up to her mouth. "Only he was also soaked. His clothes were still dripping a bit, I think. I hadn't really noticed, then. There was so much else going on. But it wasn't storming or raining on Sunday."

"Not where we were." Vitus was having to think through the implications, too. "But I'm fairly clear they're not all in a room at the top of the Keep. For one thing, all five of them, or all four, at once? The tower isn't that big. Maybe there's a portal or something like it that takes them somewhere else. I don't know that we'll ever know, and maybe we shouldn't? But whatever else, I think Childeric was in a storm. Only, what does that even mean?"

"It means he's dead." Thessaly said it slowly, deliberately. "It means I can't possibly marry him. All the marriage agreements are void." She swallowed. "And you and I, even if I could, I don't…."

Vitus shook his head. She'd said it, he could bear to think of it, he knew she was the better strategist here, too. "Doing anything right now, the next few months, it would ruin your reputation forever. And it'd ruin mine. That wouldn't do either of us much good. You can't marry Childeric. You can take whatever time you want to decide what to do next. Emeline will glare at people, and the Scali will be a wall between you and people demanding things.

Except, well, the Fortiers. Who don't have the right to ask anymore, but I don't think that will stop them."

Thessaly shivered. "No. Probably not." She twisted again. "Vitus? What do you want?" There was something more urgent in her voice now.

Vitus swallowed. "What's fair? What's good for both of us? I don't know the answer to that, not yet."

37

THAT AFTERNOON

Thessaly listened hard for whatever Vitus said next. She knew she wasn't really in her right mind. Not yet, not for a while, maybe. There had been far too much, all at once, and then the drawn out agony of the visible grieving and wondering what the Fortiers would do. She repeated herself, because she wanted to know the answer to this. "What do you want?"

She felt him shift, then he began to speak slowly. "I don't want to rush. For many reasons."

"But also your profession." Thessaly tried to make herself think through this like a duel, one of the ones that was six different things going on, and she had to pay attention to all of them. "I understand that."

He shrugged the shoulder under her head. "I don't. I ought to be flinging myself at you, by any sensible sort of maths." Then he said, "It would, erm, ease my worries about bills. Which is a terrible reason to— whatever it is we're doing or want to do. But many people find it compelling."

Thessaly managed a mock-solemn reply. "The Scali made a point of commenting on that. Both in the general and in the specific." She hadn't known how to bring this up. "I have some leeway for sensible investments, proper plans. And I talked to them - when was it, a fortnight ago, now? Some people Aunt Metaia invested in, materia, they wondered if I'd be interested. I don't know if I have her eye for it, but some of it includes stones. Gemstones and crystals and minerals, all sorts of things."

"Oh." His voice had gone entirely neutral.

"If I did that, I'd see if part of the terms were that you - and Niobe Hall, if you like - could have a first look. First chance."

"Oh." The same sound came out completely different now, suddenly warm and full of depths. "You thought of that already?"

"You've put a tremendous amount of time into learning how to do what you do. And you're going to keep wanting to make things, different kinds of items and magic, I'm fairly sure. Even if I didn't want other things, the ones we're still figuring out together, I'd want that. It seems a good thing in the world. Certainly better than coal mines or huge factories, or the sort of materia that means a lot of innocent animals died."

"Gemstones, also from mines that aren't wonderful places," Vitus said, softly now. "It's not an innocent trade." He shifted back a little, and she did the same, so she could watch his expressions better. "If I want to make my name, I'll need a lot of people to think my work is worth something. Some of them I don't like. I'd even take a commission from the Fortiers. Not that any of them are likely to ask."

"Aunt Metaia took commissions from many people. I've

been going through her notes." Thessaly shrugged. "Some she turned down. I bet some you'll turn down. And maybe most of them will be like Theo Carrington. I like how you talk about him. Tell me more about that?"

His expression shifted into uncertainty. "You'll be bored."

"It's you telling me, so no, don't think I shall." Thessaly considered, then leaned forward to kiss his nose. "Please?"

That made him laugh, and tug her into his lap, instead. She leaned her head on his shoulder, closed her eyes, and listened to him explain the entire process to her, after she agreed to keep it in confidence. Not that there were many people she'd have been likely to tell, or who'd have asked. Cousin Owain, maybe. "I hadn't known the process had so many parts. It's rather like a duel, the larger shape of one, laying out all the pieces, then using them, isn't it? The stone, the conditions."

"The timing, what's plausible in the time you have," Vitus agreed. Then he tilted his head. "Thank you."

"For what?" Thessaly lifted her head to peer at him.

"For caring. For listening. For—" He shifted, suddenly, as if newly focused on her presence, his gaze drifting down her body for a moment before he met her eyes again. "You've had so much to contend with. And you still do."

That shift in attention was also decidedly intriguing. "You said we might do something else together once we'd talked." Thessaly tried to remember, there was something else first. "You said something about gossip?"

"Nascent, still, but there's gossip not only about Childeric's death, but about your aunt's, and Philip's. And you, because you're a connecting point in two of the three. Or all three, depending on how one decides the Landry family is connected." One thing she loved about Vitus, Thessaly was rapidly deciding, was the fact he told her things, without hesitation, if she might need to know them. Not all at once in a flood, but well before she needed the information.

"I suppose that's natural." Thessaly considered. "I heard - not enough to make sense of it - some whispers at the funeral. Like people were there, but they were also afraid."

Vitus thought back to what he'd seen and heard himself. "That might be true. Any death out of season, people worry it might touch them too. And the Fortiers have a lot of allies, but that isn't the same as friends, is it? Did they have other people come to make calls?"

Thessaly leaned back a little, resting against his shoulder at a different angle, quietly working through it. "I wouldn't have seen most callers, not unless I was the one keeping vigil. But no. A lot of notes, I saw the staff come through with those. But not, um. Whoever Lady Maylis's best friends were, people she trusted."

Vitus hugged her more tightly at that. "I'm sorry for that. People ought to have comfort in their grief, company from those who are able." He took a breath, as if something in that fundamentally offended him. "If something happened to one of my parents, or…" His voice cut off, and she was sure he was worried about his brother. "There would be people. The Deschamps cousins, Mama's side of the family. We spend time with them regularly, suppers and outings. Not just family, but people I like, who are friends. Niobe. People I know from Salmon House, from the Four Metals."

"Oh!" She kissed his nose. "You had said. People you like?" He'd mentioned, briefly, that he was a member because of his current project. But she hadn't really thought about what it meant in terms of people.

"Some I'm closer to than others. But - for something

like that, they'd turn up. I didn't know that before? And now, I guess I do." He sounded very thoughtful about it. "That's not the same for you, is it?"

"Not really. As the past few months have shown. A lot of people who think about how the thing looks, not how it feels. Not what matters in the heart." Thessaly let out a sigh. "It's not that I'm lonely most of the time. There's so much to learn and think and try, with magic and duelling and whatever else I'm learning."

"But that's not the same as a good time with friends." Vitus nodded once. "In due course, maybe I can introduce you to some of them, and see if they like you as a person, too. You're curious about what people do. That goes a long way to making friends with anyone in the Four Metals."

Thessaly nodded, not that she could think about that for a while. She took a breath, circling back to the original problem of the gossip. "Would you keep an ear out? For what people say?"

Vitus promptly nodded. "Of course. Is there something you're worried about in particular?"

Now she closed her eyes, focusing. She hadn't wanted to name her fears, but if he were going to listen for anything specific, she had to. "I'm worried they'll take their anger out on someone. Maybe not me. If it were going to be me, they would have already. But someone on the Council. Cousin Owain, maybe. He's the one who got me away. Magistra Hereswith. Anyone who they could target."

"The other Challengers. Cyrus. Theo. Anyone who helped them." She blessed the fact that while Vitus might not think in these terms on his own, he saw the problem promptly. "I'll listen. And ask a few people to listen too, in general terms. The ones who'd understand why I was asking."

"Mistress Niobe." Thessaly said, mostly because she

wanted to see his slight smile at that. He had a far better relationship with her than Thessaly did with her own Mistress North, and she envied that more than a little. "I might ask Emeline to go into Trellech and see what she picks up. Or Collins. But right now, I ought to care, and I really can't bring myself to. You're right here. I suppose you have to go sometime. You have a whole other life." Thessaly was, honestly, exhausted by the expectation she care about what anyone else thought.

"Is that a hint?" Vitus swallowed now, looking shy. "You've not done much of anything with anyone, have you? Even Childeric?"

"Childeric insinuated a few things toward the end. But no, he didn't bother me that way. And agreements obliged me to come to the marriage bed a virgin." Thessaly offered after a moment what she thought might be the right metaphor. "A stone waiting to be shaped and inscribed. Or to shape or inscribe myself, never mind, that image doesn't quite hold."

It made Vitus laugh, though, and she was pleased by that. "I said we wouldn't go too far today. Not until you've had time to recover. Until it's about us, and about what we both want, and not everything else hanging over us. But I think you might enjoy a few things."

"Show me." It came out of her mouth like an eager child, taken to the Solstice Faire, promised excitements to see and taste and touch. "Do I need to move?"

That, startlingly, got a grunt out of him, like he'd just permitted himself that luxury. "I like you in my lap." He swallowed, his voice lower. "If you move - gently, please - you can feel how I like you. When I get hard like that, it's wanting. You don't have to do anything about it. Just it's a thing you should know."

In some part of her head, to be examined later, she

wondered now why Childeric hadn't ever shown any desire for any greater intimacy than the socially expected kisses and dances. There had been that flash in his eyes at the idea of getting her in bed, but that hadn't been attraction, that had been control. Thessaly set it aside for now. This was not the time for any of his nonsense. She took a breath, and then shifted in Vitus's lap, carefully. She felt how he reacted to it, not only that hardness she could feel against her thigh, but also the way his chin came up and how he inhaled. Most especially, she noted how his eyes widened, how there was something actively wanting there.

It was a particular power, and a kind of control that her family had not wanted her to have, that the Fortiers had not wanted her to have. That made her want to grab for it with both hands. Aunt Metaia had implied she'd had it, and enjoyed it - and that whoever she'd been with had also enjoyed it. That would be an interesting puzzle to consider if she knew any of them. Or if there was anything in Aunt Metaia's library that might give some ideas.

Now was for something else. "You like that. What else do you like?" This wasn't a duel, this wasn't remotely antagonistic, even in play, but she could figure out how to go forward the same way. One person did a thing, the other reacted, trading back and forth. She knew well how that went.

"I'd like to touch you." Vitus leaned forward to kiss her cheek, then whisper in her ear. "As soon as you hugged me, I realised you weren't wearing a corset, or a bustle. That there's nothing between me and you but the fabric."

That made her arch, moving against him, both the whisper and then the way his hands pressed against her back. She twisted to lean into the touch a bit, and he encouraged her to move a bit more. Then he inhaled and kissed her.

It was and wasn't like the previous times. Those other few moments, he'd held back somehow, he hadn't pressed. Now, she hovered between his mouth and his hand on her back, coming up between her shoulder blades. His tongue pressed into her mouth, deeper and more urgent than he'd tried before. And his other hand came to rest on her shoulder. She tried to get into the rhythm of it, rocking a little as she did.

Vitus pulled back to catch his breath, his eyes glowing now. "You are a fast learner. And I think you like that very much, yes?" She nodded once, completely unable to get words to form in any useful way. "May I do a bit more? Touch you, on your breast, and perhaps beneath your skirts?"

She had, when Matron had explained things at school, considered that somehow not terribly relevant. Now she liked the thought of it very much. "If you like?" There, she'd managed a few words. "I don't know if I like it. I want to find out." Those were even better. "Show me?"

Vitus broke into a grin again. Then he encouraged her to shift a bit more, so she was more or less straddling his lap, one leg on either side of his. Her gown was bunched up and flowing back behind her. Before she could get nervous again, he was kissing her, encouraging her to put her arms around his shoulders. Then, once she knew what to do there, his hand stroked down her shoulder, petting and touching, easing her into something new. His other was on her hip, then pulling the silk of her gown up on that side. All at once, his fingers were touching her bare skin, in the split in her drawers. His right hand was flat, first, letting her get used to it, then he slid it up and toward where her legs met, deliberately.

It was a distraction from his other hand. Thessaly found herself caught between the two - and his kisses, which were even more urgent now. His left hand moved to cup her breast, the thumb sliding against the inside curve, just as his fingers brushed a spot between her legs. Now she understood why he'd had her move, why she needed her arms where they were. Thessaly wanted to touch him, but she couldn't figure out how. Instead, she curled her arms around his shoulders for support, and kept reaching for something she only barely understood.

When he pulled back from the kiss this time, just long enough to speak, he sounded so happy. "I'm going to touch you a little more. Let yourself enjoy it, Thessaly, please. Whatever that is for you. I want to see you enjoy it." There was almost a growl, no, more like a purr, to it, something fiercer than he'd let her see so far, so determined to draw a reaction from her. Then he was kissing her again, and his hands were moving. The one between her legs slipped in smooth dampness, here and there flicking her. That brought sensations like the good kind of lightning, luck and joy striking out of the heavens. She found herself pushing against his hand, leaning into the fingers that cupped and kneaded her breast, frantic.

She could hear him breathing hard, then his hips moving against something. He twisted his wrist a bit, changing the angle, and the sounds he was making changed in pitch, sharper and higher, like he couldn't get enough of it either. Before she could figure out what he was doing, his fingers found the perfect spot. The pleasure hit her like a great wave on the ocean, flinging her a far distance, in a burst of delight and need. She bucked against him several times, wanting more of that, to find that perfect moment, and she felt it again and again, though not quite so strong as the first.

He pulled back from her mouth. She could hear him in a low, repeated murmur. "More, oh, please, like this, do you feel it?" It was a chain of unanswered questions. A second later, he was pulling her tight against his chest. His own hips jerked against her a dozen times, maybe, before he let out a long sigh and let himself lean back against the sofa.

Thessaly let herself fold forward against him, her head on his shoulder, her entire body tucked up tight against his. She did not know how long they lay like that. Minutes, certainly, probably not hours. When she peered out of one eye, the light hadn't changed much. Eventually, he nuzzled at her neck. "There'll be more of that, when you want."

The way he put it, the way he was insistent about her choosing, made her laugh. She moved enough she could see his expression, because she wasn't entirely sure about this question. "And you. At the end, that was you feeling that way too?"

"Oh, yes." It came out more as a groan or a sigh. "Very messily, men are like that. Splendid, though. And there are charms for the mess." Vitus beamed at her, rather foolishly. "Entirely at your disposal for such pleasures."

"You are persuasive that we should have more. Not today, though. I— you're right, about one thing at a time. And I'm now rudely very tired."

That made him laugh. "That's not uncommon. Rude for me to roll over and go to sleep on you, less rude for you to fall asleep. But you said you hadn't been sleeping well. How about we tidy ourselves up enough, you walk me out, and then you can rest?"

It was a sensible plan, even if she rather wanted to take his hand and pull him back to the bedroom now. They could be sensible. There would be other times, she was sure of that now. She nodded. "Show me the charms?"

Five minutes later, they were, in fact, tidy enough for a walk to the portal. She let him out with one last, much briefer kiss. And more than a few promises about future opportunities. She turned back, intending on a nap before maybe seeing what sort of books Aunt Metaia might have tucked away in unexpected corners. If not that, something that suited her current mood, at the least.

38

SEPTEMBER 29TH AT VITUS'S HOME

"Anyone about?" Vitus heard his brother's voice from the hall. The library door was cracked open, so at least he didn't have to shout.

"In here." Vitus had been at the table by the window, staring out of it, for at least half an hour. Now he turned in the chair, then stood up. "How are you?"

Lucas strode over, giving him a firm hug and thumping his shoulder. Then he stepped back. "What's wrong?"

"Not so loud." Vitus glanced up. "Mama's napping. Papa's out, he'll be back in an hour at the most."

"None of that is an answer to the question." Lucas pointed out.

Vitus shrugged and turned to fold himself onto the sofa. "How much of the last week's news of Albion have you caught? Since Sunday evening?"

"Council Challenge, Childeric Fortier's dead, that's most of it. I know the funeral - did you actually go?" Lucas's eyebrows went up and up. "You did."

"So did Mama and Papa." Vitus said. "I didn't talk to

Thessaly, other than in the line afterwards, just a word. Nothing out of the ordinary. And Papa had to go, so. There were hundreds of people there."

"Huh." Lucas collapsed next to him, knee to knee. "Tell me about it? And then answer my question, you."

Vitus tried to figure out how to get all of it in order. "Theo Carrington was pleased, even though he wasn't successful. His sister stopped flirting with me. That was also excellent. She's an interesting conversationalist when she's not on that particular hunt." Vitus looked up and considered. "I could introduce you?"

"When, brother, when? I like my Sundays here too much to share them." Lucas chuckled. "And?"

"And they told us Childeric Fortier had died. They took the Fortiers and Thessaly off before that, they told them privately. From what Thessaly said, it was all incredibly awful."

"Then the funeral, I suppose? How did you feel, knowing that she wasn't betrothed anymore?" There was a slight creak from the door, and Vitus looked up to see his mother standing there.

"Mama." Vitus stood with Lucas a beat behind him, and she waved a hand at them.

"Lucas, dearest, did you just get in?" Lucas nodded, entirely like a retriever puppy, sure he'd done something wrong, waiting to be scolded. Vitus rather felt like that too. Lucas went over to kiss Mama's cheek, and to rearrange a chair for her at her gesture. "Now, you were talking about the funeral?"

Vitus had, rather carefully, not been talking to either of his parents about Thessaly, not since the gossip began. They hadn't asked, for one thing, and preserving the fiction of what they didn't know worked better if both sides avoided the topic. Now he folded his hands into his lap. "We were, Mama."

"And you were talking about Thessaly Lytton-Powell. How do things stand with her at the moment, then, dearest?" That was exactly the sort of question Vitus couldn't duck. It wasn't as if he wanted to lie to Mama, he just did not know how to put any of this into words. He blushed, and that made Lucas chortle again.

"His expression tells a fair bit, doesn't it, Mama? He's as red as my uniform coat." Lucas settled back down on the sofa.

"Vitus?" Mama's voice was deliberate. "I have ears. I would like to know what isn't gossip, please. I might have a few relevant thoughts."

Vitus rubbed his nose. "Thessaly is staying at the house she inherited from her aunt, up in Wales, near Snowdonia. It has a portal, but it's warded here and back again. She has to let people into the property itself. I've been there several times. Yesterday, most recently. She was at Arundel most of the week, until the funeral. It was apparently entirely awful. They have very particular customs. Someone mentioned mostly French."

"I heard about tossing - were they bees? - into the grave?" Lucas said. "That made no sense at all."

Mama tutted. "A symbol of the Merovingians. Honestly, have you forgotten your history, Lucas? Our family doesn't trace back as far as the Fortiers, but your father's people are respectable Third Families that way."

"They were badly cast bees, on a technical level. I don't know if they were supposed to have magic imbued in them, but I sensed nothing terribly strong, if so." Vitus shrugged. He added to Lucas, "I spent a lot of the next bit of waiting thinking how I'd do it better. Not that I wish for any funeral where I'd be providing copper bees."

Mama smiled at that, so at least he was amusing someone. "There were a number of other customs, too. They kept vigil, that's common enough, but no talking in the house, sitting separately, from the death through the funeral. Was Mistress Lytton-Powell all right when you saw her?"

It made Vitus blush again, nearly as much as before. "You might reasonably refer to her as Thessaly in conversation, in private, Mama, if you would like. Whatever else there may be, we are friends, it seems."

"More than friends, yes?" Mama tilted her head just so. The pose that made it clear she'd been in Owl House at Schola, with their long and accurate view of prey waiting to be pounced upon. Never mind Owl's ability to hold dozens of pieces of information in a pattern at once.

"Yes, Mama." Vitus looked down at the floor. He absolutely couldn't look at her and say this. "We have done nothing that would have broken her marriage agreements, but we did things that infuriated Childeric Fortier. And we did, erm, a larger range of those things yesterday. Though not all the things we would like to do when it's a better time. Is that a delicate enough phrasing?"

The first response he heard from his mother was a gentle laugh, followed by Lucas's deeper one. Then Lucas's hand came down on his knee, reassuringly. "You are tender about it, brother."

Vitus nodded. Tender was an excellent word, really, like everything was far too near the surface. It got quieter until Mama spoke again. "Look at me, please, Vitus?" Vitus looked up, and Mama went on. "You truly are fond of this woman?" He nodded again, unable to bring himself to speak. "I wish to meet her when appropriate. You should know there is more gossip about her, gossip that you should know and factor in."

"Factor in?"

"By which I mean you should bring it to her and see what she says. Both because it concerns her, and because I suspect she is far better at navigating that sort of thing than you are."

"I'm rather abysmal at it, so I certainly hope so. I do not need to excel her in all things, nor do I want to. That would be foolish for so many reasons." Vitus might certainly want to teach her a few things, joyously and collaboratively, in bed. That was an entirely different sort of question and project. "The gossip, Mama? And I will ask her about when she might feel able to call for a private family supper. It will be some time, I suspect. The chance of being seen in public being what it is, even just at the portal."

"That is true, I suppose." Mama tapped her forefingers together. "You remember, I hope, Amalia Helling-Macintyre, who was a year ahead of me in Owl?"

"A particular gossip, isn't she?" Lucas asked, mock-innocently.

"It has been very helpful for your father's business more than once. Don't you impugn the benefits of information." Mama said, though she wasn't really scolding Lucas. For one thing, she had just as hard a time scolding him as anyone else in the family. "She came up to me when we were doing the shopping in Trellech yesterday, all a flutter. Checking that 'that sweet boy of mine' wasn't thinking about Mistress Lytton-Powell, because she'd heard such a thing."

"Sweet boy?" Vitus and Lucas said it in unison, stared at each other, and laughed.

Lucas elbowed him. "Guess I'm not the sweet one, then."

"Hush." Mama looked amused, though, for all the seriousness of this conversation. She'd smiled a lot, and she hadn't coughed once. Vitus was counting both. "There is gossip about Thessaly, about whether she might have had some part in Childeric's death. Not that anyone had any idea how, given that he absolutely died in the Council challenge, but gossip is not logical."

Vitus sat bolt upright at that. "People really think that?"

Mama nodded, just the once. "Tell her when you can. What do you think of it?"

"I think that there is a lot going on that I don't begin to understand." He glanced from Mama to Lucas and back to Mama. "May I lay it out? See if you can see a thread I'm missing?" He got a nod from both of them. "We have two deaths, still unexplained. I don't think Thessaly knows much more than I do. Her aunt, and then Philip Landry, within a day."

"That seems an odd combination." Mama said. "And there's no reason Thessaly knows of that might connect them?"

"Her aunt was investigating something. But she does not know what that something was, not yet. Nor how it might connect to the Landrys. Her aunt had concerns about Childeric, entirely accurate ones. But murdering a Council Member when she couldn't have prevented the marriage going ahead without excellent cause seems, well, not up to the usual Fortier standards of political plotting."

That made Mama smile again, as horrible a concept as it was. That was true, though. One expected better strategy from the Fortiers. "And more recently?"

"I am aware," Vitus considered how to put this. "Both of some separations in the Fortier family and some of the other pieces. Dagobert is rather on the outside, at the moment, and has been since summer solstice. He's been at several of the scientific lectures. I know he has been doing some reading about electricity, and I think perhaps others in the family." Which got him to the complicated bit.

Lucas spotted him stalling first, but of course Lucas was closer. There was the elbow again, though more gently. "Yes?"

"Childeric Fortier. It looks like he was killed by lightning. There's a particular burn mark that can happen. Thessaly saw it. She didn't know that was what it was at the time, across his chest. And his clothes were soaked. She didn't get a close look, she didn't want one, but that much?"

"And that's not what would be shared in gossip." Mama considered. "Surely the Guard has some ideas, though."

"Not, apparently, about Metaia Powell's death. And there's been no announcement about anything with Landry. Henut Landry isn't landed, but she certainly knows a few people to ask. She's done enough consulting for key families over the years. And Fortier's death was in the Council Keep, in a space forbidden to all but the Council. Or at least that's what I assume. A trifle difficult to investigate."

"And you won't," Lucas cleared his throat. "You are committed to Thessaly."

"To being her friend, to whatever else we figure out together, yes. And she can't be forced into the same sort of agreement now. She's not dependent on her parents, and she has other people with an eye to her own personal well-being, like the Scali, as trustees."

"And what do you want, brother?" Lucas's voice was quieter now.

"I want to understand," Vitus said. "I want there to be space for her to be happy. Ideally, I wish to be there, being happy with her. I do not know how to get from here to there, though."

The thing of it was, it all came out to love, one way or another. He wanted time with Thessaly, without being hedged around with assumptions and expectations. Vitus wanted her on his lap, in his arms, to soak in the way she listened and to share the joys of whatever they explored together. He wanted to know what she was like in far more ways in private, and what she was like with a family who cared about each other. The one Vitus had now, and the one he wanted to build with Thessaly herself. It wasn't just about any one facet of her, her beauty or her wits or her birth. Or even her skills or her passion or her magic. It was about all of her, and all of him and what that made between them.

Lucas, next to him, cleared his throat. "So. Love, then?"

Vitus couldn't look up, but he nodded. "Yes, love."

Before anyone could say anything else there was a sound from the front door, Mama looked up. "That's your papa. I will talk to him about this in due course, but for now, best let it rest."

Vitus nodded. "As you wish." He was sure he and Lucas would talk about it more when they got a chance, whenever that was. And it felt better to have said what he wanted, even in so vague a way, and to know Mama knew. That would have to do for the time being.

Elemental Truth, the third and final book of this trilogy will be out on December 13th, 2024 (with a happy ending for Thessaly and Vitus).

If you'd like to learn more about my books, please sign

up for my mailing list to get all the latest news and fun extras.

Your reviews (on whatever review site you use) are much appreciated, too!

Read on for more historical details about *Silent Circuit.*

AUTHOR'S NOTE

Thank you so much for coming and joining me for the second book in the Mysterious Fields trilogy, Silent Circuit! Don't worry, Thessaly and Vitus are going to get their happily-ever-after in the third book, *Elemental Truth.*

I owe so much thanks to my editor, Kiya Nicoll, who has as always vastly improved the plot. Particular thanks to Elise Matthesen for a number of detail points on various stones (as well as the sources I talk about below.) My early readers have also been fantastic at helping make sure the trilogy ties together well.

I won't repeat the notes about the trilogy as a whole from *Enchanted Net* (we'll recap them in *Elemental Truth*, book 3). I continued to draw heavily on a couple of particular titles for the talisman work that Vitus and Niobe do. Two key titles are *A Lapidary of Sacred Stones: Their Magical and Medicinal Powers Based on the Earliest Sources, Includes More than 800*

Gems and Stones by Claude Leconteux as well as *Stars and Stones: An Astro-Magical Lapidary* by Peter Stockinger.

In this book, we get to see a wider range of talismanic work in the pieces Vitus makes for Theo Carrington, and in the stones the Council has on hand in case of need. I really enjoyed getting to explore more of the lore around specific stones, and the ways that Vitus thinks about them in particular. (I am particularly fond of his metaphor about the poetry inherent in alluvial sapphires, honestly.)

On to the chapter notes!

Chapter 10, of course, has a number of stone references. **Amber** was known originally as electron in Greek, and it's where we get the word electricity from in English. However, while it can produce static electricity sparks (rub it on some wool!), it is not pizeoelectric. That's a different quality of stones, produced by high pressure. That sort of pressure would destroy amber. For a fun fact, bone is also pizeoelectric, but this wasn't discovered until 1957.

Burma rubies are indeed known for their particular colour, pigeon blood. They're also unfortunately one of the mines that have a long history of being conflict stones. In 1889, as this chapter takes place, the Burma mines had only been taken over under British control within the last two or so years, and so Burma rubies were becoming more common.

Aquamarines and **emeralds** are both beryls (along with a number of other kinds of stone) but they're interestingly treated as distinct types, for reasons that aren't always very clear. They do have distinct colouration, though, which does help. Emeralds have a great deal of lore associated with them related to chastity and faithfulness.

The lore that Vitus refers to here is that if an emerald is given as a wedding or engagement ring (or similar) and the recipient cheats, the stone will turn brown. In Albion's customs (especially in the upper classes), this would mean going outside the marriage agreements, which do often allow for extramarital liaisons in specific circumstances.

If you're interested in a more narrative look at the history of stones, both Victoria Finlays *Jewels* and Aja Raden's *Stoned* have a number of stories about the histories of particular stones, mines, and more.

Chapter 18 has a brief reference to something that used to be fairly common. In library collections that had (or in a few cases, still have) **loan cards** tucked in the back of the item, it becomes possible to trace someone's interests across different books or music. In my younger days, I certainly did that and discovered some amazing music. (If a couple of particular people in my music classes had checked something out, it was worth my time to listen to, basically.)

These days, the combination of digital circulation systems and a much greater attention to library patron privacy means this isn't possible in most libraries. The research library I work in as my day job still has cards in books (we have a web-based catalog but our books aren't barcoded, so we enter loans manually in a notes field). However, our stacks are closed, so the only people who look at the cards are library staff, when we're checking something out or returning it to the collection.

I was delighted to discover that a British classic humour book came out in August of 1889 and could thus appear as a new release in this chapter. That book is **Jerome K. Jerome's *Three Men in a Boat (To Say Nothing of the Dog)*** which follows three men and a dog in a journey down the Thames and back. A lot of the places they stop are still open as pubs and inns. While critics panned it, it was immensely popular with readers, and remains so.

Chapter 34 **:** On a more serious note, we end with the Fortier **mourning customs**. The majority are drawn from French Victorian customs at the time. These include the sitting in solitary silence, keeping a constant vigil with the body, the women sewing the shroud and covers for the mirrors, and the general arrangement of the processions. They also have the same customs around mourning dress, the length of time it should be worn, and so on that Victorian British society does (and that Albion also follows).

The Fortiers, of course, add their own customs. Childeric I (for whom Childeric here is named) was a Merovingian emperor who died around 480 CE. If you're unclear on Merovingian history - most people are - they were followed by the Carolingians. Charlemagne (crowned in Rome in 800 CE) is by far the best known Carolingian.

Childeric I's grave, found in 1653, had over 300 gold and garnet bees in it. Unfortunately, many of them were stole in the 1830s, but a few survive and they are stunning works of metal and stone.

Bees were a general symbol of the Merovingians, and the Fortiers (descended from the Merovingians) have kept the symbology. As part of their rites, they throw a bee (gold for men, silver for women, copper for everyone else) in the grave. Unless, of course, you're Henut Landry who makes her own rules.

~

Elemental Truth (the last book, with the happily-ever-after) will be out on December 13th, 2024. We'll be following it with some extras, but *Grown Wise* (which takes place in

1947, with Laudine and Dagobert's granddaughter, Ursula, at the centre) will explore some pieces of this story and the lasting legacy of the Fortier choices as well. That will be out in May 2025.

My newsletter has all my updates and news, as well as additional information about where I am and what I'm doing online. Until next book, happy reading!

ENCHANTED NET SUMMARY

Enchanted Net, the first book of the Mysterious Fields trilogy, begins with **Thessaly Lytton-Powell's** betrothal to **Childeric Fortier** in March 1889 at his family's demesne estate, **Arundel**.

The betrothal is the event of the season, a gathering attended by nearly every powerful person in Albion (Britain's magical community), and everyone the Fortiers want to impress. Along with members of Albion's **Council**, the guests include many allies of the Fortiers such as the formidable **Henut Landry** and her sons **Philip** and **Alexander**. Henut and Philip are established magical specialists, while Alexander is almost finished with his time as a student at Schola, about to depart on a Grand Tour.

Thessaly comes from good families with powerful magic - the Lyttons and the Powells - but neither have the same kind of social power. Marrying the golden son of the Fortiers is quite a step up. Thessaly's willing. She understands the family expectations and obligations - or at least she thinks she does. Her apprenticeship in illusion work is going well, even if Thessaly does not expect to need to make her living at it. Besides, she's also a duellist, skilled in using her magic and her wits to reach her goals.

Marrying into the Fortier family is a particular kind of challenge, though. They are a family of strong magic and stronger opinions. The Dowager Lady **Chrodechildis** still rules the family with a strong hand, even though Lord **Clovis** and Lady **Maylis** Fortier's sons (Childeric and **Sigbert**) are young adults. **Dagobert** (Chrodechildis's younger son) and his wife **Laudine** maintain a little more space from the family, but are at all the necessary events with their 9-year-old son **Garin**.

The Fortier marriage agreements are clear about what is and is not permitted and expected. Thessaly is committed to marrying Childeric and doing her best to provide him with children, but other relationships that do not interfere with that are possible. Certainly, Childeric's taking advantage of that clause.

Vitus Deschamps comes from a less distinguished family, with his father acting as a man of business for various Fortier client families and his brother **Lucas** serving in a non-magical cavalry unit. Vitus has been travelling on the Continent, learning from talisman makers and gem cutters as he comes to the end of his apprenticeship as a talisman maker. His apprentice mistress, **Niobe Hall**, welcomes him back warmly, wanting to set him up to succeed for the future. His return also lets him reconnect with the **Four Metals**, a secret society focused on crafting and innovative magic.

When Vitus meets Thessaly at a costume gala, they immediately find each other to be kindred spirits, interested in exploring the artistry that magic makes possible, as well as the function of different enchantments and forms of magic.

As spring turns into summer, however, there are some worrying signs. Childeric alternately ignores Thessaly and becomes increasingly controlling of her behaviour. Both Vitus and Thessaly have also become aware that a number of people around their age are not fulfilling their magical promise the way anyone expected - there are failed apprenticeships, complications for expected marriages, and more.

Vitus spends his spring developing his own connections, both within the Four Metals and consulting with Philip Landry about a particular technique. He knows what he needs to do to conclude his apprenticeship: gather a few more key examples of his work to present to his guild. Vitus also needs to set up his business and ways to establish his skills and differentiate himself from Niobe.

As Thessaly and her beloved aunt **Metaia** (a member of Albion's Council) are getting ready for the Council rites on Summer Solstice, Metaia asks some probing questions and shares her worries about Childeric, as well as making it clear Thessaly has her support. The evening is a shining show of magic and prestige, as expected, but Vitus and Thessaly do get a chance to dance together.

When Metaia is found dead the next morning, Thessaly - and her family - are shocked and grieving, especially Thessaly's mother **Sioned**, Metaia's older sister. More puzzling, there's another death, that of Philip Landry. Thessaly is desperately trying to figure out what happened and what it means, and Vitus offers what comfort he can - if constrained by proper behaviour and his own social station.

The funerals raise questions, odd moments of behaviour that don't make sense. The Fortiers have retreated into their estates, barely making the necessary condolence calls. Vitus and Thessaly both notice several odd reactions at Philip's funeral. Vitus begins to try and figure out what might be going on, even though he has very little information to work with.

Ten days after Metaia's death, Thessaly is summoned to Arundel with no explanation. She's shocked to hear Childeric announce that he intends to challenge for Metaia's open seat on the Council. She's rightfully upset that he didn't discuss it with her, or give her any warning of what he had planned. And yet, while she's furious, she can't go against him - not in public, and not in private.

Vitus has his own unexpected conversation when Henut Landry asks if he would take over the lease on Philip's rooms, solving his search for his own professional space. He agrees, once she makes clear what the catch is. Vitus is, after all, more likely than a stranger to let her know if some odd object or paperwork turns up. He also takes on a commission from **Theo Carrington**, another of the declared challengers for the open Council seat, for a talismanic piece that will support his magic.

At the end of the book, Thessaly and Vitus manage to get a chance to meet and talk. When Vitus admits he wishes he could kiss Thessaly, she agrees that she wishes he would. They kiss, but almost immediately are discovered by one of the worst gossips. Vitus walks away in order to offer Thessaly the scant protection he can.

Now you're ready to read Silent Circuit! (The link will take you back to chapter 1).

Also by Celia Lake

The Mysterious Fields Series - Victorian

Enchanted Net

Silent Circuit

Elemental Truth

The Mysterious Charm Series - 1920s

Outcrossing

Goblin Fruit

Magician's Hoard

Wards of the Roses

In The Cards

On The Bias

Seven Sisters

The Mysterious Powers Series - 1920s

Carry On

The Fossil Door

Eclipse

Fool's Gold

The Hare and the Oak

Point By Point

Mistress of Birds

The Mysterious Arts Series - 1920s

Bound for Perdition

Shoemaker's Wife

Perfect Accord

Facets of the Bench

Charms of Albion - Victorian standalone

Pastiche

Sailor's Jewel

Four Walls and a Heart

Land Mysteries - 1930s and 40s

Best Foot Forward

Nocturnal Quarry

Old As The Hills

Upon A Summer's Day

Illusion of a Boar

Three Graces

The Magic of Four

Other stories

Complementary

Winter's Charms

Forged in Combat

Learn more about the world of Albion and future books at my website, celialake.com. Additional information linking characters, places, and timelines is available at my authorial wiki at bit.ly/celia-lake-wiki (or get there from my website under the menu that says "more information").

Sign up for my newsletter to be the first to hear about future books and learn about fascinating bits of research. Happy reading!

www.ingramcontent.com/pod-product-compliance
Lightning Source LLC
La Vergne TN
LVHW050929080826
845145LV00001B/273

* 9 7 8 1 9 5 7 1 4 3 2 6 2 *